The Rooming House Diaries
Life, Love and Secrets

Bill Mathis

Published by Rogue Phoenix Press
Copyright © 2019

ISBN: 978-1-62420-422-7

Credits
Cover Design by Ms G
Editor: Sherry Derr-Wille

Dedication

To Betty Jo Mathis
Poet, Writer and Mother to All

And to
Ron Schmidt
A true Chicago Sout'west Side Guy

Prologue

4822 South Justine, Back-of-the-Yards Neighborhood, Chicago, IL
Wednesday, June 10, 2009

Five people were present for the funeral and interment of sixty-nine-year-old Manuel (Manny) Rodriguez. Two of them, Manny's nephew, Andres Rodriquez, and Andres' partner, Josh Sawicki, shared their sparse memories of the man. Two priests read scriptures and prayed over the urn. The fifth person was the female undertaker. The service was over in nineteen minutes.

After the ceremony at Oakwood Cemetery, Josh and Andres returned to the old rooming house that was now theirs. Both felt sad over the passing of someone they barely knew, yet excited over the fact they now jointly owned a three-story building with plenty of space for Andres to make art. The building was narrow, but deep. The first floor held a spacious four-bedroom apartment, behind it a small one-bedroom unit. Each of the two upper floors held fifteen rooms, long unused.

They sat down at the kitchen table in the large apartment. The table was fifties-style, chrome with gray faux marble. A red Aunt Jemima clock ticked on the wall. Josh shifted a tangled pile of keys and pulled a handwritten note across the table. He edged his chair closer to Andres so they both could read it.

Josh and Andres,

Just a few notes.

These are all the other keys Manny gave me. Good luck figuring them out! Father Frank and I got to know Manny better the last few months of his life, to the point we assisted with all the paperwork turning this place over to you two. During his last few days, Manny frequently spoke of diaries and secrets. He said four diaries are contained in the numbered ledgers on top of the buffet. They're mixed in throughout the records of the tenants who used to reside here. He thought there might be two other diaries, but was vague about their possible locations.

The diaries seemed very important to him and he so much wanted you to know about them and read them. Manny frequently spoke of this place and how some of the occupants became his family. We were surprised to discover that both of you have ties to the place. He said you'd both learn a lot about your DNA and non-DNA families. In fact, he wrote the last diary. He strongly expressed his desire you not sell the house. He wants you to live here. He said the place is in better shape than it looks, and it would make a stable home for you, plus space for Andres to make art and possibly display it.

Please keep Father Frank and myself informed as to your plans. We live close by, in the rectory at Saint Bobola's. We will be glad to assist you in any way possible. I hope you two decide to keep the building and live in this community. We always need energetic, young folk establishing roots. Keep in touch, we're extremely interested in hearing what you learn from the diaries, especially the secrets, and what you do with the place. How exciting.

God Bless You!
Father An

Diary 1

Josef Sawicki

Born November 3, 1858, Olsztyn, Poland (East Prussia)
Died April 19, 1936, Chicago

Diary found in Ledger One and translated from Polish to English with occasional comments by Mae Sawicki, Josef's daughter-in-law.

Chapter One

Yesterday, I noticed several flecks of blood in my spittle. I don't feel sick or any worse. To be truthful, I am old and don't intend to live forever. I can't wait to be with Walentina again, God rest her soul. So, today, February 10, 1934, is the day I shall write my story down so my progeny may refer to it and know the many wonderful things I have accomplished, as well as all the truth about me. Not that I'm a dishonest man, but there were times, not many, where I left out a few details. First, I must take a piss, being old has affected such things. I used to have a bladder like a horse, now it's like a puppy.

Now I continue my writing, even after being rudely yelled at by Henryk. I refuse to call my son Hank, like the rest of the world. I named him Henryk, it's a good Polish name. He yelled at me for carrying coal up to the hall stoves on the second and third floors. He said I should at least get dressed first, that limping around in my dead wife's nightgown was not proper and I looked godawful. He says that a lot when I don't dress and stay in her nightgowns, "You look godawful." He doesn't understand sleeping alone is lonely and her old flannel nightgowns make her feel closer to me. I miss her so much. He says fifteen years should be enough.

See, I've been wearing them since the night she died. Except for around the shoulders, they fit me. She always sewed them extra big. She didn't like anything tight around her when she slept. Of course, they tore out around my arm pits so I sewed some longer threads on to connect the sleeves. Mae finally added some material and made the arm holes bigger. "Crazy old man, I don't want you shutting the circulation off to your arms," she said.

He's right. Back when I did it, I figured he'd eventually lose the need to sleep in them. Now, I hope they hold together till he dies. They're getting hard to keep fixed, but he can't live without them. Mae

I've been through some bad things, but losing my wife was the worst. That first night I kept crying and tossing all over the bed. I grabbed Walentina's pillow to hug and felt her nighty under it. It still smelled of her. I hugged it, kept wiping my tears with it, covering my face with it.

Without thinking, I got naked and pulled it on over my shoulders and down around my body. Since then, only when I'm in her nighty can I sleep. We'd never slept apart and that was the best I could do.

Just wait till Hank's all alone forever and misses Mae's warm body every night. I know he will, because he sure gets his sausage in her enough, they have seven kids and who knows when they'll start another one. Soon, I bet. Plus, they are not quiet when they couple. Of course, neither were we.

My Young Life

I was born November 3, 1868 in Olsztyn, East Prussia.

Aha! The truth. The old man always said he was born in 1866. Ouch. This baby just kicked me hard. Lord, let it come quickly, I'm huge. Mae, May 1, 1934.

I grew up speaking Polish and German. I'd spit at that word, German, but Mae took the spittoon away, said my old friends would have to spit outside, she was tired of cleaning out the vessel and around the floor where they always missed.

My father was a gem of a man. He was a teacher, a writer, and a dreamer. He was also a Patriot. A true, brave Polish Patriot who hated the Germans for partitioning our part of Poland. He hated the Russians even worse, and wasn't fond of the Austrians, either. He was tall, about five-ten, wide-shouldered with blue eyes that were set so close together, some wondered if he was cross-eyed. From him, I inherited his eyes, the mole on my left cheek, and my wide shoulders and brains. Plus, his bravery.

My mother was small, tiny, maybe five-foot-one. She was also very smart, and spirited, very spirited. From her, I inherited more brains and my spirited voice. *He meant his big mouth! Mae.* Also, my bravery. She too was very brave and strong. They were not peasants, thank God, not like many of the Polish coming over here like lemmings who could barely read or write, if at all. Couldn't figure, only knew Polish.

My father owned a small, private school where well-off people sent their kids. Several rooms were attached that were our home, and everything sat on three hectares of land where vegetables, fruit, sheep and a cow were raised. My mother taught writing, music and art. She also supervised the girl's dorm. Father taught history, languages, science, math, and supervised the boys.

My father became more and more involved in the resistance and started to neglect his educator duties. When I was eight, he was killed, **Assassinated**, by them goddamn East Prussians for what they said was treason. Treason! He was a Patriot trying to keep the Polish culture alive. Those bastards!

My mother tried to keep the school running, but it was too far in debt so she sold it, paid off the liens and we moved near Posen where she soon met a man and married him. He was a widower, about forty-five, almost fifteen years older than my mother. He was not a peasant either, but he was not educated. He owned one hectare with a small home, one room with a loft, where I was sent to sleep after they saw me, awakened by their moans, observing them couple.

My stepfather raised a few sheep to sell wool and mutton, he was a skilled leatherworker and he had a blacksmith business. He also owned a male donkey and a female horse that he would breed every other year and sell the mules that were born. The mare usually birthed twins. He also rented out the donkey's services as a sire. In fact, that became one of my first duties. Leading or riding the donkey to wherever the peasant or person needed a horse or another donkey bred. Sometimes, I would leave him there, especially when the female wasn't receptive, but when she was ripe, I would stay all day. I watched till they coupled at least three times and were worn out. I could then lead him home. After almost getting kicked, I learned to wait till he was tired out before trying to take him home.

My stepfather was a man who used his words sparingly, like he might not have enough to last a lifetime. Silent Cal, you could say, after our former president, Calvin Coolidge. I think Stepfather was also quiet because he didn't feel as smart as my mother and didn't want to make a fool of himself. He also couldn't figure. Shortly after we moved in, I noticed Mother always showing up when it was time for a customer to make right with my stepfather. I knew how to figure, read, write, and could find most known countries on an atlas. I loved globes and we had one, something few people had in their homes at that time, especially in Poland. I rarely call it Eastern Prussia. That is an insult!

One day, Mother was not feeling well from another early pregnancy and asked me to run down and help Stepfather figure a customer's bill. When I got there, I noticed he was having problems and was ready to undercharge the customer so I turned in front of him and whispered, "Stepfather, you forgot to carry the numbers. It's double that amount." So, he told the man the correct cost. The man seemed surprised, I think he was used to getting undercharged.

After the man left with his leather repairs, Stepfather shook my hand like an adult. He said, "Thank you, Josef. I am not good adding numbers. I am a proud man, but think my pride has kept me nearly destitute. I will make sure either your mother or you are here when it's time to settle accounts."

I felt very proud. First, because he shook my hand. Second, he actually smiled a little and seemed warm and human instead of like a cold forge.

My mother said she got pregnant easily, but couldn't carry a child for long. She was cursed, she'd say. I didn't know what she meant until a neighbor's mare aborted early in her pregnancy. I was ten or eleven. My stepfather and I went to help bury it and I realized it was a partially formed colt. I told Mother how sad it was and she said, "Yes, I know. The same thing happens to me, a lot. I don't know why I'm cursed."

My new life, with no children around, was a big change from being a school teacher's child living with other students constantly around in an atmosphere of learning, fun learning. My parents had different ideas on how children should learn. It wasn't the strict, smack your hands if you get the wrong answer like the nuns used on my children and still do on my grandchildren over at St. Bobola's School. I told my wife, and later, Mae, how I do not want to hear about the kids getting smacked for stupid reasons. It upsets me too much and I want to go set them idiot teachers straight. If my progeny gets in trouble because of their behavior, I want to know and will also discipline them, but not for other dumb reasons. About a year after my daughter started school, I was not welcome because I disagreed with their teaching methods. I had no problem telling those withered-up, crabby, self-righteous old nuns and priests exactly why they didn't know how to teach and how they should teach to each child's inner spirit. Finally, my sweet, but spicy wife, God rest her soul, told me she would tell me when she needed my help, otherwise stay the hell away from the school. So, I did, and from the church, too. That's one of the reasons I rarely go near the place. There are more reasons you may discover.

Mother informed my stepfather she would school me one to two hours a day. After that, he should teach me as much as he could about his work. So, he did. He didn't use many words, mostly demonstrated what he was doing, then watched as I tried to repeat it. I was a quick learner, I always have been, though I had to learn to do things differently as I'm left-handed. I wasn't as interested in blacksmithing, but I did learn the basics. I loved building things. Stepfather also did some rough carpentry and occasional finish work. That was my favorite. Measuring, figuring out the supplies needed, and how things fit together. Building was all post and beam construction with wooden pegs, no nails and screws in the old country. I learned how to dig and install foundations, though I was a little small for moving the big rocks into place.

I also learned how to deliver baby sheep. Sometimes, they are such a helpless animal, dumber than a rock. Late winter, our six ewes started delivering. When I was eleven, Stepfather woke me one night and said he wanted me to see lambs being born. I'd seen puppies born, so figured this would be similar. It kinda was, till Stepfather said this ewe was having trouble. "Over an hour of labor and only a small bag of water showed and broke. She's in trouble. Come here," he said, "I want you to learn how to do this. Rinse your hands off in that bucket of water I had you carry."

Wow! Why did I need to do this? I didn't say that, this sounded urgent.

"Okay, now put your thumb against your fingers and slightly cup them. Now, slide one hand into the ewe and tell me what you feel."

Well, I looked at him like he was crazy. He wanted me to put my hand inside the rear end of a moaning, heaving sheep? I knew it wasn't her shithole, but still.

"Look, Josef, this lamb may be our meat for next winter or we sell it to buy things we need. There is at least one, maybe two more behind this one. If they die, the ewe might die. We can't afford such a loss. Now do as I tell you."

Slowly, I slid my hand in. "Keep your fingers together as much as possible. Slip it around. What do you feel?"

I did. It was slimy and warm, strange, but kind of exciting, like a whole other world I'd never thought about. The whole back end of the ewe and the area around her smelled of damp wool, piss and shit. Carefully, I moved my hand around, then realized I was feeling its nose and jaw. I told Stepfather and he asked, "Do you feel its feet or legs? They should be alongside the head." I moved my hand some more, shook my head, said I couldn't feel any feet or legs. "Okay, because you're small, you'll need both hands now, get your right hand in there. Push the lamb back into the canal a way, then follow the body around on each side till you find a front leg, see if you can get both of them, next pull them forward."

I did. As soon as I got the feet and legs alongside the head, that little lamb slid out like it was greased. I couldn't believe it! I'd just helped birth a baby lamb and Stepfather said it appeared healthy. His messy hand shook mine and he smiled at me just as the next lamb, a boy, slid out. Stepfather clapped me on the shoulder. "You saved two lives. I don't think a third one is coming. This boy is good sized."

I stayed out the whole night to help him. While we waited, he told me about other positions the lambs can be in and what to feel for and how to turn them in the uterus, not the canal. I was pretty proud of myself. Later, I thought about killing the lambs after they'd grown for meat. I remembered how that might have upset me when I was younger. After several years on the little farm, I realized how life worked and felt good about helping our little family survive.

As I grew and started to fill out, I began working around the area, doing whatever I could. Mother also hired a tutor to teach me some basics in algebra and geometry. I spent the summer I was fifteen working for a survey crew to map and improve the area roads and bridges. William I, the Prussian ruler and German emperor, wanted to improve our transportation methods. I also helped build a barn. Stepfather said I could keep half of what I earned, the other half went to Mother and him to help pay my keep. Mother agreed. I saved almost all my money; there wasn't much to spend it on. Chasing girls seemed like a waste of time and money. Not that I wasn't interested in them. Mother told me to wait till I could afford my own home and support a wife and children before I even nodded to a girl.

Chapter Two

Becoming a Man

I was sixteen, it was after lambing and Mother finally carried a baby through its eighth month. All three of us were excited, but dared not say much. *Don't divide the skin while it's still on the bear.* That was the old saying we observed, but still the glint in everyone's eyes each day was hard to miss. And Mother said she was feeling well.

Every spring and fall, Stepfather put his anvil and tools into the wagon and took off for one to two weeks around the countryside. He'd stay a few days in various small towns and hamlets where he'd shoe horses, repair harnesses, even people's shoes, and fix anything he could. I went with him for the two years before, but I stayed home that year with Mother being so pregnant.

I was outside, doing chores for the afternoon. When I came in, Mother was on the floor, sobbing, her dress pulled up, underclothes off, blood and liquid flooding around her. "The baby is early. The midwife is out of town and I can't push it out. Something's wrong."

I was stunned, what could I do? I didn't know how to deliver babies. Did they come out with their arms and hands alongside their head like a lamb does with its front feet?

"What can I do?" I whispered. "Just tell me."

She groaned and tried to push, but the pain was too great and I could tell she was getting weak. I rinsed my hands in the basin. Kneeling in the bloody mess between her legs, I put my hands on her thighs. "Mother, tell me how the baby is supposed to come out. Mother, tell me now."

"Its head, then shoulders, I think they usually turn a little for the shoulders, then the rest just follows. Oh, son, I'm not sure I can do this."

"You have to, Mother." Carefully, I put my thumb against my fingers like I did with the lambs and entered her, quickly finding skin. Feeling around, I realized it was the baby's butt. "Mother, don't move, don't force. Its butt is trying to come first, I will try to turn it."

She weakly moaned and I wondered if she even heard me. Slowly,

I pushed the baby back in and gently turned it around till I knew its' head was aimed downward. "Push, Mother. Push!"

Mother gave a big push, enough that I could grasp its head in one hand and slip my fingers under its shoulder and slide it out with only a few tugs.

"It's a girl, Mother. A girl!"

I grabbed a towel and rubbed it off. The baby gasped and cried out. It was the greatest feeling I'd ever experienced. The other stuff inside Mother soon followed and she weakly told me to get some string and a knife and how to cut the cord. She had me unbutton her top and lay the baby on her chest so it could nurse. When I did, I noticed a small cloth bag tied around her neck.

"Mother, you're still bleeding. Shouldn't it stop now?"

The baby was fussing, trying to nurse. For something early and so tiny, she was feisty. "Josef, untie the bag around my neck. Quick, tie it around yours. It's your future, from your father. Your stepfather knows it's for you. I think my future is almost over. Now wrap the baby and take her over to Mrs. Gorski. She has a two-year-old and is still nursing him."

I threw a blanket over Mother and ran the baby over to our nearest neighbors, about a quarter mile, close to a half kilometer. I held the tiny bundle close and tight as she kicked and screamed the whole way.

"Mrs. Gorski," I gasped, "can you feed the baby, Mother can't."

That was when I started crying, almost as loud as the blood-streaked baby. "Her name's Eugenia. My mother's name."

Wow! I never knew that. I wonder if Hank did. Mae. November 15, 1934.

Writing this is hard, there is water in my eyes, remembering all this. It feels like it was yesterday. Even so, I will carry on. If I don't, I won't sleep all night, or I'll get drunk and get yelled at by Henryk.

I rushed back to Mother. She was still alive, but barely. I checked under the blanket and could tell she was still bleeding. I knew nothing about what was causing it or how to stop it. I got down and lifted her up partway into my lap and stroked her face. My heart was pounding, I thought it might break, and my gut was churning like I could throw up. I think now it was all fear. What happens if Mother dies? What about the baby? I need Stepfather here to help, but he's been gone five days, where could he be? How will we live without Mother?

My mother opened her eyes. "Son," she whispered, "help your stepfather for a while, then go to Chicago. You need to start a new life. You're smart and will have more opportunities there than here."

"What about the baby?"

"Your stepfather will make sure she's well taken care of, he will love her as much as I have you."

Her breath caught. I kissed her on her forehead, my tears flowing and mixing with hers.

"I named her Eugenia, after you," I said.

She smiled, just a little. Her body shuddered like she was chilled, and she stopped breathing.

I felt the bag I'd hastily tied around my neck. It contained gold coins and several pieces of jewelry. I remember thinking how I preferred having my mother alive over owning the valuables.

~ * ~

Oh, my God. This is too much. I can feel it all over again. Her weak voice, her shudder, her breath stopping and her body growing cold as I held her. I can't keep writing this.

I need *Piwo* or *wino*. I'll sneak downstairs to the special laundry room Henryk and I set up during prohibition. We still make some wine and good Polish beer. It's still better than that legal three-two shit they try to call beer now.

I remember finding him almost passed out, crying down there, the lights off. He hadn't come to supper and the kids couldn't find him, so I went looking. He wouldn't tell me what he was upset about. I didn't know he started writing his memories. He was still in his dead wife's nightgown. I swore I was going to steal those rags and burn them. That would probably kill him and I couldn't have that on my conscience. I made him pee in one of the empty bottles, dragged him upstairs and threw him in bed before Hank got home. I took him some food later. He was hung over the next day, looked like hell. And me with a two-month old, Nina. Mae. December 15, 1934.

~ * ~

It's almost Valentine's Day. I can't write, all I can think of is Walentina, God rest her beautiful soul. Besides, I'm still hungover. I snuck back down to the special laundry room last night when the house was quiet. Quiet, except for the springs bouncing and all the moaning from Henryk and Mae's bedroom above me. A four-month-old baby and she still likes coupling. A woman like that is hard to find. I know, I had one. Hey, Mae took my suggestion and named this little one Nina. About time, I've been asking her to do so for years.

That's right, I liked it. There ain't much other good news during the depression. Crazy old fool, listening to us make love all those years. Mae. June 6, 1935. Glad I finally named a girl Nina. Mae.

Now, I write again. I will try to give less details. When I do, my emotions overcome me and I get drunk and in trouble with Mae and Henryk, who can't understand the reason. I'm not yet ready to tell them about my writing. I'd hate being laughed at as a crazy old man who's getting drunk over trying to write his memories down.

THAT CRAZY OLD MAN doesn't get in trouble. He makes Hank sound like a real grouch. He's not. He rarely seems upset to me over his dad. I think when he sees the old man in a nightgown, it just reminds both of them of Walentina's death and they don't know how to talk about it. Men! Mae.

Sometimes I wonder, who has suffered more than us Poles? Maybe the Jews, from the rumors coming out of Germany. There's some bad Jews too, like the lout I met on the ship. That jerk made me leery of them all. Still, most of them don't deserve the cruelties they've endured.

Fucking Germans and Russians. Look at all the misery they've caused. This is only the start of my suffering. There is much more to be written.

~ * ~

So, my mother died in my arms. I went to the priest who, the bastard, told me I first must give him money to cover his expenses to help

14

me. Up front, right then. That homosexualist! I'd heard rumors about him and other priests.

I paid him out of my own funds. Only then did the jerk organize several women from the parish to come prepare her body and clean up the floor and arrange food for the gathering. Of course, they got paid nothing from him.

The news spread word of mouth through the Polish underground and reached my stepfather. Still, it was two days after the funeral before he made it home. He was distraught. I'd never seen a man weep like he did. I didn't know he had that much emotion in him.

Several days after Stepfather returned, I told him about the priest charging me for what neighbors said he never charged anyone before, how they thought he was trying to take advantage of an orphan. Stepfather was ready to tear the man apart. *"Pocałuj mnie w dupę*—kiss my ass," he yelled at the guy. At that point, he grabbed the priest by his shoulders and whispered in his ear. I couldn't hear most of it, but it was something about Stepfather catching him and another priest down by the river and they weren't fishing or praying. The priest gave me my money back.

So, at sixteen, I helped birth my sister, held my mother in my arms as she died, handled all the details of her funeral and burial, of course with the help of several wonderful neighbors. There was damn little help from that short, fat, obnoxious homosexual priest.

I need a spittoon!

Mrs. Gorski offered to keep Eugenia as long as needed. For a very reasonable cost, she offered to feed Stepfather and me an evening meal and pack us a lunch. So, every night, we went to her house to eat and hold Eugenia. We both adored the baby, and soon enjoyed Mrs. Gorski's three children as well.

When sober, her peasant husband could be a decent man. He did day labor, unskilled peasant work, whatever he could find. Local people who hired him tried to give his wages directly to Mrs. Gorski so they had enough to live on. Unfortunately, people further away would pay him in person and he would drink most of it away, which happened more and more. At those times, he was a stupid, mean, ugly drunk who terrorized his wife and children.

One evening, about three months after Mother's death, while we were there, eating and playing with Eugenia, Mr. Gorski came home drunk. He started getting violent with the kids. I grabbed the baby and three children and ran them to our home. Shortly, Mrs. Gorski came over, crying, her right eye swollen, bruises on her cheeks.

"He started to beat on me," she said. "Your stepfather threw him out of the house and told him he'd kill him if he came back tonight. He left, but your stepfather stayed over to make sure he doesn't return."

I took the two bigger kids, they were about three and five, up to the loft to sleep with me, while Mrs. Gorski went to sleep on the bed with the two-year-old and my baby sister.

The next morning, I was outside doing the chores when I saw Stepfather and two men from the village enter our house. I heard Mrs. Gorski start wailing. I went inside to see her beating her fists on my father's chest. "Did you kill him?" she kept asking, hitting him over and over.

He grabbed her hands. "No. I did not. I spent the night waiting for him to return. Even then I wouldn't have killed him. Beat him up maybe, but not killed him. These men found him in the creek this morning, drowned."

I watched Mrs. Gorski collapse into my father's arms and knew our lives were going to change again. Could she still care for Eugenia? How would they survive? She was unskilled. Could she keep the half hectare they owned? How would we care for Eugenia? Who could wet nurse her? Would my baby sister die?

~ * ~

A break from my memories.

Mae just came in and found me sniffling, my eyes dripping. So, I told her how I'm writing my memories and need her to translate them. "You crazy old fool," she said. She sat down, grabbed the ledger and started reading at the beginning. "You crazy old fool," she said again, but she was smiling. "Lying about your age all these years. Are all these memories why you keep getting drunk?"

I sniffled and nodded.

"Tell you what," she said. "You write during the day. When you're done, lay the ledger on the counter by your kitchen door and when I have time, I'll work on it at night after the kids are in bed. It may take me a long time."

"It doesn't matter if you finish it after I'm dead," I replied, "just as long as you do. My grandchildren and theirs must know their rich heritage and what I've gone through for them to be successful in America."

"Not only are you a crazy old fool, you sound like a pompous one as well," she said.

She kissed me and left the room.

So, here I go again. This time with a relief in my heart that Mae knows and approves. Who cares what Henryk thinks? Mae will keep him in line if he does say anything mean about it.

As if I needed to! Mae.

~ * ~

After the husband's funeral, Stepfather offered to rent the Gorski land, said he would raise more sheep on it and plant a bigger garden. Things continued as before, almost better. About six months after that, I was watching Eugenia, now nine months, crawl around, pulling herself up to a chair, babbling and happy, when I noticed Stepfather look at Mrs. Gorski in a strange way. Not bad or mean, just a spark of some kind. That night, he stayed later than I did, much later. The same the next night, and I realized what was happening.

"Stepfather, I need to talk with you about my future," I said one evening when he came home early.

He carried Eugenia for a visit at our house. She was almost ready to walk and we didn't want to miss her first steps. He nodded for me to continue. "I think it's time I went on my own. I want to go to America, to Chicago. There will be better opportunities for me there than here." I didn't look at him.

He sighed, then waited till I looked at him.

17

"Son, I will miss you, but I think it's a wise decision. I only ask that you wait six months. I need your help putting an addition on the house. Mrs. Gorski and I plan to marry."

All the confusion and loss and tension, plus fear for my own future erupted. "Why? Why should I wait around?" I shouted even louder. "My mother is dead, her body is barely cold in the grave and you're going to remarry some woman whose husband is still warm. Are you sure you didn't kill him? I can't stand being around here any longer!"

I stormed off down the dirt road with no idea where I was going. It was dark and chilly. I grew tired, stumbling through the late evening on the rough dirt road.

Suddenly, I remembered, he called me son. He never did that before. I saw the tears in his eyes when I asked if he'd killed Mr. Gorski. Plus, I recalled how Mother married him less than a year after my father's death. I turned around and slowly walked back home. He was sitting in a chair, holding Eugenia who was fussy from cutting teeth. She gnawed his thick finger. He never winced as her six little razor-sharp teeth bit into him.

"I'm sorry," I said. "I shouldn't have said those things."

He nodded, looked at me as if he understood. I couldn't help asking, "Why did you call me son?"

He blinked his eyes and looked away for a moment. "Because you have been the best son to me a man could have. I have three adult sons who rarely speak to me. I was not a good father in my first marriage, too impatient, too angry with my wife and sons, too stubborn. Your mother and you helped me be a better person. I never knew how to tell you."

I picked up the baby and winced as she chomped down on my thumb. I found the whiskey bottle. It was never imbibed. We used it only for medicinal purposes. I dipped a finger in and rubbed Eugenia's gums. I nodded toward the door and said, "It's time we took her back to her mother, Dad. How soon can we start the addition?"

Holy Lord Jesus! The splotches on this page are from my leaky eyes. I need to take a break from interpreting this stuff. Crazy old fool, making me cry like this. Besides, I think I'm going into labor. Number nine. I gotta figure out a way to make it my last. I can't keep squeezing out these babies, as much as I love them. But when Hank's sausage starts poking against me, I don't know how to tell him no. What's more, I don't want to. What the hell am I going to do? Mae. August 10, 1935.

Stepfather, I still couldn't call him Father, even though he'd been my stepfather for as long as I had a real father. Sometimes I managed to call him Dad or Pops. I could tell he liked that when I did, but I think he understood why it was still hard. Anyway, Stepfather put me in charge of the addition, drawing it out, laying out the lines on the ground, finding and buying the beams and lumber, even hiring some labor at times. It went up quite fast.

One evening, Mrs. Gorski brought over supper so we could eat quickly and keep working into the evening light. She watched me write and make some figures on one of the drawings. She touched my shoulder, then lowered her eyes. "Could...Could you teach me how to figure? Just the basics? I want to be able to help your stepfather when his customers make right with him."

For some reason, I took her chin, gently, in my dirty hand and raised it till she was looking into my eyes. It was the first time, other than a hug after Mother's death, that we touched. I looked into her eyes, they were beautiful, realized she was young, probably not twenty-five yet. "I would love to," I said. "Maybe we should ask your oldest child, she's six now, to join us. That way she can learn, too." Her face widened into a beautiful smile. I could see why Stepfather may have fallen in love with her.

"I got two years of schooling when I was little, so I can read a bit and know my numbers. I hope I'm not too old to learn more."

I told her she wasn't, and she wasn't. In fact, she and her daughter caught on quickly. So, that's another trait I possess—the ability to teach others in ways they can understand. Another fine attribute I inherited from both my parents!

The addition was roughed in, the fireplace put up and we started the inside finish work. My stepfather and Mrs. Gorski had a simple church wedding, followed by a reception in the unfinished house. I think by then they had a new bun warming in the oven.

I was eager to leave. I possessed nearly all the money I'd earned from outside jobs, minus what I'd paid Mother and Stepfather, plus the gold coins and jewelry in the pouch Mother gave me at her death.

Stepfather surprised me one morning when he told me not to work on the addition that day. He wanted me to get a haircut, a full bath, and buy some new clothes and boots. When I returned home, he gave me a heavy envelope. Inside was a train ticket to Hamburg leaving the next day, a ticket on the S/S Hammonia out of Hamburg to New York, plus a train ticket on to Chicago.

"This is for all of your work on the house," Stepfather said. "The money in here is the half your beautiful mother and I collected from you as your share of the household expenses. It's yours. Try to get some land and a house as quickly as possible."

He shook my hand, his eyes watering.

The next morning, while Stepfather hitched the horse to the cart, Mrs. Gorski, now my stepmother, pulled me into a gentle hug. I could feel her enlarged belly and remember thinking how fun it would be around another baby. Her three children danced around and Eugenia, oh my God, I'm weeping again, my little Eugenia was tottering all over the place, babbling Mama and Dada. I picked her up, but couldn't tell her good-bye. How I hated to leave her. How do you tell a little toddler you may never see her again?

Stepfather came in the house and for the first time in my life, hugged me, too. "Son, it's time we leave."

I was sad-faced all the way to the train station and numb the long train ride to Hamburg.

I never saw my baby sister again. When she was around eight, she started writing me a letter at Christmas, which meant I received it months later. Her letters ended when the Great War started. One letter a year, first printed in a child's big block letters, next carefully formed cursive, eventually beautiful adult penmanship. She talked of her mother's, Mrs. Gorski's, commitment to her education, told of helping her father feed the lambs, later delivering them, of struggling as a woman to get an education, how irritated men made her. She spoke warmly of a female friend, another teacher that she lived with, and how, together, they taught the children in the village to read and write and figure. They had a keen desire to run a real school. Guess that runs in the family. She is how I knew Mrs. Gorski bore two more children, both boys, and Stepfather died at age seventy-two, suddenly, while shoeing a horse. My sister never married. I think she died during the war. Maybe she was a true Patriot like her natural mother and my father.

Her letters were in an old envelope buried beneath his raggedy socks and underwear. I kept them, though I added my tear splotches to his. They're now in the back of his first ledger. Mae.

Chapter Three

Getting to Chicago

The S.S. Hammonia set sail October 18, 1885 and arrived at one o'clock in the morning on October 30. After processing at Castle Garden on the tip of Manhattan Island, I was herded onto a ferry, then to a train station where I waited 'til they had enough to fill the immigrant train, which was what my ticket was for. I think the regular passenger trains made the journey to Chicago in forty-hours. The immigrant train took over three days, it had to pull over for oncoming freight and passenger trains who had the right of way. It was the worst part of my journey to Chicago.

Now the ship, that was an interesting experience. I almost kissed a girl for the first time, plus I got in a fight with a Jewish bastard and was locked in the ship's brig. My incarceration lasted only until the captain listened to me. I got seasick, but not for long. It was during a good storm, but I think it was from drinking too much spirits one night with the crew.

The steerage deck was the third one below the main. It was seven feet high and was near the huge boiler area. You could hear and feel the engines pound every minute of the trip. There were several rooms for single men. Each room contained four triple-bunks, two wide, a low board separating the two men at each level. Twenty-four men were squeezed into a tiny area. It seemed at least half of them were snoring or farting most of the night. Most of them were good guys, peasants, a few skilled laborers like me, and several loud-mouth assholes.

Our food was included. Each person brought their own metal dish, cup, fork, spoon and knife. We rinsed them off in a communal bucket after each meal. The women on the trip thought that was gross, but there wasn't much they could do, other than nag the cabin boy to bring more fresh water, always in limited supply on a ship.

For some reason, either at Stepfather's word or in confusion, the ticket master issued my tickets with my age listed as nineteen. I was seventeen, but didn't try to correct things. I easily looked nineteen and it gave me a shot of maturity, a sense of accomplishment. Made me puff out my chest a little more and think how a nineteen-year-old man would handle things. One way turned out to be with my fists with that Jewish lout.

A father, his eighteen-year-old daughter and a gaggle of younger kids were traveling in the family section of steerage. The youngest child was a little girl of about two. It was hard to keep my eyes off her after just leaving Eugenia. The older girl was downright pretty and at times seemed nigh wore out from keeping tabs on her younger siblings. Several of her brothers took a liking to me, they were friendly little guys, so I started taking them on walks around the ship, exploring. I tried to teach them what I was learning about how the ship operated, how it was steam powered and sail powered. I got them as close as I could to see the huge engines. One of the crew saw us and gave us a little tour. I was excited and those boys were enthralled. I was their hero.

At supper that night, the father thanked me and herded the clutch off to bed. I was having some coffee and a cigarette with a couple of the single men when that little girl tottered out through the curtain of their room, pleased as punch with herself and absolutely fearless. She ran, you know how babies that age run, all from the waist down, across the narrow dining room. Just before she got near our table, the ship took a little roll and I grabbed her up just before she fell. I pulled her onto my lap where she immediately giggled and wanted to take off again. I tossed her a little way into the air and caught her. Tears were coming to my eyes, she so much reminded me of my Eugenia, tiny, energetic and afraid of little. I kept tossing her and zooming her around. It wasn't safe to let her run around. The other single men laughed along with her. There's something contagious about a little one's laughter.

The ship was rolling, not severely, but enough to caution your walk. After several tosses in the air and her pulling on my hair and nose when I made a horn sound, we heard a commotion from the family area. "Papa, where is Genina? She was right here, almost sleeping. Papa, is she by you and the boys?" Some more words were exchanged, the papa's voice calm, the daughter's panicked. The papa opened the curtains and peered out. He saw me tossing and playing with the baby.

"She escaped, we were hoping you wouldn't notice for a while, she's a fun one."

He shook his head with a smile and gingerly made his way across the rolling deck to us. Sitting down, he held his hands out to her.

"No, no, no." We all laughed. He waved back at his daughter peering anxiously through their curtain.

Yohan, that was his name, stayed for nearly a half hour till Genina, they called her Nina too, began to get sleepy in my arms. He told me his wife died two months after giving birth, something not related to her childbirth. Nina was their seventh child, his oldest, Stefania, was eighteen. I quietly shared with him about Eugenia and her mother's death, that she now had a wonderful stepmother, how I was going on to Chicago. He nodded thoughtfully when I said that, said goodnight, gathered little Nina into his arm, and carefully made his way to their berths.

The next morning at breakfast, the little boys pestered me to go explore the ship again. Their papa said he would come along. That way, Stefania could help her sisters take sponge baths in their room.

Their papa was strict, but allowed his three boys lots of room to experiment. I could tell he was similar to Stepfather in that he showed or gave brief explanations, then allowed them to figure things out on their own.

It was cool, but sunny as the ship plowed through the waves. We watched the boys talking with one of the crew as he explained how the sailing system worked.

"So," Yohan asked, "what will you do in Chicago? Do you have any skills?"

"I love working with my hands, carpentry, I read, write and figure well. My stepfather put me in charge of designing and constructing the addition we put on the home just before I left."

He thought for a minute, glanced at the boys who were watching the crewman teach them how to tie a knot. "We're going to spend some time in New York with my late wife's relatives, then maybe go to Chicago."

I nodded, a little disappointed they weren't going onto Chicago on the immigrant train. I wanted to get to know Stefania.

Yohan continued, "My cousin works for a contractor in Chicago who buys land and builds homes on it. He says building homes is better than working in the stockyards or steel mills. He said it's hard for skilled people to get started and noticed in the stockyards, that's why so many peasants are going there, most of the jobs are unskilled. My cousin's name is Zygmunt Olanski, and he works for Rothman Builders. They're German, but fair to Poles who know their stuff."

"I speak German almost as well as Polish," I said.

"Even better. Be sure to look them up. They're headquartered on Ashland Street, in Back of the Yards, close to the stockyards. It's a hellhole, smelly, dirty, but people need housing and things can only get better." He started to leave to gather his boys. "Oh, one more thing. Their construction is much different. They call it balloon construction. I too am a builder. After dinner, let me show you how it's done."

He made sketches, explaining how a skeleton of many small pieces of lumber were structurally as strong as thick pieces and how using nails and screws was faster and just as strong as notching.

It was a good education for which I am eternally thankful. He said I was exceptionally smart and would go far. He also said rooming houses were in big demand and shared with me his idea of what one should look like. Turns out he lived and worked in New York for six years and studied housing needs for immigrants and this was his second time going back to America.

I made sure I ate at the same time Yohan's family did. Mostly because it felt good to be a part of a family, but also because Nina insisted on sitting on my lap, and, well, because I was also attracted to Stefania. So much so, I started to dream about her one night and had to open my pants and exercise myself. From the sounds of things some nights, I wasn't the only one doing such. When you're single and young, occasionally relieving that pressure becomes a necessity.

I wasn't the only one who noticed her shy beauty. Several other guys in the room mentioned her, but respectfully. One night, one of the crude oafs, an oversized Jew, said how he wanted to shove his tree into her. I told him to show respect for a woman. The man growled and asked if I was some kind of a fucking Catholic priest. I ignored him.

The next morning, I was bored. Yohan took the boys and two of their sisters for a walk and some fresh air. I wandered around and slowly made my way back to the steerage area. I noticed Stefania carrying the baby, and the lout who yelled at me closely following her. When she stopped to talk with me as Nina held out her arms, yelling for me to take her, he stepped around her, toward the sleeping berths. Grasping Nina from her sister, our hands touched and I felt a zing run through me. Maybe she did as well, because her face flushed and she looked away. We talked about me going to Chicago, how thankful I was for her father's good advice. She wanted to become a midwife, her mother had been one and she assisted her. I told her one time was enough for me. She smiled in understanding.

I jostled the baby till she was almost asleep, then slipped her back into her big sister's arms. Stefania shyly glanced at me. I wanted to embrace her so badly, but instead muttered, "Maybe I can talk with you more sometime." I felt my face turn bright red as I turned and walked down the deck, away from the sleeping areas.

A few minutes later, I heard a shriek, "No!" It sounded like Stefania. I remembered the lout was in the area, his disgusting talk last night, and how closely he'd been following her. I rushed toward the family section, then heard a loud moan and muffled scream. I pulled the curtain open to see Stefania with a kerchief tied through her mouth so she couldn't speak. The lout held her pinned to the bed with one arm while his other had pulled up her dress and was pulling her underclothing down, his member already sticking out of his pants.

I grabbed his arm and yanked him up partway, but that gave him enough room to swing at me with his other arm. He hit me on the side of my head, just above my ear, enough to slightly jar me, but not enough to make me let go of his arm. I yanked again and this time, got him off the bed where I kicked at his sausage, trying to get his two *jaja* as well. He groaned, then lurched at me. We tumbled out of the room and into the dining area, half-wrestling, half-swinging, pushing and shoving. We got to our feet where I finally landed a good left hook to his jaw, which momentarily slowed him down. He grabbed a dining chair and jammed the top rung into my throat. I gagged, grabbed it away from him and was going to swing it on him when four or five crewmen rushed in and separated us. They dragged us to the ship's brig where they threw us in separate cells, I think there were only two. They tossed buckets of salt water over us till we looked like drowned rats. They left us there for hours, shivering in the late fall sea air.

Eventually, the captain came. A short, heavyset German. He asked in German, "It doesn't appear you were drinking. Why were you fighting?" The lout couldn't understand him, so a crew member beside him repeated it in Polish.

"He was trying to accost that girl and I had to stop him," the lout yelled, pointing at me. "He's been making up to her the whole trip, pretending to like her baby sister, all the time he's just been waiting till she was alone so he could rape her."

I was shocked. Him blaming me? I was ready to explode, but remembered my mother's words to always stay calm in tense situations. Getting angry wouldn't help. I took a deep breath, looked at the lout in disgust, then addressed the captain in perfect German. "Sir, most respectfully, the man is lying. I found him holding down the lady whom he already gagged so she couldn't cry out, with his pants undone and his member out. He was removing her undergarments when I got there."

The lout yelled and hollered I was a liar. I waited till he quieted down before continuing, "And sir, he grossly boasted last night in our room how he wanted to stick his tree in her. I thought it might be alcohol talking so didn't think he was being truthful. I guess I was wrong."

The captain said nothing, turned and left. About an hour later, he returned. "I spoke with each crew member who broke up your fight. Two distinctly remember you," he pointed to the lout, "tucking your member back in your pants. Further conversation with the young lady and her father confirmed the facts. You are confined to this cell for the duration of the voyage, after which you will be consigned to the police in New York who will probably ship you back in chains on another ship. It won't be on this one. If it was up to me, I would throw you overboard now, bound and gagged."

He instructed the men to unlock my cell, help me out and give me a towel to dry off with. He stuck his hand out. "I want to shake your hand. You saved a young woman from having her life ruined by this bastard.

Thank you and good luck in America. I'm sure with such integrity will do you well. I'm proud of you."

I still remember his firm grasp and his voice as he spoke those well-deserved words.

News travels fast on a ship. I was lauded as a hero by others, including several first-class patrons who came up to me after being pointed out by the crew as the man who saved a lady's virtue. I remember hearing one first-class woman nearby snort, "Well, it's good to know there are some women of virtue and gallant men in steerage on this ship."

I ignored her rudeness.

Yohan brought his children to supper that night without Stefania. He warmly shook my hand, told me in an aside, "The lout has actually made several comments to Stefania during the trip, but she was too shy to tell me. Now, she is embarrassed and doesn't want any attention, but she sends her thanks to you."

"Please give her my regards and tell her I understand her embarrassment, but she did nothing wrong. She should walk with her head high." An impulse of chivalry swept through me, so I added, "In fact, I would be delighted to walk her around the ship. We could even take Nina and the kids."

Yohan tried to smile, said he'd pass my gallant offer on to her.

That night was our last full night on the ship. We were scheduled to arrive the next evening. I noticed one of the children fix a dish of soup, or gruel, or whatever they called the food to take to her. By that time, we were all tired of the monotonous fare and the digestive issues it brought to our bowels. Of course, Nina insisted on sitting on my lap and feeding herself, getting as much on her and me as in her.

Several of the single men and I remained at the table as the others went to bed. We were surprised when three crew members joined us, the same ones who dragged me to the brig. Two spoke Polish so my friends could enjoy the conversation. We started telling our backgrounds and why we travelers were going to America. The crew were decent men. Soon, one of them produced a bottle of spirits and passed it around. I was not used to such concentrated drink, so I gasped and wheezed on my first sip. I poured a little in my cup and added some water. Shortly, we began singing Polish and Prussian folk songs like we were brothers. That was the night we hit some cold winds and the ship bucked and tossed the entire night. As did my stomach and many others by the smell and looks of things in the morning.

Everyone was hoping our last day at sea would be clear and smooth so we could see America as we approached. It wasn't. It stayed rough and slow going until we entered the Hudson River. Finally, the winds died down and the sun appeared for several hours in the evening. It was glorious, in spite of my hangover.

Standing on the deck, watching the country and city grow, I felt someone touch my elbow. It was Stefania and Nina. "Nina wanted to say goodbye," Stefania said.

She blushed and looked away, then whispered, "So did I."

My heart thumped, my head got light as I touched her arm. She looked into my eyes, hers gorgeous, blue, shimmering. We hugged awkwardly with a two-year-old wiggling between us. "Thank you. I'll miss you."

She grabbed Nina and ran toward their berth, leaving me standing alone beside the rail, wiping my eyes. Other than a glimpse of them hurrying down the gangway in the middle of the night, I never saw her again.

Damn. If I only knew this much about the old man's life, I might have thought she would be my mother-in-law. Mae. September 12, 1935. No baby yet.

Chapter Four

My First Day in Chicago

Yohan was right. Chicago was a hellhole. I was used to smells, after three weeks of travel, sleeping and living in the same clothes, I stunk, too. However, the closer I walked toward Back of the Yards, the worse the stench grew and it wasn't mine. I didn't need a map, just followed my nose.

I walked by the meat-processing factories, huge buildings full of steam and noise. The stockyards were where workers unloaded the cattle, sheep, hogs, and horses from rail cars, then herded them toward various chutes that entered the processing plants. I could hear the squeals, see the confusion and growing fear in the animals' eyes the closer they got to the chutes, smell the blood coming from the killing line just beyond.

My God, I thought, did I just change my whole life to come here? I remembered hearing other passengers on the ship, Russian Poles and some Jews, tell how they were fleeing their homes, expelled because they were Polish or Jewish. There was no way I would return to face that uncertainty for Prussian Poles like me. I walked by and turned south on Ashland.

I noticed a sign that read, "Day Labor, seven a.m." in Polish and English. So now I knew what those words meant in English and where to show up for work. An old woman was selling kielbasa on the wooden sidewalk, I bought one.

"This shit is full of gristle. Don't you know how to make good sausage?" I barked at her.

"Fresh off the boat, huh? Well, make some money and you can afford better. This is the best I can do, my husband can't work, busted his leg up in the yards."

"I'm sorry," I said, a little embarrassed at being so critical.

She grinned at me, rotten teeth, several missing, but I could see she wasn't as old as I first thought. "You're young. What ya looking for? A lady? A room? Maybe you should start with a bath and getting your clothes cleaned."

I blushed. "I could use a room with meals, a bath, my clothes cleaned, and a job."

The woman chuckled and asked where I was from. I told her. I also told her I was hoping to find work with Rothman Builders, how I was to find Zygmunt Olanski.

Her eyes got large, then suspicious. "Why the hell you think you can work with them? They don't take dumb Polish peasants."

I bit my tongue, but could feel my anger rising. Who was this poor woman selling sausages on the street corner to speak to me in such a manner? Pulling myself up, I replied, very curtly, I might add, "I am a laborer skilled in carpentry, surveying, repairs, animal husbandry and I read, write and figure in Polish and German." I started to walk away.

"Hang on, hotshot. I didn't realize I was speaking with a Polish prince."

Just the way she said it made me realize I'd acted haughty, something my dead mother warned me about at times. "Just because you have skills and are literate doesn't mean you are better than other people. We're all God's people," she told me once when I was mouthing off about some dumb villagers in typical teenage fashion.

"I'm not," I said to this woman now. "I can do about any kind of work and do it well."

She smiled, her eyes twinkling at my youth. "Go see my neighbor, tell her the dumb sausage seller sent you. She's looking for a good, smart, clean, polite, humble boarder. Her food's pretty good, too. Better than my kielbasa you just complained about."

She gave me directions and added, "After that, go take a bath, there's several places on Ashland, they'll even clean some of your clothes while you soak along with a few other services." She winked at me, then gave me a gentle push away. "Learn all your smarts in English and you'll do fine here, boy."

Mrs. Gola answered the door of her small home on South Laflin Street. She laughed when I told her who sent me. The house smelled of good food and of the stockyards. "I only have one room I rent out, and it's with a double bed," she said. "You can share it with Pawel, he can't afford the place alone. I'll split your room fee and you pay full board. Plus, for ten cents more per week, I'll do your laundry and you can use the bath tub Saturday nights after my family is finished."

She agreed to accept payment after I changed my money. I walked the few blocks over to Ashland, desperate for a bath. First, I changed some Prussian coins for American at a bank. Two doors down, the sign said 'Baths' in big Polish and English letters, with several smaller words in English I didn't know. Later, when I learned some English, I knew they said, 'Clean Services for Discerning Gentlemen.' Not every bath establishment said that, in fact, some stated, 'No Services Provided,' but I didn't realize that on my first day.

A well-dressed woman greeted me in Polish. "You look like you just arrived." She smiled at my nod. "In that case, why don't you take a nice long bath while we clean some of the travel off your clothes." She collected my money and led me through a door to a small waiting room with comfortable stuffed chairs. Two clean, well-dressed men waited on a red divan. They smirked when I sat down. The woman said, "Lilly will show you to your bath shortly. She will take good care of you. Just remember please, you are never to repeat her name outside of this establishment, it's for her safety."

I was confused. All I needed was a bathtub with lots of hot water and some soap. Why couldn't I repeat the name of the girl who was going to hand me a towel and some soap? One of the men winked at me and said something in English. When he saw my confusion, he asked, "German? Polish?"

I shrugged to indicate either.

"My German is better. I told you, Lilly has wonderful hands." He laughed at the shocked look on my face as it dawned on me that Lilly might be helping me with my bath. "We're each having other services necessary for good health and release," he added as two young, scantily dressed women entered the room and led them off.

I was horrified, but didn't have time to make up my mind to leave as Lilly walked in, dressed not quite as scantily, but still enough to make my heart race. "Your first time here?" she asked. I nodded, sure my face was turning red. "Please follow me."

She led me into a dim room with a large tub, a thick red and black

Turkish rug on the floor, and hooks holding long towels and robes. The room smelled of lilacs. The tub was already half filled. "Please undress, we will take your clothes and boots while you are soaking and clean them as much as possible." She stood there as if she expected me to undress in front of her. "It's all right, I will turn my back when you remove your drawers," she said.

Said it casually, like men undressed in front of her every day. I realized they did, which only deepened my embarrassment. Slowly, I undressed. When I got to my underwear, she politely turned her back while I slid them off and stepped into the steaming water.

I slipped down into the water, amazed at the luxuriousness of the warmth. That tub was at least six-foot long and wide enough for two people, which I realized was a distinct possibility. I slid down till just my face was out of the water, so enthralled by the water, I was unaware Lilly was still in the room. Her voice reminded me she was still present. "Do you have anything in the pockets?"

I jumped, suddenly aware she could have been picking through them. I was glad all my money my mother gave me the night she died, including my change from the bank, was in the pouch, resting on the edge of the tub.

I shook my head, sat up a little and watched as she gathered my clothes and left the room. Slowly, I surrendered myself back to soaking, only to feel her hands lightly touch the back of my head. I startled and sat up. She'd returned and I never heard her.

"Relax," she said. "I'm not here to hurt you." It took me a while to do that. But her movements were so gentle and rhythmic as she lifted each arm and washed it to my fingers, through my pits, pushing me forward to get my upper back and neck. Frequently, she grabbed a kettle and added more hot water.

"Look at this water, you have been traveling a while," she said. Lilly stood, picked up a long heavy towel. "Stand up, and wrap this around you while I drain the tub and add more water." I did, hoping she wouldn't notice my enlarged member.

As she pulled a plug from the end of the tub, I was amazed to hear the water drain into pipes which ran under the floor, and not just spatter directly onto mud below. Several other women rushed in, wiped my grime and dirt from the tub and around my feet, and with hot water—some cold—quickly filled the tub again.

"Turn your back to me and loosen the towel," Lilly ordered.

I did and she began to scrub my back with a brush, loosening the towel so she could do my buttocks. Next, she yanked the towel off me and told me to sit down again. This time, she used the brush over my chest and sides, then down my legs and feet. Of course, I was erected, and kept trying to poke myself down and hold it between my legs.

"Quit wiggling, just let it float," she said, further increasing my embarrassment which she seemed to be shyly enjoying.

Lilly asked me where I was from, why I came to Chicago. As I talked, she gently began scrubbing me with a soft cloth and flowery-smelling soap. She told me little about herself. Still, I sensed there was something sad to her story.

Her hands kept washing lower and closer to my genitals. Part of me wanted to grab the cloth and wash myself. Wasn't a single woman washing my privates wrong? Her hands felt so wonderful. I decided I would not touch her, but she could me, only with her hands. Soon, I was groaning in desire for release. Using both hands, she expertly fulfilled that desire, laughing lightly at my expressive sounds and gasps.

Oh, my God, that was so wonderful. I wish my juices were still flowing today, but they're not. I will simply savor that memory and many more.

A heavy-set washerwoman barged in and set my clothes on the chair. She stepped over by the tub, glanced down at me, checked out my nakedness, and said, "Ooh, Lilly. He's a cute one. Maybe you should check him out in a back room, then keep him and marry him." She marched out, her fat rear end wiggling from her laughter.

I peeked up at Lilly, who appeared almost as flushed as I felt. "I—I try only to do the baths," she stammered, not looking me in the eyes. "I—I—I hate working the backrooms, but sometimes, I'm forced to. A man wants me to bathe him and then lie with him." She added, "I'm only eighteen, an orphan, and need income."

My eyes started to film over. "I wish I could help you. I think you're a good person."

She turned her back as I dried myself off and put my drawers on, still warm from the iron. Once I was dressed, Lilly pulled a brush through my hair, took a tiny pair of scissors and trimmed my mustache. Standing on her tiptoes, she kissed me on the lips. "You're a good man." She opened the door and led me to the waiting room.

I blushed like a shy groom seeing his bride naked for the first time.

I never forgot her. What a fine young woman! I met her again, but I'll leave such details a mystery for now. Right now, I need a drink.

What the hell is this crazy old fool talking about? He meets a hooker at a bath house, thank God they finally closed the damn place, and wants us to believe he met her again. Like it's some big mystery. She was probably just leading him on with that sad story about not liking the back rooms and he went back for sex with her and he wants to tell us all about his first time. Good grief!

I'm way behind. Interpreting this is going to take forever. At this rate, my grandkids will be doing it, if they'll even be able to read Polish. Mae. November 28, 1935.

Chapter Five

Working and Purchasing Property

It took me six months to get a job with Rothman Builders. Six long months, working in the stockyards and killing livestock. Some days, I gathered with the other men trying to get a day job. Other times, I worked for days, sometimes weeks, usually on the killing line. Several boss-men loved me, but the skilled labor men hated me because I was so damn good. Anything I did was better than they could do, and I was just a nineteen-year-old kid (*seventeen, Mae*).

My first job at the stockyards was unloading the livestock from the train cars and moving them to the pens where they were supposed to be fed and watered overnight so they could gain a little weight back.

My next job was on the cattle-killing line. The cattle were moved through a narrow chute where a man stood on a platform and hit them in the head with a large maul, a big hammer. The hit knocked the animal unconscious. As the animal slumped to the floor, three or four of us quickly, and I do mean quickly, swung the side of the chute open. Each of us grabbed a leg and dragged the animal several feet where we tied its rear legs to a large hook attached to a chain and pulley. Another man pulled the pulley chain, raising the animal up in the air, head down. The assembly track caught it and moved it down the line. The sticker stepped in and slit its throat and the beast moved on to processing.

Cows bellowed, pigs and sheep squealed on the other lines, the floors were a slippery sea of blood and shit and piss. The line moved fast. Slow men were fired on the spot or sent out to the yards to chase animals around in knee-deep shit.

On the third day doing this, (that meant the boss liked me, he put my name down for the recruiter to ask for me at the day labor office), I noticed the hammer-man was slightly off on his timing, sometimes needing to take two swings. This threw our rhythm off a bit and the boss anxiously kept checking back. I saw the hammer-man wince as he swung, then his face turned white. Before he hit the floor, I climbed over the chute, picked up the hammer and stunned the cow, keeping the line moving.

I swung at the next one. Bang! One shot, right between the eyes, probably killed the poor thing. I paid no attention to all the commotion going on with the old hammer-man as they hauled him off in a wheelbarrow. I just kept swinging and dropping them.

The boss walked up. I could see him out of the corner of my eye, but didn't stop swinging that maul. I didn't have time to be nervous. He yelled, "You're standing the wrong way, switch your feet."

"I'm left-handed," I yelled back, never missing a beat. Just to be a smart ass, I switched my grip and feet around and hit the next one with a right-handed swing. Next, I hollered, "Speed the lineup. Let's get these bovines out of here."

That night, the boss told me he wanted me back doing the same thing the next day. That lasted several days, till the other hammer-men started complaining I didn't wait in line to move up to that position like everyone else. So, I was shifted around, outside, inside. A few times, I did the sticking. I was good at that as well. All along, I wanted to be outside, building homes.

Every week or so, I stopped into Rothman's office. Ollie, that was the name of the office manager, always told me Mr. Rothman was out on a job. So next, I'd say, "A relative of the firm has recommended me and I am to ask for Zygmunt Olanski."

Ollie would laugh the same laugh and say, "A relative? Really think I believe that shit? Besides, what the hell do you want with that old Polack?"

"I'm a skilled carpenter," I'd politely say, "and will do a good job for the firm."

The second time I replied that way, he told me to learn some English, that I was in America. So, I started taking English classes at a settlement house.

Several weeks later, I walked in and said in English, "Good evening, Master Ollie. How are you this fine morning?" Of course, my accent was awful.

"I'm terrible, just like always," he replied. "Now which is it, morning or evening?"

"It's Saturday," I replied, trying to smile. English is a crappy language to learn.

He laughed even harder. "Leave me alone, my ledger columns won't balance and I don't have time to waste with such peasant ignorance."

He leaned over his books and forgot I was there. Someone from the back yard where they stored lumber and supplies yelled for him to come outside.

I was injured from him calling me an ignorant peasant. How dare he? He didn't even know me. When I realized he wasn't coming back in for a while, I thought I'd show him I'm not a peasant. I went behind the counter and started looking at his columns. I could see the rows and the columns weren't balancing, so I started to go line by line, working my way across and discovered the mistake. I used his pencil to circle the mistake, wrote in the correct amount, then drew a line through each of the incorrect totals and wrote in their corrected amounts.

I walked over to the window and watched the people, horses and wagons flow by. I turned around when I heard Ollie return and say, "What the hell."

"I am not an ignorant peasant," I said and headed toward the door.

"Wait, wait!" He ran around the counter and blocked me from leaving. "How long did it take you to find my mistake?"

"Not long." In English, I said, "Excuse me, good day."

He laughed so hard, I thought he was going to choke to death. I even started laughing just because he was. Finally, he asked, "Why are you always asking for Zygmunt Olanski?"

"He is the cousin of Yohan, who is now in New York, building houses. Yohan recommends me to Mr. Olanski. That is why."

"Yohan! Cousin Yohan is back in New York? Why didn't you tell me that at the beginning? I'm Zygmunt, but everyone knows me as Ollie and everybody who walks in here has the recommendation of some cousin back in the old country."

He slapped the closed sign on the door, locked it and dragged me across the street to a bar where, after telling him all about my trip with Yohan, he hired me, first to straighten out his ledgers.

38

That's how, about nine months after I arrived in Chicago, I came to purchase the residential lot at 4826 South Justine. After the commercial lot on the corner, it was the second residential lot on the west side. The first lot was already sold and construction started by a man named Anton Drabik, I spit at his name, who the best thing he ever did was die so I could marry his beautiful widow.

Oh my God. How many times will I keep saying Oh my God? Is that how he got our home, at 4822? A widow? Did she have kids? This is getting better than a cheap novel from Woolworths. Mae, January 2, 1936.

Chapter Six

I Marry the Most Wonderful Woman

Drabik, I spit again, must have had some money because he paid cash for his lot and hired the foundation and basement dug for a two flat. The deal with Rothman Builder's was they would sell you a lot very reasonably, three hundred dollars, even on time, but you had to buy your lumber from them which they sold at good prices, plus they gave you advice, even occasional help. They also would build the entire house and sell it to you on credit as well. I think around two thousand dollars for a small home.

One evening, late summer of '86, I was out walking around my newly acquired lot, well, it wouldn't be fully mine until I paid the two-hundred-and-fifty-dollar balance. I was feeling very good. Here I was, almost twenty (*eighteen, Mae*), had a good job, my own lot and still most of my money in the pouch around my neck. Drabik walked over and introduced himself. He explained he ran the floor joists across the foundation and covered the back half with a tarp until he could install the flooring, He and his wife were living in the basement, under the tarp. At least the bastard built an outhouse back by the alley for his wife.

Over by his place, he showed me the foundation and joists. Good construction. He could have built ten stories on the foundation. He hollered, "Walentina, get out here and meet our neighbor."

I could hear her rustling around in the basement, but she didn't come out. "Guess the little bitch is being shy today," he said.

Right then, I knew I wouldn't like him, he sounded like the lout on the ship, only not Jewish. Two days later, I helped the delivery crew take a load of lumber past their place, further down Justine. After unloading, I sent the crew and horses back to the yard and jumped off the wagon at my lot. Walking around my lot—it was twenty-five feet wide and a hundred thirty-five deep—I heard the Drabik outhouse door shut and saw a tiny woman limping toward the basement, bent over, holding her stomach and crying.

She jumped when she saw me approach and turned her face away from mine. "I, I'm Walentina, but please go away." She turned further away so I couldn't see her face. "Please, I don't want you to see me this way."

I left with this nagging thought that she seemed familiar. The next week, I was installing some fence I'd scavenged from the lumber yard. I planned to buy some chickens so Mrs. Gola from the boarding house could have more fresh eggs. Walentina was doing laundry in tubs over a fire in the back yard and hanging it up to dry on some poorly installed clotheslines strung from the outhouse to a weak, skinny, tree limb.

I muttered to myself, 'What kind of man puts clotheslines up like this for his wife?' As usual, I was right, because the limb snapped and the clothes dropped into the dirt. I ran over, picked up the broken limb and said, "Walentina, I'll hold this up so your clothes are out of the dirt. Go find me a hammer and nails and I'll make it stronger."

I was holding the clothes up high, so I couldn't see her face. A few minutes later, from behind a wet hanging towel, she slipped a hammer and some nails into my hand. She pulled on the ropes, her back to me which gave me some slack as I nailed and retied the lines to the trunk. When I turned around, she was gone. Just like that.

Some of the sheets and clothes had dirt on them which I started brushing off, hoping she would reappear. I wanted to see what this person looked like. Instead, someone hollered at me. Drabik staggered up, drunk. "What the hell are you doing? You hanging around my wife? I'll teach you a thing or two."

"Your crap-ass clothesline broke and I just fixed it. I don't know where your wife is," I replied.

I started to walk away, but he lunged toward me. I cold-cocked him with an upper left and left him lying in the dirt. Maybe I should swap my lot for one further down the street, I thought. I could hear sobbing from the basement as I walked by.

Oh, my God. Don't know what to say. Don't have time anyway, this ninth one's going to make Eleanor Roosevelt look slow. Almost three months, and he's already rolling over and wiggling around his bed. Mae. April 10, 1936.

I stayed away for two weeks, didn't go finish my fence or buy them chickens. It was fall and the rains set in. Everything was muddy and slippery. The ditches the city dug for run-off water and sewage were full, some drunk always falling into them and having to be hauled out, sometimes dead. You can't do much construction in the rain we were having and I was getting bored.

Sunday, October 11, 1886 was the day it all happened. It was dry for several days, but gloomy and humid. That Sunday, the sun came out and I decided to get out of the Gola's house. I made my way around the puddles, through the thick streets, headed to my lot. Wanted to see how muddy it got. I noticed Drabik had the side wall studs up two stories, with a couple of rafters tying them together. It seemed floppy to me. A good wind might knock those stud-walls over. I could see he'd rough-floored the main level at the back. I wondered how the two of them stayed dry down in that basement, even with wood over them instead of that tarp. With the front half of the main floor still open between the joists, a lot of rain could muddy up that dirt basement. I could hear Drabik yelling and cursing at his wife.

On a lot further south of mine, a German couple with several little kids built a house. Actually, Rothman Builders built it and I even worked on it. For German people, they were nice enough. The dad was out on the porch. He waved me over. "Hey, neighbor. Come over, the wife won't let you in the house with your boots on, but we can enjoy a smoke on the porch." As we're chatting away, we heard more shouting, then silence. "That man is a beast. He beats his wife all the time now. The first day they moved down into that basement, nearly a year ago, we walked over to visit. My wife carried a dish for them, just to welcome them, you know?"

I nodded, sipped my beer and winked at his little girl peeking at me around her daddy's legs.

"The wife was all friendly and chatty. Drabik started to say how he was building a two flat and she stopped him and said maybe they should think about building rooms up there, said they could make more money as a rooming house." The German took a drag on his smoke, then went on, "The look he gave her. He even made a fist, then he yelled, 'Why, so you can make even more money spreading your legs?' He shoved her, hard, and told her to get her ass into the basement. We were shocked."

So was I, but I didn't know what to say. It did explain her distant, mousy demeanor the times I saw her.

"So, my wife turned and walked the hot dish back to our house. The next day, while Drabik was working, she went over and Walentina had bruises on her face. It's been like watching a kerosene lamp go dim in that woman. She barely talks to us now. Most times just waves us away. She keeps losing babies, too. My wife says she keeps losing babies because he beats her. He's a bastard."

We talked, maybe ten more minutes, enough time for the children to warm up to me, and let me tickle them. As I started walking back, I saw something large dangling by a rope from the second-floor rafter. I watched in horror as the weight of the object, I could tell it was a body, pulled the shaky structure down and the stud-walls collapsed and tumbled down on top of the floor and the body.

"Walentina," I screamed, "are you down there? Are you alive?"

I pulled two-by-fours away till I found the steep stairs into the basement. With a knot deep in my belly, I inched down, still calling her name. In the light from the unfinished floor at the front of the building, I could see Drabik's head and shoulders dangling through the joists. I was worried, scared almost to death. Did he kill her first, then himself? Finally, I heard a whimper.

"What happened?" Walentina said, filthy with mud, peering out from under a table. I noticed blood on the back of her lower clothing as she crawled out. A dishtowel covered her head and part of her face. She held a small pistol in her hand. As I pulled her to a stand, she saw her dead husband. She startled, turned away from me. "Did I really shoot him?"

I took the pistol from her hand, the barrel was cold, the whole thing rusty. "No, you didn't. He hung himself."

"You can go now. I'll be fine," she said, still turning away from me.

I pulled the towel away and gazed into the eyes of Lilly from the Baths. She stared straight back at me, not flinching. "Now you see why I didn't want to meet you. I was afraid you'd be ashamed of me or look down on me."

I shook my head, stunned. Looking down at her dress, I asked, "Are you all right? Is that blood?"

"I lost another child, my third one, that's what started the row today. That, and him being drunk. Last week, I found this pistol in the ditch. I dried it off. Today, he started beating on me again. I decided I couldn't take it anymore. He's beat me down so bad, I don't know who I am. I pulled it out and told him I was going to kill him or he could go kill himself. Either way, I was leaving and taking one thousand dollars. It was his choice. I didn't even know if the gun had bullets or worked. I just knew I had to get away from him. He left and I didn't hear anything till the lumber crashed."

She started to cry and weave around on her feet, like she might pass out. I pulled her into a hug and her tears truly flowed. I wasn't used to women crying so I just kept patting her on the back. She eventually stopped and said, "Who do I see about getting his body out of here? I have a house to rebuild and this time, it's going to be done my way."

I started to reply how I wasn't sure, being new to Chicago, but she interrupted me. "Quick, drag some boards across the mud and carry this chair over under him."

I looked at her like she was crazy.

"You have to help me before the undertaker gets him. There's a black leather pouch in his front pocket. I have to get it. His money is in it."

The next thing I know, I'm standing on a chair, trying to move a dead body around that's draped over a floor joist. Move it enough to get to the front pockets. His eyes were open and staring at me, his tongue, all thick and blue, was sticking out, the rope around his neck still tight. By then, he'd pissed and shit himself. Walentina kept giving me orders, roll him this way, put your hand there. Finally, she jumped up on the chair beside me and as I pushed his gut up and away from the joist, she pulled the pouch out.

"We make a good team," she said. She dropped to the seat. "I'm not crying over him. After raping me every night and beating on me." She

44

waited a moment, shook herself and stood up. "I'm glad he's gone. But I am sorry I lost another baby and my stomach is cramping."

I could hear neighbors and onlookers chattering outside. I climbed out of the basement and asked who to see about the body. Said the man committed suicide and his widow needed the body removed. One offered to go get the police who would get the coroner and the undertaker.

One woman in the crowd said loudly, "Ain't this brand-new widow the whore who used to work at that bathhouse with them girls and she tried to marry up? Maybe she killed him and made it look like a suicide."

"Madam," I replied, my eyes blazing. "I own the lot next door and none of my neighbors will ever be referred to as a whore."

The woman put her head down and slunk away. The German and his wife both nodded at me.

I convinced Walentina to take my room at the boarding house—Pawl had moved out—till she was better physically. I slept on the dining room floor. The next day, I went to her house and pulled all the lumber down and resorted it to make it easier to rebuild, plus I made a rough wooden floor in the basement.

"What are you going to build on your property?" Walentina asked me at dinner one night at the boarding house.

"Someday, I want to build a rooming house. I think there's a need for one."

"Tell you what," she replied. "You help me build mine and after that, I'll help you build yours." She grinned at the shock on my face. "You don't think I know anything about building or running a rooming house, do you?"

I didn't know how to answer her, but somehow, I knew I'd find out, so I just smiled, didn't shake my head or nod. "I think no matter how I answer that, it will come out wrong."

She laughed, pulled some butcher paper and a pencil out of her bag and began showing me her plans.

I listened and asked some questions, then said, "Those are great ideas, but why not extend the building back twenty-five more feet. You would need a foundation, but not a basement, and add a third story?"

I know where this is going. He marries her, they build this place and somehow split his lot, because we sit on a lot and a half. Okay, he married a prostitute, though it sounds like she was a reluctant one. I've always wished I knew her. You just never know about life... Wonder what Hank will think? Mae. April 17, 1936.

~ * ~

The old man is dead. He died yesterday, while we were at church, Sunday, April 19, 1936. I didn't know when to note this down in the ledger, now or when I finish translating. The old man wrote a long story, I checked and he seemed to finish it. It will take me years to translate so decided to note it today.

I pulled Sunday dinner out of the warming oven and was nursing the baby, we named him Joseph Joshua and call him Joey, as the kids changed their clothes, then set the table. I sent Nina, she's two and a-half, to go get Grandpa. The old man was tickled pink when I named number eight Nina and number nine Joseph—he didn't even complain about the American spelling. She came back and said, "Gampa no wake."

I put the baby to bed and went back there. He was in his rocker, still in a nightgown, head slumped, gray and cold with a copy of the 'Dziennik Chicagoski' folded on his lap, showing the story of the Hindenburg flying back to Germany from South America. I kissed him, closed the door and decided to wait till Hank got home. He was working a Sunday, no overtime. They killed the unions. In these tight times, he takes anything he can get and the old man's not going anywhere. Mae. I'll translate more when I can. April 20, 1936.

~ * ~

I tell you, Walentina was growing on me. It was like watching that dim kerosene lamp the German neighbor mentioned brighten up with added fuel. She was smart, brave and could be competitive. She stayed in my room at the boarding house. After discovering people were stealing the lumber, I installed a small wood stove and slept in the basement. She walked down during the day and, even if I was elsewhere working on a job, she'd pull nails, straighten them, do anything she could to help. One day, she started nailing the first layer of floor boards to cover the front half of the main floor. When I got there, she wanted to race me, see who could measure, cut and nail the fastest. That little rat gave me a run for my money.

I took my dinner every night at Mrs. Gola's. About a month after Walentina started staying there, Mrs. Gola started acting strange, short-tempered, haughty to Walentina. One evening, with her husband present, she informed us that Walentina should look for another place to stay.

"Why is that?" I asked.

"I've b—been hearing rumors about Walentina and c—c—can't have her kind of person living in my respectable establishment."

Establishment! I was about ready to explode, the woman only rented out the one room. Walentina motioned for me to stay seated and calmly asked, "What rumors are those? And who did you hear them from?"

"Well. Well, th—that you are a woman of ill repute, that you worked at the full service Baths. I heard that your name is Lilly."

Her husband turned red and looked like he might faint.

"Well," said Walentina, "who told you I was called Lilly?"

Mrs. Gola stammered her husband told her.

"In that case, Mr. Gola must have frequented that particular bathhouse, because all of the clients are warned to never repeat the names of any of the women who worked there." She smiled as Mrs. Gola glared at her husband who looked like a fish gasping for air.

Walentina waited a moment, then quietly said, "It's true. I did work at the baths and I was called Lilly there, though I hope that name never leaves this room. I mostly gave the men baths."

"Wife, that's all I got there, honestly, that was all. A bath. I didn't go to the back rooms," Mr. Gola pleaded with his wife who turned her head away from him, but wouldn't look at Walentina either.

"Mrs. Gola, do you know why I worked there?"

Mrs. Gola glanced at Walentina and shook her head. "It was either that or become a street prostitute downtown." She waited till all three of us were looking at her. "You see, I was orphaned at twelve and placed in a Catholic orphanage. At fifteen, I met a young man, seventeen, we ran away and married over the line in Indiana. That same day, his parents tracked us down, had the marriage annulled because it wasn't consummated, and I ended up back in the orphanage. At sixteen, the nuns got me a job washing clothes at a laundry behind the Baths with room and board. They didn't realize the laundry owner was the same as the owner of the Baths, or so they said. Soon, I was bathing men, either that or go on the streets. I hated giving myself to men in the backrooms. I can't say I always hated giving them baths." She flushed a little, then looked down.

Mrs. Gola gasped. Mr. Gola's face looked as if a fond memory passed through his mind, one he would never forget. I knew I would never forget mine. I thought if Mrs. Gola held a fry pan, he'd been laid out cold on the floor.

"I met Mr. Drabik, he seemed charming and rich and quickly fell in love with me, so I married him. It seemed a way out of the Baths." Walentina paused, pain on her face. "The truth is, it was worse than coupling with men in the back rooms. He was a beast who raped me nearly every night and punched me frequently. I lost several pregnancies. I'm glad the bastard is dead."

The only sounds were people breathing and maybe thinking. This woman was full of surprises and I admired her even more. In fact, I think that's when I realized I was falling in love with her.

The Golas changed their mind, said she could stay till I wanted my room back. I knew that wasn't going to happen soon. After the Golas went to bed, she and I stayed at the table and talked. Told each other about our backgrounds.

She told me her father was a jeweler back in Warsaw, kind of a radical type person who spoke his mind, especially about Poland still being partitioned. Her mother died when she was eight and her dad thought it time to leave the country and move to Chicago. He died when she was twelve.

She and I worked on the house plans on bad weather days. On good ones, we started rebuilding the walls, framing the place in with the idea we'd do a third story, plus an addition off the back. One day, we calculated the costs and she told me she would run out of money, maybe we should keep it to two stories. I said I had enough to pay the third, plus hire the foundation for the addition dug and installed.

"In that case, we need to be legal partners," she said.

Before I could say anything, she moved closer to me and lifted my hands to her shoulders and looked up into my eyes. I waited, not sure what to say. I knew what I was feeling. I wanted to say to hell with just being business partners, let's get married, but was too shy to say it. After a minute of staring into each other's eyes, she said, "The answer is yes."

I pulled her into a hug that wanted to go on forever. Eventually, I asked, "How did you know the question?"

"I could see it in your eyes and knew you were too shy to ask. I love you," she said. "You'll never regret marrying me."

I never have.

We got married the next week at city hall, she didn't want a priest or church wedding, which was fine with me. We spent our first night in a hotel downtown, and stayed at the Gola's as a couple till the weather broke and we got a roof up on the front section of the rooming house. We made so much noise coupling our first night in the hotel, we decided, after our return, to do so only in the basement during the day. We thought we might disturb the Golas. Didn't want to make Mr. Gola jealous. Ha, ha. I bet it was a long time before his wife let him get close to her. As for us, it's amazing we got anything done on the house those first couple of weeks.

The day after our wedding, she led me to a tiny jeweler's office almost hidden in the back of one of those high-rise buildings going up like saplings downtown. I handed her my packet of jewelry and she went into the back room with a tiny man who wore a little magnifying glass. They argued in a language I didn't understand. It wasn't Polish, German or English. They finally came out, he sighed dramatically and gave her cash for the pieces he selected.

On the way down the stairs, she said, "We got way more than those Polish jewelers would have given us. That was fun. I haven't bartered for a long time. I'm surprised I remembered the language."

Before I could ask which language, she pulled my face down into a big kiss. We caught the streetcar and went directly to Rothman's where we ordered more lumber, then tried out the bed in our basement before going to Mrs. Gola's for a big wedding dinner with several of the neighbors.

Chapter Seven

Our Magnificent Rooming House

We hired some help for the addition and finishing off the house. We built it extra strong and tight. Mr. Rothman and Ollie told me I was crazy, building it so tight, but it paid off in the long run. Our roomers didn't freeze from drafts and gaps and the heat didn't escape. With Walentina supervising and me helping every extra hour I could spare from Rothman Builders, we finished and opened the place in October 1887.

The final building was twenty foot by eighty. The first floor held the front apartment with four, yes, four bedrooms, plus a small back apartment. It was a magnificent show of our creative and carpentry skills. We poured all we had into it, both in money and our physical labor. Each of the bedrooms, which weren't tiny, by the way, contained its own closet. We even built a room for the bathtub, which later, thanks to our far-sighted thinking, became the bathroom.

The second floor held a total of fifteen rooms, thirteen of them were approximately eight-by-nine, each with a window. The two smaller rooms didn't have a window. One was for the men's supervisor who got his room for free for doing very little and the other one was for an indigent old man who couldn't pay the full going weekly or monthly rates. It was close to the bathroom and the stove. I figured we should share our blessings and that was the least we could do. One old guy lived there for a good twenty years. I figured helping him out didn't hurt with the man upstairs, if there is one. I cross myself.

The third floor held thirteen rooms similar in size to the men's floor, but were for women. At the rear, we built a double size matron's room with an efficiency kitchen and cold water. We also added a shared kitchen area near the heat stove and tub room. Outside, near the alley, we built a second outhouse, a double one for the men. Of course, they didn't get much use after we added full plumbing.

We did it up big when we opened, advertised in the paper, put posters up. We were not a boarding house, we wanted single people who could afford to eat elsewhere or purchase their food and eat it in their rooms. We advertised we had a matron who lived on the third floor to supervise the women so they would feel safe and have a small space for shared cooking. We didn't trust the men to cook for themselves. Ha ha.

On the men's floor, we provided the tiny room without a window to a reliable, strong man who would manage the men. He lived next to the stairs so every man coming and going had to go by his room. If someone did try to sneak upstairs toward the women, they only did so once. A man getting thrown down the stairs is not a pleasant sound. The same for anyone caught sneaking in someone for sex. If they were drunk and disorderly, they were given one warning, a second time and they were out on their ear. That's when we developed the ledger accounts and started the annual census. We ran a respectable place and soon had no problems filling the twenty-seven paying rooms. I bought a Kodak Brownie camera for Walentina one Christmas and we started taking pictures of the roomers, just for fun. They loved it when we gave them a copy.

I remember, shortly before we were to open, a building inspector from the city showed up. The city was called Lake back then, just before it merged into Chicago. I was upstairs, planning a sticky door edge and heard a man's voice downstairs talking to Walentina in English, accented with Irish.

"Madam," he said in a very patronizing voice, "who may I speak with knowledge about this home?"

"I am very knowledgeable about this place. What would you like to know?"

"I must speak with the man who owns this place. You will not do."

They stood just inside the front door entry while I waited on the third floor landing to see how my saucy wife would handle this.

In decent English, my wife replied, "The ownership is in both our names. If you would look at the records, you would see such." It was quiet a moment. "See? There at the top of your paper. Those are both our names. Now how can I help you?"

From her tone, I knew she wanted to slap him for speaking down to her.

He stammered a minute. "Well, this area is zoned residential and our records indicate you were building a two-flat home. This looks like a rooming house, not a residential home. Plus, it's now three stories. Something must be done to correct this situation."

"It's both," Walentina said. "This is our residence on the first floor and there are residential rooms on the second and third floors. What actually needs to be corrected? Your records? That should be easy, just write in building modified, then approved."

The man stammered a bit more. "It's not quite that easy. Such changes are difficult and expensive. I may have to bring my supervisor back. Hmm, there must be a way to work this massive problem out."

I heard Walentina step into our house and return. "I'm sure a good-looking man like you is married, right?" He must have nodded because she went on, "This is an expensive gold ring with a ruby that was my grandmother's in Warsaw, Poland. I think your wife would love something like this to add to her collection of fine gems." I heard the guy shuffle his feet, then start to open the door. "Sir, I think you need to correct your records now and make sure you mail us an updated copy for our records."

I came down the stairs after he left. "What did you give him? One of your grandmother's rings?" I was aghast that she would give up something so valuable.

"No, Josef. It's a piece one of the girls stole out of the pocket of some man in one of the back rooms. She thought she could sell it and retire from pleasuring men. I told her it was worthless. She took it to a jeweler. I was right. It's gold paint, not even gold leaf, and the ruby is glass. His poor Irish wife will never know the difference. He can barely read or write, much less notice a painted ring."

A week later, our corrected land title arrived. That would not be the first time we befriended inspectors.

This rooming house was a lot of work back then, way more than now. Water had to be carried to each floor, where the residents could fill their pitcher in order to wash up in their bowl. They set their bowls with the leftover water outside their doors where, during the day, we emptied them and wiped out the bowl. We had one coal-burning stove in the center of the hallway on each floor which we lit at night from mid-November to

April. Sometimes, on severe winter nights, the men would sleep on the floor around the heater. The women seemed comfortable leaving their doors open.

Every room except two held a window which was screened for milder weather and lined up with the door so they could get cross ventilation in warm weather by leaving their door ajar. Plus, we had a window at each end of the hallway for ventilation. We supplied one candle per week to each resident. After gas arrived, we installed a light in each room. Later, we added electricity and a big coal, then oil, furnace with heat vents to the hallways. As soon as water and sewer came through, we added toilet rooms and a tub room on each floor, plus a small sink in each of the woman's rooms, and a bathroom into the back apartment behind us. We only rented the apartment to married couples, usually young newlyweds who we asked to leave after they had a second child, and sometimes to older couples with no children. The place was easy and quick to rent and never was vacant more than a few days. Nearly fifty years later, this place is still solid as a rock. We knew what we were doing. Walentina and I were a good team.

Chapter Eight

Whereby We Have Wonderful Children and Join the Church

Walentina lost her first pregnancy six months after we married. Her second one was successful and Eugenia, named after my beautiful mother and little sister, was born October 19, 1889. Walentina was like my mother, she could get pregnant, but couldn't hold on to them. She lost the next four babies, usually six weeks to ten weeks after conceiving. Though one was five months along, that was a tough time, we knew it was a boy. On September 10, 1895, Henryk Josef was born. He was a chip off the old block, strong, shy, charming, and very smart.

Before I forget, I got to mention the Chicago World's Fair and Chicago Columbian Exposition. It opened in May of 1893. I'd worked a little on it as a carpenter so had a good idea of the size and magnificence. I didn't work on it much because our carpenters from Rothman kept leaving us to work on the fair. I think mostly they did so because it was so exciting. That meant I was usually doing the work of two or three men.

Anyway, that June, I read they were a bit disappointed in the numbers of people coming to see it so I took a day off. Walentina wasn't pregnant and was feeling good, so our neighbor agreed to watch Eugenia and we rode the streetcars and walked part of the way over. She was amazed. She loved the art and cooking and international booths, even got up next to the stage and danced a little to a Polish song. She refused to go on the wheel, that huge Ferris Wheel that stuck up something like two-hundred-and-fifty feet into the air. I did. Thank goodness the lines weren't long so I didn't have to wait. She wandered around while I rode it. It was the most amazing thing I ever been on. I even maneuvered around the people in my car to see our house. I still shiver when I think about it. We talked about that for days. I'm just glad we saw it when we did. It got really crowded later that summer and fall.

We didn't get to the Chicago World's Fair in '33 and '34. Too broke, the old man was too sick, too many kids, though I think a few of the older ones snuck over there on their own. Plus, I was either pregnant, nursing, doing diapers or cooking. Hank was trying to work or help the roomers find enough work to pay us a bit each week. We figured a few cents coming in was better than nothing, besides, who wanted to put guys out on the street? So much for a century of progress in the middle of the depression! Mae.

Several weeks before Henryk was born, we walked. Well, I walked, Eugenia skipped in excitement as Walentina waddled, over to St. Bobola's school to register Eugenia. We started attending church, though not regularly. I even threw a few cents in the plate each time we did visit. If God truly noticed those things, I figured it wouldn't hurt. We thought that now having a child, we should raise her in the church, even though neither of us felt too religious. I still carried hatred toward that homo priest who took financial advantage of me when my mother died.

That bastard! I spit! (I'll clean it up later before Mae comes in).

The principal was a skinny, hawk-nosed, old nun who looked over her glasses at us. She tried to smile at Eugenia who stared back at her.

"Have you joined the church?" the nun asked.

We shook our heads.

"Well, you must first join the church. Were you married in the church?"

"No," I replied. "We were married at city hall eight years ago." I told her eight years, the truth, just to make sure she didn't think Eugenia was born out of wedlock.

She pursed her lips and frowned, shaking her head. "Well, you are Catholics. Correct? Do you have baptism records or something to prove you are at least Catholic?"

"Sister, we are both immigrants. Whether I have my baptism record is doubtful. I came over as an orphan. Besides, we told you we are Catholic, we will join the church and I have the finances to pay the tuition." I was beginning to get a little testy.

Walentina put her hand on my arm as she said, "I too am an immigrant who was orphaned as a child shortly after arriving and was raised in Our Lady of Hope Orphanage." She seemed tense also.

The nun's entire body jerked. Her face tried to control her shock. After a moment, she managed to say, "I am well acquainted with the orphanage, I used to serve there. When were you there? What did you do after the orphanage?"

At the nun's reaction, Walentina's hand squeezed my arm tighter.

"Sister," I said, "I'm losing money by not working this very hour. How do we join the church and how do we register this little girl for school?"

"Well," she sniffed, "this seems unusual, with only a city hall wedding and no baptism records. I've rarely met anyone, immigrant or not, who doesn't at least have those records. I think the good Father should meet with you. I'll go see if he's available."

She left the office and Walentina pulled a mantilla out of her bag and put it on her head. It was a long one and covered the sides of her face. Still dazed from the nun's reaction, she half-smiled at me and tried to joke, "Do I look more Catholic now?"

She glanced out the door and gasped as she saw the priest approach with the nun. Her eyes looked frightened again. She sucked in her breath, turned and with one of her brilliant expressions, said, "Father Bazlyi, how good to see you again." She took off her mantilla as his face turned pale, then red.

"Good—good day, Mr. and Mrs. Sawicki," he gasped as he sat down behind the desk. "What seems to be the problem?"

He didn't look at us, just at the desk, then he tried to force a smile at little Eugenia who studied him carefully.

"Why, Father," Walentina said sweetly, "all we want to do is join the church and register our daughter for school. That's all. Does it truly matter we didn't have a church wedding? Say, I think you've gained a little weight since I last saw you this close. I think that was nearly ten years ago, wasn't it?"

I thought he might pass out as he quickly pulled out some papers for us to complete and sign. The nun glanced at him, then stared hard at Walentina. A look of recognition crossed her face. She opened her mouth, but before she could speak, I handed her the money for tuition, thanked them both and quickly guided my family through the door.

That night in bed, Walentina curled up against me and cried. I wrapped my arms around her enlarged body, put my hands on the baby to feel it kick. She fought back sobs. "I'm so sorry. Just when I think my past is over, we run into someone I recognize who remembers me. You'd think a priest would be the last person to recognize me. And that nun? She's the one who sent me to the laundry." Struggling into a sitting position, she said, "Josef, there is more. I don't mean about men, but more about me. It's important and it is the last piece about me you don't know and you can never tell anyone, not even our children, not till after I am dead. Promise me?"

What could I say? I loved this woman. I didn't think there was anything she could say that would change my mind. Of course, I promised. She whispered her secret to me, said she would write more details down later so I knew her entire story. I tried not to gulp or act any different as I promised not to tell anyone till after her death. To say the very least, I was stunned.

Months after Henryk was born, she gave me her story, neatly written, and I read all the details. I read it by myself, where no one could see my tears. Afterward, I promised myself not to show anyone her story until after my demise. I hid her story where no one would notice it. This is partly why I'm writing my memories. This woman surprised me all our life together, God bless her soul.

~ * ~

Mae just brought me a beer. She checks in on me more often, especially when I'm writing. I wonder if she senses my time is getting short, like I do.

Now I will write about my four children, but not in their order of birth. I may need more than a beer when I'm finished. Anyway, I shall carry on!

Chapter Nine

Eugenia

Oh, our Eugenia. Where do I start? It seemed she was born evaluating life around her. Always looking around, taking everything in before deciding how to react. She smiled, giggled and laughed, always taking a short pause to test her surroundings, make sure her reaction was appropriate. She was a quick learner, asked good questions, did well in school, in fact, loved learning, but usually in a quiet, deep manner. She behaved well; that is, until she started becoming a woman. Even so, her behavior was not extreme, at least to me. Walentina thought otherwise.

Eugenia was an only child for six years, but seemed to adapt well to being a big sister when Henryk was born, and four years later when Alicja was born in 1899, quickly followed fourteen months later by Genowefa, our tiny angel.

Eugenia devoured books, so much that by age eight, her mother began taking her on the streetcar to the big library downtown. It was good for her mother and me as well, because we learned to read and speak better English, listening to our daughter read aloud. Eugenia would read to Henryk, which I think is why his English became so good. She asked questions, serious ones, and once she had the answer, she rarely repeated the question. I don't think the nuns and priests appreciated all her questions. One of them told her mother, "Eugenia is very bright, but some of her questions are not good for her soul. She needs to accept the answers we give her are correct in the infinite wisdom of a Holy God."

"They're not answers," Eugenia cried out when her mother related the conversation at supper that night. "Honest, Papa and Mama, they don't answer my questions."

I was ready to go give those so-called teachers a piece of my mind, but once again, Walentina told me it would only make things worse. Eugenia learned not to repeat her questions of the nuns and priests and to give them the answers they wanted. I think that's why she loved going to the library and discovering things herself.

By the time Eugenia was fourteen, she was an attractive young woman, which scared the hell out of her mother. That's when the friction started. Eugenia wanted to take the streetcar downtown by herself to the library, but her mother refused. She must either accompany her with the three younger children or she didn't go. Eugenia's friends could have accompanied her, but they were dropping out of school to work and were becoming man-crazy, which scared Walentina even more.

Eugenia grew interested in woman's suffrage. Read everything she could, the English newspapers, pamphlets, books, the names of the women leading the movement.

I hadn't said much to her about my feelings. On the one hand, I was married to a strong woman and liked it. She was smarter than me. Ollie and the other men at work and I engaged in many conversations about women voting and getting more rights. I mostly listened, but tended to agree with them that women might need a bit more freedom, but not the right to vote. Just seemed like something only men should do. I didn't think that much about it, thought it was a phase Eugenia was going through.

One Saturday, I was not working and Eugenia, who must have been nearly sixteen, pestered us with questions and opinions. I informed her of mine, the one I heard most from the other guys. "Women are just as good as men, but they have certain roles God gave them. Voting is not one of them."

"Husband," my wife yelled, "how many nails have I pounded into this house? How many times did my good planning save us money and time? Who keeps this rooming house running when you're working six days a week?"

I gulped and sat down. I knew she had me.

"If you died tomorrow, do you think I couldn't carry this place on by myself?"

I nodded, a shit-eating grin on my face.

"If I died tomorrow, could you carry this family and the rooming house on without missing a step?"

"I understand," I yelled, "but I don't think women should vote. Enough of this nonsense." I wanted a beer, but now I had two women climbing down my throat.

"Yes, Papa, if Mama can manage as well as you, then please tell me why she shouldn't vote?"

Walentina looked at the clock. "Daughter, I'm in need of a break. Let's you and I go to the library."

"Go ahead," I said. "I'm going to work on a squeaky door on one of the rooms."

"Not unless you can do so with three kids helping."

Walentina winked at Eugenia and the two of them marched out the door, leaving me with a ten-year-old son, a six-year-old daughter, Alicja, and little, sickly Genowefa, five.

"Papa, we're hungry," Henryk said.

"Genowefa needs her diaper changed, Papa," said Alicja. She looked at me. "Papa, do you even know how to change a diaper?"

"I doubt it," Henryk said, a touch of disgust in his voice. "I do, I'll take care of her. Papa, warm some milk up while I change her. Not too hot, all she can eat is bread dipped in warm milk."

Genowefa was born early, tiny, she almost fit on the palm of my hand. She never grew right. At five, she was still like an infant, only longer. I warmed up some milk and watched Henryk tenderly feed his sister.

"How do you know how to change her and feed her?"

"Mama taught me when Alicja was one, she said men should know how to do this, that it shouldn't be all women's work." He smiled at me. "It's okay, Papa, I can show you, it's not hard, just smelly sometimes."

Well. If my ten-year-old son was man enough to change smelly diapers, then so was I! He showed me and of course I quickly learned. While he was showing me how to change and feed Genowefa, Alicja, unbeknownst to me, decided to slice the bread for our lunch. On the last slice, she cut her finger and started howling. I wrapped a wet rag around her finger until it stopped bleeding. Henryk found a soft clean rag and showed me how his mother would wrap it. Finally, we ate, bread and butter with jam, plus some pickles.

"I like fixing our own dinner," Alicja said happily. "It's different than what Mama makes us eat, we usually don't get jam and pickles."

My wife and daughter arrived home, seemingly thick as thieves now, to find me dozing on the couch, cuddling Genowefa, Alicja asleep, curled up next to me with jam still on her face, and Henryk playing with the kittens who were not allowed in the house.

Eugenia slipped the baby out of my arms. We still called her a baby because she basically was, and started giggling at the manner in which I'd arranged her clothing after changing her diaper.

That night in bed, Walentina cuddled under my arm. "We need some help," she said. "I know you don't want women voting, but..."

"Oh, after today, I think women can vote as many times as they want. Why, what do you need?"

We both laughed like teenagers.

"Your daughter and I are attending a women's suffrage march in two weeks. Could you make us some signs, stay home and watch the little ones?"

I groaned yes. What else could I say?

Eugenia finished high school at seventeen and was like a cat on a hot stove. She got a job in an office downtown, but hated it. "The men chew tobacco, smoke cigars, spit and yell. I could do a better job than them, but they won't let me even try. I want to leave, go somewhere else."

We both told her she was too young to be out on her own, so she yelled at us, "I'm too young? Mama was an orphan at twelve and Papa, you left home around my age to come to Chicago. How can I be too young?"

"Because I said you are too young, that's why." I shot back, stung at the realization she was exactly my true age when I left home for good.

Two weeks later, she didn't come home from work. Walentina checked her room and found some of her clothes missing. A note lay on her bed.

Dear Mama and Papa. I have to leave. I love you, but I can't stay in Chicago. I left on the train for Cheyenne, Wyoming this morning. They need school teachers and I am confident I can teach elementary students. I will write you in several weeks after I have found housing and a position. Do not worry, I will be fine. You have raised me well.

Sincerely, Eugenia.

I sat down on the edge of her bed, put my head in my hands and let several tears slip down my cheeks. What did I do wrong? Why would she leave this safe, warm home filled with love?

Walentina sat down beside me, put her arm around me and leaned her head on my shoulder. In a teary voice, she said, "It's all right, Josef. She's right. She will be fine. We did raise her right."

I had to think about that. The part where she would be fine. In Wyoming? Even in 1906, the place was filled with Indians, but more so those cowboys, all wearing guns, drunk, their juices flowing, looking for a woman to carry off to some lonely ranch. Eugenia would not be happy stuck in some hovel, raising babies one after the other while caring for sick calves.

As usual, Walentina read my mind. "Josef, she's looking for a school-teaching position. She knows she's too young to want a husband."

"Are you sure?" I whimpered. "What happens if..."

Walentina pulled my hands from my face, wiped my face with her small hand, then squeezed my nose hard enough to make me wince. "You're a good papa, now let her go. She's now a fledgling ready to fly on her own. We're the ones not ready, but now we have no choice."

Three weeks later, we received a letter from her.

Dear Mama and Papa. To allay your worries (Papa), I have not been swept off my feet by some cowboy, though enough have tried.

"See," I yelled, "I was right, she's in trouble. Wire her to come back home immediately."

"Josef! I will read the letter, you listen and can talk at the end."

Walentina's laughing at me didn't help allay my sense of fear for my beautiful daughter living in a wild land a thousand miles away.

This is beautiful country. The elevation is six-thousand feet and will take some time for my breathing to adjust. There are tall mountains in the distance, I hope to see them closer someday. It is sunny, quite warm, but with little moisture in the air like Chicago. The wind blows most of the time, sometimes strong. To say nothing about the smell, well, even on the days they drive cattle through the streets to the train yards, the smell is still fresh and clean compared to home. I can't believe there are places where the air actually smells GOOD. You can see forever! Miles and miles and more miles of open space. Even the town has only twelve-thousand residents, less than we had in our neighborhood. It almost makes me feel like dancing around and waving my hands to be so free of tall buildings, tons of people and those smells. (Don't worry, Papa, I haven't lost my reserve, those are just my feelings at discovering such a new place and life).

Two days after my arrival, I spoke with a school administrator. He gave me a test to determine my competency for teaching elementary students. I passed, he said I impressively passed, considering Polish was my natural language. Next, he recommended I go to the University of Wyoming in Laramie to take a competency test for teaching high school. I took the train to Laramie, was interviewed and took the test. I passed it with the provision I needed to study more science and higher math to teach those subjects in high school. So, you will be proud to know I am now approved to teach every subject through eighth grade, plus all subjects in high school except higher math and science! Guess I got more from those old nuns and priests than I thought. Maybe it was all those trips to the library.

Most people here are intrigued by my accent and ask where I am from. Chicago born, I reply. One lady asked where my parents were born so I told her. After that she spoke to me in Polish. She said her grandparents were from Poland (she won't say East Prussia either) and her parents homesteaded in Nebraska to get away from the city. Now she's in Cheyenne, married to a grocer. It is nice to speak Polish with someone.

Well, hopefully, this relieves your worries. I AM FINE. Oh, I am boarding with a nice family. They are Methodists, there aren't as many Catholics out here. I heard they plan to build a new Catholic church.

I was informed it is proper protocol for single female teachers (there aren't too many male teachers) to join and regularly attend a church. I know there's an Episcopal, a Presbyterian and the Methodist. I think I will keep going to the Methodist. The school superintendent also attends it. I think he will be pleased I'm not a rabid Catholic. Besides, I've had enough of nuns and priests to last me a lifetime. I do have to say these Methodists have some crazy beliefs compared to us Polish

Catholics. Well, maybe some of ours are crazy as well.

Anyway, I love you. Someday, I want you to visit out here. You will be amazed! It's doubtful I will ever move back to Chicago.

Eugenia

There were tears in both our eyes. Tears of missing her, the house seemed so empty without her quiet presence, tears of Henryk and Alicja asking when she was returning. Now we had to tell them she wasn't. There were also, tears of relief knowing she was safe and doing well. We read her letter to the kids that night and they seemed relieved as well. Even Genowefa seemed to gurgle in joy.

I have to tell you Eugenia never returned to live in Chicago. She is still in Wyoming. She visited us twice, we never made it out there, though Henryk stayed with her for three months, after he came home from the war. He said he loved the fresh air, but the space was too open and there were not enough people around for him. I think there was another reason he needed to be with his sister.

Anyway, she taught school for seventeen years, then married a rancher, a widower with three girls. They had two of their own, then apparently adopted some teenage boy. She rides horses, kills rattlesnakes and helps brand cattle. Once a month, she writes a letter and updates us on her life. I think it's as different as me coming from a tiny village in Poland to Chicago. Wyoming seems like a foreign land. Guess that's what living in the United States is all about.

Every letter she wrote and picture she sent is in a box in the dresser drawer where we keep the ledger and other records.

Chapter Ten

Genowefa

What can I say about our little angel? She was born early, extremely early. The midwife, and later a doctor, said she would live only a short time, maybe a few weeks. In spite of their prediction, she was a tough Sawicki and proved them wrong. She never progressed, never sat up, never rolled over, never crawled or walked. She just gurgled, smiled and slowly grew longer. She was a perpetual baby, a very frail one. Many times, we thought she would die when she caught a cold, but she didn't. Then one evening, November 9, 1906, four months after Eugenia left, she died in her mother's arms. Just shuddered, looked up at her mother, gurgled sweetly, and went limp. She was six years old. Our angel went home to be with the rest of the angels.

~ * ~

Damn. My eyes are leaking onto the pages. I need to take a break, have a beer or wine, but something tells me my time is getting short. Maybe it's my cough that only deepens, or the yellow sludge I hack up, sometimes with red spots. I won't see a doctor. I am old. When it's time, it's time. I must keep writing.

Chapter Eleven

Alicja

All of our children were delightful. Alicja was probably the bubbliest, most expressive, most emotional and looked the most like her mother. Petite, dark hair, dark eyes, always on the move, always helping others. She was a Godsend with Genowefa, her younger sister by fourteen months.

Alicja did well in school, never questioned those crazy nuns and priests like her big sister, never acted out like Henryk did on occasion. She loved going to Mass and taking part in all that crazy rigmarole we Polish Catholics do. She loved jokes, laughing and found humor in nearly every situation.

I would come home from work, or working around the rooms, all tired and hungry. She would greet me at the door with a 'do-you-know' joke, or a tongue twister in English. Anything to brighten my day. After our angel died, she and her mother became active in settlement house activities. They took some training in first aid and sanitation and began going into the tenement houses and other overcrowded buildings to help the poor.

Alicja also took an active interest in the rooming house residents and the management of the place. If someone was sick, she would take them broth and toast. Soon, she was able to record their payments in the ledger and take care of simple requests. She was a bright spot in their lives as well as ours. Of course, the women's matron and the men's manager loved her and watched out for her, though there was rarely a need for them to do it.

In the winter of 1918, Henryk, then twenty-three, joined the army. It was more and more apparent the US would be fighting in The Great War taking place in Europe. He shipped out that summer and we had no idea of what he was doing or where he was in Europe. Of course, we were worried, scared out of our minds. The death rate was extremely high.

That October, the influenza epidemic hit Chicago. Alicja, nearly nineteen, and her mother volunteered to assist the Red Cross nurses. They came home with terrible stories of the sickness and the crushing results. Whole families dying, a man killed his wife and children because his fever caused him to be insane. It was a horrible, scary time in Chicago.

A woman roomer came down with it, so my wife and daughter cared for her, then a man. Both roomers lived.

Chapter Twelve

The Trials of Job

One night, Walentina woke up complaining of a high fever, she was burning up. I ran into Alicja's room to find her almost as warm. I bathed them in cool water, tried to make them drink. The women's third-floor matron helped me. I wired Eugenia to come home at once. For three days, Red Cross nurses, a doctor, the matron and I tried everything known. Eugenia arrived two days after my wire, on an evening. The following day, October 23, 1918, her mother and sister joined our little angel, one at six in the morning, the other at eight that night. My life as I knew it was over.

In fact, I must take a break from writing about it now.

~ * ~

Eugenia contacted the Army who wired Henryk's commander in France of his mother's and sister's deaths. The local officer told her they thought the war would be over soon and the battles were so intense, he doubted if Henryk would receive the message for several weeks. Of course, we didn't know if he was alive, dead, or would live long enough to see the message. That's how horrible the Great War was.

The officer was correct. Later, Henryk told us he received the news in mid-November, after the armistice on November 11, 1918. He wired back how upset he was, and hoped to be returned to the States during the winter. However, he was reassigned to stay until June. The good news was Henryk was well and uninjured; he spent most of his time away from the front lines, repairing airplane engines. He was still devastated over his mother and sister when he returned, though at times, I thought something else was bothering him. Maybe it was all the bloodshed and chaos he endured.

Eugenia stayed ten days, then returned to Wyoming so she could continue teaching her beloved students. She never mentioned moving back home to care for me and, knowing how much she loved the West, I didn't have the heart to ask her.

The matron was very helpful, fixing my meals, doing my laundry, showing me how to cook some basic things myself, sobering me up on occasion. She wormed her way into my life, but never my bed, though I suspected she wanted to be the next Mrs. Sawicki. She left several months after Henryk came home. All in a huff because he told her she was a gold digger and would never marry his father. I think he was overprotective of me and his mother's memory. I knew no one could ever replace Walentina, but losing that woman's touch in my life hurt. Henryk sure as hell couldn't cook well or clean!

Chapter Thirteen

Henryk

After he finished eighth grade at St. Bobola's, we sent him to public high school. He'd worn out his welcome with those nuns and priests. He wasn't bad, just inquisitive and mischievous. I think mostly because he was bored, plus his friends were wild Indians.

"Here's another note, Pops," he said one day after school, probably around sixth grade. He acted like he was going to hand it to me, then swooped it to his mother, big smile on his face. "I'm hungry, can I have some cookies?"

"What's it about? I want you to tell me before I open it," she said. "No. You may not touch a cookie till you tell us."

"Umm. Well, Sister Johanna wants both of you to come to a meeting with her tomorrow. Some other parents are supposed to come too."

He looked like it was no big deal, but his mother smelled a rat. So, did I.

"Tell us more." Both of us glared at him.

"Well." He turned away, his shoulders wiggling as if it was all he could do not to bust out laughing. "An explosion happened under Sister Mary Margaret's chair in the lunch room and she fell over and it took two priests and three big eighth grade boys to get her back on her feet."

Walentina and I looked at each other, trying not to smirk. We had to cover our mouths not to bust out ourselves as he continued.

"Oh, Mama and Pops. Her spaghetti spilled and you should have seen those guys slipping and sliding around, trying to get her to her feet. It was like they were on ice."

We gasped and choked to keep from laughing, and almost gave in when he said, "Her habit flew up over her head and we saw her legs. They're like huge rolls of pink blubber on top of more blubber."

He sat down in a kitchen chair and gave into his own laughter, tears streaming from his eyes as only a boy that age can laugh.

"Don't move," I managed to growl as I walked through our living room to our front door, into the entrance-way, and climbed up the inside stairs toward the rooms.

I heard a door close and knew Walentina went out the kitchen door, down the half flight of steps to the outside, walked around the end of the house, and stepped up the open-air back stairway to the third floor. We met in the hallway where, holding onto each other, we tried not to laugh too loudly.

Sister Mary Margaret was the size of an elephant. I swear she joined the nuns for their free food, intending to eat her way to heaven. She was close, but I think she totally missed those verses on gluttony.

"Henryk, we have to get serious. Explosions don't just happen by themselves when our son and his friends are around."

We wiped our eyes and slowly walked down the stairs and back to the kitchen where Henryk still sat, the cookie jar on the counter untouched.

"Can I go outside now?" he asked, a little too sweetly.

"No," we both said together.

His smile lost its shine.

"So, what was the explosion caused by? Who caused it?"

He frowned, shook his head. "Okay, I'll tell you the whole story. You'll find it out anyway. Could I have a cookie while I'm talking? I might pass out from hunger before I finish."

His mother shook her head, yet handed him a cookie.

"So, it was Butchy, Andrew and me. We each had one firecracker left in our pockets from this weekend down by the ditch. Butchy said he wanted to light his and throw it in the garbage can in the dining room, do it during lunch. Andrew said let's tie all three together, that will blow garbage higher. So, we tied them together, but I lit them too soon and they were going to blow before we walked them to the can. So, I grabbed them and whipped them at the floor and we ran out into the hallway. They didn't go off, so we walked back in, but then they did go off. They'd slid under Sister Mary Margaret's chair and she jumped up, knocking her big plate of spaghetti over. She fell over and couldn't get back up."

He couldn't help laughing again. This time, we didn't join him, just glared at him.

I sternly asked him, "Was the Sister injured?"

"She didn't hit her head and I don't see how she could have hurt anything else because she's so f..."

"Enough! Somebody might have been hurt."

"I thought Father Nathaniel was hurt after he fell trying to help her and she rolled over on him, he's not very big. He said he was fine. So, nope. Nobody got hurt."

That school meeting was one of the few I attended. I kept my mouth shut as the boys got yelled at and threatened with hell. In the end, the boys apologized and had to clean and mop the entire lunch room every night for three weeks.

Henryk sincerely apologized to Sister Mary Margaret. The brat turned around and invited her for Sunday dinner. Next, he invited Father Nathaniel. "My mother is a very good cook, probably better than the food you eat here," he said, sounding oh so innocent.

What do you say when your kid's just raised hell and now invites a nun and priest home for dinner next Sunday? Walentina flashed her best smile. "We have been meaning to invite you and this is wonderful. I'm glad Henryk did so. Is chicken all right?"

Of course, both leeches agreed. The chair I guided the Sister to held up well, though I think we went through two chickens and half a garden of potatoes and home-canned green beans. Actually, I hate to admit it, but looking back, we did have a nice time, even though, after watching her eat, I still didn't believe the good Sister's excuse she had glandular problems. Father Nathaniel and I became friends, kind of secret ones. I think he realized I didn't want to be seen too close to the clergy. Once he tasted my homemade beers, he loved to slip over and come down the side-entry stairs to the basement where we talked about lots of things besides church. I figure knowing him won't hurt my chances with the big guy upstairs, if one truly exists. Cross my heart and say a hail Mary.

~ * ~

Henryk did well in public high school. He was able to take some carpentry and mechanic classes along with his regular classes. He worked after school and Saturdays for Rothman's, cleaning up the lumber yard, organizing the bins of nails and screws. He started repairing tools, replacing handles on saws and hammers, sharpening files and saws, all kinds of stuff that impressed people with his energy and skills. He started to go out on jobs, at first to clean up, then to start swinging a hammer and sawing wood.

Henryk was intrigued by autos. Old man Rothman bought himself a 1911 Model T Ford. One day, it wouldn't start, so Henryk started tinkering with it and soon had it going. To thank him, Rothman took him for a ride and let him drive it. That boy was in heaven.

He left school around seventeen, wasn't much else to learn. For several years, he worked at Rothman's, then found a part-time job fixing cars at one of the new dealerships. I think it was on the west side.

One time, when he was around seventeen or eighteen, still at Rothman's, I came into the wood yard from being out on a job. I didn't see him, which surprised me. Ollie said he didn't know where he was, told me to go on home, he was sure Henryk would be there or would arrive shortly. Just the way he said it made me suspicious. So, I hung around the yard, watching to see if he'd come back or not.

Sure enough, he came across the street, hair wet, smelling like lilac, big look of satisfaction on his face. "Hi, Pops. I just got a bath. Man, do I feel good."

"Umm. Front or back room?" I tried not to frown.

He looked at me in surprise, like how did I know about front and back rooms. "Front room, Pops. I haven't ventured to the back ones yet. How do you know about those baths anyway?"

"Well, son," I paused.

How much do I tell him? I need to be careful in my reply. No way did I want to slip up about his mother working there, how degraded she felt, or that's how she met both her husbands.

"Well, my first day off the train, the first thing I did was find a boarding house, the second a bath. Not reading English, I was a little surprised at the personal service. In fact shocked. I didn't know there were other bath houses without the personal services. Still, I've never forgot it. Just do me a favor, stay away from the back rooms. I've heard you can catch things you don't want to pass onto your future wife."

I turned my head and coughed. Didn't want him to see the smirk on my face. He was definitely a man, a young one, but with those juices rising. It would be hard to yell at him. Yet, his mother would be devastated if she found out.

"I know all that, Pops. Don't worry, I'm not going into the back rooms. Lilly sure had nice hands and it's a lot more fun than those other places that just give you a towel and bar of soap."

I tried not to choke. "I think Lilly was the name of my bath-girl too."

He looked at me, all excited.

"No, it's not the same person, unless it was some ancient old woman."

He shook his head as it dawned on him Lilly was a name repeated in the business. "Just do me a favor, son, let's not pass this conversation on to your mother."

"You think I'm stupid, Pops? Of course not, this is my second time there and this time was a different Lilly." He threw his arm around me as we walked home.

If he only knew, I thought. Maybe that's why I'm writing my memories, so he will.

He continued to live at home, occasionally dated. Every so often, he brought a girl home for Sunday dinner. After he took her home and returned, he asked his mother, "So Mama, what did you think of her?"

"Well, son. What do you think of her? That's most important."

"Oh, Mama. She's kind of clingy," he said.

Other times the girl was desperate to get married, too shy, or too bossy. Something was always wrong with her. I think he just needed his mother to remind him to take his time and not be anxious to find the right one.

I already told you he went in the army, how his mother and sister died and he didn't get to come home till that summer. Once home, he took a variety of jobs, then spent three months with his sister, Eugenia, in Wyoming. Came back and got a good job, full time as a car mechanic, plus he helped me around the rooming house as well. It was pretty lonely, just the two of us and the matron trying to keep us fed and making up to me all the time, till she quit over Henryk's rude comments.

One Saturday night, he went to a public dance. The next morning, I asked him how it went, if he danced much or met any gorgeous women.

"I only danced a few times. The place was crowded and started getting rowdy the more alcohol people drank. But..." His voice trailed off a moment and I could see a different look in his eye. "...I am going to a street dance this weekend."

The next Sunday morning, I asked him how the street dance went. "Terrific, Pops. Would you mind if I brought this girl home for dinner next Sunday?"

"No, but who the hell's going to cook?"

"She will. She wants to. We already talked about it. We didn't dance much. Just went out for a walk, then rode the streetcars instead. Seems like we talked the whole night. Her name's Mae."

I nodded. Didn't know what else to say.

Mae was the freshest thing to enter our house since Mother and Alicja died. She was lovely and energetic. She brought a bag of groceries in case we didn't have what she needed. Henryk picked up a pork roast from the butcher the day before and put it in the ice chest.

She shook my hand, stood back and looked me up and down. "How long since you've had a bath and washed your hair?"

Henryk turned red, but I laughed. This girl had spunk. I hadn't been around any women with spunk since my wife and daughter died. "A long time. Can you tell?"

"Yes, old man," she said. "If you think I'm going to slave in a hot kitchen, making you a meal to impress you forever, the least you can do is be presentable."

I slapped my leg. "You've got some spunk. This old man better get going."

"While you're at it cut your nails, they look like a witch's. I'll put some water on to boil for the bath," she said as I headed for my bedroom to get some clean clothes. "Crazy old man," she said as I passed her in the kitchen, going toward the bathroom. Said it with a big warm smile. That's what she's called me to this day. I still take it as a compliment.

Dang, I thought I had him fooled that I didn't like him. Ha ha. Crazy old man. Mae.

Two months later, they were married and moved into the back apartment. I switched apartments with them when she started popping those kids out. At the rate she's going, they'll need the second floor someday. She recently had number nine, a boy. They named him Joseph. They spelled it American, but he is still named after me. Mae told me. She lets me hold him, if I'm not coughing and spitting up blood. Which I've been doing most of the time these last few days. I'll miss the little guy. I'll miss all of them.

I'm tired. I sat up all night to finish this. I think I have enough time and energy to dig out Walentina's letter and leave it here in the Ledger. This will surprise the hell out of them.

First, I'll take a short nap in the rocker, then get it out.

Where the hell is Walentina's letter? It's not in the ledger and not in the dresser. I'd 'a found it by now. I've been translating this crap since the old fool died. Nine years. <u>What is the secret about Walentina</u>? Crazy old man! Mae, April 1945.

Hope he's met our John up in heaven. The old man is not the only one to sacrifice. Oh, but HE would be happy to know I'm expecting number ten. Rhythm method and change of life don't go together. What am I going to do with a baby at age forty-five? Hank's barely speaking to me. He doesn't want to be a father again at fifty.

Diary 2

Mae Sawicki

Born: January 3, 1900, Chicago   Died: April 1, 1980, Chicago
Diary found scattered throughout Ledger Two.

Chapter Fourteen

November 3, 1945

I bought a new ledger. We'll need it eventually to record the annual census and roomers. The old one is nearly filled, especially after the old man's story and me translating it. Still, I figure no one will get into this one for a while, it's only me and sometimes Hank who use them anyway, and he probably won't even notice if I start halfway into the pages, typical man.

I gotta start writing stuff down. Maybe getting some of it on paper will keep it from constantly running through my mind. Keep me from exploding at Hank or the kids or running down the street, screaming at God. What kind of God gives a woman a baby at forty-five? Nine years after her last one. After she's already a grandmother? What kind of God doesn't provide a woman that old with extra patience? A huge dose of understanding? A sense that you love this one the same as you loved the first nine? A sense that, somehow, this baby knows I didn't want him and has been fighting me since he could move in my belly?

Tommy, Tommy, oh, my Tommy. This kid was big and kicked the hell out of me for five months. I thought I had Esau and Isaac down there. It got so bad, I went back to the doctor, the one who first told me I was pregnant. I'd never gone to a doctor for regular care, always a midwife. This time, even the midwife wasn't sure if I had two or not. She'd never seen a baby so active.

"There's only one, he's big and I'm concerned about your age and the stress you're under after your recent tragedy." That's what the doctor told me. Next, he said, "I want you to keep visiting me and have this baby in the hospital. Also, we may have to induce it early."

I liked him, even if he was Jewish. He came over from Poland when things got bad before the war. I said, "Can't you take him now, Doc? I know it's a boy. It feels like I got Joe Louis and Rocky Graziano in the ring going at it nearly full time."

He laughed, made me start seeing him every three weeks. Which didn't help at all, other than the kid fought his way out two weeks early and still weighed nine pounds, four ounces. I even needed stitches. Can you imagine needing stitches after your tenth kid? By that time, they should fall out from passing gas. They kept me in the damn hospital for five days, treated me like an invalid. The nurses even joked if they kept me much longer, Tommy would walk home on his own. He grew like a weed in a crack, and just as stubborn, too.

Hank's trying. He really is. I can tell he has the same feelings I do. The ones we won't talk about. Hank's like his dad was, the old man. Always liked babies and kids. Only this time, it's different.

Once, after I found out I was pregnant, Hank and I talked. Just once. Near to four months along, after Patricia, my big-mouth daughter, told me you don't get fat from menopause and get to the doctor. Hank and I both cried over me being pregnant.

Finally, he said, "Maybe God's giving us a replacement for John." We both broke into sobs, so hard, we had to hold each other up.

Our son, John, was killed November 3rd, 1944. Japanese attacked Saipan. The bastards lost, but so did our John. I musta got pregnant that month. What kind of God allows your oldest son to die in a war and lets you get pregnant when you should be in menopause? While grieving your dead kid? I don't think Hank figures Tommy is God's replacement for John, either. It seems more like something the devil would do. What the hell did we do to deserve that?

I'm going to drink some chamomile tea, I throw in a little fennel, helps with digestion for both of us, nurse Tommy, and take the streetcar over to Oakwood Cemetery. Just hit me, one year ago today, John died. Of course, we didn't find out for several days. Maybe that's why I'm so fussed up today.

I'll bundle Tommy up good and put him in the fancy stroller the big kids all went together on and bought us, as if after nine kids, we couldn't live without one. It's sunny, so maybe I'll walk some too instead of just the streetcar. Talking to John always helps, crazy as that sounds.

Chapter Fifteen

February 4, 1946

Can't believe I haven't written anything in three months. Guess it's not like I'm a thirteen-year-old writing her secret journal about girlfriends, boys, mean parents, or still have six kids living at home, plus one buried and three out of the house, all married with a total of four grandbabies and another on the way.

Just got back from Oakwood. Took the streetcar over, but walked most of the way home. For some reason, Tommy seems to love being outside, even if it's colder than heck. That's why I take him out so much during the day when Hank's working and the kids are in school. I don't know what I'd do without Joey and Nina. Joey's nine and Nina eleven. The minute they get home from school, one of them starts playing with Tommy while the other does homework, then they switch. The older kids help as well, but they're teens and doing things teens do. Tommy can't get enough of them, all of them. It's like he craves attention and still isn't satisfied unless someone's right with him, moving around and playing with him. At six months, he's rolling wherever he wants to get, starting to scootch himself, and trying to pull himself up on things. He doesn't care if he falls or bumps his head, doesn't cry unless he's mad, he's definitely got a hard head.

Hank's back to stopping off at Polish Joe's, the little corner bar, for a draft on his way home. Think he's realized the kids can keep Tommy occupied better than him. I don't care, but I do worry about when Joey and Nina are older and won't have time after school to play with Tommy. Then what? Hell, we'll be older then too. I hate to think about how old we'll be when Tommy graduates high school, if we survive that long. Ha, ha.

Today, John told me to try to take things one day at a time. That sounds strange, like I'm crazy. No, I didn't hear those words out loud from his grave, but I did hear them inside my head. They're words he used to say. He was such a calm, thoughtful kid. Not bossy like most oldest kids. Patricia made up for him, she's the bossy one. He just observed where help was needed and quietly jumped in. That's how he died. Trying to save another soldier. That boy lived, thank God. My John didn't, but we got his Purple Heart. I keep it in the drawer with the flag, too soon to bring it out and have to look at it every day.

The kid John saved came to see us last week. Name's Tony. He just dropped in. Turned out to be an Italian boy, grew up over on Taylor Street, one of the Italian areas. He and John became good friends, he said. He was pretty nervous, so were we at first. He stayed for supper and we had a good talk. We learned a lot more about the service and all they went through, saving Saipan. We all cried when he left. I think we'll keep in touch. He even said he'd invite us to his wedding next fall. He's working for his father in their Italian grocery store. He wants to expand it into a restaurant.

Just hugging him when he left made me feel like I was touching a little bit of John. The kids seemed touched, too. Except Tommy who babbled and screeched the whole time he was here. That kid has to have someone paying him direct attention or he just ain't happy.

Chapter Sixteen

February 8, 1946

Yesterday, I went to the doctor. Six-month checkup stuff. He said Tommy was doing well, way ahead of the average in terms of weight and height and coordination. I coulda told him that. He checked me all over, the woman's checkup they're doing more of now. I never thought much of the idea of a woman talking with a man about your monthlies and getting pregnant stuff, or having him look inside you. I took a big gulp and said, "Okay, Doc. My monthlies aren't back to normal, only had two light ones since the baby. Does that mean I'm really in menopause this time?" Before he could answer, I found myself crying a little, so I hurried and said, "Doc, I can't get pregnant again. How the hell do I know when to have sex?"

"So," the doc said, "that's a good question. Some women your age who have had so many kids don't ever want sex again. Personally, I think it's healthy to have sex as late into your life as possible."

"Yeah, but it sure ain't good to keep popping kids out. Doc, what do we do?"

"Well," he said. "You could still be fertile, but it's hard to tell when. The rhythm method won't work now. If you weren't Catholic, I'd tell you to make Hank wear a rubber for a year or so, till we know your monthlies are over for good." He waited for my reaction, but I just nodded. After a moment of silence, he said, "Mae, don't be offended, but I've started to stock rubbers here in the office so you Catholics don't have to buy them from the drugstore. No one else but you and me has to know."

"Do your Jewish patients or Protestant patients ever use them?"

He started laughing. "How do you think my daughter and son-in-law only have two kids after eight years of marriage? They're still young and revved up, too."

My face turned red, I mean beet red. I'd never talked with a man like this about sex. Still, I nodded. "I'll see if I can talk him into using them." I didn't say we hadn't had sex since before Tommy was born, but I think he probably figured that.

"Do you want me to demonstrate how to put them on?" he asked.

I gasped, choked, and shook my head. How was he going to demonstrate? On himself?

He turned red, almost as red as me. "Guess that didn't come out quite the way I meant." He got a brown bag from his cabinet, pulled a little packet out and explained how it was to be opened and the rubber rolled down with the tip up. "I'm also putting some lubricant in, it will work better with rubbers and your body isn't producing as much as it used to."

My face was so hot, I could 'a lit a cigar off it. I shoved that package deep into my purse, paid him, grabbed the buggy and walked home, though I did stop for a Coke at Woolworth's counter just to cool down.

Last night, old Hank almost had a heart attack when I climbed into bed naked as a two-year-old who just escaped from the tub. It was nice to know how, even after ten kids, he didn't scrunch up his face or turn away from my body, even with my milk-filled breasts and flab and wrinkles.

"We're not Catholic tonight," I said. "You're wearing a rubber till the doc says I'm through menopause."

It took both of us and some giggles to figure out how to put it on, but after that, things came naturally, just like it has for twenty-six years.

How the hell can a sexless old man in Rome tell people not to use rubbers? I can tell you we weren't moaning and groaning the Pope's name last night. For old farts like us, it was near heavenly.

Chapter Seventeen

April 21, 1946

The kid, Tommy, is down for a nap, which is rare, especially in the morning. I was going to write about something, but just read my last section and forgot what the heck I was going to say first. What struck me was Doc mentioning the rhythm method of not getting pregnant. That made me think of Sister Mary Anne over at St. Bobola's.

Joey was two months old, so that was 1936, and I'd walked over to the school with Nina and Shirley to meet with some other moms about the Fishes and Loaves dinner. After the meeting, Sister Mary Anne, the principal, motioned for me to come into her office. You didn't say no or make excuses to her, even if you were busy and one of your toddlers had dirty diapers you were waiting to change till you got home.

The Sister is thin and tall, maybe six feet or more. Rumor had it she wore thick-soled shoes to make her even taller, but no one I knew ever saw her feet underneath her habit. She looked down at you, even me, and I'm five-eight, over round glasses that slid halfway down her nose, and she had green eyes that could bore into you if she was upset. We all feared her, but not as much as the kids. We adults knew she had a heart of gold, and all she cared about was the well-being of the kids as well as families in the parish. During the depression and war, that was a lot to care about.

Anyway, she takes the two little girls, finds an eighth-grade girl and tells her to take them to her classroom and color with them. "Sit down, Mae," she said.

Of course, I obeyed. No one questioned her.

"Mae, how many more children do you plan to have?" she asked, just like that, no hemming or hawing, no hello or how are you.

My face turned red and I coughed. I thought she was going to tell me my kids were doing something bad or good. "I—I...well, as—as many as the good Lord wants me to. Children are a gift from God."

I tried to smile. How did she know I'd been worried about that? I didn't want any more babies, but Hank wasn't ready to stop having sex. I wasn't either, but who did you tell something like that to? Certainly not the nuns.

"Mae, I know my question was direct. Now I'm going to be more blunt. How are your monthlies? Are they regular or irregular? How long after birthing a child before they get regular again?" She watched me squirm on the chair. "I'm sorry, but two weeks ago, we buried Ava. She died shortly after giving birth to twins. She was thirty-nine, and they were her eleventh and twelfth babies. Twelve children in fifteen years. Mae, you've just had your ninth. I don't want the same thing happening to you."

My mouth flapped open and shut a few times. Tears started squeezing out, then I kind of snapped at her. "Sister, just what the hell am I supposed to do? It's a sin to use protection. It's a sin to say no to your husband. It's a sin not to want as many babies as you can bear. You tell me what I'm supposed to do, because I most certainly don't know." I turned my head, ashamed at how I'd just spoke to a dedicated servant of God.

Next thing I knew, she was pulling me to my feet and hugging me, like a mother hugs her kids when they're upset. "Oh, Mae, you are so right. Just what the hell can you do?" She rocked me a few minutes, then pushed me gently back into my chair. She opened a drawer behind her desk and pulled out a folder. "Look," she said, "this is a calendar. Now listen closely. I know you are a smart woman, otherwise your children wouldn't be so smart."

She proceeded to teach me how women's cycles work, when they can't get pregnant, when they can, the number of days after their monthly when they're ripe, she said fertile, how long sperm can last inside you.

"Does this really work?" I asked, skeptical.

"Now, in your mind, not out loud," she said. "I want you to think of some mothers in the parish who haven't had children in several years. Who have spaced theirs out every three years instead of eighteen months or less, like most of you?"

I nodded. I could think of several names and realized I'd always wondered how they did it, but figured they were just better at saying no to their men.

She must have read my mind, because she said, "Some may refuse their husbands a lot, but they don't have to. Just the times they are most fertile. I think Hank will respect your desire to not have more kids, or at least as many so close together. I bet he's worried about you, especially after Ava. Her husband is clueless about raising kids."

I'd already told Hank we weren't having sex till I got a period after Joey. Twice, I'd gotten pregnant a few months after birth, before my first monthly. The midwife warned me I could still get pregnant even when nursing and no period yet, but I didn't believe her. Now I did.

After my meeting with the Sister, I told Hank I needed two regular monthlies, then I wanted to try the rhythm method. I sort of explained it to him. Said I could help him out until then if needed, showed him my hands, but he was always so proud about being a strong man and thought pleasing himself after getting married meant he was weak. He groaned, it was already three months, and now I was telling him he had to wait for at least two more. That night, he didn't come to bed. I went looking for him and found him in the old man's apartment, on the couch. He wouldn't talk about it, said it would be easier if he slept apart for a while. He said he'd have to think about checking a calendar every time he wanted to have sex. I cried, but didn't want to fight with him.

This was the worst rift we'd ever had. For four months, we slept apart, and it showed. We were snappy with each other, short with the kids, everyone seemed to feel it; even Joey the baby became fussier the more tense I got.

One morning, I was up early before anyone else, fixing breakfast, packing Hank's lunch, and John walked out of the back apartment, nodded at me and went into the boy's room. A minute later, Hank opened the apartment door and motioned me into the apartment.

The big lug looked at me, all sloppy-eyed. "I've been kinda ornery lately. I'm sorry. I think we need to be sleeping in the same bed, even if it's with a calendar."

I jumped into his hug, and we both sniffled a little. That was when I smelled the bacon burning and had to run back to the kitchen. While he was in the bathroom, I ran into our bedroom and checked the calendar. Damn. As I poured him a second coffee, I hugged his shoulders. "Hank, you may want to sleep on the old man's couch for a few more nights. I'm ripe for the next three days. You can't touch me with that thing."

He tensed and I waited for him to get a little snippy. Instead, he stood up and laughed out loud. "No," he said, "I can wait a few more days, but this family can't. We need to be together."

Later that night, I spooned him. It was safer than him spooning me. "What made you change your mind?"

"Last night, John came in with a blanket and pillow and stretched out on the floor by the couch. I asked him what the hell he was doing. He said, 'No one should sleep all alone, I'm just keeping you company.' Made me feel like a fool. I didn't sleep all night, but he did." He squeezed my hand.

That's how our fifteen-year-old John helped us get over our difficulty. That's why I miss him so much. That's why we figured he would be the priest from our family. That damn war.

I gotta go feed and change Tommy. He's the proof that menopause and the rhythm method don't work together.

Chapter Eighteen

March 29, 1948

Son Mark was home for Easter weekend. He's twenty-one now. One more year at Loyola, then he'll be up in Mundelein at St. Mary's, the seminary. Hard to believe this is the son that's going to be a priest. Not that we pushed any of them. We're Catholic, but ain't all goody-two-shoes about pushing our kids into being a priest or nun just so we'll have a better spot in heaven or get out of purgatory quicker, however that works.

Still, John was going to Loyola, planning on St. Mary's after that to be a priest. It fit for him. Instead, he went in the army, didn't even try to be a chaplain's assistant, said he could minister better without some collar around his neck. Guess that's what he was doing, ministering to that nice Italian boy, Tony, when those Japs got him.

Mark was seventeen when John was killed. Couple of months later, he said he was going to be a priest. Hank told him he thought he'd make a better cop. After all the crazy stunts he pulled and the cops coming to our house to ask him questions, Hank figured his youthful escapades would give him a leg up on keeping law and order, he'd know what to look for. Ha ha.

Mark did seem to settle down. We were never sure he'd changed that much or just got better at hiding his antics. He was very competitive, played every sport possible. He was so aggressive and rough, the coaches sometimes benched him. He loved wrestling and boxing, did both all over the city. Being the middle child, I figured he was just trying to make a name for himself, to stand out after living with a perfect first-born brother and three strong sisters who wanted to tell him how to live his life. He did all kinds of crazy things, tipping over outhouses, soaping store windows when it wasn't Halloween, shooting out street lights with a BB gun, taking chickens from back yards and switching them with ones from other yards. Mostly just crazy boy stuff. He got caught running through the laundry over behind the Baths and kicking dirt up on the sheets. The guy that caught him and his buddy tried to give 'em the belt, but he grabbed it from the man and tied him up with it. A couple of days later, he and his friend, a little wop, snuck up the back steps to the brothel, lit some firecrackers and yelled, "Fire," so they could watch the naked girls and johns come busting out of their rooms. Mostly crazy stuff like that, but during the war, no one needed the aggravation.

The police came over a few times about his fighting. For some reason, he hated Negroes and Mexicans. He went out of his way to attack any that came into the neighborhood. I can't say we loved them, but we still tried to raise our kids that people are people and have the right to walk down the street. After Mark said he was going to be a priest, he told us he wasn't doing those things anymore. We both knew he snuck out some nights and was gone all night. We never knew just what he was doing. Hank didn't think he was chasing girls.

Mark now lives and works over at the Catholic Boys Home near the Loop. Goes to school and works with the boys there. Helps with the boxing program and does a lot of sports with them. He also helps keep them in line. Saturday, he took Tommy out and tried to wear him out. Tommy's talking now and tell us when he has to pee, but still poops in his diaper. Mark brought him in to pee and told him if he needed to poop, to do it in the toilet. Tommy said, 'No poop.' He peed, then less than five minutes later, pooped his pants. Mark brought him back in, cleaned him, and spanked the hell out of him. Just blistered his butt red.

"Ma," he said, "you two are treating him like a grandchild, not your son. Quit being so easy on him."

Tommy did the same thing later that day, so did Mark, but on Sunday, Tommy told us every time he needed to poop.

I'm still not sure what kind of a priest Mark will make. He seems so intense. I'm his mother, I think he's hiding something down deep, but for the life of me, can't figure out what.

Chapter Nineteen

October, 1950

Dammit. What am I going to do with this kid? Tommy loves it when the grandkids come over. At least four are older than he is and he's their uncle. I kind of like it, too, because it means they help keep him occupied. We carved some pumpkins for Halloween. Afterward, I told them to read to each other or do something quiet in the living room while I went downstairs to do some laundry. I was way behind, been doing some for a couple of the residents, extra money for me and helps them out. After a while, I went up and the house is dead quiet, not a kid in sight. Those little buggers, I thought, they've snuck upstairs to the rooms again. The third floor is empty now. We haven't been trying to take any women, thinking we may put more men up there, but haven't decided. So, I grabbed my thick yardstick and snuck up the stairs, taking my time. Well, just before I hit the third-floor landing, I heard a commotion and three or four kids went racing down the hall and out the back stairway. I moved quietly and looked in the open door to see Tommy, butt naked, lying on top of his four-year-old niece, also naked.

I grabbed him up, saw his penis all stiff, and lost my head. I whaled on him with that yardstick. My granddaughter started screaming, "We was playing doctor with the big kids."

Tommy is yelling his head off. "Ma, Grandma, Ma. The big kids was playing doctor on us, then Zach told me to lay on top of her, then they run off."

I still kept whacking on him. What would possess a five-year-old boy to lay naked on top of a little girl?

I got them dressed and hauled them downstairs where the rest of the kids were reading, trying to act all innocent, as if they'd been there the whole time. "All you kids were up there playing doctor with them, weren't you?"

They wouldn't look at me, but all shook their heads no. So, I picked up Zach's. Where'd they get such a name, Zachary? It sure ain't Polish. I picked up his pumpkin, carried it out on the porch and smashed it on the sidewalk. I did the same thing with the rest of them, one at a time. They sat there with their mouths open and tears running down their cheeks. They'd never seen me that angry. "Don't ever lie to me again. Now go clean that mess up while I call your mothers to come get you."

Oh, the wailing and sobbing that went on, but I bet it's a long time before they sneak off to play doctor.

Chapter Twenty

December, 1950

Father Joe stopped by to pay rent for Katerina's room up on the third floor. She's in the efficiency, the matron's old room. We never did put more men up there, and are letting several women stay there now. We like Father Joe. He's about thirty-nine, friendly, funny and shows real concern for people. He also keeps an eye on Tommy in the school. Tommy's as big as kids two grades up, and tries to act like they do which doesn't go well with his first-grade teacher. He's a handful in school as well as home.

Father Joe had one of Hank's home brews; they've always been popular with the priests. Hank likes Father Joe a lot, always tells him to stop over anytime. That's why Hank agreed to take in Katerina Koslowski, before he even heard my objections.

One night, middle of October, Father Joe came over. Said he had a personal favor to ask. His kid sister, nineteen, needed a place to live until she could get herself on her feet and independent. He paused. "Well, the problem is, she's in a family way. She said she was engaged, but the boy went off to Korea and she hasn't heard from him. He doesn't know she's expecting. She doesn't know if he's been killed or abandoned her. Anyway, last night, when my dad found out she's pregnant, he threw her out on the street." He sighed and didn't look at us for a minute. "She can stay in the rectory with me for another night or two, but I need someplace close for her, so I can help her out. She's a good kid, won't cause any trouble, I just think they got things out of order a bit and she got burned."

Hank didn't even say we need to think about it or talk it over, just looked at me and said, "Father, we'll be glad to have her as long as needed."

I glared at him. I mean, why borrow trouble? Even so, I didn't say a word. The next morning, while Hank was at work, the good Father brought her over. The three of us went upstairs and started cleaning up the room. Mostly dust and grit from being empty for a while. Father Joe was getting in the way, trying to clean the fridge and stove, making a bigger mess. It was obvious this girl knew how to clean and we didn't need a man to help us. Even if he was a man of God.

"Joe," she said, "I love you, but not your cleaning. We don't need you for this."

I turned my face so they couldn't see me keeping a laugh in. Father Joe chuckled, touched her shoulder and left. We quickly finished up, didn't talk much. I didn't want to get close to her. I had enough problems of my own with Tommy without taking on a pregnant girl who didn't know where the father was. Finally, I said, "I may have an old rug in the basement and some beat-up pots and a few dishes. Let's go look at them."

The girl had nothing, but some clothes in two paper bags. I'd helped her hang them up and put them in the drawers, and I knew she wouldn't be fitting in them for long, she was due in January.

We went down to the basement, found the rug and stuff. She didn't try to chitchat. I think she knew I had reservations about her. Anyway, she saw some old cans of paint and said, "Would you mind if I did some painting on the walls and floor? Oh, do you have any old curtains or drapes I could remake to cover that couch and chair?"

I grunted, kind of grumpy, said okay, found her the stuff. Down deep, I was impressed. This girl was in a bad position, but she was going to make the best of things, I could tell.

We didn't say much about her to Nina and Joey. Did say we had a new female roomer in the efficiency and she was pregnant as well as single. We warned them not to ask any more questions and I'd appreciate it if they both didn't try to hang around her much. Just leave her be. I didn't want my seventeen-year-old daughter being friends with a pregnant teen and thinking she wanted a baby. Not that I hadn't had a talk with her. I did with all the girls, made sure they knew how sex worked, but didn't want her getting all excited over a baby. Maybe if Katerina's mother had done the same, she wouldn't be in this situation. Joey, at fifteen, he thought he was God's gift for women. No way I wanted him hanging around her, he was good-looking and looked older. Nope, I most definitely didn't want him hanging around someone who already knew the ropes and was ready to have a kid. Of course, as big as she was getting, I doubted if she was interested in boys at that time. After she had the kid, who knows? I just wanted to set the limits early on. Like I told all my kids, nature is nature. Unless you're ready to support a family, marry and raise a kid, there's some nature you need to stay away from till you're set.

Several weeks after she moved in, I started noticing leftovers from the fridge or pantry shelves missing. At first, I figured it was Joey. He was never full up, but he said it wasn't him. Nina ate enough to live on, not enough to get fat or thin. One day, I took some mail up to the roomers and thought I'd go on up to say hi to Katerina. Actually, I wanted to see what she'd done with the room with those scraps of cloth and old paint.

I about fell over when she opened the door. That little bird painted the walls. One was a light yellow, one a blue and the other two a green. She cut and sewed the cloth to make covers for the furniture. She painted the little table and the floor where the rug didn't cover. Somewhere, she scrounged orange crates for shelves, painted them and had curtains hanging over them. My mouth dropped open.

She smiled. She has the sweetest smile. "My sister, Ginny, snuck my sewing machine out of the house and called Joe to pick it up. I can't live without my sewing machine." She turned her head, wiped her eyes, and next said, "Later, Joe went back and told them he and I would never talk to them again until they apologized for throwing me out. My dad said goodbye and don't let the door hit your ass on the way out."

We were both quiet. I wanted to give her a hug, but forced myself not to. I did not want to get too involved with this girl.

I saw one of my serving dishes, an old one I don't use much and kept in the back of the cupboard. She picked it up and said, "Do you want to take this now? Hank said to just leave it outside my door and he'd pick it up later."

I nodded, tried not to look surprised.

"You are a very good cook. Thank you so much for thinking of me."

That night, as I was cleaning up from dinner, I handed Hank a small dish with some stew in it. "Here, I'm sure you know someone who can use this. I think she lives on the third floor."

His face turned a little pink. He took it from my hand. "Thank you." He patted my bottom and bussed me on the cheek. "You're a good woman."

"You're an old softie," I said. "Getting almost as daffy as your old man. Next thing, you'll be running around in my nightgowns."

"Doubt it, woman. You're going to outlive me by a long ways."

Now, couple of times a week, I fix extra and hand it to Hank. Don't say a word. He just winks at me, takes it upstairs and comes back with a clean empty dish. "She loved it," he always says and pats my butt again.

Chapter Twenty-One

February, 1951

We got us a baby up on the third floor. Krystina Koslowski, born January 9, 1951, and she's a little beauty.

After dinner on the ninth, Hank took a dish up to Katie, that's what she wants to be called. He came right back and told me, "You need to get up there. That girl might be in labor."

I rushed up there and she was half-sitting on the couch. "Mae, I think this baby is coming. I've had funny pains all day, but just thought they were from the baby adjusting itself. I'm due, but the midwife thought I might go for another week or two. Then this big pain hit me, and I've had them every couple of minutes, harder and harder. Can you call the midwife for me?" All at once, she gasped, "I just wet my pants."

"Little girl, your water just broke. C'mon, we're going downstairs to my place. The midwife can check you down there." I helped her down the stairs, but could tell the contractions were coming closer and harder. Going through the living room, I hollered at Nina to put the plastic sheet over my bed. I thought she was going to jump out of her skin when she saw me holding Katie up, the front of her legs all wet.

I had Katie lay down and pulled her bottom clothing off. Hank started to stick his head in the door, looking all concerned. "Hank, go boil water, lots of it."

Nina asked what we needed the water for and why so much.

"Mostly to keep him busy," I said. "Now go call the midwife, then get back in here. This baby ain't going to wait much longer. You and me may be delivering it."

Nina came back, her face almost white, "The midwife is out delivering another baby. They said she'll come straight here as fast as she can." Her eyes were big and scared.

"Well, Nina, this will be a good lesson on why you keep your legs closed until you're married." I looked at Katie who managed to nod, then she screamed as a big pain hit.

I had Nina get me some baby blankets and towels. I showed her how to check Katie for how far down the baby was. Whatever the baby was, I could see lots of black hair. Finally, about forty-five minutes later, Katie pushed out a beautiful little girl who started crying right away. I cleaned her up, cut the cord, and wrapped her in a blanket. As I leaned over to hand her to her mother, I kissed Katie on the cheek and muttered, "You did perfect. You'll be a great mother."

I had to wipe my eyes quick. Didn't want her to see me too lovey-dovey around her, even if I did know both were extra special to me now.

"She's so beautiful, she's got her father's hair. How much does she weigh?"

I took the baby back, handed her to Nina and told her to go weigh her on the kitchen scale. Six pounds, eight ounces, and healthy as all get out.

The midwife arrived, checked Katie all over, inside and out. She told us we did a good job. She even insisted maybe Nina and I should go into the midwife business. I laughed. Nina didn't. Since then, she's been talking about becoming a nurse in the delivery room.

For a girl who came here with only two paper bags of clothes, Katie is in good shape for this baby. Crazy old Hank called our big girls and told them we needed baby clothes. Girl clothes, diapers and whatever else babies need.

Poor Katie was overwhelmed those first few days with the Sawicki girls along with their kids showing up with stuff and having to see the baby and ooh and ahh over what Katie did with her place and telling her what tea to drink to keep her milk flowing and what not to eat that would give the baby gas. You'd think the Sawicki clan never saw a baby before. Well, guess they haven't on the third floor of a rooming house.

Chapter Twenty-Two

Sunday, February 14, 1956

Last night at the dance, Hank said, "You going to write about this night in your journal?" He patted my arm and winked when he saw my surprised look. "Woman, I've been reading it ever since I needed that ledger to record the roomers. It wasn't hard to figure out. Especially when you leave the pencil right where you left off."

I told him yes, so that's what I'm doing.

Last night, Saturday, we were at the school, in the new all-purpose room. I call it a gym. Father Joe and the principal arranged for an adult-only Valentine's dinner and dance. The high school kids had their dinner and dance Friday night, now they were serving their parents.

It seemed a little foolish, me fifty-four and Hank, fifty-nine, getting all dressed up. But I could tell the other parents felt the same way, at least the older ones. Hank bought me a corsage, but I had to pin it on myself. He said he was afraid he'd poke one of my mammaries with the pin. I told him, "Honey, after ten kids, those things are almost like leather gunny sacks, I doubt if you'd hurt me." He just laughed and patted my butt.

There was a live band who knew how to play jazzy dance stuff and polkas. Flowers on the tables with cloths and real napkins and china dinner service. A couple of nuns, Franciscans, from another parish, are known for their cooking, so they came in and fixed those little chickens, Cornish hens, baked potatoes with sour cream and chives, broccoli, rolls, and sherbet for dessert. Not the typical church potluck food. I guess they figured we get enough of that.

Hank looked at his plate and said, "That baby chicken looks like about two bites worth and where the hell's the moldy lime green Jell-O with cottage cheese, crushed pineapple and cherries?"

I wanted to hit him, but everyone at the table laughed like they'd never heard anything so funny. One of them even told Father Joe. He told our Joey to come over and make our table behave.

We danced a while, then sat down for coffee at one of the little tables for two scattered around the dance area. Hank edged his chair closer and reached across the table and took my hand. "Remember the first dance we met at?"

I squeezed his hand. "The first one where you stared at me all night, but were too shy to introduce yourself and ask me to dance? Or the second dance where we actually danced together?"

We both laughed.

"I don't think I'd have met you without your cousin Luke setting us up. I was smitten with you, but still was getting used to Mom's death." He paused and wiped his eyes with his left hand. He looked away, then seemed to force himself to look at me. "Mae, I had so many thoughts of Simone still running through me, even though I'd been home two years, both of them were still weighing on me." He looked away again.

I don't think Hank ever got over his mother and sister dying while he was fighting in France, not being able to come home for seven months afterward. Speaking of Simone, this was the third time he's mentioned her name since we met. I know he still thinks of her, not as often. There were times, the first few years we were married, where I'd catch him staring out the window, oblivious to what was going on around him and I knew he was thinking about her.

All I know about her is they met right after the Armistice and were madly in love, then he had to come home without her. Of course, he came back to a home with no one left but his dad, who was wandering around, wearing his dead wife's nightgowns. There's always been this part of Hank I can't touch.

He shook his head and said let's dance another one. We did and sat back down. Joey brought us more coffee, said he might be home late, he was going to a party with a girl. He's eighteen now and graduates in June. The girls love him. I don't blame them, he is a terrific looker, plus has a great personality. Hank looked up at him with this quizzical look.

"Don't worry, Pops, I'm always careful," Joey said with a wink.

I looked at Hank and asked, "Does that mean what I think?"

He nodded, turned a little red. "Yeah, I love grandkids, but I ain't Catholic enough anymore to not buy rubbers for my boys." He coughed and wouldn't look at me.

I patted his hand. It's the 1950s, I didn't want Joey having to get married, to start out adult life with a baby in some girl's pouch. Maybe I'm just getting old, which I am, or maybe because I know what it's like to enjoy sex without wanting a baby, or being tied down with one or two or ten. "Let's dance," I said, pulling Hank to his feet. "Let's show these young ones how to cut a rug." And we did. We were gasping for air when we finished. People were clapping like mad, including all those smart-aleck high school kids.

Hank sort of shut down when we got home. We were both tired out from dancing, but it wasn't that. No, ever since Nina and Joey were babies, he gets quiet at Valentine's time. Like he's going through the motions. I was glad to see him let go and enjoy tonight, but once home, it was back to his funk. Before, he loved Valentine's, always making a big deal out of it, making sure the kids did something or another, made me a card, baked cupcakes. He always made sure I got a flower, too. Once in a while, it was a live one. Usually, because we were so broke, he made one. On the wall over my kitchen cabinets is a row of handmade wooden tulips, all painted bright and shiny. I love tulips even better than roses so he'd go downstairs and cut, sand, and paint me a new tulip every year. Except he hasn't done that in over fifteen years. I think it has something to do with Simone, but can't be sure. What happened in the mid-thirties to make him stop, to close down at this time of year?

We sat next to each other on the couch, not talking, each in our own world. The house was quiet. Nina was home for the night from Cook County Nursing School to babysit Tommy. Both were asleep in their beds.

After a while, Hank startled a little, shook his head and put his arm around me, cuddling me closer, moving my head into his shoulder. "Where would we be if I didn't run into Luke, your crazy cousin, that night I saw you?"

"Well, I'm not sure," I said, "but Luke would've been dead."

"What do you mean, he'd have been dead?"

"Because I told him I wouldn't dance with him anymore until he told you I was coming back the next week and wanted a dance with the man who kept staring at me all night."

We both laughed. I cuddled closer as he said, "Well, I'll be damned. You never told me you sent him to find me. I was standing in line, waiting to take a piss, when he slipped up next to me. How long before you were going to tell me?"

"When the time was right."

We both laughed some more.

"I miss Luke," Hank said quietly.

I almost fell over. Hank never said that before. He usually smirked when Luke's name came up. The only argument we had before getting married, which was six weeks after we met, was about him not wanting Luke to stand up with us at our small wedding.

"I don't want a faggot standing next to me at our wedding," he said.

I understood, still it hurt. He still doesn't know how hard I cried that night. Luke was my first cousin, the same age. We grew up best friends, always playing together and dancing. We began entering dance contests at twelve and managed to win a few. Even in high school, the dance floor would clear when we came on. People just loved to watch us dance. I think I knew he was a homosexual before he admitted it, but I loved him so much, it didn't matter. He joined the army right after high school, but came home a year later, said they didn't need him anymore. Years later, after I was married, popping out babies, he told me the army kicked him out after two weeks because he was too feminine acting and he'd spent the year in New York City, too ashamed to come home, but also enjoying life with other guys like him. He had a rough time back home, so moved back to New York. I only heard from him once or twice after that.

Still, I was floored to hear Hank say he missed him after thirty-four years. "I miss him too, but why do you?"

"I don't know. He just had this spirit about him. He was so light and joyful and wanted people around him to be happy." Hank wiped his face. "I think I was afraid of him. All of us guys were. It's like if we got close, laughed at him, or invited him along, we'd been thought of as faggots. He wouldn't have hurt or touched any of us and I think he somehow knew when a guy was like him. They had some code with where they wore their hankies. Part of their stuff is still disgusting, but he was a good guy."

I squeezed him again. We were both quiet again. We were also both tired, a bit sleepy, but not ready to go to bed. It was a long time since we just sat up and talked. I remember the first night we talked.

"Hank, after Luke dragged me over to you and said, 'This is Mae. Now dance with her,' how many times did we dance that night?"

"Once, then all I knew is I wanted to talk with you somewhere away from a noisy crowd."

"No, it was twice, back to back, a foxtrot and something slow. That was when you asked me if I wanted to go for a walk. I asked if the area was good for walking and you weren't certain, so I said why don't we ride the streetcars."

"I thought that was smart, I mean, a wise response, considering neither of us knew the neighborhood." He paused a moment, scratched his head. "Remember that lady with the babies? Trying to get home after working with her tired-out, sleeping babies?"

"That's when I knew I wanted to marry you."

"You did? Why didn't you say so? Could have saved us six long weeks of courtship."

I laughed at him. Most of our courtship was me getting his dad back in shape and the apartment cleaned. "When you helped that poor lady with those three little ones onto the seats, I knew you were the guy." We only had the table lamp on, but I could tell he was blushing. "You made my mind up for good when you moved us up by her and took that fussing little boy and held him, then carried him off and helped her get off and on her way. Even the driver agreed. Did I ever tell you that?"

Hank shook his head. "I was just trying to impress you."

I knew he was joking. "That driver said to me, 'Looks like youse got yerself a good man there. If youse ain't caught 'im yet, then hang onter 'im till ya do.' He had no problems keeping the car waiting a few extra seconds till you got her going, even though a couple of the riders were grousing."

I could feel his smile as he said, "I think we both figured we oughta hang on. Guess we still are."

He kissed my cheek and laid himself down till he was almost flat out. He pulled my body around till I stretched out half on him. Just like teens making out on the couch do when their parents are in bed. We lay there, quiet again.

I remembered how that streetcar ride lasted most of the night. We rode one after another, further and further away, up north, back, then west. About midnight, we started catching cars back toward my parents' house. He talked about his mother's death, him being in Europe when he got the word, not being able to come home right away. He got really quiet, I could tell he was sweating. He kept tapping his foot on the streetcar floor. Part of me wanted to tell him to stop it, but I figured he had something to say and I'd rather hear it now than later or not at all.

Finally, he said, "You ever been in love before?"

"No, I had lots of guys ask me out, but I didn't think any of them were right for me. So, I go to lots of dances with Luke and he keeps an eye out for someone good."

He coughed, kept tapping his foot. "Well, I think it's best to tell you I was in love with a woman in France. Actually, I could have come home two months earlier, but couldn't give up leaving her. I knew I had to come home, couldn't stay there, and realized it wouldn't work to try to bring her along. Besides, I'd just got a letter, finally, from Eugenia, telling she heard from the matron how bad Dad was doing." He sucked in his breath. For a minute, I thought it was a sob. "Her name was Simone, she was a nurse. Her husband was a doctor who died when the Germans invaded." He got all quiet again.

I was thinking I know this is the right guy for me, but after two years, is he still in love with her? Does he think I'm going to be like her and be upset when he finds out I'm not? Will I be playing second fiddle the rest of my life? Should I tell him it's over now?

"I did a lot of thinking on that slow boat ride, then the train ride home. I realized it was a unique affair, at the end of a war. Sort of being in another world and now I was going home to my world. She was a wonderful woman. You'd have loved her."

I was shocked when he said that. Telling me I'd of loved his old girlfriend. I started to pull back a little, but he took my hand. "I don't want you to leave. It's been two years and I may never forget her, but I'm all here, with you." He cleared his throat. "One more thing," he said very softly. "I'm not a virgin, just so you know."

I shrugged my shoulders. That wasn't something I'd thought about or was worried about. I mean, the man was twenty-five, been in love with a French woman and lived a few short blocks from the Baths. What impressed me more and more as we courted was that he never once asked me if I was a virgin.

We snuggled closer on the couch. I thought about my first time coming to this house, carrying a bag of groceries, part of me wondering what I was getting myself into, part of me knowing it would be okay. I met the old man. He must have been in his early fifties, but looked ninety. He smelled, greasy hair, long, dirty fingernails and was wearing a woman's nightgown. For some reason, I didn't act shocked. Hank hadn't told me about the nightgown, just his dad was still acting daffy after his wife's death two year earlier. Crazy old man. I thought if this was my tryout for marrying Hank, I best get things straight right from the start. Before I could think, I told him to get a bath and called him just that— crazy old man. I never stopped. Somehow, I knew right then it was a package deal. Hank, the crazy old man, and the rooming house all came together. Call me crazy, too, but I've never regretted the deal.

I gave Hank a squeeze and remembered how on our wedding night, in the hotel downtown, my stomach twisted. I worried if I would be able to perform so that he enjoyed it. Would sex the first time hurt so much, I couldn't enjoy it? I'd wanted to get naked with this man since I met him. Now, there I was, all jittery. I snugged up to him in my negligee. "I'm a little scared. I don't want it to hurt. I'm a virgin," I said.

He pulled me into a huge hug and whispered, "That's okay. I know how to go slow." That's exactly what he did and I soon became glad he wasn't a virgin. He knew, still does, just what to do to ring my chimes.

Thinking about that last night made me want to start making out with him on the couch, but the door banged open and Joey walked in.

"What the heck are you two doing? Don't you have a bedroom to go to?" He laughed at us, but instead of heading to his room, he pulled the old rocker closer. Hank's mother's, the one she'd rocked her five kids in and I did my ten.

We lay there, waiting. It was obvious he wanted to talk.

"I've been thinking," he said. "I don't want to go to college, most of my friends aren't, but I do want to get away from here. I don't want to end up working in the yards or plants and living my whole life around here."

We waited. Both of us nodded a little.

"I want to join the Air Force. I've been checking all the branches out, but like them the best. Even if there is a war, I wouldn't be one of the ground troops like the army. Plus, they've got bases all over, even other countries. I'd like to see a lot more of the U.S. and the world."

Hank cleared his throat. "Son, I think that makes sense." He chuckled and I knew he was going to joke. "What about your girlfriend? Can you leave her for four years?"

"You mean girlfriends. I figure in a uniform I can find a whole lot more. Besides, in four years, maybe I'll be ready to settle down for good."

Tommy straggled out of his room, all sleepy-eyed, and stared at the three of us in surprise. He was wearing his white B.V.D. underwear. I can't get that kid to wear pajamas. He stomped into the bathroom, didn't close the door, slammed the seat up, and peed. Afterward, he didn't flush or put the seat down or wash his hands. I struggled to sit up, but Joey stood and motioned for us to stay.

"Tommy, go back and put the seat down, flush and wash your hands. You're nine and know how to do this."

"Shut up, jerk," Tommy said.

"Tommy, do it or you'll regret it."

"Like heck I will."

I turned my head enough to see Joey grab Tommy, whip him around into an arm lock, then force him into the bathroom where I heard the seat slam, the toilet flush and some water run.

"Leave me alone. I hate you. Everyone around here is a damn jerk." Tommy stomped into his room and slammed his door so hard, I thought it would wake Katie and Krystina on the third floor and everyone in between.

"What's with him?" asked Joey. "If he doesn't change, he's going to need reform school. He's getting worse every day."

Hank and I groaned, got up, kissed Joey and headed to bed. So much for a fun, almost romantic evening.

All day today, Sunday, the fourteenth, Hank's quiet, off into himself. What is it about him and February 14th? If it has to do with Simone, why did it start around the time Joey was a baby? Fourteen years after he left Simone? It ain't her birthday, or the time they had to split. I don't get it. Just don't get it.

Chapter Twenty-Three

January, 1956

It's Saturday. Hank and Tommy are out sprinkling the ice rink again, the one on the empty lot between us and the neighbors. The one each of us own half of. Sprinkling just enough water to fill in the cracks, smooth it up so the boys can play. They don't care how cold it gets, just as long as it's not warm. Today, it's four degrees, but sunny.

Hopefully, Tommy learned his lesson about getting the hoses back in the basement before they freeze. Couple weeks ago, he didn't and they split. Hank made him take the money out of his piggy bank to buy new ones and the kid never threw a fit. Tommy loves doing stuff with his dad, well, stuff like hockey and sports. At sixty-one, it's not like Hank can run around with him like some dad thirty years younger.

They're going to a Blackhawks game tomorrow, probably a couple more over the winter. Unless Tommy acts up.

Krystina from upstairs, Katie's girl, is at the kitchen table, coloring while I'm writing. She'll watch cartoons in a while. She brought her little pink pencil box and brand new coloring book. Her mom came home last night with a huge pile of clothes that needed altering. I saw her lugging them up the stairs and told her to send Krystina down to me for the morning so she could get some work done without a five-year-old chattering and wanting to help. I don't do that often, but I do love this little one. After all, I did help birth her.

Some boys just helped Tommy put away the hoses and are skating. They play so rough. Tommy's eleven, but the size of the big kids, eighth and ninth graders that he runs with.

"You writing about me again?" Hank just came in and put his cold hands on my ears.

He sees Krystina and does the same to her. I love to hear her giggle, so does Hank. "Hey," he says, "I'm gonna take the Ford out and fill'er up. Anything I can pick up for you?"

I shake my head and wave him away. He knows what I'd say, so why waste my breath? He just filled it up last weekend and only drove it three miles each way to work. I don't think cars need filling up after thirty miles. He's the head mechanic over at that new Ford dealership on Western Avenue. Good job, five days a week, insurance.

That man and his Ford. First brand new car he's owned. 1956 Ford Fairlane Town Sedan. He even got the V-8—the thing goes like a bat outta hell—air conditioning, a radio and seat belts, paid extra for those damn things. The best thing about it is the automatic transmission. He's going to teach me how to drive once the snow is gone. I told him once I learned, he might not see me again, especially if Tommy keeps acting up. He told me, "I'm not too worried. Tommy goes with the car." I shut up. I am excited to learn, though. Who says old dogs can't learn new tricks?

I made a big platter of bologna and mustard sandwiches and pot of hot chocolate and took them down to the basement. The boys will be cold and hungry soon. I don't let them come upstairs, they're too rough and loud. I made sure to check the lock on the secret laundry room where our homemade beer and wine are. Last month, there was some missing. Of course, they denied taking it, but Tommy just smirked.

I set some rules down. Even made a sign and posted it at the back door. They have to take their skates off at the bench outside the door. They cannot use our indoor bathrooms, the old brick outhouse still stands and we unlock it each day for them to use. Hank will bleach it out in the spring, they can't hit the hole any better in an outhouse than they can on an inside toilet. If they take, touch or break any stuff downstairs, I will personally tear their ice rink down. If I can hear them swearing or telling dirty jokes, they get one warning. After that, Miss Mae's bologna sandwich shop is closed for good. Trying to corral a bunch of boys with their juices rising, sprouting hair in their pits and privates, cussing like sailors, well, it's a bunch of bologna for a mother this age.

Katie came down to get Krystina. I told her to leave her here. I made a sandwich for her and extra hot chocolate to take back up with her. I could tell she was pleased for more work time alone. Last week, I saw what that young lady can do with remaking clothes. I couldn't believe my eyes. She showed me some of the designs she sketched out on paper. She has talent. Just hope the right person sees it someday.

Hank came back. I pretended to keep writing, kind of like I'm a reporter or something. I usually write in this thing, on the rare occasions I do, when he's at work and Tommy's in school.

I watched him sit down by Krystina, then slip a Tootsie Pop Sucker out of his pocket into her little hand. "Shhh," he said to her, "don't let that mean old lady out there see this. She doesn't want me spoiling you."

She giggled as he turned his body as if to hide her from me. I just shook my head. He led her into the living room and started reading to her, only making up the story, making it wilder and wilder the more she giggled and told him those weren't the real words.

I quit writing. Too much commotion, but I think I'll pick up later. Besides, I just noticed a fight out on the rink.

~ * ~

I'm back. It's quiet for a bit.

Anyway, I didn't say a word about the boys fighting. We learned to let these boys settle things themselves. Unless they got weapons, we don't interfere. Why bother? They'll all be good friends tomorrow anyway. The boys stormed off and I heard Tommy downstairs taking off his insulated coveralls and stomp up the steps. He can't even come up stairs without sounding like a herd of elephants. He stopped in the kitchen to set down the platter and pitcher. He crammed a sandwich in his mouth, guzzled some hot chocolate straight out of the pitcher, then looked down the hallway at Hank and Krystina, both with suckers in their mouths.

"Where's mine?" he yelled, his mouth still full. "Where's my sucker?"

"It's only a sucker, Tommy," I said. "Please quiet your voice down and go do your homework or something."

"No. Why's that little brat get a sucker? She ain't even related and her mother's a..."

"Tommy, you say one more word and you'll not go see the Blackhawks tomorrow. We're watching her so her mother can earn some money. Now, just go to your room." I was trying to talk calm before he upset his dad and that little girl.

110

He marched to his room and slammed the door so hard, the windows rattled.

"What was that all about?" Hank asked from the living room. Krystina's eyes were wide with shock.

"A sucker," I said.

Hank shook his head and pulled another one out of his pocket. "If he'd a walked in here like a normal kid, I had one for him."

Tommy must have listened at his door, because the door flew open and he charged out. "Let me have my sucker!" Hank started to reply, but Tommy started in again. "Why is she down here? Why are you always doing stuff for her and not me?"

Hank stood up, his face turning red. Krystina started crying. He picked her up, walked her out and handed her over to me in the kitchen. He grasped Tommy's elbow and marched him down the short hall and through the living room. He opened the front living room door and shouted, "Get out till you grow some sense."

Tommy smirked, which was the wrong thing to do. Hank grabbed him by the ear and hauled him squealing like a stuck pig through the main front door, out onto the front porch and threw him down the steps. He locked the door on his way back in, then closed and locked our living room door. The roomers all had keys to the main door.

Hank was panting up a storm. I got him some water. "I am too old for this crap," he muttered, wiping his face. He went down the back stairs and made sure Tommy's ice skates weren't outside so he couldn't just go skate, and locked that door as well.

Tommy pounded on the front door, then the front window. He yelled how much he hated us. A few minutes later, he ran in his socking feet through the front yard, through close to a foot of snow on the ground, and started banging on the back door. When we didn't respond, he went back to the front porch.

There was a knock at our living room door. It was Katie, wondering what all the commotion was. Krystina flew into her arms, sobbing. "There, there, little one," she said. "Sometimes kids and people get upset and lose control. He'll settle down."

I wondered if we ever would.

Katie said most of her work was done and a nap might be in order and took the little one back upstairs.

Tommy quit yelling, started making faces at us through the front porch window. A couple of his buddies came by, the older ones, and asked him what was going on. He must have told them, 'cause the next thing we could see was them pointing at him and hear them laughing. "A sucker?" one of them yelled. "You're being such a baby over a sucker."

Tommy got mad at them and started acting like he wanted to fight them, but they just hooted and ran off. He quieted down, sat in the porch swing and wrapped his arms around himself, trying to stay warm. Hank left him out there for another fifteen minutes, before opening the door. Tommy wouldn't look at us, didn't say a word, just went to his room when his father pointed at it.

The next morning, Tommy was dressed early for church, ran out and shoveled the walks, including the one to the garage. Didn't argue about riding in the back seat to church. We're driving to church now, the whole three blocks. We've walked those blocks for over thirty years, but old Hank buys a brand new car and now we're driving.

We got home from church and Hank grabbed the Sunday paper and sat down in his chair while I got the dinner on. Usually, if the guys were going to some sports event, Hank got changed, they grabbed a sandwich and left. Tommy was getting antsy. I could tell he wanted to ask if they were going to the Blackhawks game or not, but was afraid too. Finally, he took a deep breath. His voice sort of shuddered when he asked, "Dad. Dad, are we going to the game?"

"Nope. Son, if I have to explain why, then you must not be as smart as you think you are."

Tears started dripping down Tommy's face.

There was a light rap at the door. Hank opened it. Krystina, still in her Sunday church dress, held up a folded piece of colored paper. "This is for you," she said. "It's a thank you picture I drew for watching me yesterday." She saw Tommy and brightly called out, "I hope you're having a good day, Tommy. I have bad ones too, some days." She turned so her little dress whirled and skipped up the steps.

Tommy glared at her with a look of murder, turned and went into his room where he flopped down on his bed.

It's times like this I wished Nina and Joey were still home. Joey is at some Air Force base in Spain and loving it. Writes us the scenery is beautiful and so are the mountains, plains and ocean. He's in electronics, working with these computer things he says are going to change the way we do everything. Sure they will, I think. Nina's sharing an apartment with another young woman on the north side. She's working full time at Cook County Hospital, delivering babies as fast as she can. Couple of times, the doctors have been late and she delivered the baby. Says she keeps asking the docs when she's going to get their pay for those deliveries. She's dated several med students, but says she's not getting serious. "You put them through med school and residency and they divorce you or have affairs. Nope, I'll wait for the right guy, I got plenty of time." She's talking of going to college to get a bachelor's degree in nursing so she can teach someday. Things sure are different.

Mark paid a quick visit and we talked a bit about Tommy. He's the priest or almost priest, I can never tell. He's always a little vague. He wanted to know if we were ready to send him to the boy's home. He said he'd take him whenever we want. How the heck do you turn your kid over to a home for delinquent boys? Oh, Mark said it's not all for delinquents. Most of them just have bad homes, fathers dead or disappeared, stuff like that. That's supposed to make us feel better? That our home life is so bad, we can't raise him right, or that he's a delinquent? We feel bad enough about the way he's growing up. It's just whatever we try to do doesn't seem to be enough for him. Something was missing in that kid from the time Hank's sperm hit my egg. Can not wanting a baby affect the child that much? It's not like we haven't tried. I've prayed and prayed, for patience, for understanding, for more love, for more energy. I've prayed to the Virgin Mary, Jesus and every saint I think could help. Change me, change Hank, change Tommy. But nothing. It's like they're all deaf. In confession, the former priest always told me God was working things out, he was still in control, just love and trust Him more. He must have told Hank the same hogwash, 'cause Hank's quit going. Of course, I don't go as often anymore either, even as much as we like Father Joe who doesn't say things the same way. I still hear that old goat's voice, just like he tape-recorded it for me special.

Chapter Twenty-Four

April/May, 1958

Didn't think I'd ever talk with a lawyer and have to go before a judge about giving up our legal parent guardianship and transferring it to Mark. Never thought I'd have a kid try to molest a little girl right in our own home. Or know he's out on the streets and the police are looking for him as a runaway. But we are. We go to court tomorrow with the lawyer.

After Hank caught Tommy with Krystina, we called Mark to come get him. Tommy ran off when Mark tried to take him to the boy's home. Said he'd live on the streets before going to the Boy's Home.

We collapsed on the couch after a bit of supper. At first, we just held each other, too stunned to talk. Trying to absorb how our boy—thirteen years old, but in a man's body—tried to...I can't even say it. The idea our son was molesting a little girl, why, I could hardly put words to it. Still can't.

Finally, Hank moaned, "I can't keep doing this. We can't. We are just too old for this kid. What happens if he comes home?"

I squeezed his hand. "What happens if the police find him, but he won't stay with Mark? Then what?"

The front door opened and Mark walked in. He hadn't found Tommy yet. "The police will find him eventually, but you need to tell them to bring him to me."

"What happens if he won't go, or worse yet, won't stay at the boy's home? We're still his parents and responsible for him." I started to cry again.

Mark was quiet, this serious, almost mean look on his face. The look I've never been able to read. "I'll take guardianship of him. You have to sign away your parental rights and transfer guardianship to me, legally. With a lawyer, before a judge."

We both gasped. I started to shake my head, but Hank said, "Mark's right. I can't handle him anymore, nor can you."

That's what we did.

I can't say if the pain of burying John was worse than admitting before a judge that you can't parent your own son, or not. John's death is never over, but the ache gets less, the loss more manageable. I will always remember him as the young, smart, funny, wise man he was the last time I saw him alive. Tommy will grow up now, only several miles away. He'll only visit us with Mark, and probably hate us for legally saying we don't want him as our son. This is a whole different kind of pain. Yet, I feel some relief. I don't know which is worse, this kind of pain, or the guilt of feeling relieved I'm no longer responsible for him?

~ * ~

The police found Tommy and brought him home yesterday. He'd been on the run for a week. Hank did what we'd agreed to do. Sent them over to Mark at the Boy's Home. Told them Mark was his guardian now, that we'd signed over our parental rights. The police wanted to know why, but Hank told them he didn't have to tell them why. Something else we'd agreed on, with the help of a lawyer and at Katie's recommendation.

She said, "He doesn't need a police record, they don't need to know. I'm not pressing charges, but he can't be around my little girl. I'll understand if we need to move out."

The cops walking toward the porch, me inside the storm door, I'll never forget the look in Tommy's eyes. Or his words from the back seat of the police car, "Please, Ma, please. I'll be good. I promise." They sounded like a three-year-old, but they were coming from a thirteen-year-old who needed a good shave and was almost the size of each of those policemen.

He looked filthy, hungry and scared. Police said he'd worn out his welcome at his friends' homes and was caught sleeping in the park. They suspected he was the one who'd been threatening young kids for their pocket money to buy himself food.

It was all I could do not to open the door and pull him into my arms, like the prodigal son's father did. There was still something in his eyes. Something I couldn't touch, a place I couldn't get to. Plus, the image of him with his pants down, trying to force himself into Krystina's little mouth kept flashing through my mind. That's what Hank caught him trying to do. That's when Hank managed to get him into his room, threatening him with the crowbar in his hands. That's when we called Mark to come take him and he ran away from Mark getting into the car.

I closed the door and turned away so not to see my youngest son leaving in the car with two cops. I didn't know for how long. Would he change? Get better? Mark said they had good therapists at the home who would work with him. How long would that take? Was he a sexual pervert, or just a messed-up kid who could grow out of it?

We both cried in shame and failure and loss and love. We cried all that night. What had we done?

Chapter Twenty-Five

June, 1958

Hank and I agreed that Katie and Krystina couldn't stay upstairs in that efficiency forever and she still wasn't making enough money to move to a full apartment on her own. We told her to take the back apartment, right behind ours. A little bit more rent money, but more space and their own bathroom.

"I hope you're not doing this because of Tommy," she said. "I don't want to take it because you're feeling guilty or trying to make up for what happened."

That girl, young woman, is so sharp and direct. I'd'a thought she'd ask if Tommy was moving home soon, but she didn't, and he isn't. We've decided no matter how much he improves, it's unlikely we'd take him back to live. We did what we could do, we failed. I don't trust us or him to live in the same house together. Something broke and it ain't going back together.

Hank smiled at her and said, "Katie, we'd been thinking of this for a long time. We were concerned about how much noise and commotion Tommy made at times and figured you didn't need to be close to that." He choked up a bit and waited, wiped his eyes and went on. "I know you've told us over and over to quit apologizing for what Tommy did, so I won't." He paused again. "We decided no matter what happens, he's not going to live with us again. Several of the big kids have said they'll take him when Mark says he's ready. We'd love to have you next door instead of up two floors. Besides, that means I can see this little one more often and she can play with the other grandkids when they're over."

"When ain't they?" I muttered.

On Thanksgiving Day, everyone was home except Joey. Somehow, he wired flowers to me and a note that said, "Mom, I decided not to bring home a wife who doesn't speak Polish. All they speak is Spanish over here." What a nut.

Anyway, everyone else, plus some, were here. Don't ask me how we fit them all in. Some go to the basement, some go into the bedrooms, the men and big boys hang out watching Hank's fancy new console TV that even has a record player in it.

Patricia, the bossy one, scribbled something on a brown paper bag and banged on Katie's door. "It's official, we voted and here's the certificate," she yelled when Katie opened her door. "You're adopted, now get your skinny butts out here with the rest of the family."

Tommy came with Father Mark for about an hour. Everyone made a point of hugging him and saying they missed him. He said he's doing all right. Mark said the place, living with the other boys, is an adjustment for him, but he's catching on. He likes all the sports and physical activity they have. Tommy wouldn't look at Katie or Krystina. I could tell he was uncomfortable, but guess it could have been worse. Krystina was playing with the kids, but when she saw him, she sidled over to her mother and never left her side. Once he left, she was back with the kids just like she'd been with them her whole life.

I still wonder who her daddy was, giving her those huge dark brown eyes and almost black hair. Somehow those aren't Polish brown or black.

Chapter Twenty-Six

Friday, August 15, 1958

"The second floor is full," I hissed, looking through the window onto the front porch. Hank didn't even look at me. He was standing on the front sidewalk talking, late Friday afternoon, with some young-looking Mexican man. I kept glaring at him. Finally, Hank waved his hand at me. I knew he heard me and didn't want to. He didn't listen to me the first time when little Krystina told us a man who talked Mexican was out front talking with her mom.

They drank more of Katie's iced tea and talked a while. Next thing I knew, he walked that little spic upstairs to the third floor, came back down, got out the ledger and wrote his name in. I didn't acknowledge Hank, just kept on doing dishes. Once he left, I checked the ledger. Manuel Rodriguez, eighteen, last address San Diego, California and Tijuana, Mexico. Next to that was a note: Mae, I checked his papers, he's not a wetback.

The next morning, I was still set off. I went storming off to find that dumb polack. Give him a piece of my mind. How dare he take in somebody from Tiawono, Mexico and tell me he's not a wetback. Some smelly spic who's going to stink the place up, eating them peppers and greasy sausage and whatever the hell else they eat. Oh, yeah, rice and beans. I know there's Mexicans coming to Chicago now, and that's fine. Except they sure as hell don't need to move into my house. Put them somewhere else.

First, I checked the basement. Hank wasn't down there, mixing up another brew of beer or putzing around in his shop. I snuck up the stairway and moseyed through the third floor. That scoundrel put that little shrimp in the efficiency. What the hell for? No one lived in it since Katie moved down behind us. He must be getting senile, putting a Mexican in the efficiency.

I marched downstairs and outside toward the garage. I heard them talking inside it. I had to admit, Manuel's English was decent, heavy, but very understandable. They were talking about the '56 Ford. Same one, first new car we had. Hank was telling him he was thinking of trading in for a new '59 coming out in October, but his wife don't like the idea. He was right. I'd already told Hank I thought the '59s were the ugliest things ever created and if he bought one, I might not take my nightie off ever again. That old fart, he started ticking off on his fingers, counting. I asked what the heck he was doing and he said, "I'm just figuring out how often you take that thing off now that we're getting old. I'm trying to project ahead."

He tried to hug me, but I wouldn't move, just stood there like a marble statue. So, he patted my butt and left, whistling. Now, there he was, still talking about a new car to some Mexican we'd never met before and who was now rooming with us. Damn him.

I stopped when I heard Manuel say, "Why you want one of those ugly things? You got a gem, it's hardly broke in. Listen to your wife, man. Now, sir, hand me the new filter, please."

I almost busted out laughing, then realized I was still angry. I stopped in the garage doorway. There those two were, changing the oil on Hank's beloved car, chattering away as if they'd known each other a lifetime. Manuel down under the car, Hank handing him stuff.

I stood there, watching them, till that little guy crawled out from under the engine and noticed me. Hank turned and said, "Mae, this is Manuel. He's going to be staying on the third floor and helping us with some work around here to partly pay his room."

I glared at him, then managed to mutter, "Nice to meet you." I didn't mean it. Before I could stop myself, I blurted out to Hank, "He better not be helping himself to any of our stuff and disappear."

Hank has never lifted a hand toward me, but the look on his face told me there's always a first time. I stepped back and was going to apologize, but that little spic stepped closer to me.

He didn't smile, he didn't look angry, just real calmly said, "Mrs. Mae, I'm an honorable person. I may be poor, but give me a chance to prove I am an honest poor person." He wiped his right hand off on a rag tucked in the belt of his pants, then began checking something under the hood. I didn't even notice how his left arm hung funny and the shoulder bent out of place. That's how embarrassed I was. Maybe I was angry, or both.

I was fixing dinner when Hank came in and put his arms around me. I stiffened up. "Mrs. Mae," he said. I wanted to slap him. "Mrs. Mae, give him a chance. Give me a chance. Something tells me Manny is going to be a big help to us around here. We're not getting any younger."

Now, Hank's calling him Manny. Next thing, it'll be son. Over my dead body.

When he patted my behind, I didn't say anything, but slapped at his hand a little, in fun, like usual.

Last night, I did take my nightie off. Looks like we're keeping the '56.

Sunday

Almost forgot, it was a crazy weekend with roomers. Sunday afternoon, Hank was snoring in his recliner, watching the Sox, and I sat on the couch, doing some cross-stitch, when the doorbell rang.

Hank roused enough to mumble, "Put him on the third floor. Manny told me he might be coming by and he's a good guy."

I didn't say a word. Now what the hell, another spic? Should we change our name to Taco Rooming House? I grabbed the ledger and yanked the door open. My mouth must have dropped three feet. It wasn't no Mexican standing there. It was a man taller than Hank, maybe six-one, skinny, with pure white hair, white skin and sunglasses thicker than the magnifier I use to cross-stitch. He was dressed in a suit and tie, clean, neat, like he just walked out of a bank or office in the loop.

"I'm Mike McGuire. Manny told me you might have a room available on the third floor."

I signed him in, took his money, he paid for a month ahead, wrote down he worked at Roseland Family Bank, obvious he wasn't broke. While I was signing him in, Manny came down. He looked at me carefully as if not to upset me. "I can help him move upstairs," he said.

The new guy kind of blushed and didn't look at Manny. "Manny does some work around our bank, that's how we met. I've been looking for my own place and he told me about you."

I started to turn to go into the living room, but paused when Mr. McGuire asked Manny if he was cooking supper. I glanced back at the men and noticed Manny's nod and smile. Mr. McGuire saw my look and said, "Mrs. Sawicki..."

"Just call me Mae, I don't like this Mrs. stuff."

He smiled and I gotta say, his smile is beautiful, if you can say that about a man's smile. "Call me Mike, please. Mrs., I mean Mae, I can't wait to eat Manny's food. He introduced me to Mexican food last week and I love it."

Manny blushed a little, if brown skin can blush, and nodded his head at me. He motioned for Mike to follow him up the stairs. He told Mike where the toilet and tub were, the rules of the place. Just like he'd been in charge forever.

I closed our living room door and stood there a minute thinking. Those two men must know each other pretty well, the way they seem all friendly. I wondered how a white, albino banker and a spic can seem like such good friends. I also wondered why the heck would Mike be all excited over Mexican food? It just seemed strange. Mike reminded me of someone, but I couldn't pull it out of my mind. I went back to the couch, shaking my head. Sitting down, it hit me. That Mike guy reminded me of my cousin, Luke. Oh, he wasn't feminine, his hands didn't float all over, but there was something extra gentle about him. None of this made sense, so I decided to quit thinking about it.

"He seem okay?" Hank asked, still half asleep.

"Guess so, he looks strange. Never seen anyone that white or whose eyes jiggled around when they looked at you."

I didn't say anything about him reminding me of Luke, or how something seemed strange about these two men being good friends.

"He's an albino," Hank said. "Something to do with their lack of pigment and it affects their eyes. We had one keeping books for us at the dealership."

So, now we got us an eighteen-year-old Mexican from Tiawano and an albino banker from Roseland living on the third floor. And they seem to know each other. I'm not worried, but it still seems odd.

I quit stitching to watch the game Hank was snoring through. I like this TV, but I'll never tell him that. At supper, I asked him, all innocent, "So, how'd you like Nellie Fox's three hits today?"

"Loved 'em," he said. "I love how that man hits and drives in runs. Never miss seeing him at bat." He winked at me. "Who won?"

Chapter Twenty-Seven

Summer, 1960

Just kept Joey Junior overnight. Now they're going to call him JJ. They don't want to call him Joey Junior, so guess I'll have to change what I call him too. No way I'm going against his folks on a grandkid's name. He's a year, just started walking. Baby's only half Polish. Leave it to Joey to marry the first non-polack in the family. JJ's mama, Lisa, was tied up on some translating job and Joey was at a conference for county computer people. They asked if we'd watch him for a night and day. Didn't take long to convince us, even after twenty-one grandkids, we still love having 'em over.

Several weeks before Joey got out of the Air Force, Tony, the kid our John saved in the war, invited us to a family picnic out in Swallow Cliff Forest Preserve. We'd kept in touch, got to know his folks and some of his kin. Every summer, they had this big picnic and invited us. Tony was married and had four cute kids.

When I got the official date Joey was arriving, I called Tony, told him Joey would be home for good and I wasn't sure we'd make it.

"Well, bring him with," he said. "It's not like he doesn't know some of us." He was quiet a moment, then said, "In fact, tell him it's an order from his Uncle Wop to come with you. I have someone I want him to see again."

So, we told Joey when we picked him up at the airport. He laughed. He'd always liked Tony. Soon as we got home, Joey saw Manny up on the ladder, washing windows. He jumped right in and started helping him. Told Hank he thought Manny was a great addition to the house. Hank said, "Tell your mother, I already know that."

I just smiled and nodded, but not enough to act like he was one of the family yet. That nice Mike guy only stayed eight or nine months, I think, then showed up once in a while to visit Manny. Manny seems a bit quiet and lonely without him. Hope he's all right.

At the picnic, Tony introduced us around to the folks we didn't know. He always said, "These are the parents of the man who saved my life in the war." Of course, that always brought some tears when people realized our John didn't make it back. This year, he added, "This is their youngest son, Joey, who just got out of the Air Force two days ago."

We were chatting away when Tony brought this young lady up and says, "This is my baby sister, Lisa, I don't think you've seen her since she was young."

"I sure haven't or I'd remember," said Joey.

He stuck out his hand to her, but first, she just shook her head and laughed at him, like you're a dolt, then she took it and shook.

"Joey," Tony said, "once you hit high school, I tried to make sure you didn't see much of her. I was hoping you'd matured in your choice of women. You know, I have to be a protective older Italian brother, right?"

Lisa hit her brother and laughed. "The day I need you protecting me will be a cold day in hell." Looking at Joey, she added, "Joey, we have met before, several times. You don't remember me, do you?"

Joey flushed a little, shook his head.

"Well, that's probably because the last time we saw each other, we were both fifteen and I had buck teeth with braces, thick glasses and was still flat chested. You'd already sprouted and I hadn't. That's why."

Joey blushed a little more, started to mumble something, but she cut him off with a wicked grin. "So, Joey, tell me. Were you discharged honorably or dishonorably?"

Joey's mouth opened and closed like a fish trying to get oxygen. I thought right then, son, you just bit, hook, line and sinker.

They wandered off and never quit talking. On the ride home, Joey said, "Well, she may be Italian, but she speaks Polish. That Spanish girl I flipped over for a while couldn't, nor English."

"No way," his dad said. "Lisa speaks Polish?"

"Yup, she speaks English, Italian, Spanish, French, Polish and is just finishing a class in Russian. She's a linguist."

"A what?"

"She studied languages. She interprets at meetings for businessmen and lawyers when they have foreigners visiting. She rewrites manuals and letters and stuff from one language to another. I'm going to marry her."

Six weeks later, he did, and nine months and six days after their wedding, Joseph Joshua Junior was born. Now, we have a wop daughter-in-law who speaks Polish and who I wouldn't trade for nothing. They're buying a house in Oak Lawn. First kid to move out of the city, but don't think he will be the last.

Chapter Twenty-Eight

Tommy Dies
October 31, 1966

Halloween Day. No candy. Lights out, shades pulled, even left up the black cloth in the front window. Our kids know not to bring any grandkids around trick or treating. Any neighbors with little kids should know the score and won't bother us. This is the first Halloween we ain't decorated. Some years, it was big, lots of pumpkins, lots of candles. Sometimes, I even made up a scary old man, stuffed with rags and whatnot, and sitting on the porch swing to spook people. Not bad, just a little.

Not this year. Tommy died in Vietnam and Hank and I aged about twenty years in ten minutes. We've always been too old for that boy. I think we always hoped down deep that once he got out of the Marines, there might be a chance to establish some kind of better relationship. Guess we never figured we'd lose two boys to war, twenty-two years apart. Both getting their Purple Hearts saving others.

It was Friday, ten days ago, Hank just got back from picking up a few groceries. He stopped by the A and W place and picked us up each a root beer float. We were in the kitchen, slurping and kinda giggling on account neither of us are supposed to be eating those things. We didn't, very often. The front doorbell rung and as I walked through the living room, I could see two service men in their uniforms on the porch. Mark stood with them. "Hank," I yelled, then sat down quick on the couch. I couldn't go any further.

My heart started thumping and I started to sweat. I pointed onto the porch when he came along, and his face went all white. He managed to open our door, then the main one and motioned them into the living room. He sat down on the couch by me and we held hands.

"It's Tommy, isn't it?" Hank said.

They nodded. Mark did, too. He was almost white. He kept trying to light a cigarette, but his hands shook so badly, one of the Marines finally lit it for him. I never saw Mark that nervous. Uptight, yes, but shaky nervous, no, never ever. It's like he always figured Tommy would come home, too. The fact he was in a war and could die, and how we'd already lost one son in World War II, somehow didn't sink in to any of us. I mean, everyone thought the Marines would be the best thing for Tommy, and the war over there so far away it seemed like a dream, and Tommy being so mean and tough and ornery...Well, I never worried about him much. Like I wrote before, I was hoping for some changes in him and the chance to get along better when he came home.

I managed to tell the men to sit down, but I didn't have any energy to get up and offer coffee or anything. They seemed uncomfortable. Mark even more so. After several drags on his cigarette, he calmed down a little. The marines quickly told us Tommy died in an ambush not far from his unit's outpost. They used big words. Said it was Operation Prairie, DMZ. Said overall, the operation was going on since August and over one hundred fifty boys died so far and it still wasn't over. The commanders were surprised at the ambush on a small group of guys.

I don't even know how I remember that stuff. It didn't matter. Tommy was dead. They did emphasize he died saving four other guys' lives, and would receive the Purple Heart.

"We don't want a big church funeral," Hank said when they asked about helping us make the arrangements. "Just do something at the grave. Father Joe over at St. Bobala's will help. He knew Tommy."

Mark looked surprised. He closed his eyes a moment before saying, "I agree, Father Joe's a good man." He took a big breath and let it out. He seemed relieved.

Tommy actually died on the nineteenth, but what with the time zone stuff and getting the word back to these Marines, well, what the hell difference does it make. He's dead. We buried him fast, last Tuesday, six days ago.

All the family came to the graveside funeral. Everyone kind of stunned. Mark and a few of the priests and staff from the Boy's Home came. Other than a marine who wasn't even there saying he gave his life to save others, it seemed like no one else seemed to know what to say about Tommy. Especially when most of us knew what he almost did to Krystina on his last visit home. The very idea of him trying to force himself on her again was too much to even think about. Katie says Krystina won't even talk about it, and doubts if she ever will. No, he wasn't a good kid. Whether that was Hank's and my fault or not doesn't change the fact he was a hard kid to have around. Still, no one expected him to die. He was so damn tough and mean hearted, no one figured he'd die. Shot up, maybe, but not killed.

Hank and I did a lot of crying up till the funeral. We didn't talk much, except a few times, we laughed about some of his cute stuff, especially his ice hockey. At the same time, we'd remember the fights he had with other kids, how he talked to us, how we couldn't handle him, the things he did to little Krystina, how we legally disowned our own kid, gave our guardianship over to Mark, and everything came up our craws again, tasting all bitter. I bet we went through a bottle of antacids, but those don't stop your mind from wheeling and turning. Patricia got the pharmacist to give us some sleeping pills, but just a half of one made us each so hung over the next day, we could hardly move around.

After the funeral, it was like most of the pain and grief was over. All the family supported us like mad. No one ever blamed us. Maybe that's why we felt better after the funeral.

Anyway, it's over.

Now, I'm worried about old Hank. I know his heart isn't good, and he still looks older than seventy-one, but hopefully, he'll feel better. I'm not sure it's good for him to go out to Oakwood every day and check both boys' graves. On the other hand, maybe that's how he'll get rid of some of his grief.

Damn that boy. Damn God for taking him and not giving us a chance to get better with each other. Isn't there a word for that? Renewal? No that's not it. Rejuvenation? Lord knows we could use that, but it ain't that. Restore? Well, that's close, but not quite. Hmm. Reconcile. That's it! Why didn't God give us a chance to reconcile with each other? Reconciling. Isn't that what God's supposed to be all about anyway?

Chapter Twenty-Nine

Finding Hank
Tuesday, January 17, 1967

I stopped Manny coming in the front door. He was carrying some groceries. My hands were shaking 'cuz I was worried. "Oh, Manny. Hank went to visit the boys, but hasn't returned, it's been over three hours and it's cold out. I'm worried about him, what with his high blood pressure and all."

"I'll take my car and go check on him. Maybe he stopped on the way back for something. Either way, I'll track him down. Do you want to ride with?"

"No, I have this bad feeling. No, I'll stay here and pray."

I ain't much for praying anymore, specially after Tommy dying less than three months ago, but that seemed a good time to try. That old man, taking off and not coming right back like he usually does, scared me.

Manny said he drove straight to the cemetery. It took him a while to find Hank. It's a big place. The Ford was parked on the edge of one of those little roads, close to Tommy's grave. It was running, the driver's door hung open and Manny said it looked like Hank was sitting in it, looking down at the grave. Manny parked and walked up and said, "Hank, you okay?"

He wasn't. He was dead. Manny said his feet rested on the ground like he was either getting out of or into his car and his head leaned against the door jamb. Both hands lay in his lap, and one of them held an envelope. A letter was on the floor under the steering wheel, like it fell there. Manny touched his face and it was ice cold. He even looked in at the gas gauge and it was down a ways. Later, we figured he'd been sitting there a long time to burn through that much gas. Hank always kept the car at full, topping it off every couple of days, just for something to do, and because he loved his '56 Ford.

Manny drove to the cemetery office and told them what happened, and that he'd be back with me in twenty minutes and asked them to take their time calling anyone. No sense in calling the police or ambulance, they said. The funeral home could come get him.

I knew the instant Manny walked through that door with tears in his eyes. For some reason, I didn't collapse or bust out sobbing. Instead I nodded, got my coat and hat and asked, "Can I still see him?"

Manny said yes, and told me to contact the funeral home so I called the same one that took care of both our boys. I slipped my hand into Manny's. Somehow, I knew I needed him badly right then.

Hank's funeral was huge and we buried him at Oakwood, not far from our boys. He was seventy-one. Everyone figured a heart attack got him. I was convinced about it a day or so after the funeral. After I read that letter Manny picked up off the car floor. He mentioned there was a letter, but I should wait to read it. Later, I told the kids, "He just couldn't take any more about Tommy. His heart could only take so much pain from that kid."

I don't know if I can ever forgive Tommy for what he wrote to his dad. Oh, I know when it's your time, it's your time to go. Still, I can't help but believe that Tommy's letter pushed Hank's time up a ways. I almost want to burn his flag and Purple Heart, but I won't. Sure as hell ain't going to display it though. It can stay in the back of the closet drawer forever. Might even put it down in the old coal bin. Someone can find it after I'm gone.

Chapter Thirty

Tommy's Letter

Mr. Sawicki, Sir.

I am Ralph Morgan. I been Tommy's best friend since he came to the boy's home. I was there a year before him. We went to college together to play football to and joined the Marines together to.

Me and Tommy did everything together. We was like brothers, almost twins. If one of us got in trouble, the other one was rite beside him. We chased girls together, tho Tommy was rougher on them then me.

I know his big brother, Mark, too. Tommy hated him. So did I. So, did most of the boys in the home. We just couldn't say much because the head priest thot he was a good guy and never would listen to us boys when we tried to say Mark was mean and a homo.

Why did you send Tommy away to be with Mark when he was such a bastard? All Tommy wanted was attention from you. I figured that out soon as he came to the home.

Anyway, that's none of my business now, I guess.

In Vietnam, Tommy kept telling me if anything happened to him to get his letter to you out of his duffle and get it to you. So that's what I did.

Tommy saved my life and three other guys. He is a hero, even tho the brass was ready to put him in the brig for forcing himself on them dam gook women all the time. The last one was fourteen, her old lady worked in our little outpost cleaning up and the girl came along one day. The next day our squad was attacked out on maneuvers not far from the post. I wondered if it wasn't some of her family came after us as revenge cuz it seemed they quit when Tommy went down for good. We never could tell the good gooks from the bad.

Tommy called in the copter, then covered us as a couple guys jumped in it. Four of us got hit and Tommy dragged us close so the other guys could haul us in. Then the gooks moved around and opened up on just Tommy. The gunner inside said later they wasn't even firing at the copter much, just Tommy. Still, he earned the Purple Heart, even tho he may have got us into that shit.

I was sent stateside to the hospital, got out last week, came here. Was gonna talk to you in person, but chickened out, afraid I'd shoot my mouth off over crap that don't matter anymore. It won't bring him back and you is old as hell anyway. So I'll slip the letter in the slot instead.
Signed
Ralph Morgan. January 16, 1967

~ * ~

To Hank the Crank,
If your reading this, it means I'm dead. Ain't no big deal, I never believed that heaven and hell shit the priests and nuns said anyhow.
Not sure why I'm writing this other than to get it off my chest, let you know what I really thinked of you and Ma, but mostly you.
Did you know all my neeces and nefews called me OOPS. Always behind your backs and they're folks. Amy, Pat's oldest girl told me why. Said I wasn't wanted like all my big brothers and sisters were. It made sense. Why else would you stop at the bar when you was coming home from work? You told Ma it was for one beer, but I never knowed anybody who took hours to drink one beer. I think you just wanted Joey and Nina to watch me so you didn't have to play with me much.
You know how I liked hockey so much? It was because you did. Those was the only times I felt close to you and you'd come straight home from work to work on the rink. I wished youd of liked baseball to, that would of given us something else to do together. But you only liked the sox cuz you could sleep in your chair while they played on the radio, not go out and play catch with me or make a ball field like I always asked.
Did you know Ma beat my ass with that thick yardstick when I was about five cuz the older kids got us little ones into playing doctor all naked? She even whacked my pecker, wouldn't listen to me tellin her the big kids was in on it to.
I begun to really hate you when you liked Krystina more than me. Cuddlin her, bringing her candy, readin to her. If I asked, you never had time. But for that little bitch youd drop anything to do what she asked. And she didn't have a father, she was a bastard child whose mother was

a hore and you took them in, acted like you bred them with Ma just like everyone else but me.

Howd you never figure out Mark was a homo? And a mean bastard? Seems like you bein his dad youd aknown he was a mean one who fooled most people by always pretendin to help boys and actin like he was doin good things.

HA! Even the fuzz knowed he was queerer then a 3 cent coin. Remember how I ran away when you tried to send me to the home to live with Mark? I spent a week living in the parks and on the streets until the fuzz grabbed me. They took me home, gonna bring me in the house, but you come out and told them to leave me in the car and take me to the boy's home and how Mark was now my legal guardian.

Them cops looked at each other, then asked me who Mark was. I told them he was my big brother who grew up in the house and was now a priest. The cop said, "Sorry, kid. If we'd of knowed this we'd of left you on the streets. We knowed he was a mean faggot when he used to run the streets at night. Now you say he's a fuckin priest?"

When I got to the home, none of the boys liked him. Said he was to strict, used a paddle with holes in it alot and made team practice as bad as basic training. That's probably why we won so many games, we were tough as hell and could outlast any other team. Ralph and me laughed when we got to the Marines and all these other guys was complaining about basic. It was hard, but I will say we was prepared cuz of Mark. I can't say much else good about him.

Ralphy and me got pictures proving Mark was a homo. He exercised and shot hoops late at night twice a week when the gym was locked with a priest from Loyola college. Me and Ralphy snuck into the balcony one night to watch them. After a while they started wrestling, next thing they got naked and started suckin and fuckin. Old Ralphy joined the camera club and started bringing a camera and film. We got in trouble once over some girls at the girls home and Mark was mad and going to throw us out to live on our own. It was right before we was to graduate high school. Ralph just layed them pitchers on the desk. Week or so later we was asked to try out for the Western Illinois college football team. That coach got us accepted, said we needed lots of schooling help which he arranged. We weren't excatly high performin book guys, but we was hell on the field.

Coach switched us to men toutors after the girls kept complainin all we wanted to do was get in their pants. They were all hores anyway. Same as them bobbsy twins that gots us in trouble the next year. They weren't even students, just hung around campus acting like they was and screwin half the team. Me an Ralph gots carried away on some speed and dope after a game and kept them in a motel for two days straight. Even coach wouldn't bail us out, but he did talk with the prosecutor and said if it went to court most of his team would testify about what those girls were. Coach was tired of us, so he said he thought if they'd drop a trial, we'd go in the service.

I was surprised to see you and Ma at the court, looking all hang dog. Nope Hank the Crank, you didn't have to set thru a trial of your OOPS kid. Why the hell did you even bother to come? The judge agreed with the choice, so did the girls.

I didn't intend to rape Krystina that last time I was home. I seen her go back to her and Katie's apartment and thot I'd say hi and something nice. Then she dropped something coming out of the bathroom and was bent over in her short little plaid skirt and I could see all the way to her cute panties. Next, I noticed hangin on the wall that goddamm brown bag tellin they were adopted into the family and I lost it. That fuckin little bitch was adopted and I couldn't even come home without Mark as a body guard to keep you shitheads safe from me. Next thing I knew was that butcher nife Katie was poking behind my ear and her sayin to zip up my pants and leave before I died right then and there.

Last letters are sposed to be for sayin your sorry or all lovey like. Sorry Hank the Crank, this one ain't. I'll always hate you and wish you was dead like I am now. If there is a hell and we meet there, I'll still say all this to your face. Bet on it.

Youre unadopted dead son

Chapter Thirty-One

Mae's Note

Paper clipped to Tommy's letters was the following note.

Manny told me to wait till after Hank's funeral to read Tommy's letter. He said I'd understand why then.

I do.

He also suggested on the day he found Hank, that only Father Joe do the funeral. When I looked at him all funny, he said, "Please, just trust me."

I did and now I'm so glad I did. I couldn't imagine remembering Tommy's funeral with Mark leading part of it and knowing what I know now. Mark acted like he didn't want a part of it, after all it was his father.

It's like the punches keep coming. Tommy dies, there's no chance to make things up. Hank dies. Next, there's Tommy's letter saying Mark's a homo. A mean one. Does that mean he touched young boys or teens? I sure as hell hope not. My god, if that's the case, then we sent one perverted son to live with another. I can't even think about that part. Two perverted sons are too much for my brain and emotions to deal with.

But Mark being a homo, when I think about just that part, doesn't bother me much. My cousin Luke was a homo. He was a sweet one who wouldn't of thought to molest kids.

Seeing as Tommy or that Ralph guy didn't come right out and say Mark molested kids, I'm not going to say it either. I can live with the homo part, though I always thought homos were like Luke, kind of flighty and feminine, not hardcore body builders and wrestlers. I don't like what they do with their sex, guess I never tried to concretely figure out what Luke did with other men, and wished Tommy hadn't spelled it out so clearly about his brother. The mean part about Mark really bothers me. That and wondering if we made things worse, giving Tommy to him. Oh, God help me.

It seems like I never quite knew how to relate to Mark once he decided to be a priest. He was always so distant and tied up inside himself. I didn't know how get in next to him, like I could with most of the other kids. Well, all except Tommy, too. Now, I feel even more distant. Like I can never look at him the same way, seems it's just more distance on top of distance. Whatever that means. Think he feels the same way. His calls are even less now and shorter.

Yesterday, Mark stopped by and I showed him the letters. He shook his head, teared up a bit, blew his nose, laid them down on the kitchen table and said, "Ma, why don't you burn these. They won't help anyone." He turned to leave, but, instead, sat down. "Sit down, Ma." He didn't look me in the eyes. I sat down.

"Ma," he said. "I am a homo. I'm sorry. I've tried not to be. There are other guys like me. I think some of us are just made this way, even if the Bible says otherwise." Looking up, straight into my eyes, he said, "But Ma, I have never touched a boy or teen or any kid at the Boy's Home or anywhere else. I wouldn't do that." He coughed, blew his nose and wiped his eyes. "Yes, I'm tough on the boys. It's a mean world out there and I want to make sure they're prepared. That's all I'll say. I'm not a nicey-nice man who treats kids like they might break. Oh, one other thing, I'm taking accounting classes and someday I want to leave the Church, leave Chicago, not be a priest, and have a real life."

I stuck the letters in the ledger Hank wrote in. Never showed them to the other kids. They wouldn't have helped anyone.

Diary 3

Hank Sawicki

Born September 10, 1895, Chicago
Died January 17, 1967, Chicago
Diary written in Ledger Three. The letters from Eugenia and Arnaud
found in the dining room buffet and arranged in date order.

Chapter Thirty-Two

January 12, 1967

I've been meaning to write a few things down, kinda tell my side of a few things, explain stuff. I'm too damn tired. No way I can write a lot like Mae did, or the old man. The way my ticker feels, I'm not even sure how much longer I'll be around. I don't say that to Mae, she'd be busting my butt to go see the doctor more.

It seems since we buried Tommy, my energy has left me. I don't know if I'll ever get it back.

I can't even think of anything to write about Tommy. I have regrets, but honestly don't know what I could have done differently. They say it's hard to teach an old dog new tricks and that's sure true for me. Nine years between kids. At fifty, I was too old to be a father again, too tired to at least meet the needs of Tommy.

What am I supposed to think about having two sons with Purple Hearts? One a saint.

And the other?

It's hard to say one of your sons tried to rape your granddaughter, the same one he tried to molest when she was little. She wasn't blood, but we still thought of her as ours. Shortly after that, he gets himself killed in Vietnam, saving four other guys' lives. It's beyond what my mind can deal with, especially when you consider everything else that kid did.

I go out to the cemetery and park by John's grave, think and lose a few tears. After that I go by Tommy's grave and wonder what the hell I'm supposed to think or feel. I'm numb.

The other thing that still wears on me is Arnaud. I wanted to write about him, how I never got enough nerve to tell Mae about him, how he spent a night here when Nina was tiny and I never told Mae. How I snuck him off to Eugenia who adopted him and raised him like one of her own and he's done well. I've just been stuffing that piece down deep.

Would Mae have cared? I sure couldn't tell her when she hadn't slept for three months, caring for a cranky, colicky baby and this fourteen-year-old kid shows up on Valentine's Day, saying, "Hello, you are my father. My mother is Simone. I am from France."

One look at his close-set eyes told me he was mine and those fine features told me he was Simone's. I've never forgotten our last night together when she and I knew we would never see each other again, yet somehow ended up in bed with no rubbers. The only time we made love without them. The math fit.

I panicked, not outwardly, just hustled him upstairs to a room, snuck food up to him, managed to spend some time talking. That's another thing I never forgot. His words, "Mother told me before she died to find you. She said you were a good man who would make sure I was taken care of in the United States of America."

I think she knew I may not be able to take him in myself, but would make sure he was looked after. I couldn't believe how much she'd told him about me, all positive, or how mature for fourteen he was. It was amazing, but then, so was Simone.

I did make sure he was taken care of, entirely thanks to Eugenia. I never told anyone else about him. Somehow, the more I stuffed it down, the easier it became not to tell Mae. Would she care today? My guess is she'd want to jump in the Ford and go find him in Denver. She's always said she wants to travel. I'm just too tired to even think of bringing it up now.

After I die, I figure she'll find the tackle box with all the letters from Eugenia about Arnaud. One of these days, I might set it down on the tool bench. Hopefully, she forgives me.

Same with Walentina, my mother's letter. I found it years after the old man died. Apparently, he intended to dig it out from the closet in the little apartment and put it with the damn life story he wrote, but he died first, sitting in Mother's ragged old rocker. I think that was the last thing he meant to do, find her letter and put it with his, but he wore out first. After I saw it, I slipped it back where I found it.

I'm kinda glad he didn't get to it. Back then, it would have been a big deal. She was a wonderful mother and I was shocked to find out she wasn't who we thought she was which meant Eugenia and I, plus our kids, aren't either. But today? In the sixties, as big as our clan is, I doubt it will matter much. I don't feel guilty over keeping it a secret. I think the kids and grandkids will laugh like hell. Mae might not, but she gets over things fast and after a while, she'll laugh too. Unless she reads it and the letters about Arnaud at the same time and realizes how much I have hidden from her. Guess I'll still keep them hidden separately. That way, they'll pop up at different times.

Writing this wasn't too bad. I think I'll try to write a little next week. Maybe once a week.

Chapter Thirty-Three

Mae's letter to Eugenia
Ten years after Hank's death—January, 1977

Dear Eugenia,

I know every time I wrote, which wasn't all that frequent, I avoided talking about the letters you gave me after Hank's death. I did read through what you sent me that Hank sent you and Arnaud, but I couldn't find the ones from you he musta hid. I looked all over hell in this old place. Don't know how many times I checked his shop and got rust and grease all over myself. There were several fishing rods, along with an old tackle box stuck up in the rafters over his work bench. Finally, I realized I'd never took a look inside the tackle box. I mean, why would I? So, yesterday, I did. Snuck down there while Manny was napping. Anyway, everything you sent him was in there and not one piece of tackle. He sure hid it good and after putting everything in order like you said, I read them from start to finish. Several times.

That old coot, what did he think I'd do? Leave him? Him siring a baby with Simone was before I met him and I knowed he wasn't a virgin when we married. Thank God, at least one of us knew how to make it feel good right from the start. I think Simone taught him a lot, 'course I never told Hank I was appreciative of her. Still, he wasn't the first soldier to leave a love child over there.

I bet his love child is the first that made it across the ocean and showed up at age fourteen on their daddy's front porch and said, 'Surprise!'

Yes, I coulda got upset, especially if he told me right at the time that boy was sitting upstairs. It sure sounds like things worked out pretty quickly between Arnaud and you and that's why I can't understand why the hell Hank didn't tell me when you adopted him. Instead, he carried this guilt all his damn life, thirty-three years of it. I feel so sorry for him and he's been gone over ten years.

Now I feel bad for not knowing Arnaud. You know how we are, always welcoming some stray or cast-off into the family. Well, Hank more so than me, but I always came around. It's just so confusing. I think my kids would have been thrilled to know this boy. They sure took to Katie, Krystina and Manny, why wouldn't they have their own half brother? I just don't get it and part of me is angry which means I'm hurt at him holding out on me. The other part says that was just Hank, always trying to be the perfect husband and father.

Anyway, Manny and I will drive out early this summer to see your ranch and then go on to Denver to meet Arnaud. I'm nervous about it, but figure I gotta face my scaredness.

Let me know if any times in June won't work. Could you also check with Arnaud?

My kids tell me I'm slowing down and should take it easy, what with my sugar and blood pressure. Manny takes good care of me and we love traveling around together. The kids don't even worry when I tell them we sometimes sleep in the same motel bed when we can't get two. They say they'd worry if Manny wasn't a homo, ha ha. Actually, they say gay now.

I'm excited for the trip.
Mae

Chapter Thirty-Four

Arrival of Arnaud, 1934

Telegram
February 15, 1934
To: Eugenia Johnson, Bar X Ranch, Hawk Springs, Wyoming
Fr: Hank Sawicki
French sun arrives Friday, 1:00 pm, Cheyenne train. He will explain. Dad fine. Thanks

~ * ~

Telegram
February 19, 1934
To: Hank Sawicki
(Hold for pick up, do not deliver)
Fr: Eugenia Johnson
French SON arrived safely Saturday with telegram. Has your eyes. Will write.

~ * ~

February 28, 1934
My dear brother Hank,

I have waited these eleven days to write. I, actually we—Harry, the five kids and myself, plus Arnaud—needed some time to adjust to the shock of a fourteen-year-old French boy appearing at our door shortly after a blizzard, arriving in the big mail truck whose driver also carried your telegram notifying us of a French Sun arriving Friday. Obviously, the Chicago telegraph operator misunderstood you or mis-keyed the word son.

A blizzard hit the fifteenth and sixteenth, blocking the roads and snowing us in. Our driveway is over a mile long. It also knocked over telegraph and phone lines, plus delayed the train. In fact, Arnaud said they spent eight hours sitting, not able to proceed, just east of Ogallala, Nebraska. He said he entertained several families with younger children by teaching them songs in French.

Anyway, he arrived in Cheyenne about eleven Friday night, along with a Methodist missionary who was coming to visit my good friend and former pastor, Reverend Huggleston. The Reverend came down to pick up the missionary who was waiting with Arnaud. The night watchman at the station didn't know what to do with Arnaud and had no way of knowing who we were nor of notifying us as we have no phone. So, the good reverend brought Arnaud home with him, fed him, allowed him to bathe, and the next morning took him to the post office where the mail truck driver said he was going to Lagrange, not far from us. Arnaud was able to explain a telegram had been sent, so they checked that office, and sure enough, there was the telegram announcing his arrival and unable to be delivered because the lines were down and no one could have delivered it in the blizzard anyway. So, the driver said he would deliver both to us because his truck could get through the remaining snowdrifts. It took them over four hours, what with bad roads and several stops, before arriving at the ranch.

Arnaud later said the driver fed him half his lunch and coffee. During the ride they taught each other dirty words which I quickly explained he couldn't repeat in my house in English or French.

In case you forgot, what with trying to remember the ages of all your kids, Harry's three daughters are now nineteen, eighteen and sixteen and our two little ones are nine and seven. ALL GIRLS. For some reason, Harry-the-wonderful-Swede could only produce girls.

That Saturday, the big girls were out repairing fence and trying to start the Dodge Powerwagon, our truck. One of them was on a horse, checking for early-born calves. She found one and her father was helping her get it to the house because the mother apparently died in the blizzard after birthing it.

Everything converged at once, the truck driver waving a telegram, Arnaud trying to tell us something in French about his father Monsieur Hank Sawicki, Harry and Marti lugging in a baby calf barely able to bawl, the little girls rushing around to gather warm blankets for the calf and fill a calf bottle. Everyone talking like the tower of Babel. It got quiet for a second and Arnaud said in understandable English, "I think I will like it here." He sat down by the little girls and began helping them feed the calf.

"Who are you? Why are you here?" I finally gasped as everyone stared at this kid.

The truck driver handed me the telegram. The driver said, maybe it meant French son instead of French sun. I wanted to wipe the smirk off his face. Plus, I knew by the end of the day, all the other ranchers and town folk in the area would know we had a French son. Smoke signals travel fast out here.

Arnaud smiled and politely said, "My name is Arnaud Sawicki Aubuchon. My mother died two weeks ago. Her name was Simone Aubuchon. She had a love affair in nineteen-nineteen with Monsieur Hank Sawicki who could not take her to United States of America with him. He left without knowing she was pregnant, they didn't wear a rubber the last night. You know a rubber? A condom?"

My big girls snickered, I thought Harry was going to bust out laughing along with the driver, but I shot them both my angry-eye look. Before my little girls could ask anything, I said, "Please continue the story."

I hoped I didn't sound rude, but was still in shock that my brother fathered a son, evidently on his last night in France, which resulted in this son showing up at our ranch fourteen years and nine months later.

"My mother always told me about Monsieur Hank. How kind he was, how loving, how smart, how good at fixing things. How sad he was his mommy died and he had to go back to care for his father and couldn't take her with him."

His English is accented, but surprisingly easy to understand.

"My mother was a nurse. Her first husband was a doctor who was killed by the Germans. After the war, she became an interpreter because her English was so good and it was easier to raise me doing that than being a nurse."

He looked around at us and smiled again, like he belonged here and was perfectly comfortable.

His smile was enough to melt me, it's like yours, Hank, but even more like our mother's. His fine features remind me so much of our mother too.

Next, he asked, "Do you burp a calf?"

Of course, we all laughed at him as we shook our heads, but he wasn't embarrassed.

"So, my mother raised me with good thoughts of my father. She was very brave. Some women who had babies by American soldier men were treated poorly. She was very confident. When I was twelve, she got sick, it was cancer. That is when she started preparing me to come to the United States of America to find my father. 'He will make sure you are taken care of,' she kept saying. 'He is a good man.' So, before she died, I had train tickets to the shipping port, a ship ticket, and a train ticket to Chicago with Father's address for a taxi driver to take me to. She has no family, all killed in the war, so when she died, I called the burial man and left for here. I met my father who was very surprised. He told me he never knew about me, but believed me that I was his. He said he didn't think he could bring me into his family right then. He said it was best if he sent me here. I hope you can care for me, but if not, I hope you and my father can find another family for me. I am disciplined, friendly and will help do anything. Plus, I always dreamed of being a cowboy out west in America. Can I see your horses soon? Do you shoot guns?"

We laughed again. Couldn't help it.

He jumped up and rattled something off. Later, we made him teach us that *Ou sant les toilettes?* means, where is the toilet?

When we realized he meant the toilet, Marti took him outside and showed him the outhouse. "Wow." he said when he returned. "I can see so far out here."

I guess the idea of a freezing, drafty old outhouse didn't faze him.

We let him help with the calf a while, fixed him some lunch, and while he ate, Harry and I went into our bedroom to talk. Harry wanted to know if I had any idea you had a son in France. I said no and was sure you didn't know either, but I told him you were madly in love with Simone.

"What should we do?" he finally asked.

"I think we need to give this a few days. Give us some time to think. I'll telegram Hank he's arrived and we'll write later. We can't just send him on his way to fend for himself."

"Where can he sleep? The bunkhouse?"

"No, I don't want to put him out there. He'd be all alone. He can sleep on the couch by the stove for a few nights and we'll see how this goes."

Hank, you won't believe this, but I jokingly told Harry he'd always wanted a son. Harry just looked at me and nodded. Right then, I kind of knew Harry didn't want to send the kid on. Still, I said, "Let's give it a week. After that we'll have a family meeting to see what everyone thinks, including Arnaud. He may want us to find him another place."

Hank, it didn't take a week. Three days later, I came down early to start breakfast and Arnaud was standing looking out the window. His shoulders were shaking. "I miss my mother." I put my arms around him and rocked him a bit, trying hard not to cry myself. Can you imagine your mother dying, getting on a ship, then two trains and ending up in the middle of nowhere in Wyoming on a ranch that just got electricity? No family, except a father you'd never met and whom you still trusted to see that you would be taken care of. Oh, how my heart melted. Holding him against me, I could tell he definitely takes after his mother who looked tiny in the pictures, he showed us, as well as his grandmother, our mother, Walentina.

Harry saw us and patted his back, then winked at me as he went toward the door.

The little girls came down in their pajamas, dragging blankets. They sat on the floor beside us and wrapped themselves up, looking scared at his sobbing.

"Are you worried?" I asked him.

"Yes, and no," he said. "A little bit worried about having to go someplace else, then not worried about it." He sniffled a bit more. "It's just I've never lived without a mother and calling you Eugenia, or Aunt Eugenia, sounds so odd."

"Mom, I know he's not your real son, he's your nephew, but

couldn't he still call you Mom?" It was Tina, my youngest. She patted at my leg. "After all, the big girls call you Mom and you're not their real mother. Their mama died, too."

Arnaud, teary-eyed, looked at me like he was afraid to ask. I nodded. "Why not? Six kids calling me Mom can't be much different than five."

He hugged me and whispered, "Mom, *merci beaucoup*. I only called my mother, *Mere* or Mother, never *maman*, so I will like calling you Mom."

"Just don't call her Ma," yelled Tina. "She hates to be called that. Don't ya, Ma?"

I shook my fist at the little scalawag and pushed Arnaud away. "Go help Dad with the chores and take your shoes off at the door when you come back in."

The little girls figured out by themselves that their playroom could be his bedroom. It's small, but has a window and enough room for a single bed and a dresser and some hooks. He was thrilled. Said he'd shared a bedroom with his mother all his life. The big girls got a kick out it when he said, "When I started achieving my manhood, my mother put up some bookcases and hung a blanket so I had my privacy. A room all to myself is fantastic."

Hank, that was a week ago. This sounds odd, but everything around here is about as normal as it ever is. By rights, I should shoot you on sight. I've helped you out, did you a huge favor and will keep your secret. However, it almost feels like you did us a favor by sending him here. Of course, I do owe you for taking care of the old man all these years. Somehow, I don't think I want to trade. Ha. How is he doing? Still wearing Mom's nightgowns? Smoking and drinking?

We'll keep you updated on Arnaud. I know you don't have any more money than we do, what with this depression, but we grow our own food and the ranch is paid for, so we're probably better prepared to care for him anyway. Don't worry about his expense. We aren't.

Love Eugenia, your big sister who just did you a huge favor, but

150

who loves you more than ever. Thank you! Say hi to the old man and that we love him.

Oh, Harry said to tell you this kid will make a great cowboy. He's a natural with horses.

Chapter Thirty-Five

Hank's Reply

March 18, 1934

Dear Eugenia and family,

I cannot thank you enough for taking in Arnaud. It was a shock to open the front door and hear him say, "Hello, *Monsieur* Hank Sawicki. I am your French son. Simone Aubuchon is my mother. You did not know about me, *nestpa*?"

I had to have him repeat himself several times. I asked him his date of birth. It was February 14, 1920. I'm trying to do the math in my head when he said, "My mother said I was created your last night because you forgot about rubbers. She was so glad because she had me to remind her of you and your love."

My head was spinning. I knew one of the kids would soon open our living room door to see what was keeping me, or the old man would wander out, asking questions, so I rushed Arnaud up to an empty room, showed him the toilet and said I would be back. Mae was not feeling well, wore out from Nina who is three months old and a colicky baby and doesn't sleep at night. I needed to slice the bread and dish the soup for supper. Most of all, I was afraid to tell Mae. Not then. I was still in shock. It never dawned on me Simone became pregnant our last night. We meant to say goodbye and I would walk away. Things happened and we couldn't part from each other till early morning when my train left.

I was in such distress over leaving her, then coming home to an old man wearing my dead mother's nightgowns. Well, as I said, I never dreamed of a child with Simone. However, the math checks out, more importantly, he has my close-set eyes and the same mole on his left cheek. Plus, he showed me pictures of Simone and I together in France. One I had not seen was of us taken on our last day, both of us with our eyes swollen from crying. There is no doubt he is my son.

I feel ashamed I can't claim him, take him in, raise him. He's about a year and a half older than John, though much smaller. I know he was dying to meet the family. I took supper up to him and we talked a bit.

152

When the house was quiet, I went back up and we talked several hours. He is a bright young man who is very mature for his age. Simone did an excellent job raising him. I had no idea what to do with him until I was telling him about the family and mentioned I had a sister in Wyoming.

His eyes grew big and he jabbered something in French. I had him slow down and speak it in English. "I have always wanted to be a cowboy out west in the United States of America. I read many books on horses and cowboys and cattle. Do they have rattlesnakes there?"

That's when the idea of sending him to you struck. I slept on it and the next morning, I wasn't called into work so I checked the train schedule and telegraphed you, praying you could at least help me until I could figure something else out. I'm glad it seems to be working out. I am forever grateful.

The old man is the same, well, slowing down even more, but still stubborn as hell. He looked like he was writing something down in the ledger, but wouldn't tell me what.

Hank

Also, don't worry about sending letters to me. Mae and I never open each other's mail. Her sister's letters are opened by her. My mail is opened by me. We share the information later. Maybe put anything specific about Arnaud on a separate sheet or in a second envelope.

Chapter Thirty-Six

Eugenia's Update and Request

April 3, 1934

Hank,

Arnaud continues to do well. He has moments of grief over his mother, but we have learned to leave him alone if that's what he wants. Sometimes, he asks me to hug him. Apparently, Simone was a hugger, probably more than me. It's okay, I don't mind. Sometimes, he wants an animal to pet or hold so he will get a kitten from the barn. I've relaxed my standards and let him bring it in, but just for a while. I can't stand cats roaming around inside the house. So far, he obeys such requests, though Harry thinks he's leaving his bedroom window cracked at night and one of the older kittens is sneaking into his room for the night. I'll play dumb as long as the dang thing is gone in the morning and never runs loose in the house.

Listen, brother. I have a big request to make. I want you to send us a letter stating you are his father and you are relinquishing your parental rights to Arnaud so that we may adopt him legally. You need someone to also sign as a witness and a notary public to affirm the letter. Please don't delay.

This is a community of tiny towns and spread out ranches, but everyone knows everything about each other. Arnaud was very open about who his father is and how he came into existence. Several small-minded parents and their kids have called him illegitimate, a bastard child, and on and on. Most of the kids in school are good to him and love him, as do the teachers. We figured it will calm things down if he is legally ours. We've talked with a lawyer and a judge. Both said it will be simple, especially with all the legal papers he brought that his mother arranged with help from the U.S. embassy. Apparently, she did a lot of work there and they were very willing to assist.

His legal name will be Arnaud Sawicki Aubuchon Johnson. The judge said when he's eighteen or older he can always drop the Johnson, which would be fine with us. This is important. Please don't delay. We have assured Arnaud he will always be your son, but this will give him a better sense of belonging around here. He is worried about your reaction, so maybe you could address that in a separate letter to him. He has also stated emphatically he will not Americanize his first name. "People have to learn how to pronounce it," he says. The teachers tell me he is quick to correct kids when they want to call him Arnie. "No, my name is Arnaud and you pronounce it like R-know."

So now the kids sing out when he comes up to them, "I know, it's R-know."

One other thing. Can you buy a soccer ball and ship it to us? We will reimburse you if necessary. These local kids and their parents are quite isolated and the only sports they know of are football, basketball and track, with a little baseball. No one in these parts has seen a soccer ball, let alone do Cheyenne stores sell them. Arnaud is quite adamant that true football is what we call soccer and not played in face masks and shoulder pads. The gym teacher, basketball coach is getting tired of reminding him basketballs aren't soccer balls, likewise the volleyballs. So, I figure if he has a true soccer ball, he can demonstrate his skills and maybe some of these ranch kids can learn something else about the world besides French names for cursing and body parts. He is all boy! Especially compared to raising girls...

By the way, Arnaud has his own horse now. An older horse trained for roping. He is learning to rope and runs around on his feet, practicing on everything, including the girls. The cats, dogs, calves and any tumbleweed drifting by are all lassoed with vigor. Harry plans to start him roping from the saddle shortly. He is still amazed at how quick this kid picks up ranch life. Now, if only I could get him to bathe more often. Boys!

Eugenia, Harry, five girls and now a boy

Chapter Thirty-Seven

Adoption

April 11, 1934
To Whom It May Concern:
This is to confirm that Arnaud Sawicki Auchubon is my biological son born of Simone Auchubon, now deceased. I relinquish my parental rights in order that my sister, Eugenia Sawicki Johnson and her husband, Harry Johnson, both of Hawk Springs, Wyoming may legally adopt him.
Signed: (Henryk Sawicki, Chicago)
(George Rastas, Chicago)
(John McGurty, Notary Public)

~ * ~

April 11, 1934
Dear Arnaud,
I have signed papers that will allow Eugenia and Harry to adopt you. I think this is an excellent move and gives you a solid family. I am sure you will be happy with them and it sounds like you already enjoy being with them.
I am still sad I could not think of a way to bring you into my family. I still haven't told them about you, but will someday when the time is right. Hearing how much you like ranch life, I also think their home on the ranch is better for you than the big, smelly city.
I am proud of the mature way you have handled so many changes in your life. I will always be proud of you. I know your mother in heaven is as well. She was a wonderful woman and did a great job raising you.
Best Wishes,
Hank Sawicki

Chapter Thirty-Eight

Letter from Arnaud to Hank

May 1, 1934

Dear Biological Father Hank Sawicki,

Please do not think me disrespectful when I did not address you as Father or Dad. Harry is now my legal father. I call him Dad. He is an excellent father who teaches me many things and sometimes corrects my exuberant and youthful behaviors. He does so calmly. I call Eugenia Mom. She does not want me to call her Mother because I had a wonderful mother. She is a wonderful mom who enjoys my humor and the way I act with the girls, even when I tease them like a brother. Which I now am.

She does yell at me to change my underwear more frequently and take a bath, but I think all moms do that. My mother, when she was strong enough, told me the same thing.

I am even happier here now that you sent me two soccer balls. Merci beaucoup. I demonstrate how to kick them and handle them with the feet to the other kids. They are impressed, but like their pigskin ball better. I am learning to catch the pigskin ball because the coach thinks I could make a good receiver because I am small and fast. I'm not sure I like the idea of getting tackled by ranch boys much bigger than me. I will try to learn how to throw it as well.

In two weeks, I get to attend my first rodeo. I can't wait. Someday, I hope to participate in them. Dad says I am learning fastly and will be able to compete by the end of the summer.

Well, I must say goodbye and thank you for making sure I am well taken care of. I never dreamed it would be this way or this good.

With appreciation,

Arnaud Sawicki Aubuchon Johnson

~ * ~

June 3, 1934

Envelope from Eugenia with three photographs.

157

Photo 1) The entire Johnson family in front of a horse with corrals and the open prairie in the background. Arnaud is holding the reins. On the back: The Johnsons! May 1934. L to R: Arnaud 14, Harry, Marti 19, Sally 18, Jessica 16, Eugenia. In front: Tina 7 and Jenny 9.

Photo 2) Arnaud on his horse

The French Cowboy!

Photo 3) Arnaud swinging a rope at a cat.

The mighty roper!

Chapter Thirty-Nine

Letters Regarding Josef's Death

Dear Hank,

I am so sorry I cannot attend our father's funeral. As I said in the telegram, Marti's wedding is this Friday and we have already postponed it twice. Once for her fiancé's broken leg in January, the second time for the death of his mother in March. I feel so torn, but hope you will understand my decision to be here for their wedding. Plus, the train schedule was not conducive to making it to Chicago and back in time.

Besides myself, Arnaud seems to feel the saddest. Even though he never met the old man, I think it's because his mother's parents died in the war and now his only blood-related grandfather is dead. I have to say, there are times I see flashes of the old man in him with his extreme self-confidence and feistiness. He is growing into a wonderful young man. We are proud of him. Harry keeps close eyes on him. His exuberance (he loves that word so we all use it now) is challenging at times. Based on rumors, all 13 girls in the high school call him, 'the French Kisser.' He swears it's all in good fun, but he is certainly different than the big girls were at his age. Hopefully, the younger ones take after their big sisters and not their brother.

Please express our sorrow to all of your children and friends. We are with you in spirit and will be forever. The old man was a good father. I wish I could have been there to cry and reminisce with you.

Love,

Eugenia, Harry, Marti and Lawrence, Sally, Jessica, Tina, Jenny and Arnaud

~ * ~

April 29, 1936

Eugenia and family,

Thank you for your nice note. I had no expectations you could attend the funeral, the distance being so great and the time so short. I think the old man would have agreed with your decision. He liked life and always acted like that was more important than death.

A wedding. He would have been thrilled. He's already bugged our John, still in high school, about getting married. John never had the heart to tell him he planned on going into the priesthood. He knew exactly what the old guy would have told him, "That's a hell of a waste of your manhood, keeping your juices all bottled up. Get a woman and make babies."

It is different around here without him. These last years have been hard with him being so grumpy and opinionated. The thing that kept him busy, however, was, about two years ago, he started writing his memories in one of the old ledgers. Mae found him working on it, so she's been translating it into English in between doing all she does with nine kids.

I haven't taken time to look at it, but did glance at the last page. He said something about finding our mother's letter she'd written and kept hidden because of some surprises about her life. Do you know anything surprising about Mother?

Maybe the old man was off his rocker more than we thought.

Congratulations. Hope the wedding was wonderful. Best wishes to the new couple.

Arnaud does sound a little like the old man. Of course, he didn't inherit anything from me!

Hank

Chapter Forty

November 1, 1936

Dear Hank,

Enclosed is a clipping from the weekly paper about Arnaud's sports abilities. He continues to grow into a respectful, outgoing young man. We are proud of him and everyone that meets him loves him. However, I'm not saying he's perfect. In mid-September, we noticed a smell of smoke, cigarettes, coming from him. Both Harry and I do not approve of smoking. I realize we are in the minority on this idea, but have told all our kids it's their decision after they are out on their own and financially independent. The first couple times I mentioned it to him, Arnaud said one of the kids he rode home from practice with smoked. After that Harry caught him smoking behind the outhouse. Harry chewed him out good, even told him he'd call the coach himself if he caught him again. Arnaud said he'd quit. A week later, on a Saturday night, he came home late from some kid's birthday party drunk as a skunk! Stumbled in the door, fell up the stairs, knocked a chair over, laughing and giggling. I thought Harry would skin him alive, but instead he quietly got him to bed, didn't yell or say much, even picked up the chair. Old Harry was laughing when he crawled into bed. "Know what that dumb kid told me?" Of course, I didn't. "Well, he kept telling me over and over how I was the best dad in the whole world, of course he could hardly get one word out after the next. Finally, he said, 'Dad, at least I wasn't smoking. Right, Dad? Right?' Honey, he reeked of smoke. Between his beer breath and smell of cigarettes coming off him, I thought I'd get sick."

We both laughed and Harry said he'd give him a lesson he wouldn't forget. We aren't much for drinking alcohol, but do keep some wine and spirits on hand. The next morning, Harry rousted Arnaud out of bed at five thirty and pushed him out to the bunkhouse. He carried a bottle of cheap red wine and an old cigar given to him from some celebration. Let's just say that Harry got that boy so sick he looked pale for several days. I think we knew he'd learned his lesson when his littlest sister asked him to sneak her some wine. He almost gagged and he looked ready to kill her until he realized she was teasing him. She's such a dickens!

Word got out around school, I told you there are no secrets in Wyoming, and the coach has threatened he'll send any of his team members caught smoking or drinking to Mr. Johnson. That's in addition to whatever their parents might do.

Well, brother, enjoy the clipping about your almost perfect boy. I'm sure you've never faced anything similar with your other sons!

I know nothing of any secret about our mother, other than she was fantastic.

Love,
E.

~ * ~

Goshen Weekly Times

LGHS Frenchman Quarterback Impossible to Translate
By Clyde Smits, Sports Editor
October 7, 1936

He's a junior. He's small. He's from France. He can run and pass and the area teams facing LaGrange High School this fall have no idea what to expect when he takes the snap behind LaGrange's big front line.

Arnaud Sawicki Aubuchon Johnson weighs one hundred twenty-five pounds. His name is almost bigger than he is. He's the starting quarterback this year and the team is five and two. The kid passes quicker than a rattler can strike and he's accurate. No one open to receive? Give him the tiniest hole and he takes off running faster than a jackrabbit.

"I hate to get tackled by all those big guys," Johnson says in his charming accent while laughing. "That's why I run so fast. I want to live a long full life."

Johnson insists on using all four of his names, even on his

162

school papers, because each has a special meaning to him. Sit down with him and he'll tell you his unique story of growing up in France while dreaming of being a cowboy, his mother dying and him coming here at age fourteen to be adopted by Harry and Eugenia Johnson of Hawk Springs.

"Arnaud would rather play soccer," his dad Harry says, "but no one will play it with him. He's making the best of it playing football, which he calls pigskin ball because true football is soccer, as well as pole vaulting and running track. He also is winning rodeo awards in roping and team roping with me."

It's plain to see his dad is very proud of him.

I spoke with several coaches in the conference about playing LaGrange this year. "We still ain't got him figured out. Is he gonna throw? Is he gonna run it? He's like trying to watch one of them hummingbirds that go in all kinds of directions." That was Coach Smith of Burns.

"We're used to grinding it out, going up against some speed, but this kid is like an angry yellowjacket flitting around. You never know where he's going to sting ya at." Coach Barry from over at Sidney was still shaking his head after their twenty-eight to nine loss at LaGrange last Friday night. "We gotta figure out a way to net that little guy next time, or we're not going back to state this year."

When asked about playing basketball, Johnson laughed again. *"Non merci, monsieur. Je risque assez de football."*

I think that means he feels safer playing football than basketball. Must be those oversized pads he can barely keep on him. Think how fast he'd be on a court without equipment.

Chapter Forty-One

Graduation Invitation

March 3, 1938

Dear Biological Father,

I will graduate from high school on June 4, 1938 and request your presence. I would be honored to have you here and Eugenia and Harry would love to see you.

Remember the newspaper story Mom sent you about me raising the champion steer last summer for the county fair? Well, I saved most of the money from selling it which is more than enough to pay your train fare here, maybe for your wife, Mae, too, or one of your children, the half siblings I have yet to meet.

It would be very meaningful to me if you came and paying for your ticket would be my way of saying thank you for finding me such a great family.

After graduation, I will stay on the ranch. Dad bought the neighbor's ranch, it's more of a wheat farm. Dad says they went belly-up from the depression. He was able to negotiate a loan from the bank because he owns his ranch free and clear—I think that means no mortgage. Lawrence, Marti's husband, will farm the new one.

I also have a girlfriend. Her name is Agnes. We are in love, but our parents keep telling us we're too young to marry and they watch us like hawks. I think we're quite mature for our ages, though she doesn't want to be a ranch wife and I don't want to live in town.

Please come to my graduation. That way, you can see your family and meet Agnes. I'd say you could ride a horse too, but Mom tells stories about you staying in Cheyenne with her for two months when you were young and hating horses. Riding around in the Powerwagon is fun, so I could show you all over the ranch and where the rattlesnakes are.

With appreciation,

Arnaud Sawicki Auchubon Johnson

I never found that newspaper. Don't know what happened to it. Mae.

~ * ~

May 15, 1938

Hank,

Arnaud waits for a reply regarding his invitation to graduation. We would love to have you and whomever you can bring. If you haven't told Mae, now may be a good time to do so. How long are you going to put this off?

We're busy, barely keeping our heads above water, but still better off than many others out here. We're grandparents and love it and think we'll be planning another wedding. This one for Sally. Like I did, she's been teaching school in Cheyenne where she caught the eye of the new single Methodist pastor. They think they've been discrete, but half the state knows they're sparking, so I'm sure they'll announce their engagement soon.

Brother, I hope to see you in June.

Your sister who's not happy with you right now.

~ * ~

June 10, 1938

Dammit, Hank!

Couldn't you have at least acknowledged Arnaud's invitation? Sent a 'sorry I can't come' note? Sent a congratulations card with a dollar in it? Anything?

Do you have an explanation? A reason? Or is my straightforward brother losing his integrity?

He is still your son!

E.

Chapter Forty-Two

Arnaud's Wedding

October 1, 1938
Hank,

I'm not sure why I'm writing you, seeing as you haven't sent anything our way in over two years. I know times are rough, but surely you can afford a stamp. Still, I feel responsible to update you about our family and especially about Arnaud.

Marti and Lawrence had a second baby, born too early and it died. It's sad, but they're young and plan on trying again.

Sally and Larry married in the Cheyenne Methodist Church on September 3rd. A big wedding, what with all the parishioners so excited. I now have a son-in-law named Lawrence, thank God he goes by that, another one named Larry, and a husband called Harry. I told the other girls they must marry someone whose name is not close to their father's or in-laws. Tina informed me she is never marrying and plans to be another Amelia Earhart, only she will succeed at flying around the world solo.

Now for the big news. Not necessarily good, but big. On September 17th, Arnaud and Agnes married in Larry and Sally's parsonage in Cheyenne. Only immediate families were present. Neither set of parents are wild about this marriage. We both tried like heck to supervise them and not leave them alone for long. Arnaud bought a Model T at a ranch auction. Harry and Lawrence helped him get it running and the rest is history. Once a young man's got wheels, you can't keep him home on the ranch twenty-four hours a day.

Right after graduation, Agnes' parents bought a grocery store in Torrington and moved there. We both were relieved, but Arnaud got that damn car and thought nothing of driving the forty-five miles up there. Anyway, they're living over the store and expecting a child in April.

Both sets of parents worry about them. They're about as opposite as you can be, and not in a good way. Maybe a baby will focus them. It's just hard to think of Arnaud inside all day, cutting meat and shelving canned goods. Don't know how long he can keep his good attitude up.

Please, Hank. Whatever burr is under your saddle, get it out and communicate with us. We're far apart enough as it is without at least some written communication a few times a year.

We all love you, including Arnaud.

Eugenia

Chapter Forty-Three

Hank Responds

January 1, 1939

Dear Eugenia, Arnaud and family,

I am sorry for my distance and not writing. I have nothing against you, especially Arnaud. It's just that whenever I make up my mind to respond or write, my mind fills with thoughts of what a failure I've been in letting Mae know about Arnaud.

I planned to tell her. Made up my mind I would right after I got Arnaud's invitation. It made so much sense and I was getting excited about telling her. That night when we went to bed, I lost my nerve. I told myself it was okay to wait till the next night, but she didn't feel good and so I put it off another day. After that one of the kids got sick, then another.

Plus, the rooming house has been challenging. There is so little work, guys can barely feed themselves let alone pay weekly or monthly rent. The girl's floor sits empty. Single girls can't get a job when all these men are willing to do about anything. It's almost a daily thing with guys ringing the doorbell to tell us they won't have their full rent. We take what we can. Sometimes, it's a dime a day. Once in a while, they catch up or come close, but easily get behind again. Neither Mae or I have the heart to throw them out on the streets. Especially the ones that been with us a good while or we know are out there hustling every day. There's been a couple we had to throw out, but it was more for their behavior than their lack of money. Still, we felt terrible.

Thankfully, the place is paid for so we have no mortgage, but still heat and lights for 3 floors and all these rooms is a lot. I get a little work at the meat plants maintaining equipment, but it's hit and miss, so I well understand the guys not finding much work. I'm skilled, the meat plants can't do much without keeping their equipment up, but most of the guys with us aren't all that skilled, or their skills aren't needed. It's a damn shame. Roosevelt says things will get better, but I'm not seeing it yet.

Mae works her butt off with all these kids, plus on the days I do work, she hauls the coal up to the stoves, cleans the toilets and mops the hallways. Of course, the big kids help out, but it wears on her, too. Once a week, she's been making a big pot of bean soup, no meat, and sending it upstairs for the guys. That way, she says they have at least one good meal a week. If she has enough flour, she'll make them some fresh bread, too. Of course, she grumps about doing it, but even the kids know she's doing it out of kindness, not because she has to.

Maybe that's why I get in these dark moods where I try to avoid things like telling Mae about Arnaud. I tell myself it's easy to keep busy with nine kids in the middle of the depression and with the rooming house, but telling Mae and writing an occasional letter shouldn't put me into such a slump. But it has. I'm sorry. Truly sorry.

Today is New Year's. I make no resolutions, but did write this. Please take it as my apology and my desire to do better. I do love you.

Have a good new year.

Hank

Chapter Forty-Four

A Baby Boy

Dear Brother,

Apology accepted. These are depressing times and you're certainly around more depressed people than we are. I'm sure Mae will know her stepson someday.

Tuesday, Arnaud and Agnes had a baby boy. Six pounds, four ounces and healthy. They still haven't chosen a name. Arnaud insists at least one of the names be Hank/Henry or Harry. Agnes refuses to consider either of them. Right now, we're calling him Baby J for Johnson. Agnes is a snit. I have grave worries about her ability to mother. Arnaud does everything but nurse the child, and even then, she acts like that's an imposition. Her parents are concerned as well. Agnes calls him up from the store whenever the baby needs changing or is fussy. He's running up and down those stairs constantly. He is very excited over the baby and I think will do whatever it takes to be a good father.

In other news, sadly, Marti keeps losing pregnancies, the doctors are worried if she will be able to carry another one, something about her uterus. She and Lawrence live about four miles away on the farm we acquired. Out here, that is close.

Sally and Larry are doing well and are expecting in September. Larry says thank god for those three months before she got pregnant. He didn't want to hear what his parishioners would have said if the first child came at nine months or slightly before. Ha ha.

With love,
E.

~ * ~

April 20, 1939
Dear Arnaud,

Congratulations to you and Agnes. I wish you the best. If you haven't chosen a name yet, I will not mind if mine is not included. Harry would be a much better choice. He is someone who has parented you way more than I have.

Hank

Chapter Forty-Five

Book of Job

October 12, 1940
Brother Hank,

Sorry I haven't written sooner and this will be short. A short version of the Johnson book of Job. Marti had her womb removed. Doctors said any more pregnancies would kill her. She and Lawrence are disappointed, but bearing up with the realization they will only have one child.

A month ago, Harry's horse fell on him, breaking his left hip, ribs and leg in several places. He just came home, but is immobilized for some time. Arnaud and his baby, James Harry, are moving home with us next week. He has filed for divorce from Agnes for desertion. Personally, I think she should be arrested and jailed.

The good news is that Tina is now twelve, Jenny fourteen and both very helpful. Jessica, twenty-two, is taking a leave from the family she nannies for in Denver to come home until the first of the year. Plus, having Arnaud home will take a lot off me in terms of the ranch as big Harry will take much of my time until he is mobile again. Doctors will make no predictions on his physical abilities once the body cast comes off.

Maybe we should all jump on the train and move into the rooming house with you!

With love,
E.

Chapter Forty-Nine

Birthday Thoughts

February 14, 1941

Dear Hank,

I have much to update you on. Today is my 21st birthday. Instead of celebrating, I am reflecting. Life is strange and mine has been much stranger than many people. It is still good, but hard.

I now have a better understanding of how much love it took for you to acknowledge me as your son and make sure I was well taken care of. Even though you have shown fear in telling Mae and your family of me, I now have a better understanding of such matters. I too am in an awkward situation regarding my son and part of it involves my future.

It took us several weeks to name him James Harry. Agnes was adamant his first name be James. She had no family named James, but it was the name of a former boyfriend. I finally gave in on the name. She quit nursing the baby at six weeks, which meant I had almost full care of him, plus working in the store. Three months later, she told me the baby might be James' and left me to move to Laramie to be with James who is a student at the college. No matter who was the baby's father, she didn't want it, neither did he. I started calling the baby Harry. Her parents helped some with the baby, but not enthusiastically. Three months after that, the store failed and they moved to South Dakota. I moved back home with Mom and Dad where I am very busy. Dad is just starting to move some on his own. His leg is still in a cast, but he can get around with crutches inside.

Even knowing there's a possibility Harry may not be mine, I love him dearly and he also seems to have my looks, especially the narrow set eyes I inherited from you. I don't worry about that part. I also want him raised in a stable home with no shadows hanging over him. That led me to think about my future. I love the ranch, but also realize I have interests beyond strictly ranching. I want to train horses. I would like to run some kind of other business as well. I'm good at buying and selling cattle and horses. I study the markets as closely as possible. I just have this strong sense that I will not stay on the ranch when Dad recovers. Which has made me consider the issues of raising a son by myself when I start out on my own. How fair would that be to him? Especially if he could be raised with a loving mother, too. Also, I'm not jumping into another marriage just to have a mother for him.

In December, I began talking with Marti and Lawrence who can't have more children. They have enthusiastically agreed to adopt him legally with the stipulation his first name be Harry and they choose a different middle name. It is a load off my mind, but a heavy feeling still weighs on me that I failed.

I let my exuberance and lust take over and will always regret it. However, knowing Little Harry will be well taken care of balances out the regret.

The hard part is, as long as I stay around here, I will now be seeing my son raised by a couple in a close family where I will be known as his uncle. Marti and Lawrence have asked the family to not discuss my parenthood of him in public or amongst the family. It is over. He is their son; I am his uncle. They feel any rumors in the community will not last and will be done by the time he starts school. I don't know about that and can only hope they are correct.

My mother raised me with no secrets about you. It is hard to be in a situation where there are family secrets. Of course, she had no other family to keep anything secret from. I understand better the pain you have been going through, keeping me a secret from your family. The advantage for you and me is that we don't get to see each other frequently. However, I will see my son grow up before my eyes, calling me uncle. That's another reason I need to move on with my life elsewhere. I can't do that for some time, not till I know Dad is better or Lawrence could assume the full attention of the ranch if necessary. I am desperately needed here right now and will be for some time.

With ever more respect and understanding for you,
Arnaud

Chapter Forty-Six

Enlisting

February 17, 1942

Dear Eugenia and family,

John enlisted in the army. He leaves next week. He dropped his studies up at Mundelein with the Catholics and refused to consider being an army chaplain. He said, "God calls me to be with the men fighting, I can minister and fight." It's hard to argue with him and God, especially when I enlisted to serve my country.

What about Arnaud? Will he be able to get a farm deferment?

The stockyards are preparing for more work, hopefully that means more cattle from you guys. I'm working more, keeping things repaired, and expect to be full time again soon. That's the only good news. Other than the kids are all healthy and we've managed to keep Mae from getting pregnant again.

Hank

~ * ~

February 23, 1942

Hank,

Arnaud also enlisted, army, sounds like the same week. He leaves tomorrow. He says the army is excited to have him because he speaks French so we expect that is where he will go. He wouldn't consider the idea of a deferment. Like you, we are proud and worried stiff. Harry installed a higher antenna for the radio so we can get the news better. Don't know if that's good or bad, but it sounds like this country is going to gear up fast on two fronts. The government's already asking us to increase beef and wheat production as quickly as possible, so we will be busy.

Arnaud said he'll try to write you and us, but we aren't holding our breath. Just praying he and John both come home safely.

The kids are all well. Harry is almost back to normal, just not roping much or cutting cattle and can't stay in the saddle as long as he used to. Still, it's a blessing to have him back running this place.

Marti asked me last week if all three-year-old boys are as rambunctious and full of the devil as Harry Joseph is. Yup, they chose our dad's name for the middle, coincidentally, it's Lawrence's dad's name too. Ha ha. I told her, "No, not all three-year-olds act like him, just the ones who are part French and Polish." She wasn't sure whether to laugh or cry. He is a dickens! I told her his bad side was from his biological mother and the good side from Arnaud. I don't think she wanted to hear that. Don't worry, that little boy is loved and well cared for. We just aren't used to raising little boys. Maybe you and Mae could come out and give us lessons.

Prayers for our boys,
E.

Chapter Forty-Seven

Telegrams and Condolences

Telegram
November 7, 1944
To: Eugenia Johnson
Fr: Hank Sawicki
John killed 11/3. Await body. Praying for A.

~ * ~

Telegram
November 9, 1944
To: Hank Sawicki
Fr: Eugenia Johnson
Sorrow and Prayers. No word from A.

~ * ~

November 17, 1944
Dear Hank,

We are so sorry for the loss of John and wish we could have been present to share your grief at the funeral. Getting a passenger ticket was nearly impossible, given the war demands on the railroads. Receiving a Purple Heart may not be of solace now, but in time, I trust it will be. John was a priest to the end and that proves it. What a sacrifice he and so many other boys have made and are still making.

Still no word from Arnaud, don't know if he's in France (we suspect he might be working with the underground), or Germany, or anywhere else they're fighting. Will keep you informed.

All our love,

Eugenia, Harry, Marti and Lawrence and kids, Sally and Larry and child, Jessica, Jenny and Tina

~ * ~

December 1, 1944

Dear Sister and family,

We appreciate your kind words and thoughts and I pray Arnaud comes home safely. Not sure if I could take another death in the family.

Thanksgiving was quiet. Mae broke down several times. Thank God there are now several grandchildren whose spirits can't be quiet for long. They helped lift ours at times, but other than the funeral, it was the roughest day of my life. At least three other boys from the parish have died in the last two months, so we, mostly Mae, has someone else to sympathize with. I even had a telephone installed so she can call them. I know life will go on, it always does, but it's hard to get through the next few hours right now.

Our priest is worthless as tits on a boar. Just keeps saying it's all in God's plan. I told him that plan was bullshit and I would return when someone new replaced him. He's old, so hopefully that won't be long and his replacement will be someone young with a brain and the ability to sympathize and who's not half-pickled all the time.

Enough of my sorrow. Secretly, I'm praying for Arnaud, for whatever good it may do.

Love,

Hank

Chapter Forty-Eight

Last Letters Found

September 15, 1945
Greetings, Hank!
Mom and Dad decided not to tell me while I was in combat, that my half brother John died while fighting the Japanese. I am so sorry about this. I have wept many times since coming home.

While I'm thankful I survived, I'm not going to tell all about the war. I think you understand from your personal experience and losing your son. It was hell most of the time. I will say part of my time was as a liaison to the French underground and was very thrilling and dangerous at times. I did fall in love, but soon recognized how insane it was to think she could come home with me. There was no love child.

I came home to the ranch and stayed for one month and moved to Denver. I love the ranch, but they can run it without me now, and I couldn't see my son almost daily and continue to look at him as my nephew. Though I do feel comfortable and at peace about him. Mom says he's got a lot of Sawicki and me in him. He's a wonderful, exuberant (that word has stuck) boy.

I saved my money, and Dad loaned me some, enough to purchase a section of land just north of Denver. I plan to keep eighty acres to develop a horse-training facility and subdivide the rest into five acre home sites. All these GIs will want a place to build a home and these Western guys like their space. Enough to have a nice house, a garden and a horse or two. Dad and I figured once we sell fifty lots, we will buy the next section—that's six hundred and forty acres for you Chicago folk—and subdivide that. We have an option on two more sections after that.

I've also taken a job with a horse and cattle broker. I think I will do well with it and there's a good chance I can take over the business eventually. The owner's son was killed in Italy, so we've bonded quite well.

I wish you the best as you deal with your grief.
Much love,
Arnaud

~ * ~

February 14, 1948
Dear Hank,

I'm sorry you never replied to my letter several years ago. I imagine knowing you had one son die and the other, one you didn't raise, survive would be troubling. Still, I love you and would like to hear from you.

I am doing well, very well. I train several horses at a time for whatever their owner needs. General ranching, cutting, roping, show, barrel racing. There was even an article in the paper that called me the 'Man with a Horse Spirit,' for the way I communicate with horses. I'm also busy brokering cattle, which is up and down with the economy, but people still want beef. My boss joined Dad and me in a partnership subdividing the land so we have expanded that.

I don't have a wife, not sure I want one, but keep getting invited to events and dinners where single women always seem to be introduced to me. Ha ha. Some of them are very, very nice and very, very friendly. Don't worry, I'm not going to get trapped until I want to.

I do hope you find the time to drop me a note.
Arnaud

~ * ~

March 1, 1948
Arnaud,

You wrote me on your birthday. Happy birthday! I'm sorry for my late reply, that's a bad habit or trait I have. You were right, having two sons in the war, one died, the other didn't, was hard for my weak mind to grasp. I am thrilled you lived, but it's hard for me to keep my guilt of keeping you secret from Mae and the kids beat down inside myself. I know the answer is to share the information about you, apologize for keeping it a secret, and move on. Somehow, when I get ready, it seems something blocks me.

Another reason I didn't write was that shortly after John's death, Mae got pregnant. Number ten, a boy, Tommy was born in August 1945. Talk about a surprise! It was nine years after our last one, we thought we were done. It's a cruel surprise, as far as I'm concerned. I was fifty and have no desire to crawl around on the floor with babies and toddlers unless they're my grandchildren, and them, I can send home.

Mae and I are trying, but it is not easy when our son has nephews and nieces older than him. Plus, this kid is demanding. He wants every bit of me and his mother to himself. He's big, rowdy, and the word 'No' simply means to keep doing whatever it is he's supposed to stop. I have no idea how we will get him to adulthood. The only child I've ever seriously thought that about.

I've even talked to our new young priest, Father Joe, about Tommy. At least Father doesn't give me some canned tuna scripture verse or saying like the last jerk. He at least seems to understand and is a good listener. Not even God has an answer to this or my feeling that I never wanted this kid and still don't.

So that's not an excuse or a reason, but may have something to do with my not writing. I'm sorry.

I do love you and am proud of you.

Hank

~ * ~

March 1, 1948

Wow, Hank! A tenth child. Thank you for telling me. I can only imagine how you must feel, especially at your ages.

Best wishes to you. I love hearing from you, but will understand when you don't reply for some time.

I wish I could say something that would help you deal with your guilt over not telling Mae about me. I would love to meet her and my half siblings, but in saying that, I'm probably adding to your guilt, so will shut

181

up.

I am doing well. Life is good. All my enterprises are breaking even, most are making money. I plan to build a nice home on my horse-training land. It will be large for lots of guests and a family, if I ever decide to have one.

Good luck and good thoughts.

Arnaud

Attached note: *I never found any other letters or photos and I looked good. Mae.*

Diary 4

Katie and Krys Koslowski

Katerina (Katie) Born: September 16, 1931
Krystina (Krys) Born: January 9, 1951
A red leather diary discovered between the back of an armoire and the wall in the efficiency apartment.

Chapter Forty-Nine

The Interview Weekend

May 25, 1949

This is Katerina, but I think I'm going to start calling myself Katie. Hello, brand new diary!

That sounds so funny to write, as if a diary is a person. Maybe it is. Having an official diary sure sounds different from writing stuff down in leftover school notebooks.

Mom gave you to me and you are beautiful. Light red leather. Real leather. With a clasp and lock. Big enough to write lots in, pages big enough so I don't have to cramp my hand, but small enough to fit into my purse or shoulder bag.

Mom waited till Dad left the house to give it to me. I don't know if he went off to work or drink. Either way, I knew he'd have yelled at Mom for spending the money, even for a graduation present. Poor Mom. I don't know how she does it. Six kids twenty years apart. I'm the youngest, Joe is the oldest, he's a priest and we're best friends. Mom had a bunch of miscarriages in between us kids. I love her, but she's so worn down and tired out, I try not to bother her with things in my life. Not that I have many things to bother her with. Still, it would be nice to know she could help if I ever needed it.

I am so excited. Friday, I go to Dr. and Mrs. Kaplan's for the weekend, till Monday, Memorial Day. My Home Ec teacher, Mrs. Sorenson, the one who wants me to go to clothing design school downtown in the Loop, told me the Kaplans were looking for a nanny, part-time and sometimes full-time. She gave them my name and had me talk on the phone from school with Miriam, Mrs. Kaplan, who told me not to call her Mrs. because it made her feel old. Mrs. Sorenson told me she and Miriam went to college together and have stayed friends. They're calling it a weekend trial interview, but Mrs. S. said not to worry. She thinks we'll hit it off very well.

I want to save money for design school, but Dad already told me

I have to give most of it to him for my room and board once I graduate in four weeks, even if I'm not living home full time. My older sister Ginny just hands him her pay every week and he gives her a few bucks back for spending. It's not fair, but she's not as strong as I am. I'll find a way to keep most of mine, even if I have to lie, which I don't like doing.

Monday Evening, May 30, 1949

I forgot to take the diary with me to the Kaplans. Maybe that's just as well if I don't write in it every day, but in chunks and this is going to be one whale of a chunk. What a weekend!

I love the Kaplans. Doc, Miriam and little Esther and Ruth. Miriam is slender and tall, maybe five foot, seven inches. Taller than my five one. She has curly brown hair and big brown eyes and a most friendly look. Doc is shorter than her by at least two inches. He's a little pudgy and balding. He has hazel eyes and wears round glasses that make him look very serious, almost like an unfriendly, stern doctor.

The first thing Doc said was, "Call me Doc, that way, you only have to learn three old testament names, Miriam, Esther, and Ruth. Besides, Levi sounds so orthodox New York Jewish. Oh, that's right, we are Jewish and from New York and still sound like it." He patted my shoulder like I was an old friend and said, "Hey, Katerina, think we'll ever sound like native Chicagoans?"

Of course, I giggled, he was so funny, but I did speak back, "Call me Katie, please. It's more Chicagoan and less Polish." They both laughed. His laugh is catching.

Their big home is in South Shore, near the lake and is beautiful. It's all brick with a fireplace, a huge kitchen with a separate dining room for guests. Upstairs are four bedrooms. The girls' bedroom has its own bathroom with another door into my bedroom so I'm close to the girls. Miriam said it's called a Jack and Jill bathroom. Doc and Miriam's bedroom has its own bathroom, too. I'd never seen a house with so many bathrooms. Downstairs is another one off the kitchen, and an enclosed back porch, Miriam called it a sunroom. AND in the backyard surrounded by a wrought iron fence is an in-ground swimming pool. I couldn't believe it! I knew doctors make lots of money, but I never thought about them living like this.

"You can't take the girls in the water unless the lifeguard is present," Doc said. He winked at me. "Of course, our lifeguard is cute too, but you're not to fall in love with him, he's a much, much older man, probably close to thirty."

Miriam told him to be quiet and quit joking around like that. "Eddie maintains the pool, the yard, the cars and sometimes when we're not here, he takes the girls in swimming. He's a certified lifeguard. He works at that YMCA over in Roseland. Most of the time, he lives there, but sometimes he stays over in the apartment above the garage. Sometimes he even babysits for us. The girls love him and so do we."

All at once, Doc and Miriam looked at their watches, then each other. "Wow," said Miriam. "We need to get going."

I must have looked a little shocked, because Doc said, "We decided that if you didn't seem like an ogre, we would leave you with the girls while we go to Friday services at the synagogue. We'll be back in several hours. Here's the synagogue number if the girls escape. Hopefully, they don't tie you up first."

Miriam showed me what was in the oven for dinner. On her way to the door, she said, "Katie, don't be alarmed. We are not usually this casual with new sitters and nannies, but Mrs. S. has told me so much about you and recommended you so highly that after about three minutes, it felt like we've known you a long time."

I told her I felt the same way.

Everything was so organized. In the fridge was a salad and the oven held two dishes. One was macaroni and cheese and the other baked hot dogs. I didn't think Jews mixed some foods, but couldn't remember which ones. I had no trouble helping the girls eat, mostly Ruth, she's almost two. Esther is four and very self-sufficient. If you're not sure, she'll tell you.

Both girls 'helped' me clean up and do dishes, it's obvious they each have little chores they're expected to do. I didn't know much about Jews, but thought they kept pots and dishes separate for some things. Yet, everything seemed to be mixed together in the cupboards. Still, after we dried them, I left the dishes out to ask about when they got home.

After we cleaned up, we read some books and played with their huge doll house, then went upstairs where I had no problems finding their nightclothes. We read some more in their bedroom. They told me I was supposed to wait in my room with the bathroom doors open until they went to sleep. That way, I could hear them. Of course, there were several potty and drink calls, but they did fall asleep without a fuss.

Diary, get this, I have my own radio in the room. A Philco clock radio that sits on the dresser.

When they arrived home, Miriam asked how the girls were, but Doc cut her off. "I'm more worried how you are, Katie. Any bite marks? Broken limbs? Scratches? Bruises? Concussions?"

I couldn't help laughing at him, he is such a nut.

He said he was going to bed because his answering service at the hospital told him a woman was having trouble delivering her baby and he might need to perform a C-section in the middle of the night.

Miriam kissed him good night and said she and I were going downstairs to get better acquainted over a cup of chamomile tea. She noticed the dishes out and looked at me kind of funny. I blushed and said, "I wasn't sure if you kept your dishes separate. I heard Jews do that."

She squeezed my shoulders. "Oh, Katie, orthodox Jews do. They won't mix dairy products and meat at the same meal and insist on separate dishes and pans for each." I looked at her, confused. She laughed, and explained, "We are not orthodox. In fact, we're quite liberal in our beliefs and practices. I understand your confusion over seeing hot dogs and mac and cheese in separate dishes in the oven, yet for the same meal. See, the hot dogs are Kosher and all beef and even though we eat meat and dairy in the same meals, sometimes I forget." She sighed and shook her head. "It's hard to get Kosher out of my system. Especially when I'm cooking. Sometimes I automatically put things in separate containers, but then I still put them in the oven and we eat them together. Isn't that silly?"

I nodded. "We usually cut the dogs up and heat them with the mac and cheese and save a pan."

Miriam slapped her thigh, laughing. "Oh, Katie, that makes so much sense. Get this. I only buy kosher hot dogs, yet, at times, we eat bacon and pork. Just don't tell Doc's parents, they'd *kvetsh*." I shook my head as I didn't understand that word. She said, "Oh, that means they'd whine and complain. Isn't that a great word?" I nodded, it did sound great. "Also, don't tell them, but we even put up a little Christmas tree with presents under it. Santa Claus is a great tradition."

I must have looked concerned, because she said, "Don't worry. Doc's parents only visit once a year when there are no Jewish or Christian holidays in sight. They only stay two nights, thank God, and they want to eat every meal out at kosher restaurants because I won't turn my kitchen kosher for three days. I'll warn you when they're coming, they're a hoot."

We sat in the sun porch and talked and talked. She's a social worker, but only works occasionally, now that she has the two little ones. Once they're in school, she'll work more. I tried not to look surprised that she had a college degree, or still worked after children. She wanted to know how much I would be available after graduation and I told her as much as possible.

"Living away from home won't be a problem?"

I told her no. I wanted to say I'd like to move out for good, but didn't think that was appropriate. I almost fell out of my chair when she asked me, "Katie, does your father expect you to give him part of your earnings?"

Before I could think, I blurted out, "Almost all. That's what he does with my sister. He takes it all, then gives her two or three dollars for spending money." My face turned red and I looked away from her.

She didn't say anything for a minute, then said, "Katie, if you could save money, what would it be for?"

"For clothing design school!"

I went on to tell her how much I liked sewing and designing clothes and making things over. I showed her what I'd done with my dress and told her what Mrs. S. said about my skills.

Finally, she said, "Katie, I know you don't want to lie to your father, but I think we can work out a way to pay you a certain amount that you can tell your father is your pay. We, Doc and I, will put another amount into a piggy bank, kind of a forced savings for you. Does that sound all right?"

I almost cried. It was such a relief to have someone understand my situation without me giving all the sad details about a mean, drunk father who beats his wife so much, she's afraid to think for herself.

Miriam hugged me. "You have a bright future. I think you will do well with us."

I heard a phone ring in the distance. Miriam sighed. "That's Doc's business phone line. I bet it's the hospital calling him to do that C-section. He does all the hardest deliveries, the ones that may not turn out well because they're so complicated, breach births, premature babies, obese women, sick women, sometimes little twelve-year-old girls who don't even know how they got pregnant from their father or uncle." She wiped her eyes a moment. "That's why, most of the time, Doc is so funny and goofy at home. If he loses a baby, mother or both, when he comes home, he goes straight to our bedroom for an hour or so. I know he's crying, but I leave him alone and don't let the girls go see him. Later he comes out like nothing is wrong and acts like a nut." She sniffled and wiped her eyes again. "He's a wonderful man, I'm glad you can get to know him."

Saturday morning, I got the girls dressed and helped with breakfast, then assisted Miriam with folding some laundry while the girls played in the sun room. She showed me her chart of which chores get done on which days, and their social calendar next to it. "Are you flexible in what you do around here?" she asked.

"I can and will do anything. I'm not afraid of work," I replied.

"That's good," she said. "How about travel? Could you travel with the girls and me for several weeks this summer?"

"I'd love to." Anything to keep me away from home sounded good. I'd clean their toilets with a toothbrush if needed. Just not my own.

I noticed Ruthie pooping her pants in a corner, hiding behind their recliner. I carried her into the bathroom and changed her on the changing table, then rinsed her poopy diapers in the toilet. Miriam told me where to put the dirty ones in the basement laundry room. Downstairs, there was a new Bendex Deluxe automatic washing machine and a tumbler dryer. "Miriam," I said after I ran back upstairs, "you have an automatic washer and dryer, you'll need to show me how they work."

I blushed over my getting all excited over modern appliances, but even our school didn't have machines this nice and at home, we had an ancient wringer machine and dried clothes on the line.

Miriam chuckled and said she'd be glad to show me. "Next week, I'll save all the laundry until Saturday so you can help me," she said.

I am so happy I'm coming back.

I was helping Esther write her numbers and letters on her little blackboard when she jumped up and ran to the window with Ruthie. "Eddie's here! Eddie's here. Can we go say hi?"

Before I could answer, she opened the door and they both ran outside onto the patio, squealing for Eddie. He squatted down and hugged them. Seeing me rushing after them, he asked, "Girls, did you have permission to come outside?"

They shook their heads.

"It okay, Eddie. We luv you," Ruthie said.

"You still have to ask for permission from your mother or...?" He looked up at me, a twinkle in his lovely brown eyes.

"I'm Katie, I guess I'll be working here sometimes." I stuck my hand out and waited till he disentangled himself from the girls and shook it. I was glad he's a lot older than me, he's a very attractive man, but definitely doesn't look close to thirty.

He told the girls he had work to do, but in the afternoon, if they took good naps, he would take them swimming. "Do you swim?" he asked.

I shook my head, embarrassed that at seventeen, I'd never been in a pool and only waded in Lake Michigan a couple of times.

"Well, you should learn. That way, you can take the girls in when I'm not around or their parents are busy." He hurried off to the garage.

While the girls napped, Miriam asked, "Do you swim? Did you bring a swimsuit?" I told her I didn't know how and didn't own a suit anyway. Next, she said, "Hmm, you could wear one of mine and go in with the girls." My eyes got big as she said, "Oh, wait. I'm much taller. Mine would hang to your knees." She laughed, then winked at me. "I'll bet you could wear my two-piece."

I turned so red I could feel the heat rising off my cheeks. I gasped, "A two-piece? Me wear a two-piece?"

Miriam laughed so hard at me that I couldn't help but laugh along. "Oh, Katie, I don't think you realize how attractive you are. You would look wonderful in a two-piece or a full-length suit." When she quit laughing, she asked, "Could you sew a suit?"

"I'd need a pattern and the right material."

"Good, I'll have both for you next weekend. In between doing laundry, I'll make sure you have time to sew yourself a suit. Now, two-piece or regular?"

"R—R—Regular."

I turned red all over again. What a little goose I am. Most girls have swimsuits at my age, many can swim, but not little old Katerina Kozlowski. Except now, I'm Katie.

Miriam helped me get the girls into their cute little suits and I took them out back and watched Eddie explain the pool rules to them. He must do it every time, because the girls repeated them back to him. "Hey," he called to me, "I need you to come through the gate and sit in that chair or on the edge of the pool with your feet in. Either way, take off your shoes. It's safer if another person watches." He asked Esther, "What is Katie to do if someone needs help in the water?"

"Get the long hook thing and reach it to them!" she shouted.

I looked around and saw the shepherd's hook and nodded at Eddie. I was impressed with his safety measures.

"One more thing, Esther. Katie can't swim. Should she go into deep water to help someone?"

"No! Only reach something." Esther looked at me with a look of wonderment that I couldn't swim.

I watched Eddie use a combination of play and instruction and safety exercises with the girls. Esther was able to float on her stomach and turn over and float on her back, plus do the beginning of a dog paddle, that's what beginner swimming is called. Eddie would tell Ruthie to take a big breath and then he and she would go under together, facing each other and blowing bubbles. She seemed to like being under the water as much as on top. I wondered if I could learn to swim. I'm quite old to learn, but if I'm going to sew myself a suit, I might as well learn to use it for something other than just sunbathing.

Miriam came out in her two-piece. She looked beautiful. She was followed by Doc who came out in bright yellow swim shorts that came down to his knees. He did some cannonballs and played with the girls. Soon, they were all splashing and shouting. I felt jealous, and determined I will learn to swim. All at once, Esther started splashing me and trying to pull me in. I panicked a little. It's my time of the month and I didn't want to go in. I looked at Miriam and shook my head. My eyes must have told her why, because she grabbed Esther and said, "We're going to wait till next week to get Katie wet. She'll have her new suit then." She winked at me and mouthed, "Monthly?"

I nodded, my face was beet red. I didn't look at anyone for a few minutes while they continued to play.

Later, we grilled all-beef hot dogs and hamburgers, and played croquet. Croquet is something I can play well.

"Mommy," Esther asked while we were eating, "can Katie take us over to Rainbow Beach to play on the swings and in the sand?"

Her mom looked at me and I nodded. "Sure, Mommy and Daddy have a party to go to, but she could take you two over there. We'll give her directions."

While Doc and Miriam dressed for their party, I put the food away, cleaned up and changed the girls. Their parents said good bye to us and left. On our way to get the stroller from the garage, Ruthie said, "Me want Eddie go."

"Well, Eddie is busy. See, he's cleaning the pool."

"No, Eddie go too." This time, she yelled as only a toddler can. I started to remind her Eddie was busy, but she dropped to the driveway and began screeching, "Eddie go. Eddie go. Me want Eddie."

I tried to pick her up, which made her madder. Eddie heard the ruckus and came over. From the look on his face, I could tell he was enjoying watching how I would handle the situation. I dropped down beside her, staying calm. Two-year-old tantrums didn't bother me, but with him watching, I flushed, my stomach tightening a little. Ruthie would have none of my calm reasoning. Looking at him, she yelled, "You always take us, not her."

Next, Esther joined in. "Yeah. Eddie always takes us and HE buys us ice cream from the old man in the hut."

I'm usually not a slow thinker, so I said, "I think we both should take you to the beach." I hoped I didn't embarrass him. I didn't look at him for a moment.

"Yay," the little girls yelled.

Eddie grinned. "Good thinking. Let me get a shirt on and my shoes and lock the garage and pool gate, then we're off. I'll grab the other stroller so you don't have to push both of them together." A few minutes later, as we walked down the driveway, he paused and looked at me. "Do you have the diaper bag?"

"Do I look incompetent?" I shot back. Who'd he think I was, some little nincompoop who didn't know enough to carry supplies for a toddler?

Little Esther chimed in, "Yeah, Eddie. Katie is smart, too. Just like you."

He shook his head and laughed, "Guess I walked into that one."

I love his laugh, it comes so easy, so natural. I'm glad he's a lot older than me, even if he doesn't look it.

Lots of kids and their parents were at the park, on the beach, and playing on the equipment. Several kids knew the girls and Eddie. A couple of parents kept staring at us, especially at Eddie. It dawned on me that they were probably trying to figure out if we were the parents or not because I looked so young. Eddie went off to use the bathroom and, on his way, back, I noticed two men stop him. It looked like they were mad at him. One man spit in the sand as Eddie left them.

I must have looked concerned when he got back to us, because he said, "Some people are so ignorant." He gazed wistfully out at the lake.

I didn't understand what he meant.

As we were loading the girls into their strollers, a young boy and girl ran up, yelling, "Hi, Esther. Hi, Ruth. Hi, Eddie."

Their mother hurried after them. "Hi, girls. Oh, Eddie, how are you? How are your college classes?" she asked, brushing sand off her children's behinds.

"Hi, Mrs. Rockingham. My classes are going well, I'm done for the summer in two weeks."

I realized the man lugging an ice chest about fifteen feet behind her must be Mr. Rockingham, the same man who spit by Eddie. He caught up with his family and glared at Eddie. Turning to his wife, he said, "Why are you speaking to this spic?"

I couldn't believe what I just heard.

Mrs. Rockingham narrowed her eyes and forced a smile on her face. "Honey," she said, "this is Eddie, the young man who taught our children to swim last summer in the Kaplan's pool. I'm hoping he has time to teach Aaron the front crawl this summer."

Eddie quick stuck his hand out, grinned real wide and waited for Mr. Rockingham to take it. "Hi, I'm Eddie. I'll make sure to find time this summer to work with your children on their strokes."

The man sort of choked and limply shook Eddie's hand, then turned, picked up the chest and walked toward the cars.

The girls were quiet on our way back to the house. If we had more than the six blocks, I think they'd have fallen asleep. I kept glancing at Eddie to see any reaction on his face. He caught me looking at him, and shrugged his shoulders.

A few steps further, he said, "Sometimes, things happen when your name is Eduardo Vargas."

His voice was sad. He didn't look at me.

So, Eddie was a Mexican and in college. Was he really close to thirty? I was beginning to wonder. Maybe twenty-four, that's still a lot older than me, but not like thirty. He sure is easy to be with and wonderful with kids. I wonder why he lives at the Y. I wondered about him as I went to sleep and was glad to see him at breakfast Sunday morning.

Chapter Fifty

Miss Pearl

Sunday, Doc got called in to the hospital. He thought he would have several deliveries and would be gone most of the day. Miriam and I packed a picnic lunch and drove the girls to a private club on a small lake near Indiana where Jews were accepted. They weren't welcome at the beautiful South Shore Country Club which was near their house. I'd heard of country clubs, but never knew what they were. This one had a big pool, tennis courts and a golf course, plus a beach with lifeguards. I seemed out of place, especially when some of the girls around my age looked at me as if I didn't belong. I soon realized I wasn't the only nanny. Miriam asked me to watch the girls along with another nanny for a little boy named Samuel while the two moms played tennis.

Shirley, the nanny, was from the North side, near Lincoln and Belmont, and was German. She had Mondays off and visited her family then. We got along easy enough, though she mentioned several times she wanted to nanny for a family who wasn't Jewish. "I still think the Jews killed Jesus," she whispered. "That's why I want to work for a Protestant family, maybe someone on the North shore."

I didn't know how to respond. My dad always said he hated Jews, and also the colored, Chinese, Irish, and the Mexicans. Anyone who wasn't Catholic Polish like him. Although most Polish Catholics I know, and that's a lot, aren't all like my dad.

A heavy-set colored woman walked by, holding the hands of two small boys, about Esther's and Ruth's ages. The boys yanked their hands from the woman and ran up to our beach towel where the girls and Samuel were eating cookies and grapes. "Hi, Essie and Wuthie! May we have some?" one of the boys asked, very politely.

"Of course," yelled Esther, "we got lots." She handed each of the boys a stem of grapes and two cookies. "These are my club friends," she said to me.

By then, the colored woman was by us. She had a wonderful laugh. "What you two little scalawags doin', beggin' off people? You

195

gotcha own green grapes and cookies layin' out on our blanket down the way." She laughed again. Looking at me, she asked, "You da new nanny for da Kaplans?"

Without thinking, I jumped up and stuck my hand out. "Yes, my name is Katie."

She shook it strongly and held on to it. "Well, you gots a wonderful fambly to work for. I hope you know dat. Dey don't come much better den da Kaplans. Old Doc delivered my youngust when I was havin' awful troubles." She let go of my hand, then pulled me into a big hug. "My name's Miss Pearl and I kin tell you'll be real good for Doc and Miss Miriam."

After she walked off with her two charges, I noticed Shirley still sitting on the towel with the kids, her back now turned to me. With a sneer, she hissed, "Why did you touch her? Why did you let her hug you? She's a nigger working for Jews. I'll stay here while you go wash yourself up, get those colored germs off you."

I dropped to our blanket. It all happened so fast, I didn't realize Miss Pearl was the first colored person I'd met up close or shook hands with or got a hug from. Now Shirley was telling me to go wash off the colored germs? Should I? Was I wrong for being so friendly? What else should I have done? Ignored her? Like Shirley did. Tell her to stay away from me?

Tears welled up in my eyes, several slipped out and down my cheek. Little Ruthie noticed and crawled into my arms and hugged me. Esther lifted one of my arms and pulled it around her and snuggled in close. "Why you crying, Katie?" she asked. "Was we bad?"

"Oh, heavens, no, you're both wonderful."

Shirley looked at me, stood and gathered Samuel and their gear into her arms. "That was disgusting." She marched off in a huff.

A few minutes later, Miriam walked up, all sweaty in her white tennis outfit. She was smiling, but her eyes seemed wary. She looked at me a moment, then the girls. Taking a big breath, she said, "Well, I just ran into Shirley. She told me you need to wash yourself up before hugging my kids." I dropped my head as she continued, "Just before her, I saw Miss Pearl who congratulated me on finding you. Told me she has a good feel about you. Did Miss Pearl hug you?"

I nodded slowly, not knowing what to expect. Was I in trouble? Would I need to find another job because I touched a colored person?

"Oh, Katie," Miriam exclaimed, "doesn't she give the best hugs? Every time she hugs me, I feel like I'm being held by my grandmother and there are no problems in this world. She is wonderful."

I shook the tears out of my eyes and stood up, but was still uncertain. "So, I shouldn't wash myself off?"

Miriam gazed into my eyes. "What do you think?"

I stared back, then slowly shook my head. "I think I want another hug from her."

She took my hand and pulled me with her down to the blanket. Ruthie and Esther scrambled quietly into our laps. "Oh, Katie. What kind of a world do we live in?" She looked out at the water before continuing, "Millions of my people were just exterminated in Europe, several of them my distant relatives, and several were Doc's uncles and aunts and cousins. Here you have Shirley, who's only two years older than you, telling you to wash those colored germs off of your skin. Sometimes I just don't understand life."

We were quiet on the ride home. We bathed the girls and put them down for their nap. Miriam poured us iced tea and we sat in the sun room, both of us thinking.

Doc came home. He was quiet, too. Poured himself a glass of red wine and sat down on the glider. He took several big sips, set the glass down, stretched and smacked his fist into the palm of his other hand. Miriam asked if he wanted us to leave or if he wanted to go upstairs to the bedroom.

"No," he snapped. "It's just I saw a young woman today who should deliver in several weeks." He fisted his palm again. He looked like he should be on the front line with the Chicago Bears. He was that tense. His voice changed, became forceful. "This woman just turned twenty, isn't married and her boyfriend deserted her. I understand that happens, but what really ticks me off is that I had a talk with her mother a year ago when she began dating this guy." He picked up his wine and nearly drained it. "Her mother was a bit slow and has nine children. I told her several times about rubbers and diaphragms and she finally agreed to a diaphragm after her husband refused to wear the rubbers I gave her." He sighed and leaned back in the glider. "I told the mother she needed to explain what I told her to her daughter and she said she would. When the daughter came in pregnant, she acted like she knew nothing about contraception." He leaned forward again, sucked the last drops of wine out and said in a mean voice, "There is no excuse for her to be pregnant. I know contraception doesn't always work, but any woman who's in love or think they are should be responsible enough to prevent a pregnancy, or at least try, until they want one." He stomped into the kitchen and refilled his wine. He stood silent a few minutes, took a big breath and slowly let it out. I could see him relaxing as he did so.

He walked back into the sun room, stretched out on the recliner and flashed a nearly normal smile. "Now, I'm almost all right. The first two deliveries went very well. The last one was twins, full term, almost six pounds each. They tried to come out together. By the time we got the first one out, the second managed to wrap the cord around his neck and nearly strangled. He's alive, but I fear brain damage." He stuffed a pillow under his head. "Damn. That little one won't have much chance at a life in a poor colored family." There were tears in his eyes.

I didn't know what to think. I never expected to see Doc that intense or as angry about the girl not using rubbers. I'm sure my face was red. I never saw a doctor about women things before and Mom never talked about rubbers or diaphragms. Never. Her big thing for us girls was to not have sex till we were married then it didn't matter when you got pregnant. Being Catholic, you should have lots of babies. I looked at Miriam. She put her finger to her lips and pointed at Doc, whose eyes were closing. We sat in silence. I tried to sort out what I just heard and saw, but it was hard to make sense of it.

Doc dozed about ten minutes, then sat up. "So, how was your day? Katie, did you have fun at the club? Meet any cute guys who asked you to elope with them?"

I couldn't help giggling as I managed to say, "No, but I did meet Miss Pearl."

"Miss Pearl. Now there is one of the best persons I've ever met.

Did she hug you?" It was like he never changed from his usual self. I wondered if his intensity happened often.

"Yes, I hope I see her again. I want another one."

He laughed, then his face became serious. "Miss Pearl hugs everyone, she has a heart of gold and I don't think many people, white people, can hazard a guess how much she sacrifices to make us feel good."

What did Doc mean? She seemed so happy and loving. What kind of sacrifices did she need to make to be that way?

Doc saw the questions on my face. "Katie, Miss Pearl works twelve to fourteen hours a day, six days a week, making sure the Mayers have a clean house, good meals and loved children."

Miriam walked over and sat next to him. She smiled at him to continue.

"Miss Pearl has five children of her own. She lives in a tiny, two-bedroom apartment with her husband, his parents and her sister and husband who are expecting a child soon."

"You're kidding me. That's twelve people." I couldn't grasp it, and I was used to big families living together, but usually in a house or big apartment.

"I'm not. Their apartment building is crammed with people, plus it's poorly maintained, has only one toilet for the whole floor, maybe twenty-five to thirty-five people. Her husband works, usually day labor in the area, her in-laws work as much as they can and still, they can barely get by financially."

"How do you know all this?" I asked.

"Actually, I don't know much else. Miss Pearl never complains, even when she almost lost her life delivering her last baby. Once, I asked her if moving up from Mississippi was a good move for her family. She teared up and said, 'Mister Doc, this ain't the promised land, but it shore 'nuff beats share cropping.' After that she said something I will never forget. 'Doc, I could tell you all about it, all about my life and what we go through just to survive and what we go through to make sure white people succeed. You being white, well, I don't think you'd understand. You and Miss Miriam are about the warmest, most understanding white people I know, but your white minds can't appreciate what us Negroes go through as hard as you might want to.'" He hugged Miriam. Shaking his head, he said, "She's right. I don't. I can't understand. That's why I charge all my rich white women as much money as I can and cover over at County Hospital on the high risk cases for the poor people. They never see a bill from me." He refilled his wine glass.

No one said a word till the silence was broken by two mad bombers who rushed in from their naps, begging to go swimming with their daddy.

Oh, diary. Just writing this almost makes me cry all over again. I learned and experienced so much in only one weekend. I don't know what else to say or think. I hope it wasn't wrong to write Miss Pearl's words like I heard them. I'd never heard a colored person speak up close and I loved her voice and the way she talked. I hope I meet her again.

Chapter Fifty-One

Memorial Day

Monday, Memorial Day, was quiet. Eddie was back and worked on the lawn. Doc wanted to listen to a White Sox game on the radio, so Miriam and I walked the girls over to Rainbow Beach and played in the sand and on the swings. Ruthie and Esther exclaimed over all the flags flying for the holiday and the decked-out cars returning from parades. They loved seeing the sailboats zip around and the people swimming and picnicking.

I started to wonder how I would get home. Mrs. S. drove me over, and I figured I could take the bus and streetcars home, but would need to ask Miriam for fare money as I had none. I realized that wouldn't be a problem if she paid me. Silly me, I didn't even know how much I would get paid or when.

Every week?

Once a month?

How was she going to work out the piggy bank thing for me?

Back at their house, I made chicken sandwiches that we ate outside at the picnic table. The girls wanted to picnic like all the people at the park were. Doc looked at Eddie and said, "If you don't mind, why don't you and I drive Katie home. The buses are on a slow schedule today. After we leave Katie off, I'll spend a few minutes at the Y, looking over your final science assignment."

"Sounds good to me," Eddie said. "That's my toughest subject."

"Oh," said Doc, "and let's take the Caddy. In fact, put some of those flags on, the top down, and Miriam and the girls can go with. We'll have our own Memorial Day Parade."

Doc made Eddie drive and me sit between the two of them in the front. Miriam and the girls rode in the back seat. I think I blushed most of the way. People would honk and wave at us. I guess 1948 Cadillac convertibles, light green, are not common. There sure aren't in my neighborhood.

It was so much fun! The wind blowing my hair, feeling the sun on my cheeks and neck, Doc laughing and teasing Eddie about being the chauffeur in our one-car parade. Lots of cars were parked on my street, so Eddie parked several houses down, just past our raggedy-looking home, the worst looking place on the block. He let me out, got my little overnight bag from the trunk, and walked me toward my house. Doc, Miriam, and the girls chatted away in the car.

"I'm sorry," I said to Eddie. "My house is, well, my house is quite run down."

"Never apologize for what you can't control," he said. "You should have seen some of the places I lived in before my mother died."

He was going to say more, but as he opened our sagging gate, my father threw open the door, stomped onto the porch and bellowed, "Get that fucking spic out of here." He reached inside the door and grabbed the baseball bat he kept there. Waving it and starting down the steps, he roared again, "I said get the fuck away from my daughter, and don't you ever come near here again."

"Go, Eddie, just go. He's drunk. Run, fast." Out of the corner of my eye, I noticed Doc start running up the sidewalk toward us. I stepped back through the gate, pushed Eddie ahead of me a few steps toward Doc and put my hand up.

Dad stepped down onto the walk and bellowed, "Is that the kike doctor you're working for?"

I gave Eddie another shove and said to them, "Don't bother. There is nothing you can do. You'll only make things worse."

Doc's eyes got big, he nodded. "I get it. A spic and a Jew. Will you be safe?"

"Once you leave, he'll go back inside. I'll wait for a bit. He won't hit me. I'll give him the pay Miriam gave me, and he'll probably head to the bar. Thank you." I motioned for them to hurry. "Now just go."

Reluctantly, they walked to the car and drove slowly off. I tried not to look, but couldn't help turning my head a little. Enough to see Miriam hugging the girls heads tight against her as tears rolled down her cheeks. Eddie and Doc looked like they wanted to jump out of the car and attack my dad.

I waited on the sidewalk till after Dad went inside, about ten minutes. I hoped he would be cooled down or have left for the bar by the time I went in. I refused to cry in front of him or our curious neighbors who were used to his outbursts. At least he had clothes on today. Last week, he yelled at someone walking their dog while he stood outside in his baggy underwear, his fly half-open, groin hair showing.

But Dad was still waiting for me. Waiting for my money. "Why the hell were you walking with that damn spic? Why was he carrying your case?"

Mom stood in the corner, head down, not looking at either one of us. I knew if she said anything, she'd get yelled at, too. Maybe worse.

"You sure you ain't lying to me? Were you really working or just running the streets with that little greasy taco eater?"

I handed him the ten-dollar bill. "If I was running the streets you think I'd be handing you my money?" I stomped my foot and glared at him till he lowered his head, brushed past me and lurched out the door, leaving the screen wide open.

Mom hustled to close it. As she came by, not looking at me, I touched her shoulder to stop her. "Mom, he works there too. He and the Kaplans drove me home. I hope Dad didn't blow this job for me."

She raised her eyes a second, nodded, and looked away. I stomped up the stairs and slammed my door.

I waited till then to cry. Waited till I was in my room, the one I share with Ginny, my sister, who's working today. Waited till I quit shaking.

How can a person go from a home that is loving and kind to this madhouse? How will I survive till I can live on my own? With my head held high, enough money in hand to start design college, enough self-confidence to figure these things out? Will I still have a job Friday? Will Doc and Miriam be so embarrassed and ashamed of the way my father acted that they'll want to find someone else from a normal home? What will I do? At least if I can work for them, I can spend some time away from here after I graduate in two weeks. Should I try to call them from school tomorrow? To apologize, beg for my position?

I must have cried myself to sleep. When I woke up, there was a plate of cold macaroni and cheese waiting on the dresser. Ginny was already in bed. We're usually not close, but tonight, she put her arms around me and hugged me. "Mom told me how Dad acted. That doctor must be rich to have a Cadillac and a spic chauffeur. Did you have a nice time? Were they nice?"

I started to tell her all about it, but decided not to. What happens if I don't have the job? Anything I tell her, she'll tell Mom who will tell Dad who will holler about anyone rich enough to have their own pool and Cadillac should pay me more. "They're okay, decent enough, kind of dull, other than the ride home. Good night."

Chapter Fifty-Two

Mowing Lawn with Eddie
Tuesday, May 31, 1949

Today, I went to school with my stomach all twisted up like clothes coming through the wringer. I even felt hot. How much should I tell Mrs. S.? Well, diary, Mrs. S. saw me in the hall and called me into her classroom.

"Are you all right?" she asked.

I looked at her, my eyes big.

"Did your dad hurt you? Miriam phoned me last night and told me all about dropping you off. They are so worried about you. They almost called the police and asked them to check on you. I told her not to. I would check with you, and if anything were wrong, would call her. She said if necessary, you could stay with them until graduation, and she would drive you back and forth to school."

I had to sit down. I felt light-headed. "You mean they still want me? I thought, after seeing my dad and our house, they might not want anything more to do with me."

"Oh, Katie. If I don't call Miriam back between classes this morning, she's liable to drive over here to check on you herself. They absolutely love you and want you to spend as much time with them as possible. Do you like them?"

All I could do was nod. I couldn't speak because of my runny nose and leaky eyes.

"Miriam said to tell you that she will pick you up directly from school this Friday. Have fun sewing your swimsuit."

I flushed a little, then became confused when she asked, "So, did you like Eddie? Isn't he a cute, nice young man?"

"He's very nice and good with the little girls, but I don't think he's very young. He's nearly thirty. That's not young."

"Really? Almost thirty?" She looked like she was going to laugh.

I nodded. "Yes. That's what Doc said. Before I met him, he said he was cute, but too old for me because he was nearly thirty."

Mrs. S. turned away, as if she had to hurry off. "Hmm, well, okay. You better get to class now." She looked like she was laughing as I left the room.

I wondered what that was all about.

Okay, Diary. I'm not going to write about every day at home. I try to stay as late as possible at school, come home, do some chores, get supper started, go to my room and sew or design clothes. That's my life and will be till I graduate and can spend more time at the Kaplans. I can't wait till Friday!

Monday, June 6, 1949

Back at home till Saturday evening. My last day of school is Friday and graduation is Saturday morning. Two weeks after that, Mariam, the girls and I leave by train for New York City. She's talking of coming back through Washington, DC. I can't believe my life.

This past Friday night, I watched the girls while Doc and Miriam went to synagogue. Saturday morning, we started the laundry and Miriam set up her sewing machine in the sunroom. The bathing suit material and pattern were perfect! She bought two shades of blue, said she knew I could figure out a way to use both shades. I did and the suit is wonderful. While the girls napped, she took me in the pool and soon I was floating on my back and doing the dead-man float on my stomach, even kicking my legs a little.

Eddie was gone all day, taking training on the lakefront beaches where he'll lifeguard weekends this summer. During the week, he'll teach swimming and lifeguard at the Y. Except Wednesdays, when he'll give private lessons in the Kaplans' pool and also clean it and do the lawn. I admire his energy and drive.

I don't know why I keep thinking about him, but I do.

Saturday night, the Kaplans were out and Eddie came back tired and hungry. I fixed him some leftovers. While I put the girls to bed, he checked the pool and yard and washed one of the cars.

He came into the sunroom after I came downstairs. We both sat, quiet. I tried to think about the throw-over I was going to make to cover my new swimsuit, but my mind circled with questions I wanted to know about him. Was he truly almost thirty? How did his mother die? Where was his father? Why did he live at the Y? What was he studying for?

Finally, he stretched like he was tired and asked, "Do you know how to mow lawn?"

I burst out laughing. "Is that what you've been thinking about?"

He blushed, shook his head, but didn't say anything. His face seemed to ask, 'what were you thinking about?'

"Yes, I do know how to mow lawn. Why? Is that now part of my job as well?" I was still laughing.

His eyes crinkled as he said, "Maybe. I've never met a nanny as hardworking and willing to do anything as you. I'm going to be up at Y Camp Cutten near Lake Villa the week after next, training their summer waterfront staff. Last year, Doc hired a local lawn guy while I was gone, and he did a lousy job. I figured if you could at least mow the lawn, I can catch up the rest."

I laughed even harder. "So, do you always ask the young, new nannies to do your work?" It was kind of flirty, but he was so sincere, I couldn't help tease him a bit.

He blushed again, as if he didn't know whether to laugh or be offended. Quickly, I said, "I was just teasing. I'll bet I can do as good a job as you. Just show me what to do."

He grinned, then yawned. "I'm very tired and need to get to bed. Could you meet me at seven in the morning and I'll show you? The girls will still be sleeping and it shouldn't take long."

I agreed and fell asleep, wondering about all the questions I wanted to ask him, but didn't dare to.

The next morning, he showed me the section of the garage with the lawn tools. I was glad to see the hand-pushed reel mowers, two, one set high, one set low, as opposed to those noisy gas engine ones I'd heard. I didn't want to learn to use one of them. I made him show me the clippers, rakes, how to oil and sharpen the mowers, and other yard equipment. He was so proud of the yard he walked me all over it, showing me what he'd planted, when to trim various plants, his hidden hoses for sprinkling, and where he put the clippings to use as mulch later.

When we got back to the garage, I grabbed the high-set mower and started down the drive.

"What are you doing?" he asked.

I almost burst out laughing at the look on his face. "Nobody's going to be up for at least a half-hour. I figure I can get the first pass done on the front section and you can follow in a bit with the low-set mower."

I could tell he usually mowed in the same pattern, so I began mowing a slant pattern, angling across the yard, something I'd learned in the yard and gardening class I took in high school. I lined myself up with a fence post and walked straight lines.

Eddie stared at me, shaking his head, then, after I'd made several swipes, pulled the low-set mower out and began following my pattern. As we passed each other, he said, "Why did you cut in this direction?"

"Because I could tell you've been cutting the other pattern for some time, and it's good for the grass and looks better to vary it."

He shook his head, but kept sneaking looks at me as we mowed. I kept sneaking looks at him, too, but don't think he knew it.

We were almost finished with the front yard when Doc stepped out on the front porch, holding a large cup of coffee.

I startled and stopped mowing. "Are the girls up?" The color rushed from my face. Here I was, mowing lawn with Eddie when I was supposed to be caring for the girls. What happened if they'd been crying and I wasn't there?

Doc tried to frown, but couldn't hold it. He shook his head a few times, like he couldn't quite believe what he was seeing. "Don't worry," he said, "they're still sleeping. I thought I was seeing double and had to check it out."

Now Eddie was blushing. "I—I thought when I was gone. Well, you know I thought the man who covered for me last summer did a horrible job. And, well, I wondered if Katie could do it." He turned his head and looked toward the street. "Now, the thing is, you may want her doing it all the time now instead of me. She's good."

Doc almost choked on his coffee.

I rushed through my last passes and pulled the mower near the

208

garage where I hosed it off, oiled it and hung it on the wall. I kicked my grass-stained Sears sneakers off and rushed into the house. It was still silent.

Doc came in the kitchen, poured a cup of coffee and handed it to me. "You realize you don't have to cover for Eddie when he's gone, don't you?"

"I know, but it's something I can do, even if I don't think I'm as good as he is—he hasn't seen me trim yet. If it will help, I want to do it." I didn't want to say it might also keep me away from home a bit more, but just from the way he nodded, I think Doc understood.

"That's fine," he said. "I think you're a gem, but don't repeat that to anyone. I wouldn't want you getting a swelled head." He winked and poured himself more coffee.

My cheeks turned pink. Thankfully, I heard the girls squeaking and ran upstairs before they woke Miriam.

I totally blushed when, after breakfast, Miriam handed me a pattern and more material for a two-piece. Doc saw it and hooted, which only made me redder. I wanted a pan of ice water to dip my face in. When she saw my embarrassment, she told me I could make it when I stayed there during the week and it would be only us girls at home during the day, no men around.

That evening, Eddie and I rode the buses back to the 111th Street YMCA. My house is six blocks from there. We sat next to each other. I didn't know what to say, what to talk about. I had all these questions, but didn't know where to start, or if I should. He seemed the same way. Several times, we started to say something at the same time, then stopped and smiled at each other. We had no problems talking at the Kaplans', now it was like we were strangers. Finally, I blurted out, "How did your mom die? How old were you?"

His face became long and he glanced out of the window. "Mom died six years ago when I was almost fourteen. My father left when I was nine to find work out West. It was still the depression. We think he died in California." He stared out the bus window again. It was almost dark. "My mother had cancer for years and knew she was dying. She asked the Y director if I could live there. I'd been hanging around the Y since I was little, helping out, taking classes, washing dishes, anything to eat and stay warm. He and a member of the board of directors took guardianship of me and put me in the empty maintenance supervisor's bedroom in the basement." He paused, his eyes moist. "They kept a closer eye on me than four mothers could have. That's why I want to work for the Y, be a director, to pay back what they've done for me."

I nodded. I thought living with a drunken father was rough at times, but I still had a roof over my head and both parents alive. I wanted to say that, but instead, heard myself say, "Then you're not almost thirty years old?"

He looked at me in surprise.

My cheeks burned. I felt so stupid for saying it, not something about how sorry I was about his parents. "Doc said you were. Well, he said you were nearly thirty."

Eddie burst out laughing so hard, the bus driver looked up in his mirror and smiled back at us. "Doc said that? What else did he say?"

I could tell he was teasing me. Afraid to look at him, I was already embarrassed enough, I mumbled, "He said you were cute and nearly thirty and too old for me."

Eddie laughed harder as my face turned even pinker. I couldn't look at him. He gently bumped my leg with his. When I didn't look at him, he elbowed my arm till I turned and looked at him. He smiled. It was an understanding one. "Want to know what he told me about you?"

"I—I think so." I couldn't help but grin back, he was so easy to be with, and I could see he wasn't making fun of me.

"Before you came, Doc told me he heard you were cute, but you were young, only fifteen, and I wasn't to get any ideas."

I gasped and laughed out loud. "I'm not young! I'm going to be eighteen in September."

"I know I act like I'm nearly thirty," Eddie said, a kind smirk on his face, "but I'm going to be twenty next week. Think you're old enough to bake a cake for me?"

"Does that mean you're not old enough to bake your own?" I asked, giggled, felt my cheeks warm.

He nudged me with his elbow again. It sent shivers through me. I glanced at his face. He was blushing, too.

We didn't speak, just rode next to each other. Once in a while, he'd turn his head and smile at me. Other times, I did the same to him. Something happened. I couldn't put it in words, but I think we both knew we would make a good match, a team.

The bus stopped, this time, it waited longer. The driver called out, "Hey, Eddie, you and the lady thinking of getting off or are you going to ride all night?" He laughed as we jumped up, both so lost in our own thoughts, we didn't notice we were at Michigan Avenue and 111th.

"Umm, I guess I could bake a cake for your birthday. What kind do you like?" I asked as we stood on the sidewalk. I didn't want our time together to end. I think he felt the same way.

He walked to the front of the Y and leaned against the building, waited till I followed. "Anything is fine, but I love Dutch Chocolate. Is that something a fifteen-year-old Polish girl can make?"

I punched his arm. "You mean at thirty, you don't know a Mexican recipe for a cake? I'm Polish, what do I know about making Dutch cakes?"

"Well, it's rare for me to eat Mexican food. They don't fix that in the Y cafeteria or at the Kaplans. Any nationality cake is good, as long as it's chocolate."

We both laughed. He asked me about my family. This time, I wasn't embarrassed to tell him about them. My dad being an orphan who never got over his abuse and became abusive himself. My brothers and sisters, especially Joe, my nieces and nephews who rarely visited because of my father. How I couldn't wait to become independent. I told him about wanting to design and sew women's clothing, how Miriam and Doc were going to save my money for me to go to school.

He told me about his parents being Mexicans from Texas and unwanted in most places of Chicago, his dad not able to find stable jobs so he did migrant work across the country while his mother did anything she could to feed him and his older brother, six years older. His brother left when Eddie was ten, and was in and out of jail. How his mother came to the Y to ask for help with her boys and how much the Y staff did for them, finally taking him in. How he learned to work hard and fast as a child and that his mother insisted he stay in school and get good grades and not end up on the streets like his brother.

We were both quiet after that. I glanced at my watch. "I need to get home. I'll see you next weekend." I didn't want to leave him, but standing outside the YMCA all night wasn't an option.

"I'll walk with you as far as I can. You tell me when to turn around. I don't want you getting yelled at by your dad."

So that's what we did. He didn't try to hold my hand, but our elbows and shoulders sometimes bumped, and that sent tingles through me.

Dad was gone when I entered the house. I handed Mom the thirteen dollars Miriam gave me. She gave me three dollars back. "Thanks, it's good you missed Dad," she said. "I'll use this for groceries tomorrow. He took my grocery money when he left."

"Mom, once I start staying most of the time at the Kaplans, I'll probably be paid around fifteen dollars a week, sometimes less if I'm not that busy."

I wasn't sure how much they planned to save for me, but I didn't ask and didn't want to know. I trusted them and thought if I knew, I might let it slip around my sister or mother. I hugged Mom and she limply squeezed me back, which was about all she was capable of doing. I went to bed and tried to think about recipes for Dutch Chocolate Cake, but mostly, I thought of Eddie.

Chapter Fifty-Three

Showing Off My Two-Piece and Learning to Drive

Monday, June 13, 1949

What a hectic weekend. Didn't have school Friday afternoon, so spent it cleaning the house and fixing food. Mom decided last minute to have a family graduation party for me Saturday afternoon. So, I got to fix most of the food for my own party. Which was okay. I looked forward to seeing my older brothers and sisters and my nieces and nephews.

Friday, I was making deviled eggs and Mom baking a cake, we were laughing and having a good time, which doesn't happen often, when Dad walked in, acting grouchy, like he forgot he told Mom it was all right to have the party.

"Hope we can afford this," he grumbled.

Mom handed him four quarters and told him to go to the corner store and get a box of toothpicks. He didn't come back till bedtime. Of course, the corner store is next to his favorite bar and we have several boxes of toothpicks, but the peace and quiet was worth it. What a family.

Saturday morning was graduation, and all five of my siblings were home for the party after it. Dad behaved, for the most part. When he started getting crabby, everyone but Joe left. Dad headed for the bar. Joe helped clean up the kitchen, then waited for me to pack more clothes along with my patterns and some of the material I've accumulated. He drove me to the Kaplans' who insisted he stay for a light dinner and graduation cake Miriam made.

I was exhilarated to get to the Kaplans'. It felt like coming home. Joe must have sensed that as well. He stayed past ten, talking, drinking wine, and playing with the girls. I could tell he was impressed with Eddie and asked him all sorts of questions about his classes and plans. When Eddie said he lived and worked at the Y, Joe laughed and said, "I learned to swim at the Y, but I lied a little to do so."

Of course, we looked confused.

"Well, Dad always said Catholics weren't allowed to go there. I was little, I didn't know if that was just Dad talking or true, but when my Lutheran friends said there were free swimming lessons, I tagged along with them. None of the desk staff said a word about religion when they signed me in. We were lined up, sitting on the edge of the pool, and the instructor was trying to get to know us, asking our names, where we lived, where we went to church. So, when he got to me, I nervously said, I'm Joe Kozlowski and I'm a Lutherist."

We all laughed as Joe went on, "The guy, probably only fourteen or fifteen, looked at me funny, then moved on to the next kid. I got the basics down that week. Several weeks later, my friends were going swimming there, but I told them I couldn't go because of my religion. They told me to sneak in the back door. I did and the same young swim instructor caught me. 'Why are you sneaking in?' he asked. 'Because my religion isn't allowed in here and I wanted to swim.' 'Oh yeah,' he said, 'you're the Lutherist, aren't you?' I nodded, scared he knew I was lying. 'Guess what?' he said. 'We just made a new rule, Lutherists can now come in the front door with everyone else.' My eyes got all big, this was great news! He guided me to the locker room and whispered, 'Guess what else? Catholics can come in the front door now, too.'"

We all laughed hard. Doc said, "I doubt if I'd been allowed in. A Jew in the Young Men's Christian Association? Especially when I was little, I spoke mostly Yiddish and wouldn't have thought to call myself a Lutherist."

The next morning, Miriam said we were having a birthday brunch for Eddie and showed me the ingredients to bake a cake. I made a wonderful three-tier Dutch Chocolate cake. We had fried eggs, bagels and cream cheese with lox, something I'd never seen before, but it was delicious, and fresh-squeezed orange juice.

Doc disappeared for a few minutes and came back, pushing a brand-new Raleigh Three Speed Sports Tourist bicycle for Eddie. It had lights, a back rack, plus a bag with tools in it. "This should help you get around this summer and beats the heck out of that junker you keep wiring back together."

Eddie hugged Doc, Miriam and the girls. He looked like he wanted to hug me, too, but didn't know if he should. I turned and quickly sliced a big piece of cake and handed it to him. I wanted a hug, too, but was afraid to appear interested. Doc and Miriam are such good people.

Next, Doc said to pack our swimsuits, towels and the rest of the cake, said we were all going along to drive Eddie up to Camp Cutten. So, we did. The top down, Doc drove along the lakeshore as far as possible, which took longer, he said, but the weather was too nice to be on Rt. 41. I had no idea what that was like, but along the lake was wonderful. Eddie and I sat in the back with the little girls, and Eddie taught us camp songs till the girls dozed off.

The camp had rough-looking cabins gazing over a small lake with two other camps situated across the water. The dining lodge was nifty with pine paneling, a stone fireplace, and big beams with flags and paddles on them. The staff was moving the boats and canoes from storage onto the racks when we arrived. I never saw so many young men's bare chests and legs in my life!

They all ran up the little hill to us and mobbed Eddie. "Nice wheels," one of them yelled. "No," another said, "nice girl! Eddie, is she yours?"

Eddie and I both turned beet red, only his was a darker color. "Guys," he said. "Guys, calm down. This is the family I work for and live with when I'm not at the Y. This is Doc and Miriam Kaplan, and Ruthie and Esther."

One of the guys interrupted, "They're all good-looking too, Eddie. Who's the last one you haven't introduced us to yet. Is she their daughter? Are you two sparking?"

The idea that we would be sparking struck me like a knife to my guts. How dare he suggest that? Eddie started to stammer, but I cut him off. My eyes flashed as I said quite loudly, "My name is Katie Kozlowski. I am not the daughter, but the nanny." Stomping my foot, I added, "I am not his and we are not sparking."

I glared at the boy with the big mouth. He shook his head as his mouth dropped open. I noticed Doc trying to keep himself from laughing. Failing, he leaned against the car as his belly jiggled and tears came to his eyes. Damn him for laughing at me like that. I shook my fist at him, too, which made him laugh harder. Everyone was laughing at me

A tall redhead said, "Dang, Eddie. I can see why you don't spark with her. She's a little spitfire."

I shook my fist at him, too. I wished I had time to think about why the idea Eddie and I were sparking triggered my little outburst. Maybe it was because I didn't want to admit that idea crossed my mind several times in the last few days. Just then, the camp director walked over from his office. "Hi, Kaplans. Good to see you again. You going to cool off swimming?" He turned to me. "Hi, I'm Jim, the camp director. I see you've met our wonderful crew of overly friendly, loud-mouthed young gentlemen who need to get back to work." He waved his arm at them to shoo them away, then shook my hand.

"I'm Katie," I said. "I definitely need to cool down."

He laughed, and I couldn't help laughing over how crazy I must have looked, yelling and stomping my foot at those guys. I caught Eddie looking at me, and he winked at me. He winked. What a devil. I winked back at him and laughed even more as he blushed. He turned away and followed the guys toward the waterfront.

Jim told us we could change in the bathroom of his office. Miriam and I got the girls changed, then Miriam changed while I waited with Ruthie and Esther who were eager to get in the water. In the bathroom, I reached in my day bag only to pull out my two-piece. My two-piece. Where was my regular suit, the blue-on-blue one I'd made? In my hurry to pack, I'd thrown both of them in the bag, but only intended to wear the regular one. I pulled on the two-piece, and looked in the mirror. It felt so different than my single-piece. The bottom of the legs was about the same as my single, level near the top of my thighs, with the waist part lying just below my belly-button. The top section ended about four inches above that. A wide strap hooked the top-piece in the back and two ties went from the top of my breast areas and tied in a bow behind my neck. Both pieces were lined in an off-white. I thought the blue, pink and yellow colors were striking, but elegant, and I loved the airy feeling, yet I still felt embarrassed to show this much skin. I threw my cover-up on and opened the door. "Miriam, my regular suit is missing! I can't wear this in front of those guys. Eddie hasn't even seen me in it."

Miriam couldn't keep a straight face. "Oh, Katie, I thought you packed both, too." She giggled like a teenager. "Well, I say hold your head high. You look beautiful and there is nothing wrong with that. Besides, Doc and the director are with the guys, and they'll be afraid to shoot off their mouths. I can't imagine Eddie wouldn't see you in it eventually."

She stopped talking as a strange look came over her face, almost a frown. Was it something about Eddie seeing me in my two-piece? She looked like that thought hadn't occurred to her. Shaking her head, as if to clear those thoughts, she pulled me into a hug. "Oh, Katie. I wish I had a movie camera to film you stomping your feet and shaking your fist. Those poor boys didn't know what to think, and some of their mouths fell so far open, I thought a bird was going to fly in."

Going out the screen door, she whispered, "And, Katie, Doc was rushing me around so much, I grabbed the wrong suit, too. I'm in my two-piece."

We both laughed all the way to the lake. Doc shook his head, smiling, as he realized we were both in two-pieces. As I dropped my cover-up, I caught a peek at Eddie's face. His eyes widened in awe. I tossed my head a little and winked at him. His face blanched, and he almost dropped the canoe he was moving. I waded in, splashed some water on my arms and belly like I saw Miriam just do, took a big breath and shoved off into a dead man's float and started kicking, then moving my arms. I was swimming. I nearly panicked when I stopped and tried to put my feet down and realized the water was deeper than I thought. Miriam was right beside me. Taking my arm, she said, "You can touch bottom, don't panic. We don't want twenty guys trying to save us."

I almost swallowed water, trying not to giggle, while I stretched for the bottom. The sand felt soft and yucky, but I was brave. Ha ha. I had to be, I could feel forty eyeballs staring at me. I never thought about guys looking at me and liking what they saw. This was fun. Maybe I am prettier than I thought.

After we changed, we ate some bagel, cream cheese and lox sandwiches at a picnic table by the lake and watched Eddie begin his waterfront safety orientation. There was no laughing or goofing off now. Every eye was on his face as he talked and demonstrated the overall safety procedures they would learn that week.

About five o'clock, Doc pulled Eddie's bike out of the trunk. He rolled it into the dining room as we put our wet suits in a bag and the leftover food back in the basket. As I lifted the basket into the trunk, I noticed my blue suit laying in the middle. Apparently, it fell out of my bag.

Doc laughed when I picked it up and stuffed in in my bag. "Hey," he said, "want to learn to drive? There's some good backroads up here to teach you on."

I gasped, didn't know what to say. My mother didn't drive. I never considered it. Me? Drive?

"It might be helpful at times," Miriam added. "That way, you could run some errands, and I wouldn't have to be the only one to drive when we go on a trip."

Doc opened the driver's door. "Get in. Close your mouth before the flies get in. It's an automatic, and anyone brave enough to wear a two-piece in front of twenty, drooling, bare-chested young men is brave enough to learn to drive."

Miriam pulled out Eddie's chocolate birthday cake and led the girls back toward the waterfront where they would serve it to the staff while Doc gave me my first lesson. Learning to drive was actually quite easy. Well, easy after I moved the seat up and sat on a pillow. I'm pretty short for a car that long and wide.

Doc made me practice starting and stopping and parking around the camp, then directed me out onto the country roads. I loved it. Can you imagine a little Polish girl who'd never been out of the city learning to drive in a Cadillac convertible seventy miles away from home? We even crossed into Wisconsin, though I couldn't tell the difference.

Doc and I came back to pick up Miriam and the girls. I put the car in park and shut the engine off. The guys were headed for the shower house. Eddie broke away and ran over. Leaning over, his arm along the door, he put his face close to mine. "I'll miss you," he whispered.

"Likewise," I whispered back, not daring to look at him, glad Doc was back by the trunk.

Sitting up straighter, I pushed his arm away. "Don't bother me.

Can't you see I'm learning to drive?" I couldn't help laughing at the confused expression on his face, as if he wasn't sure if I was upset. I reached out and patted his elbow and winked at him. He startled in surprise as I said, "Go take a shower, you smell."

He waved goodbye to me, tentatively, as if he wasn't sure who I was anymore. I wasn't sure either. Wearing a two-piece and driving a Cadillac convertible did something to me.

Chapter Fifty-Four

Speed Walking and the Goy in NYC
June-October, 1949

What a summer! It sped by.

After training the camp staff, Eddie rode his bike from Lake Villa all the way to the Kaplans'—over seventy miles in one day. He was tired and sweaty when he arrived that Friday evening.

Saturday morning, I was up early and saw him walking around the yard with this strange expression on his face. Not only had I mowed the grass, but I weeded the flower beds, trimmed some of the shrubs, and Miriam and I bought some additional perennials and planted them in the far back yard, beyond the pool. I took him a cup of coffee.

He stared at me, sort of in wonder and I wasn't sure what else. Butterflies started banging around in my tummy. Butterflies I felt all week when I thought of him, which was a lot. "You," he looked away, then whispered, "you are amazing."

He looked like he wanted to hug me.

Grinning at him, I asked, just as he was taking a sip of the hot coffee, "Worried about your job? What's the matter, didn't think a woman could do all this?"

He choked, sputtered and spit out the coffee. "My God, Katie. No, but you are amazing. Thank you."

Again, Eddie looked like he wanted to hug me, and I wouldn't have minded, but we heard Doc step out onto the patio. He called across the yard, "Well, Eddie, your job is still secure for a while. These women are leaving us for a month, so you got a reprieve." He slapped his belly and chortled, like only Doc can do when he's teasing.

Miriam and I spent the weekend packing for our trip to New York City. I barely saw Eddie until Sunday after dinner when we took the girls for a walk to the beach. On the way back, they both fell asleep in their strollers, which was good. They hadn't napped because of all the excitement of packing for our trip and trying on the new jumpers I'd made them.

Our arms kept brushing against each other as we walked slower and slower. I wasn't sure what to say. How do you describe the butterflies? The good tension? The anticipation something is happening you've never experienced before, but always dreamed about? We stopped under a large tree. Eddie put his arm around my shoulders and squeezed me lightly, tentatively. I snuggled closer. I wanted to throw my arms around him and hang on forever, but thought that might be too forward, plus I was frightened by the warmth and excitement rushing through me.

"Katie," he finally said, "I missed you this week. I—I couldn't believe how much I missed you."

We were both quiet, gradually squeezing closer, each still holding the handles of the strollers with one hand. I slipped my free hand around his waist and our heads leaned into each other's as I whispered, "I know. I missed you as well. I'm going to miss you this next month, too."

He held me tighter. "I don't want to think about it. I'm glad we'll both be busy."

We both turned our heads and stared into each other's eyes. *We're going to kiss,* I thought. Just as we started moving our heads closer, the light at the end of our driveway came on, and started blinking on and off.

Our faces flushed. Was someone watching us? We couldn't see Doc, but maybe we hadn't noticed him peeking through the shrubs.

"Speed walk," I said. "I'll beat you."

We took off walking fast, swinging our hips and legs like you see pictures of speed walkers at the Olympics. Miriam and Doc sat on the front porch, drinking wine and started laughing as we strained to be first without breaking into a run or waking the girls.

"Eddie, I think we need an electrician. That driveway light was just flickering." Doc winked at us.

We both blushed as we handed the sleeping girls over to them.

New York Trip

The train ride to New York was incredible. We had our own sleeper berth. Two beds on each side folded out. We had our own tiny bathroom. The attendant brought us tea and coffee in the morning and juice for the girls. We ate in this beautiful dining car with cloth napkins. The girls loved to run up the long aisles and to spend time in the observation car, high up, looking down on all the scenery.

In New York, we stayed with Miriam's aunt and uncle. All the food was kosher. They called me a goy and laughed when I looked funny at some of the food, or started to mix up the meat and dairy dishes and pans. They treated me more as hired help than Miriam and Doc did. Guess that's what I am, but somehow, I felt like family back in Chicago.

Speaking of family: I decided not to tell my folks many details about our plans. I mentioned to Mom we would be traveling, but I wasn't sure where. In New York, I sent them a postcard. "Traveling is okay. Not sure when we return. Will bring money then." I doubted if they missed me, maybe Mom did, but I knew Dad would worry about the money. What a family.

We went up the Empire State Building, out to the Statue of Liberty, even to Ellis Island where Miriam's aunt talked about arriving here in 1900 to get away from persecution in East Prussia. We visited other relatives, mostly cousins who were almost as cool as Miriam. I rode on subways, buses, in taxis, and on commuter boats and ferries. We ate mostly Jewish dishes, but also lots of Chinese, both new to me. Once, while out walking, Miriam, her cousin, and I ate a pizza pie. We never told the other relatives we chose the one with Italian sausage on it. It was so good.

We took the train to Washington D.C. to see the monuments, galleries, AND toured the WHITE HOUSE! On Capitol Hill, we met a congressman from Chicago, Sidney Yates. He made me laugh when he said, "Don't ask me many questions on finding your way around this city. I'm new, too."

Still, can you imagine me, a poor Chicago Polish girl, meeting one of Chicago's U.S. Representatives? He even sent us a picture of him with us and a note with our names on it on the back.

Next, we took the train to Philadelphia and saw their sights. Miriam had a good friend from college, a goy like me, who we stayed with. Finally, five weeks after leaving, we arrived home to Chicago. Our train was late and Doc had an emergency C section, so Eddie picked us up. The girls were so tired and cranky I barely got a chance to look at him, let alone talk.

Doc arrived home shortly before us. His eyes grew misty as he pulled the girls and Miriam into a big hug. "I never want to be apart this long again. Next summer, I'm going, too."

Two days later, after helping Miriam catch up on the laundry and grocery shopping, Doc drove me home. We chatted away, about the trip, all the first time things for me, he kidded me about the kosher relatives who mostly called me 'the goy' rather than my name. "Prejudice works many ways," he said.

He became serious. I could sense he wanted to say something else. Several blocks before my house, he pulled into a parking spot. "Katie, I'm sensing you and Eddie have developed an interest in each other. Am I correct?"

I nodded as my cheeks fired up.

"On the one hand, we think that's fine. We love both of you. On the other hand, I think we saw you as brother and sister, which was rather naïve on our parts. So, when you come back in a few days, we plan to sit down with you and Eddie to set some rules."

I nodded, whispered I understood.

"Katie, we're not mad at either of you. Heavens knows we think the world of you both. It's just we don't want anything to happen that would ruin or make your lives harder. More importantly for us, our little girls come first, and it's important how you conduct yourselves in front of them." His hand lightly fisted into his other and I remembered his intensity the weekend I started when he spoke about the unwed pregnant girl. He looked at me, not in anger, but with a seriousness I rarely saw. "That's right, Katie. I don't want anything to happen that might make your lives harder." He sighed, put the car in gear and pulled out, dropping me off a block from my home.

I was still thinking of Doc's words when I walked into my house and slipped Mom my money so she could keep some out for groceries and the rent. The rest of the week was hell. I worried about meeting with Eddie and the Kaplans. Mom was glad to have me home, but Dad wasn't working much those days, so he sat around the house, drinking or yelling about the news and the goddamn Communists.

Chapter Fifty-Five

In Love

When I returned to the Kaplans' Friday evening, Eddie and I barely looked at each other. The next day, he guarded an early shift at the beach and came home at three-fifteen. The girls were napping. We met in the sunroom.

Miriam got right to the point. "We both think love is fine, is good, is healthy, but biology also plays a part."

I glanced at Eddie. His face was turning red just like mine. Miriam's words, love and biology, struck me. I figured they probably did him as well.

"We don't want to obstruct a relationship, in fact, we think you two are..." She paused, shook her head, then started over. "It doesn't matter what we think about a relationship between you two, even though we love you both. What matters is that you both live here part or much of the time. It's not like you come to work, then go home to your own lives each night. You don't have a lot of time to date in the normal way, and you have more opportunities to be alone with each other in some ways. That's our worry, that you will want to see more and more of each other and our girls will become secondary, especially for you, Katie."

I gulped. I hadn't thought how liking Eddie might affect my working relationship. I didn't think I'd gone head-over-heels giddy for him, like some of my friends had with their boyfriends, now husbands. Still, I could see Miriam's point. No, I couldn't. How could she think the girls would become secondary to me after all the extra things I did around here? That didn't seem fair. I'm not the type of girl to get pregnant before marriage. Where does she get off talking about biology? For the first time since I met her, Miriam's words aggravated me. I caught Doc looking at me, his eyebrows raised. I nodded at him to say I was listening now.

"The question is," Doc said, "how can you two date? That is, if you want to date each other. Plus, maintain a healthy environment for our family and yourselves." He waited a minute, his face a slight frown. "You know, I frequently deliver the first child of a young married couple who didn't take the technical nine months gestation period. Understand what I mean?"

I nodded tentatively, then harder as I grasped what he was saying. I knew several girls who were pregnant at their weddings, but I sure as heck wasn't like them.

Eddie looked perplexed longer than me. He coughed when he understood and nodded.

Doc went on, still serious. "I'm also starting to deliver a few babies whose mothers are not married. I don't want to see you two in that situation, in either situation, a hurried-up marriage or a child out of wedlock."

A lead weight, like one of the long sinkers fisherman use, slid down my throat and into my stomach. From the way he gulped, I think another one went down Eddie's craw.

"Guys," Miriam said, "after dinner, why don't just the two of you take a walk and talk about our concerns and come up with some ideas or a response to our issues. We want to keep both of you. We want to be involved in your lives until you can be independent and well on your way to success. Which we both know you will achieve."

Neither Eddie nor I said a word the six blocks to the beach. Even so, our elbows kept touching, as if we wanted to hold hands.

We sat side by side on a picnic table overlooking the lake. I couldn't stand the silent tension anymore and blurted out, "Do you like me?"

"Oh, my God, yes. I think of you all the time. Even teaching swimming lessons at the Y, some little blue-eyed kid will look at me and I'll think her eyes look just like yours. At the beach, I don't know how many times I've seen a small woman walking down the beach in a blue suit and I'll startle, wondering what you are doing there without the girls."

"I thought of you all the time we were gone, too. You know all those postcards and photos we sent back?"

He nodded. They were addressed to Doc and him.

"Well, I'm mostly the one who kept doing that. I think that's how Miriam knew I liked you. She never said anything, but smiled this funny way when I suggested to the girls to send a postcard or photo to their dad and you."

"Okay. We've settled that much." Eddie stretched his back, trying not to grin.

"Settled what?"

"That we like each other." He grinned, put his arm around me and pulled me to him. "I figured out the first thing, that we like each other, now you need to solve the rest."

I elbowed him, couldn't help but giggle. "As usual, we women have to solve everything."

"Well, if Eve didn't eat that apple..."

I didn't let him finish. "No fair. You men have been blaming women for everything ever since. No. You and I will figure this out together."

He started to laugh, squeezed me, and whispered in my ear, "So, no barefoot in the winter and pregnant in the summer?"

I jumped off the table and stomped my foot. "No. There's no way in hell I'm going to end up like my mother. If that's what you want, then go find someone dumb and stupid enough to wait on you hand and foot." I started to turn away, but he stepped down from the table and gently took hold of my shoulders and pulled me into a hug.

"I only want you, just as you are, smart and sometimes sassy. I love you."

"I'm sorry, I know you were teasing, but wanted you to know what I'm not." I stepped closer into his arms, my voice breaking as the impact of what he just said sunk in. I whispered back, "I love you, too."

We kissed. A clumsy, nose-in-the-way first kiss. We gently pushed the other back and stood, looking into each other's eyes, his hands on my shoulders, my arms around his, as if knowing we both wanted way more, but now was not the time.

"So," I finally said, "how do we define the problem and how do we solve it?"

He laughed. "First, I don't think it's a problem. If it is, I want more of it, but only with you."

We were both quiet, listening to each other breathe, the warmth of his hands still touching my shoulders, mine resting on his arms, our toes bumping as we lightly rocked on our feet.

Eddie broke the silence. "I think we need a short-term plan to finish the summer." He coughed, stepped back, dropped his hands from my shoulders. "I think I need to tell you something else that affects us, especially now we know we love each other."

My face betrayed my surprise and confusion.

Taking both my hands in his, he moved closer. "I have been thinking of going into the Army." He waited till I looked him in the eyes again, mine wide. "You see, I'm only taking classes part time. Even with the Kaplans' job and Y jobs, I still can't afford to go full time. If I join the service, I will be eligible for the GI Bill when I get out in two years. When I'm out of the army, I can go full time and work less till I finish. In the long run, I think it might be faster."

I didn't know how to respond. We'd just said we loved each other and wanted to date. Now he was thinking of leaving for two years. Tears started down my cheeks. He pulled me close, wrapped both his arms around me.

"I know. I know. It seems like we just found each other and I'm talking of leaving. It is something I've been considering for some time, even before I met you."

"I understand." I sniffled and nodded against his chest. Yet, I wasn't sure I did. It didn't seem fair. I felt and heard his sniffles.

"You know, we are young and two years will go quickly. Besides, I get leave time, so it wouldn't be like not seeing each other for two years straight."

"When? If you go, when would you leave?"

"I met with the recruiter in May, and he said to think about it over the summer and let him know in August. Soon. September or October would be a good time to enter, if I choose to."

"Oh, Eddie. I don't know what to say." My tears were wetting his t-shirt. "The good thing is, maybe by the time you're done, I'll have finished design school, and, and, we..."

"Yes, maybe we could..." He hugged me tighter.

I pushed back from him. "We still need a short-term plan. Could we plan on one night a week as our date night? That way, everyone will know. Maybe we can tie it in with my day off so sometimes we can spend more time together?"

"Good idea. How about Wednesday nights when I'm done with the private lessons and the yard?"

"That means our date will either be an hour bus ride to my parents' home, or..." I giggled, relieved some things were resolved.

He interrupted, "Or you on the back of my bike."

"Exactly." I waited, feeling his hands take mine with their warmth, security, our hope for our future. "I think that's a good idea. Maybe take in a movie on our way to my parents' home. I can take a bus back to Kaplans' Thursday by myself."

"Hey, I could even ride the bus back with you." He said it like he just discovered gold. "Plus, I'll be back at Kaplans' to spend Friday nights, now that I'm working Rainbow Beach Saturdays and Sundays. I'll just plan on living at the Y more often. This should relieve some of the Kaplan's fears and give us less time to be distracted." He grinned as he said distracted.

"So, that means you'll stay at Kaplan's Friday and Saturdays and maybe Tuesdays?"

"We'll see what they say. They might think that's too much. If they do, that's fine, I can cut back to nothing if needed. As long as we have Wednesday evenings together." He sighed.

So, did I. It was logical, but my heart realized logic doesn't always make sense when you love someone.

"What about the army?" I looked away, not at him, couldn't.

He sighed again. "I think I need to tell Doc and Miriam I've been considering it, so they're not shocked when I do make the decision."

"So, you've made a decision?"

"Oh, Katie. I don't want to say yes right now, but my gut is telling me it is still the wisest move for me and both of us. Not the easiest right now, but the wisest."

"I understand, but somehow, wise doesn't feel good right now. Does it?"

He took my hand, squeezed it, and we started walking toward the house.

We sat down with Doc and Miriam. They were pleased with our openness and respected our efforts to not be distractions. They set down some parental rules. Eddie could sleep in the garage apartment Tuesday, Friday and Saturdays. We couldn't be in each other's bedrooms. We could watch TV together after the girls were in bed, or go for a walk if they were home, as long as he was out of the house by ten thirty p.m. No holding hands, hugging or kissing in front of the girls.

Doc asked one question of Eddie after being told of his desire to enlist. "What about Korea?"

It was a good question, one I hadn't thought of. I did glance at the papers and usually listened to the nightly news on the radio.

"Well, the recruiter thinks the chances of the U.S. getting involved with men on the ground is not strong. He thinks we will give South Korea money, maybe some more weapons and equipment, but not ship a lot of men over there."

We were all quiet. Not another war. Please, Lord, not another war.

I tried to smile, act strong, as Eddie continued. "He did say if we needed to send in troops, it would be quick. There's no way the Commies can stand up to us."

Doc shook his head. His face said he had his doubts about that statement, but he didn't say anything. He started to get up, then sat back down. "You know," he said, waiting as if thinking what to say next. "You know, when you're in love, your feelings start to change. They get hot. Your physical feelings." He looked at both of us and must have realized we didn't quite get what he meant. "Your desires! Your bodies want to have sex and that's natural and everyone's telling you to wait till you're married."

Miriam put her fingers to her lips to shush him.

"I'm sorry. I didn't mean to be so loud, but the fact is, it's true." His voice level didn't raise, but he spoke intensely in the tone I recalled him using about the unwed pregnant girl. "I'm not giving permission or telling you it's okay, but if things look like they might get out of control, there are methods to avoid pregnancy. Talk to me early. Don't be embarrassed to ask me about using protection, because the last thing I want is a pregnant nanny."

He stood, took Miriam's hand and led her out of the room. She looked as shocked as we probably did.

Eddie and I didn't speak, stared at each other, hugged lightly and headed toward our separate areas. I was stunned. How dare Doc talk like that? Did Eddie and I look like the type of couple who couldn't control ourselves? And that tone of voice? I hoped I never heard it again.

So that's how my dating life with Eddie started. On Wednesdays, I was through with my responsibilities when I put the girls down for their naps. If Eddie wasn't finished with the lawn, I'd jump in and help him. I needed to be back to put the girls to bed Thursday evenings.

Wednesday nights, I slept at home, helped Mom around the house Thursday mornings, did some sewing and left at three to walk to the Y and meet Eddie.

Doc laughed when he came home one Wednesday afternoon and saw us buzzing around the lawn together. "Love makes people do strange things," he teased.

For six glorious weeks, it worked. Sometimes we dated on his bicycle. We'd ride off, singing, usually *On a Bicycle Built for Two*, to the beach or a movie, occasionally all the way to the Y, an hour ride, about the same as the bus, where we'd eat a free dinner. Sophie, the cook, a big colored woman who acted like Eddie's mother, always fixed something special for us and got mad if any of the men who lived there teased Eddie about having a girlfriend. "You just be jealous," she'd holler and shake her big wooden spoon at them after she gave us each a hug. "I knowed Eddie since he was little. Only once did I threaten him wit dis here spoon."

The next afternoon, Eddie would bike me, or ride the bus with me, back to the Kaplans' and ride back to the Y. Doc was right. Love makes people do strange things, but it seemed quite normal to us.

Chapter Fifty-Six

Christmas Surprise

Today, September 18th, 1949, two days after my eighteenth birthday, with tears streaming down my cheeks, I kissed Eddie goodbye. Watched him board a train for Fort Benning, Georgia, to begin his basic training. I didn't know when I'd hear from him. He said basic was busy and he may not have much time, if any. After that, he would go on for other training. He was hoping for some type of clerk training. He could type and was good at organizing things. He thought we would be able to see each other at the end of the year.

I can't remember seeing anything or anybody as I took the South Shore Line back to the Kaplans' where Miriam and I set up a new routine. I offered to take over the yard work, so we factored that in. Before he left, Eddie shut the pool down for the off-season, even though it was still warm enough to use and the girls were upset, but it made the most sense.

We planned a little school time each morning, set up little desks, worked with Esther on starting the McGuffey Readers and her numbers. While they napped, I sewed. The word spread amongst Miriam's friends that I was a good seamstress, and they started dropping off things for me to fix or redo. Sometimes, I made their children new jumpers or play clothes. Miriam put most of that money in the piggy bank.

After his basic training, Eddie and I wrote frequently, with me usually receiving a letter every five or six days. Once a month, he called me on the phone at the Kaplans'. I think the phone calls made things worse. I could hear his voice. In his letters, I could imagine him and dream about him, but when I heard his voice, my whole body wanted to be wrapped in his arms. Suddenly, the call would be over. Clink, clink, the coins would drop in the pay phone, and Eddie would whisper, his voice hoarse, "I'm sorry, I can't afford to spend more. I love you."

Those nights, well, sometimes other ones after a letter as well, were the ones I rubbed myself till I was moaning and gasping, dreaming of being in his arms, just the two of us in a bed. I thought it was probably wrong, a sin, but sometimes I think our body knows what it wants and needs, so I didn't worry much about it. I knew boys did similar things.

Before the Kaplans', I babysat frequently for a family who had a thirteen-year-old boy, almost fourteen. One night, I heard sounds from his room, so I quietly went upstairs. His bedroom door was open, and from the hall light, I could see him lying on top of his bed with his pajamas pushed down to his knees, and he was pumping on himself. It took me a moment to figure out what he was doing. I'd heard girlfriends tell about touching their boyfriends so they didn't go all the way, but was never quite sure what they meant. Next, the boy moaned louder as creamy stuff shot out of his stiff penis.

I have to admit I was fascinated and felt warm between my legs. Suddenly, he opened his eyes and saw me watching him. "Take a picture, they last longer," he snickered. "Come back in ten minutes, I can probably jerk off again and you can watch me some more."

I turned forty shades of red as I rushed away. So that's what my friends who were engaged or dating meant when they said they jerked off their boyfriends. Several weeks later, at the same home, I put the younger kids to bed. As I passed the boy's bedroom, I noticed him standing just inside the door, stark naked, his hard penis sticking straight out. I was surprised at how large it truly was, but determined this nonsense must end. As he grinned at me with a proud, show-off grin, I said, "If you ever do this again, I will hand your father a belt when he gets home and tell him exactly why he needs to use it on you. Now close the door."

Oh, the fright that came into that boy's eyes as he quickly closed the door. I giggled silently all the way downstairs. Thirty minutes later, he tiptoed down, in his pajamas, his face still white. "I—I'm sorry," he whispered. "Are you still going to tell my dad?"

I stared at him as if I was trying to make up my mind.

"It—it will never happen again. It's just, well, I don't know why I got so carried away and wanted to show off."

"Carried away is right. Your body is changing and it's exciting for you, but it may not be for others around you. Have you shown yourself to your little sisters?"

"No, no, of course not. I swear I'll never do it again in front of you. Please don't tell my dad or my mom."

I stared at him till tears started in his eyes again before saying, "You keep that thing to yourself, and I won't tell anyone. If I ever hear a whisper of you misbehaving, I swear I'll tell your dad and mom."

He nodded and scurried off to bed.

I couldn't believe how well I handled that. Still can't. I was just turning sixteen. I sat down and smiled. I figured I'd just learned a lot about boys and how sex might work. I never could figure out how those little floppy things I saw when changing boy-baby diapers or giving toddlers baths matched up with my plumbing. Now I knew. That was the first time I started thinking of me someday having sex with a husband.

Now, here I was seven hundred miles away from Eddie and thinking of sex with him. I bet he was thinking of the same thing with me. I moaned at the thought of him naked with me.

Christmas Day

Friday, December 22nd, Miriam ran out to do some errands. Doc was home early and having coffee at the kitchen table while the girls were napping. He asked me to dust and clean their bedroom. It was an odd request as Miriam and I usually cleaned the bedrooms on Wednesdays and the way he asked me seemed strange. I said sure and hurried upstairs. I quickly dusted everything and ran the sweeper, still thinking it was strange as it was obvious Miriam did the same thing Wednesday. I did notice the drawer of their nightstand was open and contained packages of rubbers and a strange-looking thing I realized was a diaphragm. So that's how they've only had two kids, I thought. I closed the drawer, wondering why they left it open.

The next day, Saturday, I went home and spent an enjoyable Christmas Eve going to Mass, opening presents and eating a big Christmas dinner with my brothers and sisters and nephews and nieces. Dad behaved, told funny stories. I think we all wished he could be that way more often.

Monday morning, Christmas Day, after his early Mass, Joe drove me back to the Kaplans where we had brunch. He laughed at Ruthie's and Esther's excitement over the tree and little presents around it. "I could bless the tree for you," he joked to Doc and Miriam, "but I don't want to mess up your fun by doing something religious. Besides, I must get back. These old Polacks need two more Masses on Christmas Day or they don't think I'm earning my money."

Doc jumped up and refilled his coffee cup. "You have plenty of time, finish your coffee."

Joe winked at Doc as the doorbell rang. I stood near the door, thinking he was leaving, but wondering why he accepted more coffee and about his wink to Doc. I pulled the door open and screamed. It was Eddie, in his dress uniform, a huge grin on his face. He pulled me into a quick hug, shook Joe's hand and was mobbed by the little girls and Doc and Miriam.

Everyone laughed at my expression as I realized the adults knew Eddie's arrival was a surprise for me.

"Actually, the timing got a little screwed up," Joe said. "I was going to drive us by the train station and surprise you by picking Eddie up. Unfortunately, the train was running late, so I asked Father Anthony to pick him up and run him out here. Now, I really do have to leave before Father Anthony beats me back and starts without me. I think he wants to be senior pastor." He shook Eddie's hand again and left.

I shook my fist at Doc, but I wasn't mad. "You were behind this, weren't you?"

He grinned at me. "Let's just say it took some quick wheeling and dealing between the Army, the Catholics, and the Jews to make this happen."

"And," said Eddie, "some good colored folk who let me ride in their train car. There were no seats in the white cars. By the time I was notified I could take a short leave, all the train tickets were sold, except in the colored section." He shook his head in wonderment. "In fact, the white conductor told me I couldn't go in the colored section because I was white. The colored conductor asked me my name, then winked at me. 'You one of them Puerto Ricans, ain't ya?' He winked again, so I nodded. 'You dumb cracker,' he said to the white conductor. 'Don't you know a Puerto Rican is a Negro that speaks Spanish. Now, tell that guy something in Spanish.' So I rattled off something, and the white guy said it was good there weren't any seats in his section, anyway, 'cause I sure as hell didn't belong there."

Doc busted out laughing while I looked shocked.

"If it wasn't for my brown skin, I wouldn't be here," Eddie said softly. "In fact, two of the colored men I sat with were soldiers coming home to see their families in Chicago. One of them owns a car he left here, but is driving back, and I'm riding back with them. They're picking me up at five-thirty tomorrow morning. We have to be back by wake-up at five a.m., Wednesday morning, which gives us plenty of time." Looking at Doc and Miriam, he asked, "Is that okay if they pick me up here? Otherwise I can meet them someplace."

"Hell, yes." Doc shouted. "I dare any of our neighbors to say anything."

"I agree," said Miriam. "In fact, I want you to call them and tell them I will have breakfast on the table at five. And I'll send you off with that big old thermos full of coffee." She looked at Eddie, "They do have a telephone, don't they?"

Eddie nodded and went into the kitchen to call them. "They were a little nervous, said South Shore isn't the most welcoming to coloreds. I mentioned Miss Pearl knowing you and one of them knows her. They thanked you for the coffee. Said it was hard to find places to serve coloreds till we got back in the South. They're bringing all kinds of food."

We opened our gifts and ate a big turkey meal. Actually, we mostly watched Eddie eat. While the girls napped, Eddie and I sat on the sunporch and talked. He was tired and kept dozing off. It took him several trains and over forty-eight hours to get here. "Why did you do it?" I asked.

"Twelve hours with you is worth it. I love you so much." He pulled a small envelope out of his pocket. "Here, this is all I could afford. Eventually, I'll buy something to hang on it."

It was a beautiful, thin, gold chain, the kind you hang a jewel stone or ornament from. I loved it and slid into his arms for a long kiss.

"I think that's a distraction," he whispered, reluctantly pushing me back.

He napped while I helped Miriam prepare a light evening meal and prepped things for the early breakfast. Later, we watched movies and played games with the little girls. After everyone went to bed, we cuddled on the sunroom couch. Our kisses grew intense, his tongue finding mine, mine his as his hand slipped over my breast.

Oh, Lord, this was wonderful. He stretched back on the couch and pulled me on top of him his hands sliding up and down my back, over my bottom. I felt him poking me and knew exactly what it was. I started rocking against it. We groaned and rocked faster. Finally, he gasped, "Stop, I'm ready to explode."

I didn't want to stop, but I did, and slid to his side as we each caught our breath.

"I'm sorry. I shouldn't have let us get so carried away," he said.

"I'm not." I jumped up and went to the bathroom. On my way back, I brought a hand towel. Snuggling in beside him, I kissed him deeply and ran my hand down his chest to his belt and over his pants, then quickly fumbled the fly-buttons open.

"You don't...What are you doing?" he croaked.

"My girlfriends told me about boys getting blue balls. I don't want you to have any." I giggled as I fingered my way through his underwear. "Is this the right way?"

He adjusted my fingers and hand slightly, then moaned loud enough that he covered his mouth with his hand. "Go slow, stop for a minute. I can't believe you're doing this."

I never dreamed touching a man would be this exciting. I was so wet. I started stroking him again and rubbing myself against his leg. He started bucking and I knew his release was coming. I grabbed the towel and threw it over him just in time to catch his spurts and keep them from hitting his clothes or mine. When he calmed down, I pulled up my skirt and moved his hand inside my wet panties until I burst.

We rearranged our clothing and cuddled, this time sitting up. "That was wonderful. What a distraction. That was the first time I touched..." His voice trailed off in wonderment.

"I didn't think I'd like touching you, but I've been dreaming about it since you left."

"You have? I dream about you, more than I want to. Oh, my God, I can't wait till..."

"Me either," I whispered. The stairway lights flickered from upstairs, bouncing through the dim kitchen. We both laughed. "Guess that's our warning. I'll see you at breakfast."

Eddie pulled me to my feet and into a tight embrace and kiss. "I love you so much. For someone so young, fifteen, you're quite a woman."

"I love you, too. Even if you are an old man, almost thirty."

~ * ~

The next morning, Red and Lawrence, Eddie's two colored friends, showed up promptly at five a.m., all spiffed up in their uniforms. They looked around at the big house and seemed unsure of themselves as they sat down in the kitchen chairs, I pulled out for them. The little girls straggled into the kitchen, rubbing sleep out of their eyes.

"We heard something. What's going on?" asked Esther. "Who are they?" She reached out and politely shook the men's hands.

Ruthie stepped over to do the same, but tripped in her feety-pajamas and almost fell. Red caught her and pulled her onto his lap. "You look awful sleepy to be up this early," he said, giving her a little squeeze.

She snuggled up against him, stared into his dark eyes, reached her little hand up and touched his cropped, kinky, red-toned hair. Miriam sucked in her breath as Ruthie said, "Your hair is short and stiff. Mine is long and soft. I like your hair."

I realized she most likely was never close to a colored man and only saw Miss Pearl, who kept her hair made up the way colored women did.

The man laughed as she wiggled off his lap. "You're about the same size as my niece. I miss her a lot when I'm away. I bet ole Eddie misses you, too."

Eddie, Red and Lawrence ate like it was their last meal on earth. I filled the big thermos as Miriam packed a box with bagels and cream cheese and apples.

"Lordy, we got us enough food to drive clear to Alaska on." Lawrence tapped Eddie's shoulder. "Our two mamas packed fried chicken, cornbread and apple pie, plus maybe some chitlins. Hey, you

238

ever had chitlins?"

Eddie grinned and shook his head. "Sorry, men. I know I'm supposed to be Puerto Rican, but I didn't have time to cook any of that kind of food. So, I'll try your chitlins, but you have to try Miriam's bagels and cream cheese. It's Jewish."

They looked in surprise at Miriam. "Yes," she said, "we're Jewish, Eddie is Mexican and Katie is Polish." She paused a moment. "Do you men have a copy of the Negro Motorist Green Book for your trip?"

Their mouths dropped open. I looked surprised. What was she speaking about?

"Yessum, ma'am. Most white people don't know anything about that." Looking at Eddie and me, Red added, "It's a book that lists places where us Negros can find lodging, food, gas or mechanics in most of the states."

The reality of segregation hit me even harder than when the nanny told me to wash myself off after hugging Miss Pearl. My eyes grew moist as Miriam whispered, "Good. We Jews also know a little about not being accepted everywhere."

"We well prepared," Lawrence said, turning his head away as if to hide the moisture in his eyes. "I have two spare tires, oil, two cans of gas strapped down tight in the trunk, water, tools, belts, even a radiator hose. And I know how to fix about ever-thing. We should be just fine."

"Where do you keep the car? Can you park it on base?" Doc asked.

"Nah, too much red tape, especially for a colored man. I gots cousins that live near the base. They never moved north and they gonna keeps it for me. That way, next time we come home, we won't have to worry 'bout the train."

Doc pulled Eddie aside and handed him a wad of five and ten dollar bills, plus a roll of dimes. "This is for gas and to call if you need help. If there's any left over, split it up three ways. Be safe."

The little girls hugged Red and Lawrence, and next Eddie. Doc shook their hands. Miriam hugged each of them. I saw the surprised look on their faces and figured it was because a white woman would dare touch a colored man, let alone hug one. I walked out to the car, holding Eddie's hand. He pulled me into a hug and long kiss. We didn't talk, we knew what the other was thinking, it would be months till we saw each other again.

"Lord, Lord. I hope this lovesick Puerto Rican man gets well enough to help us drive. Climb in that back seat, Eddie. Hopefully, you'll look a little darker by the time we hit Albamma." Nodding at me, Red explained, "We don't want some little-town white cop to stop us for hauling a white kid around. Good thing ole Eddie's got some brown and talks Spanish."

My mouth opened as I watched Eddie climb in. He rolled down the window. "Don't worry. I'll be fine. I trust my life with these men."

"Yup, we all will be good." Lawrence sounded a little worried as he pulled his door shut. Rolling down his window, he grinned at me, big and confident, gave me a big wink as if to convince me he wasn't really worried. "'Course, he ain't ate our mama's food yet. That might do your boy in. On th' other hand, he may not wanna come back to your Polish cookin' he's always bragging 'bout."

Chapter Fifty-Seven

April Fool's Surprise

Shortly after the first of the year, January, 1950, Eddie was reassigned to Fort Lewis near Seattle, Washington. He was a D.I., Drill Instructor, training the new recruits. They've increased the draft. The papers talk more and more about going to war if North Korea invades South Korea. Eddie's letter two weeks ago said he would probably be at Fort Lewis a while, training others. His last one, two days ago, said he was most likely being shipped over, but not to worry, he would be recording, tallying all the supplies arriving by ship. He wouldn't be on the front lines.

March 31st, a Friday afternoon, Eddie shocked all of us when he showed up on a ten-day pass. He flew in. Said flying was so exciting, he wished he'd gone into pilot training. Doc and Miriam were thrilled to see him, but seemed a little upset as they were going away for the weekend. They told him he couldn't spend the night, even in the apartment, but he could visit during the day until the girls went to bed. He could even use their second car to drive back and forth to the Y. That was fine with us. We understood how it would look to have him staying here and us dating. Doc especially seemed confused. He started toward the stairs, turned. He looked at Eddie in an odd manner and shrugged when Miriam reminded him they needed to leave. It was odd.

After the Kaplans left, Eddie helped me make dinner and clean up afterward. I started some laundry for him as he read to the girls. We played board games with them, he said goodnight as I led them upstairs. I glanced back at him, and it took every ounce of determination I had not to run back and jump into his arms for a hug and kiss. He looked like he had the same feelings.

After the girls fell asleep, I left their door open and wandered downstairs, ready to cry for wanting to be with him so badly.

"Boo," a quiet voice said from the darkened sunroom. "I never left. I couldn't. Not without a hug and kiss from you."

I flew into his arms, laughing and crying at the same time. We calmed down a bit and sat on the couch, well, actually I was on his lap. We talked about his time at Fort Lewis. We made plans for me to take Monday off and spend the day downtown. I wanted to show him the design school I planned to start in the fall. He wanted to show me George Williams College where he would enroll full time after the service. A year and a half didn't sound quite so far away.

We began making out, but he stopped it. "There's nothing my body desires more than yours, but we're not ready. I'd feel terrible if the girls found us."

I said I understood, but my body didn't agree with my mind.

He kissed me goodbye, said he had some paperwork business to take care of at the Y in the morning and would be over sometime before lunch. It sounded rather fishy to me, but I didn't say anything. What kind of paperwork could he have? He wasn't in school.

He showed up about eleven, a silly grin on his face, like he had something to tell me, but couldn't. We took the girls for a long walk. Some of the neighbors waved or came out and greeted us. A man in a uniform draws attention. The old lady two houses down asked if he was staying overnight at the Kaplans. She said it didn't seem proper if he was.

Eddie laughed. "Now, do you really think the Kaplans would allow that? Nope, I'm staying at the Y and just visiting during the day."

"Yeah," Esther said. "Mommy said Eddie can't sleep over anymore 'cuz he's in love with Katie and they're not married yet."

My cheeks burned. Eddie coughed and pulled Esther into a hug, patting her head. The old lady harrumphed, "Well, it's good to know someone around here sets common-sense rules for their help."

While the girls napped, I started dinner. Eddie sat on a kitchen chair and pulled me onto his lap. While he was kissing me, I felt his fingers exploring my neck. "Ahh, you do wear it," he exclaimed as he discovered the thin necklace, he'd given me for Christmas.

"Yes, all the time, except in the shower or swimming. Why?"

"Oh, never mind. I'm just glad you like it." His eyes glinted with something I couldn't read. Definitely mischief and surprise. I couldn't tell what else.

I pulled his head into a lock and rubbed his short hair with my fist.

"Why? Tell me. You've got something you're not telling me. Now, what is it?"

He giggled. "Nope, I don't have anything up my sleeve. See?" He grabbed my hands and ran them up and down his sleeves, then, as I started to say something, he kissed me, sticking his tongue between my teeth.

"You nut." I gasped, pulling my face back. "You know something you're not telling me."

"That's simply not true," he said, sounding like a school boy. "Oh, wait, I just heard the girls." He released me and gave me a gentle push. "I am glad you like the necklace."

"Oh, wait. It's April Fool's Day, and you're acting like one," I called as I ran toward the stairs.

That evening, I knew he would be downstairs waiting after I got the girls to sleep. However, I wasn't expecting the candle and the bouquet of roses in the sunroom. As I entered, he knelt, took my hand and said, "This is not an April Fool's joke. I love you. Will you marry me?" I felt cool metal slide up my ring finger. It was an engagement ring with a tiny diamond. Simple, but elegant.

I stared at him. I was certain we were meant for each other, but I thought our engagement would come after he was out of the service. My tongue seemed frozen, thick, sluggish, like I couldn't move it. The tears started rolling down my cheeks.

He just asked me to marry him!

I nodded and managed to whisper a thick, "Yes."

I stood silent, like a statue, till he wrapped his arms around me.

"You are the most beautiful person in the world. I can't wait till we get married."

I cried into his shoulder, still in shock, my mind and body a jumble of feelings. Giddy, awestruck wonder, wanting to kiss and never stop. I couldn't believe I was engaged and to such a wonderful person. I knew he felt the same about me.

The sunroom was chilly. I pulled a large beach towel out of the bathroom closet and wrapped it around us as we snuggled on the long couch. First, we talked, both of us awestruck that we found each other, fell in love, both dreaming of marriage and now we were engaged. We talked about the possibility of being married with both of us in school, though mine was only a one year program, so I would be nearly finished when he got out of the service. We talked how we both wanted children, but not a huge unplanned family like most Catholics we knew.

"Guess that's what rubbers are for," he joked. "I think Catholics have to set their own limits, don't you?"

I nodded, thinking of the rubbers I noticed in the open drawer next to Doc and Miriam's bed that time I was dusting. Doc's intense talk flashed through my mind about asking him for protection. It made sense, but only for that moment.

We started kissing, little fun pecks, followed by longer ones, then deep tongue ones. We started moaning and grinding against each other. I started to unbutton his slacks, but his hands were already fumbling around under my blouse, trying to undo my bra. "How the heck do these things work?"

I giggled, pulled his clumsy hands down, reached back, unsnapped it and inhaled as his fingers and hands began kneading my breasts. "*Suave*. Gentle, they're not hard like baseballs." I snickered. "Though they're not much bigger."

"They're beautiful." He moaned as he carefully caressed them.

I rubbed against him. Any thought of stopping vanished. The idea to run upstairs and grab some of Doc's rubbers was nonexistent. The same with asking Eddie if he had any. Love. Sex. Lust. Nature. Whatever it was took over and it seemed perfectly natural and right. We ended up on the floor, totally naked. After the third time, we fell asleep in each other's arms for about thirty minutes.

Reality hit as we woke up and dressed and hugged. Our eyes glistened with amazement and joy, plus frustration at not being able to be together forever and ever. To not spend the rest of the night in each other's arms.

As he left to return to the Y, I grabbed the beach towel, checked it over and noticed several drops of blood, proof I was no longer a virgin. I ran it downstairs and threw it in the washer. I left a note on the kitchen counter to remind myself to dry it before Miriam came home.

At eight-thirty Sunday morning, Eddie called to say his sergeant, who was also on leave in Chicago, tracked him down at the Y to tell him their leaves were cut short and they had to be out at Chicago Air Park, oops, it's now called Midway, by four to fly standby back to Seattle. He didn't know the reason why.

We were a mixture of happiness and sadness when Doc and Miriam arrived home about two-thirty. They were excited for us, but also sad that Eddie couldn't stay longer. Doc drove Eddie to the airport while I wandered around in a daze.

"Katie," Miriam finally said, "why don't you go take a nap. The girls are sleeping, maybe you'll feel better when you wake up. I can't imagine being engaged one day and having to say goodbye again the next."

I fell hard asleep. The little girls woke me up for dinner.

Sunday, June 25, 1950

I retched into the downstairs toilet, glad Miriam was upstairs and couldn't hear me. Something about old slimy bananas did it. I was making banana bread. I knew it wasn't always bananas. Sometimes it was oatmeal, other times scalloped potatoes. Me throwing up started happening about the time I missed my second period. I was sure I'd get my next one, but I didn't. Now I missed three. I flushed the toilet and rinsed my mouth out. I had to get this bread made and start dinner. Dinner, that's what the Kaplans called supper.

April Fool's Day was supposed to be about funny jokes and harmless kidding, not for getting pregnant the first time you had sex.

I sensed my body changing, my breasts getting bigger, which wouldn't be all that bad if I wasn't pregnant. My morning sickness hasn't been too bad, I thought I was able to hide it. The girls were sick with the flu a few weeks ago, so I passed it off on that if Miriam wondered. All the time I wondered what was I going to do? When should I tell Doc and Miriam? I felt so ashamed at breaking their trust. Especially after Doc's stern warnings about unwed mothers. What would Eddie say when I wrote him? Would he be angry? I was angry at myself. Why didn't I take the time to run upstairs and steal a rubber from Doc's drawer? Oh, my goodness. Was that why he asked me to dust before Christmas? He knew Eddie was coming home, but I didn't. Was that a reminder? A hint to be prepared? There were dozens of them in there. Why the hell didn't Eddie think to bring some? I knew the answer. It was the same for both of us. We didn't expect to make love, hadn't planned on the possibility, and we both would have been too embarrassed buying or stealing rubbers. Besides, who gets pregnant their first time? Well, our first night together. We did it three times.

Eddie was getting shipped out soon and he said in his last letter he might not receive any of my mail afterward for up to a month. I must tell him when I write tomorrow. I have to think about when to tell the Kaplans.

We've been packing like we might never return. Doc and Miriam acted tight-lipped, having little conversations away from me and the girls, sometimes in Yiddish. All of us were leaving Wednesday for Philadelphia to visit Miriam's goy friend, then on to New York. I heard mention of other places. Last week, Miriam asked me to take the girls to the beach on Wednesday. She said not to bring them back before two-thirty, which was strange, but I did. Ruthie got fussy so I walked them home. It was two-fifteen and a shiny car was in the driveway with a sign that said realtor on it. Inside, Miriam was showing a man and woman through the house. She frowned a little when we came in, but introduced them as her friends who came for a visit.

Today, I came downstairs while the girls napped and saw Doc's gestation wheel lying near the phone. I saw him use it a few times, talking to some patient confused as to her due date. I picked it up and tried to figure it out. I knew the time to carry a baby was around nine months, which meant January. But the wheel wanted to know the first day of my last monthly. I put it in and felt a hand touch my shoulder. It was Miriam. "Are you late?"

I started crying. "Yes, I've missed three. I'm so sorry. It—it just happened. He didn't stay the whole night."

Miriam looked like she wanted to hug me, but she didn't. "Sit down, let's have some tea." She poured us each a cup, pushed a box of Kleenex across the table to me. "We, actually you, have to tell Doc. We're both disappointed in each of you."

I dabbed at my eyes, wouldn't look at her for the shame. Kept staring at the gestation wheel I carried to the table and now sat next to my cup. I heard a car drive up and knew it was Doc's brand-new Cadillac sedan, almost the size of a limousine. He looked at us, his eyes confused till they saw the gestation wheel. With a big sigh, he sat down and looked at me.

"We suspected. When are you due?"

"I—I didn't quite figure it out, but around January."

"Is this your last period?" He pointed to the wheel.

I nodded. "It was the first time, honest. I'm so sorry to disappoint you."

"So, is this an April Fool's conception?" He wasn't joking or smiling. "Your due date is January first, possibly later as it's your first one." He sighed. "This complicates things, way beyond you being pregnant."

I couldn't believe how changed he looked, grumpy, even angry.

Miriam sipped her tea. "You see, Katie, the reason we plan to be gone for so long is that Doc has several job offers in Baltimore, New York and Boston. He plans to interview while we're away, plus enjoy some vacation time. We were going to need a lot of help from you with the girls. Now..."

"I can still help. I haven't thrown up in three days, so I think my morning sickness is over."

"It's more than that," Doc said. He stood and started pacing, tapping the wheel against his palm, occasionally looking at it and shaking his head. "Your body will be changing a lot. You will be more tired. Your stomach may still revolt at some foods, and heaven knows, we'll be eating different foods. Plus, you're going to look pregnant." His eyes flashing, he spat out, "And just how the hell is that going to look for us? A new job, a prestigious one on the East coast, buying a new home in a better neighborhood, meeting new people. Now we have a little pregnant goy nanny trying to keep up with our children. Keep up, that is, when she has the energy, when she's not throwing up, when her belly isn't in the way." He stomped toward the stairs, stopped and yelled back at me, "Why the hell didn't you use a rubber?"

His words stung. Who was this man? Why was he so angry with me? I could understand his disappointment, but this was different. Like he was embarrassed or something. This was a side of Doc I never saw before. He was acting like the Jewish relatives in New York who looked down their noses at me for being a little, naive goy nanny. Before I could stop myself, I hissed, "Why the hell didn't you offer us some?"

"Why the hell do you think I asked you to dust that day and left the drawer open?" He turned and stomped toward the stairs.

Miriam followed him without a word to me.

Guiltily, I remembered his tone when he spoke with Eddie and me about our relationship and not getting pregnant. His offering to give us protection. I missed all the clues and suggestions he made. How stupid. I collapsed into the kitchen chair, put my head on the table and sobbed. Humiliated over my attitude that I couldn't get pregnant. I wasn't that kind of girl. I was embarrassed over my secret snotty attitude toward my girlfriends who were pregnant when they got married. Now, what would I do? Move home? I could hide my pregnancy for a while, but eventually, Mom and Dad would know. Then what? Especially when they realized the baby was half Mexican. Where then? Single, pregnant young women weren't hired for any jobs I knew of. What would Eddie say to do? What could he do? He might be on a ship or plane right now. He couldn't get out of the army because his girlfriend was pregnant and too stupid to make him wear a rubber.

I rushed into the bathroom and retched, mostly dry heaves. It wasn't from the smell of food, just nerves, I figured. How could I be so dumb? I rinsed my mouth out and stepped back into the kitchen, now hungry. I found some saltine crackers and cheese and was stuffing them in my mouth when Doc and Miriam walked in. He motioned for me to sit down. I dropped two crackers getting to the table. He sighed, picked them up and laid them down in front of me.

"We just looked at the calendar and our commitments," Doc said. "My interviews will be over by early August. I expect at least two offers which means I will have to make up my mind right away and be prepared to start work September first."

Miriam spoke next. "Once that decision is made, we will find a house to buy, then you, I, and the girls will drive back, hopefully by mid-September. I will oversee the packers and movers and finalize the sale of this house. Doc will fly back to help drive us back to the East Coast. We think we will be done with your services no later than October first."

"Thank you. I'll do my best with the girls and you."

"You want to be a dress designer. Right?"

I nodded at Doc, his eyes still cold.

"Well, start thinking how you can alter your clothes or design some new ones that look stylish and not like maternity ones." He glared at me. "I'm serious. At least you won't be around us in your third trimester."

I dropped my head, wanted to crawl under the table or into my bed and sleep forever, but my stomach growled. I shoved some cracker and cheese into my mouth. That seemed less embarrassing than retching.

Doc stood and tapped my shoulder. I looked up at him, cracker crumbs on my lips. "One more thing. You have an appointment at ten-thirty tomorrow morning with Dr. Cordelia for a complete pregnancy exam. That includes a pelvic exam, got it?"

I nodded, tried not to let my face flush. Somehow, they still cared for me, I thought. Nobody ever touched my private area, now, some doctor would be poking his hands around down there. I turned toward the door, the lawn needed mowing. Yes, somebody did touch my privates. His name was Eddie, and if it wasn't for him, actually both of us, I wouldn't be seeing some doctor tomorrow. I wished he was here to help share the blame. Maybe if he was, I could have stayed here with him till the house sold. At least we'd have figured out the next steps of our lives together. Like getting married quickly.

Marriage. What did that look like now? Getting married with a baby in my arms? At the courthouse? I wouldn't dare ask Joe to marry us, to put his blessing on us when we'd so obviously sinned. Next, I wanted to shout. What sin? It wasn't like I was a streetwalker and he paid me for a quick piece of ass, that's what I've heard some guys call it. No, we loved each other, we are going to get married. Maybe out of order, but we would get married, and when Eddie was home, none of this would matter anymore. Not even Doc's terrible attitude toward me.

I shoved the mower with a vengeance. Hypocrites. How dare Doc turn on me like this. He loved the colored folks, look at how he treated Ray, Lawrence, and Miss Pearl. He said he didn't charge the poor women for his services. Now he acted so high and mighty because he was going to be a doctor on the east coast. Was that really better than being one in Chicago? Acting all embarrassed because his goy nanny was pregnant. It wasn't like I was going to the stupid interviews with him or they were interviewing me. *Oh, yes, Dr. Kaplan. We like you, but next, we'd like to interview your nanny. You know, just to be certain she'll fit in with your new status on the east coast.*

I heard myself yell, "Bullshit."

I re-mowed the lawn in a cross pattern. I thought about packing up my clothes and calling my brother Joe to come pick me up at the corner late that night. Just sneak out and not come back. Maybe I would call that nice director at the Y, or the cook. What the heck could they do? Besides, involving them would only mean more embarrassment for Eddie someday. By God, at least that would show Doc and Miriam!

I didn't simmer down till I finished mowing and realized I still had a job, plus I doubted they would give me the money they were saving for me if I walked out, and I needed that money when this baby was born. I remained outside and weeded some beds, determined the place would be in good shape for the man taking over for the summer. I'd show them a pregnant goy nanny could still function.

The girls were up from their naps. I pasted on a big smile, acted like nothing was wrong, and asked if they wanted to go to the beach. I packed some snacks, extra for me. I was starving.

Chapter Fifty-Eight

Thrown Out
Monday, October 2, 1950

I'm officially in my third trimester. Miriam sent me over to that same doctor this morning for a checkup. He said I'm doing well and the baby is healthy. He wants to keep seeing me, but I have no idea how much he will cost. Now that Kaplans are moving, I don't think they will continue to pay. I was too embarrassed to tell him today was my last day with them or that I wasn't moving east with them.

Thank goodness I only started to really show the last several weeks. Right after Miriam, the girls and I returned home.

I didn't write in my diary the whole time we were gone, didn't even make notes. All things considered, I did quite well. Doc basically ignored me, though one day, he told me to buy some bigger bras. Out of the blue, coming out of a little restaurant in New York City, just like that, he grumped at me, "Go buy some bigger brassieres. You're going to injure your mammary glands."

Miriam shrugged when I looked at her. She pointed across the street to this little shop with a sign written in Hebrew that sold ladies foundation garments. I went in and this bent-over little lady jabbered in Yiddish and bad English as she measured me. She patted my tummy, there was a little bump, and asked me something.

"January," I replied, hoping that was the right answer. It must have been because she gave me six bras, two each in three different sizes, the last pair were for nursing.

She took my hand and rubbed my engagement ring while I turned beet red. "Where other ring?"

I shrugged and looked away.

"Where man?"

Tears slipped out and down my cheeks. "Korea."

Her eyes got big as she grabbed my face in both hands and started kissing my cheeks, one side, then the other, over and over. "Be okay. Be okay. Be okay."

"Five," she said when I reached in my purse to pay her. I'm sure those bras were at least two dollars each and handed her two fives, but she snatched one and gently pushed me out the door. The Kaplans were eating ice-cream cones from a street vendor and jabbering in Yiddish. Barely glancing at me, Doc reached in his pocket for money and bought another cone. He asked Esther to bring it to me.

The whole trip, Miriam was fair, but cool. She never hugged me or patted my back or said good job. Yet she never yelled at me or got upset. At times, she made sure I got extra rest or she quieted the girls down if they became too exuberant. The girls and I did well together, just like always, and that was all that mattered.

Doc accepted a job with a new group of physicians in New York who formed to serve the rapidly growing number of couples having babies. He also would serve in a teaching hospital two days a week. They bought a home on Long Island, a brand new one in a subdivision around a golf course. They were the fourth Jewish family allowed in the development. Their new home was not on the golf course, but was near the club part where there were two swimming pools and tennis courts. The home was almost twice the size of their one in Chicago and they planned to hire a live-in nanny so Miriam could work more with an agency that served low-income families.

The day before Miriam and I left with the girls, we were at the new house so she and Doc could order some drapes and furniture. The girls were napping in the car, the doors open. The car sat in the shade of several big old trees near the house. They were so tired of travel and living in hotels and in relatives' homes and we still faced a three-day drive home. I sat on the stoop, facing the girls. Doc walked up, a little hesitantly. "Umm, I need to say something."

I looked at him. He seemed nervous, not grumpy or happy, but uncertain. I nodded at him. I didn't know what to say. He barely spoke to me the whole trip.

"I, umm, I owe you an apology." I looked at him in surprise. "I apologize for being so crotchety with you over you getting pregnant. You see, I've been mad at myself about it. I think I blamed you, tried to put all the responsibility on you for getting pregnant, or for not getting pregnant

252

and that wasn't fair."

I wasn't sure what he was trying to say. Eddie wasn't around to blame, but what did he mean? He noticed my confused look.

"See, I know how in love you two were and how we encouraged it, though I didn't realize it at the time. I know how distance intensifies the time you are together. So, that Christmas, I knew Eddie was coming home, but I thought it was going to be for longer than one day. That's why I asked you to dust the bedroom so you could see the rubbers."

I shrugged my shoulders and squinted my eyes at him. I thought that's why he had me dust. So I would see the rubbers, figure we might have sex and take several. I didn't even know Eddie was coming home! That's why he got so upset with me later when I did tell him I was pregnant?

He must have read my mind. "I know, I know. I assumed a lot. Why I really am disappointed in myself was when Eddie surprised us on his next visit, I didn't follow my gut. We were in a hurry to leave for the weekend, but I clearly thought about him being around for a few days. I knew we would be gone for the weekend and started to go upstairs. I was going to grab several rubbers that I was going to slip to him on the side for just in case you two got carried away. Then I thought he'd be embarrassed and might be offended." Doc paused and wiped his face with his handkerchief. "I wish I went with my gut and risked him being offended. I told myself I would give him some when we got back from the weekend, or at least mention something to him. When he got called back early...Well, I hoped nothing happened."

I stood up, still not knowing what to say or whether to be insulted. He was right. Something did happen and it did so as naturally as it could be.

"All I can say," he said, "is that I'm sorry. I know how love works. What you did wasn't wrong or sinful." The girls started to wake up and I moved toward them as he said, "Thank you for being part of our lives."

I didn't know how to respond. On the one hand, I wanted to snap back, why don't you let me stay on? That was when I thought of his remarks about having a fat, unwed nanny and figured he was correct. I WAS a part of their lives. I wouldn't be for much longer. I helped the girls get oriented from their sleep. Miriam and I left with them the next morning for our long drive back.

Today, she and the girls just left for the airport to pick up Doc. The movers come tomorrow, then they're gone. I'm waiting for Joe to pick me up. We're dropping off Eddie's bicycle at the Y where they'll keep it stored for him.

Instead of going straight home, Joe drove south to a county forest preserve near Midlothian. Along the way, we stopped at a deli and bought some ham sandwiches, chips and Coke. At the picnic table, I chattered about the trip, trying to make it sound like it was as exciting as the one a year ago.

Joe put his hand on my arm. "Katie, what are you going to tell the folks?"

He walked around the table, sat beside me and put his big arm around my shoulders as I cried. He kept squeezing my shoulders, patting my arm, whispering, "I'm not mad. God's not mad. I'll do anything I can to help you out."

"How did you know?"

"Doc called me from Baltimore, right after they found the house, just before you girls were to get back."

I thought about Doc talking with me that last day before we drove back. I was still confused. In some ways, I appreciated the fact he apologized, but things happened so quickly and easily, would we have taken the time to use a rubber even if Doc was right there to hand them to us? I snapped at Joe, "What did he say? Make sure I don't look pregnant? Get bigger bras? That Eddie and I are big disappointments to him?"

He started to chuckle, but felt me tense up, ready to jump up and stomp my foot. "No, little sister. He said nothing like that. He called me to apologize for letting this happen. He feels responsible, so does Miriam."

"How are they responsible? What could they have done? Put chastity belts on us? Kept us in cages?" Am I supposed to tell my priestly brother about Doc offering us rubbers? Wasn't that a sin? How the hell could I have that conversation even if he was my brother?

Joe couldn't contain his laughter, especially after I jumped up, stomped my foot and shook my fist at him.

"This is not funny. I am pregnant. Eddie is in Korea, driving munition trucks, not working on the docks like he was supposed to be. I don't know if he's dead or doesn't want anything to do with me because since I wrote him I was pregnant, he hasn't replied." I started shaking, grabbed my Coke and took a big swig, then remembered that Miriam told me not to drink Coke or much caffeine while pregnant. I threw the bottle to the ground, watched it fizz out. "You're laughing at me and telling me Doc thinks he's responsible? And you're asking about what I'm going to tell the folks? This is a hell of a mess and it's all my fault." I dropped to the ground, sobbing, gasping for breath, like a toddler throwing a tantrum.

Joe dropped down beside me and pulled me onto his lap. "There, there. I wasn't laughing at you to tease you, just it's been a long time since I saw that feisty, sarcastic side of you like when you were little. I'm sorry. I love you. I'm worried about Eddie too." He rocked me back and forth till I stopped sobbing.

"I'm sorry I'm so emotional. It's like I swing from one extreme to the next."

"Sissy, you're pregnant. I've heard that is normal. With all the uncertainty in your life, you have every reason to be emotional. Now, when is the baby due?"

"January first, but the doctor said this morning, based on its size, it might go a week or two longer because this is my first, but it's healthy and I'm fine." I paused and tried to smile at him. "Other than yelling at my favorite big brother."

He hugged me again. "I think you should not tell the folks you're pregnant, that you will be looking for a new job. Do you have money saved?"

I told him about my deal with the Kaplans and I had eight hundred dollars saved. It was enough that I could get my own room or flat if I found some kind of job. Told him how the money was supposed to be for design school, but didn't think they accepted single pregnant women.

"Well, the folks will find out eventually and I doubt if they will accept it well, especially because Dad knows Eddie is Mexican. When they do, and if it's rough, call me. I'll come get you and we'll take the next step. At least you've got a cushion."

"Okay. Miriam gave me her portable sewing machine for my birthday last year, so I can sew for others. Thank you, big brother." I hugged him and helped pull him to his feet. "Aren't pregnant girls the ones who should need help getting up?" It felt good to say something funny.

Two weeks later, about nine one night, I was taking a bath when Mom burst in, gasping she needed to pee, she thought she had a bladder infection. One of us women in the tub and another needing to pee was not a big deal. Except Mom stared over at me, eying my enlarged breasts, my tummy.

"I thought your face looked fuller and you'd gained weight. You're pregnant, aren't you?"

I stood up, pulled a towel around me and stepped out of the tub and dried off. Pulling on my nightgown, I said, "Yes, Mom, I am. I'm sorry." I held my head high as she followed me into my bedroom. My gut churned. Where was this going to lead? Would she tell Dad? Could she listen as I tried to explain everything? Could she accept how in love we were?

"You really are pregnant." She started sniffling.

I thought she might hug me, be sad, but understanding. Instead, she stomped her foot and yelled, "How the hell did you get pregnant? Where is the bastard? Who is he? He better be white and Catholic."

I tried to stay calm. "His name is Eddie, we are engaged. He's in Korea and I haven't heard from him in months."

Downstairs, the front door slammed. I heard Dad belch as he stumbled into the living room.

"Eddie?" Mom screeched. "Do you mean Edward?"

"Eduardo Vargas."

Hearing Dad come in, I slipped into some socks and my tennis shoes, the ones I mowed lawn with, and for some reason, I pulled thirty dollars out of my stash hidden in the drawer and stuffed it into my sock, then shoved the envelope all the way back, behind my underwear. I decided to be prepared in case I needed to leave quickly.

"You're pregnant by a goddam spic? And the bastard disappeared on you?" Mom's voice shrieked like a wildcat.

Dad stomped up the stairs, bellowing, "Who's pregnant?"

"Katerina is. By some spic named Eduardo Vargas." Mom threw herself on my bed and started to cry.

"Get out. Get out now. Use those paper bags, get some clothes and get the hell out of my house and never come back." He yanked a dresser drawer open and started throwing my underwear on the bed by Mom, as if to speed my departure.

I gasped as he found my envelope with nearly eight hundred dollars. "What the hell is this? I knew you'd been holding out on me. I knew them damn Jews were paying you more than you said." He stuffed the envelope deep in his pants pocket and staggered down the stairs. Mom followed him. I heard her telling Ginny I was pregnant by a spic and they'd thrown me out.

I stuffed some clothes in the two bags, trying to think logically despite my emotions. I made sure I got the new bras, some pants and skirts I altered and some I could still alter. I felt like I gained twenty pounds when I bent over to stuff clothes into the bags, especially when I twisted my way inside our closet to find my winter coat, which I slipped on over my nightgown. I threw my snow boots on top of one of the bags, my new bras were on top of the other. I managed to get my arms around both bags and waddled down the stairs, through the kitchen, and out the back door, glad I had shoes on.

I didn't see Ginny, wondered where she'd gone, but my mind was more focused on what I should do next. I walked across the back yard, then stepped in front of the garage door which faced the alley. I sensed Dad was watching from the kitchen door. By standing in front of the garage door, I knew he couldn't see me and might think I'd headed down the alley. But to where? I had no coins for a phone booth. The only place to get change was in the bar Dad almost lived at, and the guys sitting around were all just like him. I could only imagine what they would say to their friend's young daughter wearing a winter coat over her nightgown, walking in tattered, grass-stained tennis shoes, carrying two grocery bags of clothes with her bras flopping out.

After waiting a few minutes, I realized I wasn't crying. Which surprised me. Shouldn't I be? But I wasn't.

I felt a twitch in my stomach. I realized right then a new life was truly starting. Two new lives, one inside me and my own. The one inside me just told me he or she was there with me. That little kick told me, even if I had no idea what our life would be like, or whatever happened, there would be two of us going through everything together. I was responsible for making sure we both came out on the other side safe and sound.

It was sobering, but not frightening. I can do this, I thought, as I watched Joe's old black car roll slowly up the alley.

Ginny jumped out and stared at me, her eyes dancing. "Was it the chauffeur? A damn spic? You're pregnant by a spic chauffeur?"

I nodded, started to speak. She grabbed me and pulled me into a hug. "I ran down to the phone and called Joe, told him to get here fast." She pushed herself back and with the biggest grin I'd seen on her face in a long time, said, "I'm so happy for you. You get to leave this hell hole and start a new life. I love you. Hey, that spic got any brothers I can get knocked up by so I can get out of here?" She giggled, then cried out in frustration. "You are so lucky."

She kissed me as Dad hollered from the kitchen door, "Ginny, if you're back there, get your ass in here or you can go live on the streets too."

Ginny took off running and crying across the dark, jagged back yard. Joe held up his hand toward me. "Just a minute. Stay here." He trotted after Ginny while I stood in the open car door. He yelled, "Goddammit, Dad, give me her money. You sure as hell didn't earn it."

"That little whore will never get it and I'll knock the shit out of you if you step any closer."

There were some grunts and it sounded like Dad and Joe were wrestling around on the ground. I heard Ginny scream, "Dad, put the bat down. He's your son. She's your daughter."

I heard the bat smash into wood, and the back door slam. Next thing, Joe was back at the car. "I'm fine. He tackled me and tried to swing his fist at me, but missed. When I tried to hold him down to look in his pocket for the money, he swung the bat at me. I'm sorry I didn't get it. I think he left it in the house. That old bastard is crazy." He helped me into the car, took several big breaths, shook his head, sighed and half smiled. "Got your fancy luggage, I see." He climbed in, shifted into gear and slowly eased out the clutch. "Guess we need plan B. Ginny told me when I picked her up by the bar how Dad got your money. You can stay a night or two in the rectory, but we'll have to come up with another place. I have some money set aside and earn a little each month." He inhaled a huge breath and slowly let it out. "It's enough I can cover your housing and food somewhere till you can get on your feet. I know getting on your feet is not going to be soon, so don't worry. We're going to take things one day at a time." He reached over and patted my arm and looked at me long enough to catch my nod.

"Thank you." I paused, not knowing what else to say. I couldn't think beyond the next few minutes, let alone one day. We were quiet for several blocks.

"Hey, Joe. Guess what?"

He glanced over again. By the dim streetlights, I could see his face lined with concern and strain.

"When I was out waiting by the garage, for what I didn't know, or why, the baby kicked. It kicked me easy, like it was saying the two of us are going to make it together. It was just before you showed up."

I saw tears reflected from the headlights of an oncoming car slide down his cheeks, easing those lines. The baby tapped me again. I put my hands around my tummy and gently patted it.

Chapter Fifty-Nine

The Rectory

The light blinded me as I struggled to sit up. Where was I? Why was I sleeping on a couch in someone's living room? Why was this lady asking me questions?

"Who are you? What are you doing in here? What's more, how did you get in here?"

The gray-haired woman with wire-rimmed glasses bent over, glaring at me, her face so close, I was afraid we'd bump heads as I struggled to sit up. She straightened and stepped back one step, exactly one step, as if she stepped back any more, I might have room to escape.

"I—I'm Katie Kozlowski. I'm Joe's youngest sister." I managed to sit up and remember I was in the living room of the rectory of St. Bobola's Church where Joe was the priest. I was on the couch because he didn't think it wise, I sleep upstairs where he and another priest slept.

"Listen, young lady, I don't care if you think you are his sister, but around here, he is referred to as Father Kozlowski, or those who know him better, Father Joe. A man of God is not simply called Joe!"

I managed to stand up. I desperately needed to pee. The blanket fell away from me and we both looked down at my body. Had I gained another ten pounds overnight? My ancient flannel nightgown was snug around my tummy and breasts. I looked around for the bathroom. The woman lowered her eyes as she pointed a long finger toward the hallway with the bathroom.

She was eyeing my polish suitcases when I returned, my bras still hanging out, my old snow boots barely hanging on in the other. "I'm Hannah, the housekeeper for the rectory. Been here nigh on thirty years. Is that all the clothes you got?"

I looked her directly in the eyes. "Yes. My parents threw me out of their home last night and that's all I could pack."

Hannah looked me over again. Her shoulders eased, her face softened and a light smile flashed across her face. In a friendlier tone, she said, "I met your folks once. That was enough times for me. C'mon, let's start some breakfast goin'." She straightened herself, marched ahead, then paused and turned back. "Throw that blanket back over yourself. No sense advertising the fact you're in a family way."

I didn't blush as I wrapped the blanket around me. What you see is what you get, I figured. I'm not going to be able to hide this pregnancy any longer, so I'm not going to worry about it.

I'm still wearing my engagement ring. Joe asked me last night if Eddie bought a wedding ring the same time he got the diamond. We were both quiet. I wondered if he thought I might wear the wedding ring if I had it. It might make things easier. "He didn't give me a wedding ring, just an engagement. I'll wear a wedding ring when I'm married, not before."

He reached over and patted my arm, then squeezed it as he nodded. "I love you, sis." That's all he said, but I could tell he agreed with me.

"Your brother is a wonderful man of God," Hannah said as we sipped our coffee, waiting for the biscuits to bake a bit more before we started the bacon and eggs. "He has done wonders with this church. Why, he's got people working on raising money to build a school gymnasium and more classrooms for in a couple of years."

I took a sip and looked around the kitchen. I loved it, lots of counter space with an opening to serve things buffet style to the dining room.

"So, you need some clothes?"

"Maybe some things I could remake. I'm a good seamstress." My head dropped as my situation whipped through my mind. "I guess I'd need a sewing machine, though. Mine is with my folks and they won't let me back in to get it."

"Hey, why am I smelling biscuits? What's the occasion?" Joe, my brother, I mean the Most Reverend Joseph Kozlowski, sauntered into the room. "Are you sure we can afford this extravaganza?" He grinned at Hannah as he patted me on the shoulder.

"Well, Father Joe, it's not every day we find the homeless sister of our favorite priest sleeping on our couch. How long you think you can keep her here without the nuns and that new assistant priest giving you heck?"

He laughed, then got serious. "Well, I'm planning on seeing Hank Sawicki today. He's got a new batch of beer he said was ready to taste and I'm hoping she can go there. I know they have empty rooms up on the third floor."

"Well, see him first. Don't ask Mae, she's got enough on her mind with that tagalong. He's a hellion, even in kindergarten. I'm sure Hank's working today, so catch him when he gets home. That way, Katie and I will have time to check out the closet and maybe she can start sewing some stuff to cover herself up. I think she needs to start with a new nightgown."

Chapter Sixty

Living in a Rooming House
December 20, 1950

I wonder how long old Mae is going to keep acting like she doesn't like me? Especially when, underneath, I know she does.

She barely speaks to me if she passes me around the rooming house, not that I'm out of my efficiency much. Yet every time I'm doing my laundry on Friday mornings, that's when she told me I could and I'm the only resident she lets do their personal laundry, she always pops down, asking if I have enough soap, showing me an old chair I could paint and use, dragging out old curtains and material I might want to fix the place up with. Hank keeps updating her, so I know she's dying to see what I'm doing with the place, but won't ask herself up for an invite. I'll wait to invite her. I want to do a few more things before showing her. She will be stunned, that much I know.

Hank started sneaking me food two days after I moved in. I thought Mae was sending him, so always told him to thank Mae for me. As I grew bigger, the portions started getting larger, and he or one of the kids began bringing it up right after dinner, still hot. I started to put a little paper in the empty clean dish going back with them that said thank you. After a while, I began drawing little flowers around the words, but never got a response, other than from Hank, Joey or Nina. They always said I was welcome and I didn't need to keep thanking them.

This morning, taped to my door was the note I sent down last night, only with 'you're welcome' written on it. I've seen Mae's writing, it's hers.

I have my darker moments, what with never hearing from Eddie, but overall, after two months in the efficiency, I'm beginning to feel a peace about being here and myself. The Sawickis are great, even if Mae won't act like it yet. Hannah has become almost like a grandmother I never had. Joe, well, he's always the same. I had the blues last week and started to snivel. All worried about having enough money to live on and paying him back someday, and raising a baby by myself.

"Katie," he said. "Why don't you focus on what you do have, not what you don't." Lifting my chin till I looked in his beautiful blue eyes, he added, "God knows you're a long-term project. I know you're a long-term project. Neither of us are complaining or worried, so it's about time you quit worrying." He kissed my cheek and pulled me into a hug. "You do realize, everyone is a long-term project. Don't you?"

Well, diary, I tell you, those words settled down deep inside me and I try to think of them every day. Since then, I seem lighter, well, not in weight, but emotionally. Life's a lot more enjoyable, looking on what I've got than what I don't.

I realized that, around Nina and Joey, I feel like a big sister. I never had younger siblings and these two are so much fun and nice to be around. Mae doesn't want them hanging around me much. Doesn't want them getting ideas that having out-of-wedlock babies is all right. I understand, but things happen sometimes.

I laughed when Nina told me what she replied to her mom. "Ma, if you think seeing Katie all stretched out, can't get comfortable no matter how she sits and knowing she's got a baby coming soon is going to make me want to run out and get pregnant right away, then you're crazy."

Tonight, Joey popped in, brought dinner. I try not to count on it and always have several cans of soup on hand and some vegetables, but Mae's cooking is wonderful.

"It's only leftovers tonight. Ma said you should take it easy on the sauerkraut, didn't want to upset the chipmunk." He laughed as I looked at him. "She didn't say chipmunk, that's just what I call him."

"What if the chipmunk is a girl?"

This kid is so cute. Eighth grade, nearly fourteen, dark brown hair, his blue eyes are set close like his dad's, but are so deep, they draw you in. He's going to be a lady's man and is starting to act like it.

"Well, if he's anything like Tommy, he's better off being a girl chipmunk. Dad's watching him tonight, while Ma's at some lady's church meeting. I'll have to go down and rescue him soon, he can only take so much of Tommy." He sighed and looked around the efficiency, trying to see what else I'd done to the place. "I don't know, Dad and Ma are awful old to be raising a five-year-old, I don't know what they're going to do when Nina and I are out of the house." He plopped down on the couch, covered in old drapes I'd combined into a bright throw.

I stuffed my face with sausage and mashed potatoes, only taking a couple of bites of the kraut. Joey was so easy to be with, just like Eddie was. I winced at the thought of Eddie. Why couldn't he be here with his pregnant wife or girlfriend? Would he ever reply to my letter telling him I was pregnant? Would it be okay, that I missed him terribly?

"You're thinking of him, aren't you?" It was a soft and understanding question, especially considering the kid wouldn't turn fourteen for three more weeks. "Your man, the baby's daddy."

I looked away. I'd never talked about Eddie with Joey alone, and only a little with him and his sister together. Never told any of them he was Mexican. "I'm sorry, I was. Sometimes you remind me of him, his name was Eddie, he was a wonderful man."

A look of wonderment and surprise spread across his face. "Really? I do?" He sat straighter, flexing his shoulders a bit, as if trying to be more mature.

I needed to watch where this conversation was headed, at least in his mind. Smiling, I chided, "Yes, but a much younger version."

He grinned. He understood. Glancing at his watch, he stood. "Looks like it's time I got downstairs and rescued the old man." With a teasing look, he added, "Some situations just need a younger version of a man to step in." He giggled, his voice cracking. He looked at my belly and waved at it. "Bye-bye, little chipmunk, I can't wait to meet you."

About nine thirty, there was a light rap on my door. "Psst, Katie, you still awake? It's Nina."

I pulled the door open and Nina handed me a plate of peanut butter cookies as she held something behind her. She set a tub of ice cream on my tiny table. "Isn't this about time for one of your cravings?"

She was dressed in her nightclothes. I was in the immense muumuu I'd made over at Hannah's the day after being rescued. "Honey," Hannah said, watching me cut and sew, "you made that thing big enough for a circus fat lady expecting triplets." I loved it.

Nina and I sat on the couch and giggled and talked, shoveling cookies and ice cream in our mouths as if we hadn't eaten in a week.

Another thing I liked about Nina was she didn't worry about her weight or diet. She was active, not skinny, not fat, and cared less what others thought of her. She seemed very mature for a sixteen-year-old high school junior.

"Tommy's asleep. Joey's probably checking to see if any more hairs grew in, and Ma and Dad's bed started to creak, so I grabbed this stuff and hightailed it up here." She saw my shocked look. "What? You think they're too old for sex? Well, if they are, no one's told them. At least once or twice a week, they still rev that bed up."

She laughed as I shook my head in disbelief. She put her ear on my tummy, then slowly moved it around. "I think I can hear its heartbeat, and I definitely just felt a kick, a good one."

"You think I didn't? Joey's calling it my little chipmunk now." We both laughed.

"So, what are you doing for Christmas? Going over and eating with the penguins again?"

"No, one time, Thanksgiving, was enough to last me a few years."

It was horrible. All those nuns and several priests around the big table in the rectory dining room. Everyone trying not to stare at me, the wayward woman kicked out of her house for being pregnant and no idea of what happened to the father. They all acted as if they talked to me, or got to know me, they might contaminate themselves. Poor Joe almost worked himself into exhaustion trying to keep conversation going, getting everyone singing afterward. It was terrible.

"Nope," I said. "Hannah has a small frozen turkey she's giving me, and I've invited Joe and the three girls in the front rooms over. We're sharing the cooking. It will be cramped, but anything is doable. Besides, those poor girls have nowhere to go and not enough money to get back home to their families." I waited a moment and wiped my eyes. "Plus, my sister Ginny is joining us. She's the one who snuck my sewing machine out of the house, called Joe and told him it was on the neighbor's porch and to come get it. Now, she's moving to St. Louis with my parents after the first of the year."

Nina hugged me around the neck. "That's wonderful to see your sister. Oh, Katie, you are unbelievable. Taking care of others when you have almost nothing yourself. How are you going to fix a whole dinner?"

"We've got it all worked out. Planning is the key. Sally Raye has a hot plate, so she's doing the green beans. Wilma is going to help bake the pies in here the day before. We're not stuffing the turkey, so it won't take as long, besides who needs all that bread anyway? Georgina and I will bake the turkey, plus cook the potatoes and gravy on the stove. We can't have anything else because there's no more burners. Joe's going to borrow some old plates and silverware from the rectory. Afterwards, we'll play charades, probably in the long hallway."

"You are amazing." Nina kissed my cheek, grabbed the softening ice cream container and left.

I crawled into bed. I am pretty amazing, I thought. I wriggled around, trying to get comfortable. A strong, black wave of panic washed over me. No, I'm not amazing. I'm a scared, twenty-year-old girl who's going to deliver a baby in a week or two. What am I going to do then? A baby? A real live baby who will need everything I can give it just to stay alive. I started to sob loudly. "I can't do this. I can't do this by myself."

I didn't hear my door open or realize I forgot to lock it after Nina left, but I felt someone crawl into my bed and a gentle hand start touching my forehead and cheeks.

"Honey girl, you can do this. You'll do this and do it jus' fine, or I'm not the daughter of a cotton-picking share cropper from Tennessee." Sally Raye held me and started rocking me. "I done heard you when I was a comin' out of the facility."

She called the little toilet room the facility. She joked it took her three weeks living here, using the old outhouse, because she was afraid of the modern plumbing. Hank finally told her she'd have to clean out the outhouse tank in the spring by herself if she didn't stop using it.

She kept stroking my face and rocking me till I calmed down. "I'm goin' to make us some of that comfy tea you like."

She brought me some and stuffed some pillows behind my back. "Can I check on junior?"

"It's called the chipmunk now. Hank's boy, Joey, said that's what it's to be called till it's born."

She giggled. "That boy is going to be one looker in a few years."

We both snickered.

"I know this ain't got nothin' to do with you cryin' and bein' all upset, but you know my hotplate has two burners?"

I half-smiled at her. Leave it to Sally Raye to be thinking of something else, which was probably good for me at the moment.

"Well, if I can find me some greens, would you care if fixed a few? It just ain't Christmas without some Tennessee tastin' greens. You yanks might even like'em."

As I laughed, she ran her hands over my huge belly. "Ain't you the one bin telling us this baby kicks when it wants to tell you sompthin? Well, it's sure sayin' a lot right now. Ain't it?"

"You're right, Sally Raye." Trying to copy her accent, I said, "And I just ain't bin a listenin'."

Chipmunk talked to me all night, in between pee visits to the facility, lying on my left side, my right, on my back, sitting up, it kept talking. Telling me we would be all right, but mostly telling me not to eat so much chocolate ice cream again.

~ * ~

Joey suggested the best names for the baby. On New Year's Day, I was lolling around like a pregnant whale. The entire house almost reverberated from the noise of the Sawicki clan on the first floor. Joey and Tommy knocked and came in. Joey handed me a napkin wrapped around three snickerdoodle cookies. Tommy looked cautiously around, he'd never been inside my room. I patted the couch beside me. "Tommy, there's a baby in my tummy, want to feel it kicking?" His eyes lit up as he stood in front of me.

I reached for his hand, but he snatched it away. "NO. I do it myself." He started to jab his fingers at my stomach.

I grabbed his hand, then his other as he tried to poke with that one. "Tommy, you have to be gentle, or you can't touch the baby. You could hurt me or the baby."

I was calm, but firm. His face turned red as he pursed his lips to spit at me. Switching both of his hands into one of mine, I grabbed his chin, pulling his face almost to mine. Glaring into his eyes, I said, "You may not spit at me, hit me or kick me. Now you decide if you can be nice or not."

Joey moved to pick him up, but I shook my head and kept staring into Tommy's eyes. His shoulders slumped and he lowered his head. "I be nice." He relaxed and let me gently move his hand around to the spot where the chipmunk was kicking. His five-year-old eyes lit up in wonder. "A real baby is in there? What's its name?"

"Good question. I need some suggestions."

"I know," Joey yelled. "I'll take a survey downstairs and come back with some ideas." He and Tommy trotted off as if on a mission from God.

I was quite certain of a boy's name. Either Edward Joseph or Joseph Edward. Eddie had to be in it, but whether first or middle I wasn't certain. Joseph was my brother's name. It's also Joey's name. *That's interesting,* I thought.

I struggled with my feelings about Eddie. Was he dead? Lying on some mountain or in some rice field? Missing in action? Was it possible he was ignoring the last letter I sent him? Did he buy a cheap ring just to get in my pants? I heard some guys did that with girls back home. How many nights have I lain awake, trying to figure it out and come to no valid conclusion? Torn between the Eddie I thought I knew and the total lack of communication or news. One time, I even called the Kaplans in Baltimore. Miriam was kind, but short. They heard nothing, wished me the best of luck with the baby, yet clearly were not interested in a long-distance relationship with me. I even try to read the obituaries in the newspaper when I can get hold of one, but haven't seen his name. I even went into the recruiting office and told them I hadn't heard from my fiancé in a long time. The man saw my belly and snickered. "Lots of girls like you haven't." I was too embarrassed to ask where else I might inquire.

I heard steps stomping up the stairs and Joey and Tommy rushed in again. Tommy carefully handed me a slice of apple turnover and Joey set a plate of dinner down—ham, chicken, au gratin potatoes, Jell-O salad. "Here, I fixed this up for you." Tommy leaned shyly against me and carefully reached out his hand to feel my tummy. "That's a good boy,

Tommy." I looked at Joey. "Do you have any names for my baby?"

With a flourish, Joey whipped a paper out of his pocket. I felt Tommy poking harder. Taking his hand, I said, "Easy, soft touches, Tommy." He jabbed harder. This time, I pushed him back. "You need to leave right now. If you can't listen to me, then you can't be around me. Now go downstairs." He laughed in my face and tried to kick at me, but Joey grabbed him and shoved him out the door. Still laughing, Tommy ran down the stairs.

Joey shook his head. "That kid is trouble and he keeps getting worse." Rattling the paper, he began reading. "Of course, at the top of the list for boys is Joseph, that's an excellent choice." He giggled as he rattled off more boy's names. "Now, there were all kinds of suggestions for girl's names. Every one of them already the name of some Sawicki, but I think I have the best one." He paused dramatically until I nodded for him to go on. "Krystina, with a K and a Y. I think that is the most beautiful name. It's Polish, and later she could call herself Krys, Tina, or Krysty. Isn't that just the prettiest girls name ever?"

"That is a nice name, and one I hadn't thought of."

"And," he excitedly interrupted, "it's similar to yours, Katerina, but just different enough so people won't be confused. I just love it." He began to stuff the paper into his pocket.

I tried to keep a straight face, he was so cute and sincere. I held out my hand for the paper. "Can I at least see the other suggestions?" He reddened as he reluctantly handed it to me. "What the heck, Joey? There's only two names on here. Yours and Krystina. Where's the rest of them?"

"Well, I didn't bother writing the other suggestions down, they were very mundane, too common for a child of yours." I forced myself not to laugh out loud at his use of the word mundane. He was trying so hard to impress me with his maturity. He pulled out a handkerchief, wiped his still red face and shoved his hands in his pockets. Looking at the floor, his feet shuffling, he muttered, "Actually, I didn't ask anyone else. Ma was looking at me kinda suspicious and I didn't want her to know I'd been up here."

270

"Joey, I love both these names, now get your butt downstairs before you get in trouble with your mom."

Just before slamming the door, he called back, "Dad loves both of them. Said they were good choices."

Chapter Sixty-One

Summer 1951

Having a baby is hard work. Raising one with no money and no husband is even harder. I haven't written in my diary for months. Too busy. Krystina is six months old, smiling, laughing, jabbering, crawling, trying to climb stairs. I chose Joey's suggestion for her name. It seemed to fit her to a T.

He hasn't stopped strutting around like a peacock since. Even more so since her baptism. We held a private one in the church. I didn't want a public one, didn't want to put that kind of pressure on my brother, Father Joe. I wasn't even sure we could have a public one, me being a disgraced woman. He loved the idea of a private one, even my choice of Godparents: Joey and Nina Sawicki. So, it was just Hannah, Joe, Joey and Nina around the baptism bowl with me and the baby. I made her dress out of sheer curtains and some satin I pulled off some threadbare coats. It was beautiful, probably would have won a prize for design, but those dreams are on hold for a while.

The three girls from down the hall couldn't take off work, but they surprised me that evening with a cake and ice cream party in their rooms. Several of the men roomers came, plus Hank, Mae, Tommy, Joey and Nina. I think Mae was glad no one tried to make this a typical, large, Polish baptismal party. I'm not sure she was happy about her two kids being the Godparents. Hank beamed when I told him my plans, said he'd take care of telling Mae.

At about ten this morning, Krystina and I were off to the rectory. I loaded her into the stroller Mae loaned me from Tommy. Twice a week, I go help Hannah sort clothes donated to the church's helping closet. I repair things, patch some, help launder, keep the shelves organized and labeled. Hannah loves the help and mostly plays with Krystina while I take over. Every so often, she keeps aside something she thinks I can use or remake for myself. She has a good eye for clothes and what they can become. Thanks to the Sawicki women, I need nothing for the baby. It's like a big game of swap and trade amongst them and they include me in it.

Right now, we're waiting for laundry to dry, so I'm writing while Hannah cuddles Krystina, she's teething and a little out of sorts.

Hannah put up a sign on the church bulletin board. The one with notices about needing help or being able to provide services. I get a few seamstress jobs from it, not a lot, but it helps a little. Joe reminds me I'm a long-term project and laughs when I stomp my foot and shake my fist at him. I know I'm a long-term project, but I don't want to be reminded of it. I want to be totally independent, but who would help raise my child? He keeps reminding me she's my top priority and my life will come together in God's timing. I get it, but sometimes, when all you have are two cans of soup, some wilting lettuce and overripe bananas, it's hard to stay calm, waiting on God's timing. I refuse to ask the Sawickis for food. They already send some up several times a week, plus everything else they do for me.

It's those nights my mind goes black when it's the worse. I think I'm standing on the edge of the Empire State Building where one more step or a slight slip will pitch me over the edge. I cry, sometimes sob. Almost always, Krystina kicks her little feet into my side, bumps against me, or wants to nurse. That reminds me we're still together and will be all right.

Some nights, Sally Raye bops in. I swear she has a microphone into my room. She starts fixing chamomile tea, or brings a wet washcloth to wipe my face. She yelled at me for locking my door when I'm home. "Ya'll yanks are strange. Ya'll should lock the doors when ya goin' out, not stayin' in." She's been seeing a lot of one of the long-time roomers from the second floor. Older guy, maybe thirty-five, but nice, stable, just kind of shy. I tease her she'll soon be off in their own little place and making babies. "Ain't sure I want one twenty-four/seven," she said. "It's nice gettin' chipmunk all riled up then walkin' away."

She's the only one that still calls the baby chipmunk. I do too, but only when I'm holding her and no one's around. She is such a happy little chipmunk with her daddy's brown eyes and dark hair and a touch of his tan skin. I think of him on those dark nights. Sally Raye seems to guess that and always reminds me the sun still comes up someplace in this big old world, even if we can't see it. She's right.

Chapter Sixty-Two

Nina and Joey
June, 1954

Krystina is no longer a baby. Ask her and she'll tell you in no uncertain terms she's a big girl and will get bigger someday. She is an absolute delight. She's finally given up dragging her dolly, Henrietta May, everywhere she goes. I made Henrietta out of old dishtowels I dyed, stuffed with rags and sewed on buttons and yarn. Joe bought her a real doll for Christmas, but Henrietta is still her favorite. I think partly because Hank helped her name it.

"Is this doll named Henry?" he joked when she proudly showed it to him

"No, it a girl doll."

"Oh, oh, a girl doll. Since she's a girl, her name must be Henrietta."

She nodded a little. Mae happened to stick her head into the room and Krystina hollered, "Mae, too."

"So," Hank said, "her name is Henrietta Mae then?"

Krystina nodded her head vigorously.

"Now, do you spell Mae with an e or a y?"

She furrowed her two-year-old brow in deep thought, then shouted, "A Y."

I did have to perform emergency surgery on Henrietta May after Krystina left her outside the door, in the hallway, for a dolly timeout while she took her own timeout inside. She, Krystina, had been sassy and somehow Henrietta had to serve the time too. Tommy came by, picked up the doll and carried it down the hall where he started to tear her apart.

That boy is so jealous of Krystina. Any attention his dad pays her or any of the grandchildren seems to set him off. No one, including Hank and Mae, even his teachers, understands how to deal with him. He is a handful and everyone seems afraid for the future of this mean, sneaky, rough child who loves to bully younger and smaller children.

I would love to move down to the one-bedroom apartment behind the Sawickis, but change my mind whenever Tommy acts out. Hank did mention I could use another bedroom for Krystina. "It'll give you a bit more space and we can't seem to make up our minds about renting out those rooms to women anyway." He sighed.

I don't think he and Mae have the energy to put into upgrading the third floor enough to attract more women, or even advertising it. Keeping up with Tommy takes almost everything they have.

I thought about making the room across the hall into Krystina's room. At first, I was afraid of what might happen if she woke up in the night and couldn't find me or I didn't hear her. Eventually, I realized I wasn't ready to have her away from me. I like having her in bed with me. We can make do in this tiny efficiency for a while longer, plus it's two floors of separation.

Nina is now in nurses' training at Cook County School of Nursing. She said she's getting an eyeful of real life and still loves delivering babies and working with pregnant women and young mothers. She comes home occasionally to visit and for some home-cooked meals. I miss her.

Joey grew into a handsome, kind, funny man, who just graduated from high school. He frequently comes up to chat, check on his Goddaughter, or tell me about some girl he took out. Sometimes, he'd imply they slept together. "She's a fast one, a lot of fun, but she's still looking for a ring." He'd notice my eyebrows raise and quickly add, "I'm safe. Always. Don't want to be a daddy yet. Sure as hell don't want to get married yet either."

All spring, prior to graduating, he's talked about joining the service. Yesterday, he sauntered in and said he joined the Air Force and was leaving next week. He handed me an invitation to a little party they were having this weekend. I congratulated him. I am so proud of him, but I will miss him. In bed that night with Krystina sleeping away, it hit me how much I will miss him and how much he reminds me of Eddie. I let myself have a cry. Not a sobbing, chest-pounding, gasping one, just a quiet, teary, lonely one. Krystina rolled over in her sleep and elbowed my ribs. It reminded me I was not alone and would be all right. Both of us would be all right.

Chapter Sixty-Three

Writings from Krystina (Krys)

After reading her mother's diary, Krys added the following.

I'm so glad Mom's diary was found. I realized her diary was mostly about meeting Eddie and having me. After that, I think I kept her too busy to write much. I didn't keep a diary, but have things I feel important to summarize about my life in the rooming house and what happened to us after we moved out. I think this will fill in the gaps for my children, Nate and Lacie, too.

Learning Math

My earliest memory of living in the rooming house is of counting the stairs, either the inside ones or the outside ones off the back of the third floor.

Mom believed structure and consistency were important, as well as setting expectations for my behavior. Her manner of discipline was usually to withhold a privilege or put me in a timeout.

I recall no spankings or her using a wooden spoon on my behind, but she says she did spank my bare little butt once. I was two and, according to her, doing quite well in potty training. I was out running up and down the long hallway, carrying my doll, and pooped my pants. When she discovered my odor and droopy drawers, she insisted I go into our room and get changed. She was not upset that I'd messed my pants, just wanted to get me changed. I had better things to do and put up a fuss. As she got the dirty diaper off me, I tried to jump up and run out our door. Running naked is fun when you're two.

She snatched me back and firmly told me to lay still while she put the clean diaper on me. I bit her arm, hard enough, she had a big bruise for some time. At that point, she gave me two quick cracks on my skinny bare butt. After that, she says I never bit her again and was very docile when she changed my dirty diapers. Guess I was a fast learner.

She was creative in trying to keep me busy and learning. Timeouts for being sassy took place on my little wooden stool she'd found somewhere, re-glued and painted. She'd sit me on it in our doorway, facing the fading painted plaster wall across the hallway. It was very boring, so I'd start counting or repeating my ABCs. One day when I was driving her nuts, she said, "You have entirely too much energy for this tiny room. Instead of running up and down the hallway, why don't you go up and down the back stairs? They're outside and your noise won't disturb anyone."

That sounded fun. The next day, she suggested it again, only added, "Why don't you count each step between here and the first landing going down."

I did. Soon I could tell her how many steps were between each landing. They varied, Hank said, because his Polish father mixed up his American numbers with his Polish ones. It took me several years to realize numbers are numbers. The old man simply screwed up and adjusted things as he went along.

Over time, Mom had me count them by twos, then threes and so forth. When I was in second grade, Hank was replacing some of the steps. He showed me how to measure with a tape ruler. How to measure twice and cut once. How to use a square, how to support the stairs with cleats. Eventually, he had me dividing and multiplying, even teaching me how to correctly figure the rise and number of steps needed for a given space. "With American measurements, not the old man's Polish ones," he joked.

As I grew, I loved helping him with projects around the old place, like sanding, painting, replacing windows, keeping roofs maintained. "Keeping a building in shape is more than just keeping it looking good. Anyone can slap paint over rotten wood. It's the things you can't see that you pay most attention to." This was true, because over the years, that old place looked faded, even decrepit, but I understand the bones are still strong and solid.

Obviously, learning math on the stairs as well as maintaining and fixing up old buildings affected my career. I became a Certified Public Accountant. My husband, Tim McGuire, and I bought, rehabbed, and rented out a number of two and three flats, plus several small apartment buildings, most in the Northwest side, around Wicker Park. Eventually, we sold all of them but one, which is Lacie's now.

A Pink Boy's Bicycle

Another vivid memory is of riding my bike up and down the third floor hallway and thinking how boring riding a bike was. I recall glimpses of all my toddler and childhood art work taped to the walls, on the doors of the empty rooms, taped as high as I could reach. Mom taped the higher ones.

Hank gave me a bicycle for my fifth birthday. One of his co-workers at the Ford dealership where he was the chief mechanic brought it in, said his kids outgrew it, and asked if anyone wanted it. I guess it was pretty rusty and beat up. Hank said he'd take it. A couple of guys from the body shop helped him get the rust off, repaint it pink, put a new chain and tires on, then added white handle grips with pink streamers, a new white seat, plus training wheels. The fact it was actually a boy's bike didn't bother me. What bothered me were those dang training wheels.

"Mama," I hollered, "I can't go fast with these little wheels, please take them off."

She told me the reason I couldn't go fast was because I was inside and only had about sixty feet of hallway. Still, I hollered and complained till spring came and she took me out on the sidewalk. I rode the whole block up and back, frustrated as only a five-year-old can be.

"Mama, these wheels have to come off. I can balance. See!" I jumped off the bike and stood on one foot. Holding there forever.

Mom was laughing so hard, Hank heard her and came from the backyard to ask what was so funny. "I don't like these little wheels. I don't need training. I already wear big girl pants and I can balance. See."

I remember Hank's eyes. I loved making him smile and laugh. He got a wrench and took the training wheels off. "Okay, Miss Smarty Pants, I'll give you your first push, then your mother's gotta take over. I'm too old to be running up and down the block."

He gave me a good push and I made ten feet before wobbling off into the yard.

"Not bad, not bad," he said. He raised his eyebrows at Mom and nodded for her to push me.

She did and I went about twenty-five feet before falling and scraping my knee and elbow. I didn't want her to see my tears so I hollered, "Goldarn it," real loud. She yelled at me not to use that word, or tried to. I think she was trying not to laugh. Several more tries, and I wobbled the entire length of the block without her holding me up. She showed me how to get off and turn the bike around, get on and take off by myself. That was it.

Later that evening, Hank came up to our room and handed me a popsicle, my favorite, a cherry one. He was always bringing us food or treats, telling us not to tell the boss lady. Mae would holler up the stairs, "Hank, I'm missing a cherry popsicle, know where it is?"

He taught me to holler back, "Hank's not up here, but the popsicle is really good."

"You scalawags!" She tried to sound mean, but by then, we knew she wasn't.

God, those were precious times. People ask me where I grew up, and I always say in a nine-by-nineteen foot, cold-water, third-floor efficiency room of a rooming house in Back-of-the-Yards. I would add, "It was wonderful!" They look at me in shock. Especially our Lake Forest neighbors who grew up on the North side or in the North Shore suburbs.

I usually don't tell them how little food was in our orange-crate cabinet, or in the old fridge that sounded like a motorcycle missing a piston. I also don't tell them for several years, we shared a tiny closet toilet with several other women, as well as an ancient, clawfoot, rusty tub in a separate closet where the hot water took forever to rise from the basement. That we considered ourselves the lucky ones on the floor because we had a kitchen sink and a skinny range with oven. That we never worried about the fifteen men who lived below us on the second floor. Hank and Mae ran a tight ship in who they allowed to rent there.

Chapter Sixty-Four

An Awful Day

One of my most vivid memories is coming home from school, probably February, 1958, when I would have recently turned seven.

I walked down 48th Street, holding the hand of a girl whose name I no longer remember. She was a big girl, probably in fourth or fifth grade, and I was very proud to be in first. She was quite motherly and frequently walked me to Ashland Street and watched me cross with the guard or the lights. I could get to Ashland by myself, but it felt rather nice to have a watchful older sister-type person take an interest in me, at least for those few minutes. We shivered in the cold, the wind off Lake Michigan making the smell of the stockyards and slaughter plants even worse. It was a smell people said they got used to. It seemed to my little nose, there were only bad days and very bad days. That day was very bad.

I knew the way home. I didn't the prior year when I was in kindergarten. From St. Bobola's Church and School, you walked across the playground to 48th Street. After that, you walked three blocks east. East was toward the lake, but I hardly knew what the lake looked like, we didn't own a car and never had money for fun stuff. Anyway, you walked three blocks east, then carefully crossed Ashland Street, a very wide, scary street with lots of traffic. You crossed with the walk lights or when the crossing guard, carrying her little sign, took you. Once across the street, you walked one more block on 48th to Justine, turned right and our house was on the right side of the street with the even numbers, past a big brick building that I didn't know what went on inside. I knew our address was 4822 South Justine, Chicago, Illinois, third floor. We didn't have a telephone. When necessary, we used the Sawickis', but Mom tried very hard not to use it often. I didn't know the phone number, but did know our landlords' names, Hank and Mae, Mr. and Mrs. Sawicki.

Just as school got out, while crossing the paved playground, we heard a loud crash and banging noise. As we walked down 48th, closer to Ashland, we saw a big truck, like a cattle truck with solid sides, in the middle of the intersection, lying on its side and could hear lots of noise, people shouting and sirens screeching. It was scary. It looked like the truck spilled stuff all over the street and onto the sidewalk, all the way up to the buildings. It smelled horrible and the girl said, "It's guts, oh no, I think I'm going to puke."

"What is it? I'm scared."

"It's guts from the slaughter plants, my dad works there and he calls it offal."

"Awful? What do you mean?"

She yelled, "O-f-f-a-l, not awful. Oh Mary, sweet mother of Jesus, how will we get around this mess?"

Men with shovels were trying to clear a path along the 48th street sidewalks so people could proceed to the intersection. Our crossing guard was on the other side of the mess near the traffic light and we were half a block back, totally confused as what to do. People started crowding us from behind. Kids trying to walk home from school, people who lived nearby, all were trying to see what was going on. I felt myself being moved forward. Shuffling along, I could see a narrow path shoveled next to the storefronts and hear the crossing guard calling to walk very carefully to her.

"Stay next to the buildings," she kept hollering.

Our hands held tightly, we tried to wait for our turn to proceed, but people kept pushing us. The smell became worse and we began to see innards from cows and pigs, even what looked like eyeballs, all in a thick soup of blood. Suddenly, the girl turned toward me and vomited, most of it going down my new-to-me burgundy wool coat, given to me for Christmas by the church benevolence committee.

Before she could apologize for puking on my coat, we were pushed forward again by several big kids, I think fifth or sixth graders. Someone yelled to walk single file and to be quick, but careful because it was very slippery. I started first, my arm stretched behind to hold hers, but she started to slip and let go to steady herself. I cautiously stepped most of the way over the reddish, greasy sidewalk and looked straight ahead, intently trying not to notice the intestines, and stomach linings, the eyeballs and other stuff swimming just a few feet to my left. I tried not to breathe deeply. Oh, it was so hard.

Only fifteen feet to go and the girl yelled and grabbed the back of my coat, apparently to keep from falling. I don't think she was trying to push me. I tried to shrug off her grasp, but suddenly found myself slipping and sliding. My feet flew out from under me. The girl barely made it around me without falling on top of me. I crashed to the ground, arms and legs flailing as I slid across the sidewalk, over the curb and into the street. Into the offal, screaming and screeching in desperate fear. Every time I tried to jump up, I fell again, on my back, my side, next on my stomach. All the while trying to keep my face out of the wretched smelly stuff. It seemed forever before I felt big hands grab me and carry me the rest of the way, stand me on my feet and hold me up until I could stand somewhat steady on my wobbly legs and slippery feet. My hair was matted with blood and guts. I reeked and the smell went deep into my nostrils and lungs. I was petrified, crying for my mama, my Uncle Joe.

"Who knows this kid? Someone needs to help her home. Where do you live, little girl? Hey, who knows this kid? C'mon, someone help her, she's a little one," bellowed the big man with yellow rubber boots who rescued me. He had been shoveling the offal away from the sidewalk.

I sobbed and cried harder. Stuttering, I looked up at the man. "I—I live at f—f—forty-eight t—twenty-two S—S—South Justine, and my mama's not home." I started to wail.

"Hush, hush, little girl. You'll be okay, your mama can give you a bath and wash your clothes. Hey! This girl needs someone to see her home. Hell's bells, it's only a block away! What kind of people are you? Ya just gonna stand around and watch?"

I tried to calm down and was surprised when I heard a voice say, "I know her, I'll get her home, she lives upstairs, but my ma will watch her till hers gets home." It was Tommy Sawicki from downstairs. Now one of the biggest boys in the school, he was twelve, going on thirteen, and large for his age. He took the edge of my sleeve and led me across Ashland Street. He didn't say a word, but kept me at arm's length, his other arm covering his nose. Several of his friends, older boys from eighth grade, hooted at him. He glared at them, then turned his head away from their noise.

"You wait out here on the step while I get Ma."

I tried not to cry as I waited by the sign tied to the porch railing that said, 'Rooms and Efficiencies.' Mama had to tell me how the second word sounded and that it meant a room with a kitchen, like ours, and how we had the only efficiency in the rooming house because Hank never converted more rooms into efficiencies and never changed the sign.

Mae Sawicki appeared at my side. "Lord, lord, little girl. Let's get you inside. Follow me, we'll go through the yard and down the side stairs to the basement where I can take your clothes off. Once that's done, you'll take a bath while I wash your clothes. Okay? Tommy, you did the right thing, now go inside and throw a blanket down the stairs. Next, go to the kitchen and make some hot chocolate. Young man, do not come down the stairs, got it?"

Tommy nodded, but I saw a smirk on his face. Tommy usually teased me, said bad words to me on the playground or in the yard when our mothers couldn't hear him. He was always sneaking around the rooming house and trying to scare me.

I remember shivering in the damp, stone-walled basement. I loved seeing the basement because they had an electric wringer washer with white clotheslines neatly hanging from the beams for days when things couldn't dry on the backyard lines.

Mae gingerly removed my smelly coat and laid it aside. Next, she pulled off my green plaid uniform, my little girl's t-shirt and high white socks and my plain white underpanties. She tossed them into the washing machine which was already starting to fill. She wrapped me in the blanket, picked me up and marched up the stairs with me to the bathroom where she ran warm water into the tub and told me to climb in.

"Can you wash yourself? Really good now, especially your hair. You may have to do it twice, there's the soap and the shampoo. The handle on the left is hot water, add more if the water starts to chill. You are to stay in here while I go back down and work on your coat and shoes and then upstairs to find some clean clothes for you from your room. Okay?"

I nodded vigorously. I understood and was very thankful. Despite my terrible smell, I was thrilled to be in Mae's bathtub and not having to take one in the third-floor tub. I liked taking baths at Uncle Joe's too. He was the pastor at St. Bobola's Church and School. He was my mom's big brother, much older than her, he'd joke to me. Occasionally, when Mom had work, Uncle Joe would tell me to stay after school and ask Hannah, his housekeeper, to give me a good bath. Not because I was extra dirty, but because he'd seen the tub we had to use. I loved soaking in the rectory tub, especially when Hannah added some bubble bath she kept hidden just for me. I loved her and my uncle, they always seemed to understand me and my mom.

It seemed like a long time waiting for Mae, so I added more hot water and washed my hair a third time. I loved seeing the shampoo bubbles flow down my shoulders and tummy. In Uncle Joe's tub, I would form angels with the bubble bath foam, but Mae didn't have any of those pretty bottles in sight.

I heard Mae tell Tommy she was going down to the basement to hang my wet things up, then upstairs to look for some clothes for me. She said for him to be good or he would get a whipping. He never hurt me, but once, he pushed a friend down in front of me and yelled bad words to the two of us. He played with other big boys who sometimes whispered to me, "Where is your daddy, little girl? Who is your daddy, Krystina? Do you really have a daddy?"

Clear as day, I remember hearing the bathroom door quietly open. Oh, no, it was Tommy! What should I do? Jump up, scream?

"Don't say anything or scream, little girl. I gotta take a piss and can't wait till Ma gets back with your clothes. Besides, you probably never saw a real dick before and it's time you did."

I sat paralyzed as he swaggered over to the toilet, lifted the seat and stood slightly to the far side of the toilet, purposely it seemed, so I could watch him unzip his pants and proudly pull his penis out. It looked like a hose with a pig snout on the end, but it was much bigger than the ones I saw on a baby boy Mom changed one time. I watched, in fear and fascination, as his pee tore into the toilet, listening to the sound it made. He shook the drips off the end, flushed the toilet, then turned to face me, still holding it in his hand. "It can get bigger than this. I got hair down here too, wanna see it?"

I shook my head, couldn't talk as tears formed in my eyes.

"Well, I think you should see it real close." He took several steps toward me, holding it in his hand as I watched it get bigger.

I was petrified and started to cry harder. I didn't want to see his thing. I was a little girl sitting naked in the bathtub. A little girl who still smelled cow guts in her nostrils and remembered thrashing around in that awful soup. Now this big boy was standing with his thing inches away from my face.

"Don't you make a sound," Tommy hissed. "Now be a good girl and touch it."

I tried not to sob out loud, put my little hands under my legs, and shook my head.

Suddenly, Tommy grabbed my wet hair and yanked my face closer till my lips were touching his pink, round pig's snout. "Open your mouth and lick my cock."

"No," I muttered through closed lips.

We heard Mae coming down the stairs. Tommy quickly put his hose back into his pants, zipped them up, and sneered, "Don't say a word, to my ma or yours, or I'll tell everyone your dad didn't really die in Korea like you always say. You're really just a whore's bastard child." He walked out and quietly closed the door as I rubbed my little fists at my eyes.

A minute later, Mae came in. "There, there, child, you're all clean now, there's nothing to be all upset about any more. Let's get you dressed and go have some hot chocolate Tommy made. I'll check on your shoes and coat and hopefully by the time your mother gets back from wherever she is, the stuff will be reasonably dry."

I nodded, cleared my throat and tried to talk without my voice shaking, "My mama had some work to do for a lady on the North side. She wants her to do the work at her place instead of ours."

"Well, that's good, maybe Katie can finally start getting some steady income from her seamstress work. She asked me earlier today to keep an eye on you if she wasn't back when you got home from school."

I didn't tell on Tommy. Not Mae. Not my mother. Even after he found me alone at other times and tried to do other things to me. I was afraid of him. I was afraid of other kids calling me a whore's bastard, it sounded like a bad name to be called, even if I didn't know what the word meant. I kept waking up some nights, thinking of Tommy's hose against my lips, smelling an odor of pee and something else I couldn't describe. Mom would cuddle me back to sleep. Still, I didn't tell her.

Chapter Sixty-Five

Tommy - Another Awful Day
Spring 1958

Mom got the job with Mrs. Jürgens on the North side and that was the start of a whole new life for her and me. Not an immediate big change, but one of gradual progress in her skills and self-confidence as a dress designer, and eventually, our finances. Mae agreed to keep me after school on the days Mom needed to work until five p.m.

I loved staying with Mae. They had a TV with a stereo and sometimes she'd play a record or radio music. Whenever Tommy was in the house, I would stay close to her, trying to help her, doing my homework at the kitchen table, setting the table for them for supper.

One spring day, shortly after Easter, I was staying with Mae when Tommy came home from school and told her he was going outside to play street hockey. Fine, she said, be home at five thirty for supper. I skipped up to her and asked if we were going to make cookies today.

"No," she replied, "not today. I have to go do some laundry downstairs, so you do your homework, then watch Mickey Mouse. When I come up, maybe we can play checkers. Okay?"

"Okay," I sang and ran to the couch where my folder and pink pencil box were. I was copying math problems when I heard the front door quietly open and Tommy tiptoed in.

"Don't say a word, hear? You do and I'll slap you silly." He walked over and stood in front of me, "Look, little girl, your mother was a whore and you're going to be one too. Sunday was Easter. Did you know that?"

I silently nodded, looking around for Mae, who I knew was in the basement.

"Of course, you did. Did you get any presents?"

I nodded again, not looking up at him, praying Mae or Hank would show up soon. Hank gave me a tiny, cute stuffed bunny and a big lollypop. Mom gave me a beautiful handmade card and an Easter dress she made from brand new material. I couldn't have been happier.

"Of course, you got presents, you little spoiled brat. My damn parents almost forgot to get me anything besides a chocolate bunny. They got me a shitty book. A book. I told them I wanted a new baseball glove. A goddamn book." He shook his head in disgust.

Suddenly, he unzipped his pants and pulled his hose out. It was getting big and thick. I cringed and tried to slide back on the couch. He grabbed my head, digging his fingers into my hair, and yanked my lips up to his penis. "Listen, you little whore, I want an Easter present from you. You're going to open your mouth and lick and suck me. Now open up."

I tried to shake my head and wriggle further back. Tommy dug his fingers deeper into my scalp and shoved his penis even tighter against my lips. I smelled pee, salt and body odor. I tried to keep my lips closed, hold my breath, and wriggle and scream all at the same time. Forcing himself even harder against my lips, he suddenly let go of his penis and grabbed my nose, squeezing it tightly. Through my tears, I could feel warmth, see his hair growing out of his pants zipper. I gasped. I couldn't hold my breath any longer. As I opened my mouth, desperate for air, Tommy jammed his thing into my mouth, pulling my head against him, pushing it further in, gagging me. Cutting my air off again. I could feel it throbbing, taste slime, feel its heat.

Just as I was ready to throw up, it was suddenly gone from my mouth. I watched Tommy fly across the room and crash into the corner of the hall archway. Stunned, he lay there, looking up at his father.

"Don't move, boy, or you'll be in a grave," Hank ordered, his voice low and fierce. He turned and picked me up, cuddling me to his shoulder, smoothing my hair as I began to wail. "Shhh, there, there. It will be all right, he will never bother you again."

Mae flew up the stairs and into the room. Tommy lay on the floor, his pants open, fear as well as revenge flashing in his eyes. He aimed a look of murder at his parents and me.

Mae turned to take me, but Hank told her, "Go call Mark, I'll hold her. Tommy is not going anywhere."

He turned and barked at Tommy, "Close your pants up and go lay on your bed."

I heard Mae, her voice shaking, speak into the phone, "Is this the

Catholic Boys' Home? I need to speak with Father Sawicki, please. I'm his mother, it's urgent."

She waited, her hands shaking so hard, I thought she might drop the phone. She kept glancing into the living room to see Hank holding me with his body turned so I couldn't see Tommy cowering on his bed. "Mark? Mark, is that you? Mark, we've had a problem with Tommy." She listened a minute. "Well, he apparently tried to force himself on the little girl who lives upstairs. No, no, she was fully clothed, but his pants were open. Oh God, Mark, I'm so sorry to call you, but Dad told me to and I agree, we can't handle this behavior. I just hope it's not too late for him. You know we love him. Yes, yes, I'll tell Dad what to say to him and he'll be ready at seven. Thank you, Mark, goodbye."

Mae walked into the living room and took me from Hank's arms. "Mark says to go in and talk to him, calmly, don't threaten him, simply tell him Mark wants him to come live with him at the Boy's Home and maybe that will be a better place for him. Tell him he needs help we can't give him. I think he'll be okay."

I watched Hank sigh, take a big breath, go to the front closet, take down a battered suitcase and go into Tommy's room where he closed the door. There was no yelling.

Mae sat down on the couch, holding me, cuddling me, patting my back. She carried me out to the kitchen for a glass of milk and a cookie. "Your mama will be home soon, everything will be all right. Tommy's not going to live with us anymore."

I could feel her heart beating, her body slightly shaking. Writing this today, I wonder how do you begin such a conversation with the mother of the little girl entrusted into your care? How do you tell a mother your nearly thirteen-year-old son was shoving his penis into her seven-year old-daughter's mouth?

That night, I snuggled in bed with Mom. Softly, she asked, "What happened today with Tommy?"

I curled tighter against her and began to cry. "Tommy's been mean to me ever since I started staying down there after school."

"What does he do to you?"

"He says I'm a bastard child and you're a whore so I'm a whore.

He unzips his pants and take his hose out. He wants me to touch it and kiss it. Today, he put it in my mouth 'cause he only got a book for Easter and he shows me his hair down there. He keeps asking me to take down my panties so he can see my pussy. He told me if I ever told anyone, he would beat me up. He would tell everyone at school my daddy didn't really die in Korea and that I don't have a daddy cause you're just a whore." I burst into loud, gasping sobs as Mom pulled me closer and hugged me even more tightly.

I could tell Mom was stunned. What do you say to your child, your little seven-year-old girl who didn't know the meaning of the words Tommy told her? I know Mom thought I was safe there. She had no idea Tommy was so perverted, so sick. She knew he was a bully, but it seemed Hank and Mae kept a tight eye on him.

I know she beat herself up. How could she not have seen this? Why did she stay in this dump? Why did she trust Hank and Mae? They were becoming more like parents to her every day and grandparents to me. Where could she go on such short notice? Should she ask Uncle Joe, to help her out? Again?

"Oh, baby, baby, I'm so sorry this happened to you. I'm so sorry. I didn't know Tommy was that nasty of a boy. Oh baby, please forgive me."

"Mama," I cried, alarmed to see her so upset, to feel her shaking too. "It's not your fault. You didn't know. Hank and Mae didn't know he was acting like this and I was afraid to tell anyone because Tommy told me he would hurt me bad."

At that moment, there was a knock on the door, and Mae's voice asking to come in. I sensed Mom wasn't sure she wanted to see them. I mean, what would she say? Could she stay calm? How were they going to stay in this house with Tommy still here? At that point, she didn't have a choice as I jumped off the bed and ran to open the door, flying into Mae's arms who was also in tears. Hank stood behind her, a worn, tired look on his face. Even to my young eyes, he looked ten years older.

"We hate to bother you. We understand if you never want to see us again, but we wanted to tell you a few things. May we come in?" Hank asked.

Mom nodded and they came in and sat on her old couch, me still wrapped in Mae's arms.

"Katie, we knew Tommy could be a bully and obnoxious. But we didn't know he was sneaking around, exposing himself and threatening Krystina like that." His voice trailed off.

Mom nodded with a look that said she didn't know what to say or how to respond.

Mae gently smoothed my hair and cuddled me against her shoulder. "Katie and Krystina." She gathered herself. "Tommy will not be living here anymore. His older brother, Mark, Father Mark from Boys' Home, has been telling us for some time how Tommy needs more structure. He has wanted him to come live with him at the Home. Just now, he picked him up." She paused. "Or he tried to. Tommy managed to run away before getting into Mark's car." She shook her head, then sighed. "When they find him...The police are looking for him. When he gets there, Tommy will get some psychological evaluations. Mark is quite certain Tommy is still young enough to change. We are so sorry, we tried to hold on to him too long. Please, please trust me, we had no idea of what he was doing, exposing himself and, forcing...Oh, my God." I felt her shudder. "We just didn't know."

I noticed Mom shudder, too. The impact Tommy might still be loose, running around the neighborhood, didn't enter my mind. It must have Mom's, though.

Hank patted her arm. "Katie, we really want you to stay. You're beginning to feel like family. I will stay home until Tommy is found and he will not be allowed back in the house unless Mark is with him. Even then, that would only occur on a weekend for a short visit. Please believe us when we say how sorry we are."

Mom stood and opened the door. "I have to think this over. To say I am shocked is the least I can say. I'm mostly worried about this little one and what effect it will have on her. I want to talk this over with my brother, Joe. I do feel better knowing Tommy is not in the building." She stopped, then added, "I am so sorry for you too. Good night."

Before crawling back into bed, we brushed our teeth over the rust-stained kitchen sink again. Why again, I don't know. Maybe it helped get the taste out of my mouth and Mom's mind, then we made a quick trip down the hallway to the shadowy, dank toilet closet. The wind was whipping from the North, driving the stockyard smell through the chinks around the windows.

I snuggled up against Mom. So close, Mom must have thought I was inside her womb again. "Mama, I'm sorry I did this, but I don't want to move. I love Hank and Mae, they are like grandparents to me. Grandparents I never had before. If Tommy is gone, Mama, we don't need to move."

"Baby, you did nothing wrong. Just next time a boy talks dirty to you, wants to show you his private parts, or wants to see yours, you scream and run for help. Never be afraid to tell the truth. Okay, sweetheart?"

The next morning, Mom used Mae's phone to call her boss, Mrs. Jürgen's, to say she couldn't come to work that day. With that call finished, she called the school to say I would not be attending that day and made an appointment to meet with her big brother, Father Joe.

I was excited to see my favorite uncle, even if he was the only uncle I knew. He talked lightly with me and then asked Sister Maria, the school principal, to take me to do some art projects while he talked with Mom.

In her office, Sister Maria asked me to draw pictures, pictures about who was in my family. I loved to draw. I drew a stick figure mommy and then three smaller figures, two on one side, further away from Mommy and one close to Mommy. "This is my mommy, this is Uncle Joe, I mean, Father Joe..."

"It's all right to call him Uncle Joe, only in the classroom do you need to call him Father Joe," said Sister Maria.

"Can I call him Uncle Father Joe?"

"I think that's a wonderful solution. Now, who are these two people?"

"These are Hank and Mae, don't you know them? They are almost like my grandparents who I never had before."

"Can you add some pictures of the other kids you know, especially the ones you see most often?"

I got busy, my little fingers flying, making stick figures, some big, some small. I used different-colored crayons with lots of flourishes and flowers.

"Wow, that is so nice. Who are these people?"

"These are everyone I know and like, some are my best friends."

"Do you like everyone in that picture? You can draw people you may not like too, this is only for you and me, okay?"

Ooh, did I have to? I squeezed my eyes shut for a minute. With determination, I picked up the fattest black crayon available and made a simple stick figure. I paused a minute, before picking up a purple crayon and drawing a short line at the crotch of the figure's legs. That's when I burst into tears.

Sister Maria gathered me into her arms and soothed me till I quieted down. "You did nothing wrong, you know that, don't you? This wasn't your fault. Tommy acted very badly, he's an angry boy and was taking it out on you. Do you want to talk about it, how Tommy made you feel scared?"

I sat for a few minutes, thinking. I straightened up and looked Sister Maria in the eyes. "No, he was a bad boy, but he is going away. Mommy, Hank and Mae won't let him ever bother me again. I'll be fine. Can I go now?"

Mom or Mae walked me to and from school for the next week.

I never forgot Tommy's hose swinging when he peed in front of me. Nor the other times he exposed himself and tried to force me to touch him. The smell of it, the pee taste and salty taste on my lips and the gagging as he forced it into my mouth is still with me to this day. I still recall the look of rage and revenge he glared toward me. No, I never forgot. Not even as an adult. Not even after I married and had children. I never told anyone about the lifetime of nightmares I've experienced, not frequent, but often enough to recall them for months at a time. I never discussed Tommy again, with anyone. Barely mentioned him to Tim, my wonderful husband, who has always, yet patiently, wondered about my lack of interest in intimacy.

I was a happy, smart, energetic good girl. Mom had enough on her mind, just keeping us fed and clothed, and I didn't want her to worry about me. I determined to never cause her to be upset again. Plus, I never wanted to move away from Hank and Mae's. They were the family I never had.

Chapter Sixty-Six

Adopted

That same summer of 1958, the tenants in the one-bedroom apartment behind Hank and Mae moved out. Hank asked if Mom wanted it at only slightly more rent than the efficiency. We moved in the first weekend of August, after Mom painted the walls and Hank installed new linoleum.

I was thrilled. A separate bedroom that Mom found two single beds for, my own bed. A bathroom, complete with green tile, a tub with a shower and pull-around curtain, a sink with storage below it, AND a mirrored medicine cabinet built into the wall above the sink. It seemed like pure luxury to a second grader. At least this second grader.

Mom never expected anything from the Sawickis. Meaning she never planned on them giving us some food, or took for granted Mae watching me after school. She consistently expressed her appreciation for their help.

For our first Thanksgiving in the apartment, Mom thawed a small chicken she planned to bake, along with some sweet potatoes, and a home-canned jar of green beans Mae gave her when she finished her garden canning.

We were playing Scrabble. The noise next door kept increasing as more and more Sawickis rolled in. Mae was up early, stuffing a huge turkey and boiling potatoes to mash. More smells wafted under our door as the Sawicki kids brought pies, salads, sweet potatoes and Polish pastries.

Our door suddenly burst open and Patricia, the oldest, marched in. She was well pregnant, smoking a cigarette and had a bottle of beer in her hand. I guess those weren't considered damaging to the unborn in the late fifties, as all her children turned out fine. She carried a flattened brown paper bag with some writing on it in black crayon and lots of smaller names in other colors.

"Okay, you skinny little twerps," she yelled, as others crowded around, pushing her further into our small living/dining area. "We just took a vote and decided to officially adopt you two. You're Sawickis now, but you don't have to change your last name."

She handed Mom the paper bag. "This here is a legal document, now get your skinny asses next door and quit hiding back here like little church mice." She pulled Mom and me into a bear hug, ashes dropping on us, a drop of beer spilling on my dress. "You two are so tiny. How the hell can you call yourselves Polish?"

The little kids ran up and hugged me. "Hurray! You're our real cousin now." They pulled us next door into all the hubbub.

That evening, after an afternoon of eating, playing games, racing up and down the stairs until one of the old residents yelled he was calling the president of the USA if we didn't quiet down. After all the pie was gone, the dishes done, Mom and I crashed in our apartment. Mom picked up the brown-bag certificate.

"Just think, Krystina, how lucky we are to have ended up in this old house with all these wonderful people." She managed a teary wink. "Who'd a thunk it?"

The certificate read
Hear Ye Hear Ye
This certifies that
Katie and Krystina Kozlowski
are officially ADOPTED into the Sawicki Family
November 27, 1958
(Now they're really stuck with us)

All sorts of signatures, some legible, some little kids' scribbles, surrounded the black crayon writing.

I remember hugging Mom. "This is the bestest day of my whole life. I have real cousins and real aunts and uncles and real grandparents. Oh, Mommy, I never want to leave here. We have a great big family now."

Chapter Sixty-Seven

Lessons Learned

I was seven, it was late on a Friday afternoon right after we'd moved into the back apartment in 1958. I was sitting on the porch swing, reading a book, probably Nancy Drew. I was a voracious reader and read several grades ahead of my class. I was going to solve mysteries when I grew up, just like every other little girl in our neighborhood.

Hank and Mae were out, maybe to visit the cemetery with John's grave who died in the war. Mom was deadheading some of the lilies and flowers on the side of the house. An old car with ladders strapped on top pulled up and a small man with black hair, brown eyes and brown skin climbed out. He was young, that much I could tell. When he came around behind the car, I noticed his left arm hung down, just dangled, and his left shoulder bent forward.

He gave me a big smile and paused on the sidewalk. Very politely, he asked, "Who do I see about renting a room?" His voice had an accent.

I jumped off the swing and hollered, "Mom, there's a man here who wants a room and he talks funny."

He covered his mouth with his good hand to hide his smile.

Mom came around the corner and stopped, looking at him intently, almost like she was spooked. She finally smiled, stepped closer and stuck her hand out. "Hi, I'm Katie, this is my daughter, Krystina. Sometimes she has a big mouth. The Sawickis are gone right now, but I expect them back shortly."

"Mom. Mom. Listen to him talk. It's so cool."

"Is cool a new word you picked up from TV?" she muttered, trying not to smile.

"Yes. The beatniks say cool all the time." I giggled.

I was right, they did and it was cool.

Both of them laughed at me. "I'm not a beatnik," the man said as Mom shook her head.

"I didn't realize my accent was so cool, especially around here."

He seemed to check to see if Mom was still smiling before he went on. She was, still with a look of wonderment on her face. "Well, as you guessed, I'm Mexican. I grew up in Tijuana, Mexico and San Diego, California." He glanced down at me, my eyes wide with amazement. "Those places are a long ways from here."

"Krystina, would you run back to the apartment and bring back three glasses and the pitcher of iced tea? Maybe we can have something cool to drink till Hank and Mae return."

"Can she carry all that?" the man asked in concern.

"Of course, I can. I'm not little. Watch me."

He chuckled as I marched off, almost indignant.

I heard Mom say, "I'm sorry I stared at you, but you look so much like someone I used to know, you could almost be his brother, but he didn't have any younger ones."

I finally struggled back with the glasses under my left arm, holding napkins between my fingers, my right hand carefully grasped the heavy glass pitcher with ice cubes bouncing around in it. I gripped a plastic bag of homemade oatmeal-raisin cookies between my teeth.

He was sitting on the steps, but jumped up and gently took the pitcher from me. Looking at Mom, he asked, "Is she always this determined?"

Mom had tears in her eyes, just a few, she wiped them and nodded. Then laughed.

"You know that's part of our heritage, don't you? Determination, hard work, quick thinking, that's part of our blood."

"Whose blood?" I demanded.

What were they talking about? Why did he act like he knew something about me that I didn't?

"I was talking about Mexican blood, that's all," he replied quietly.

Mom was turned around by the end of the porch, blowing her nose. "Krystina, could you pour the tea and give Mr. Rodriguez, Manuel, a glass, and a cookie on a napkin, please?"

"Please call me Manny. That's all I go by."

We sat and drank our iced tea in silence. Mom still seemed a little shocked. Draining his glass, Manny started telling us about his skills and abilities with house maintenance and upkeep. He could paint, repair, refinish, saw, pound. Anything needed to maintain or even build a house.

I kept looking at his left arm. When he wanted to move it, he picked it up and placed it where he wanted it. For a while, he had it on his legs, across his lap and held his cookie between its fingers. Once, he lifted his left hand by placing his right hand with his tea glass under his wrist, and lifting it to his mouth to bite his cookie, then lowered it back to his lap.

"How? How do you do work stuff with your left hand?"

I heard Mom cough behind me, but he just waved his good hand at her, as if the question was all right to ask. "Well, that's a very good question. I have to move it where I want it. Sometimes I wear a sling across my shoulder and chest that I can hold it up with, keep it in the same place. Once it's there, I can use my fingers some, or hold things in them."

"Does it hurt?"

"No. Not really. It looks worse than it is."

"After you move in here, can you teach me Mexican?"

He and Mom both laughed.

"I think that's still an if. A big if. So far, I haven't found any rooming houses around here that want me."

My eyes got big, but before I could say anything, I heard car doors slamming and the garage door squeaking down. I took off running around the house, yelling, "Hank. Mae. There's a nice man here who wants a room. Come meet him. He's really cool. He's from Teewanno and San Dago and he talks Mexican."

Mae stared at me, grabbed the grocery bag from Hank, and rushed toward the side door, muttering at him, "Don't you dare. I'm warning you, don't you rent to him."

"C'mon, Hank. Come meet him. You have room on the third floor, no one else is up there and you haven't rented to women in a long time." I grabbed his grease-stained, calloused fingers and pulled him around to the front porch. "Hank, this is Manny." I bowed like a princess presenting to the Queen, or the King. "Hank, you can give him the efficiency. That way, he could cook his own kind of food, he probably eats Mexican food, whatever that is. Oh, and Hank, you're getting kinda old and he can help you around here, he's very handy. See, he even has ladders on top of his car and tons of tools inside it."

Mom almost choked, she was laughing so hard. Manny's eyes were huge, like a tornado just raced through. Hank stood there, trying to be serious, but finally doubled over in mirth. I caught a glimpse of Mae looking out the living room window at us. She did not look happy.

Finally, Hank stuck out his hand and introduced himself. "I don't know. I just don't know. If I rent to you, you'd be the first spi..."

"The first spic?" Manny's eyes glared. "I prefer the word Mexican."

Spic? I could tell Manny didn't like that word. I thought it must be a bad word for Mexicans. I hadn't heard it before. Mom told me it was bad to call colored people niggers. Spic must be the same for Mexicans.

Manny paused, swallowed. "You realize there will be more and more Mexicans coming to Chicago in the years ahead. Maybe someone needs to take a chance on one of us in this neighborhood. I guarantee you, I will do my race proud, just like someone once did in your family." He turned around, poured himself some more tea and took a long swallow.

Hank almost staggered over to the steps, picked up my glass of tea, poured more into it, plopped down heavily on the middle step and took a long drink. He wiped the sweat from his forehead. He almost mumbled, as if to himself, "My parents came from Poland. My dad and mother built this place in 1887." He waited, his eyes closed, his brow creased. Shaking his head, he poked Manny with his glass. Manny turned and sat down beside him. Hank tinked his glass against Manny's, like a toast. "Ready to go see the efficiency?"

Mom looked away, her eyes glistening.

I didn't grasp everything that just happened. Had no idea Manny would be the first Mexican to live in our neighborhood of Polish and white immigrants, or the significance of such. All I knew was, he seemed like a nice young man who needed a place to stay and who could teach me a new language in a place where Polish was so common, it was boring.

~ * ~

It would be years before Mom told me I was half-Mexican. More years after that before she explained the shock on her face that day was because Manny so closely resembled my father, Eddie Vargas. That he was the first person she told since being kicked out by her parents that I was half-Mexican. How proud of me she was that I didn't see color, just a good man.

Several years ago, I asked Mom why she didn't tell me sooner.

"Two reasons," she replied. "One, in that day and age, when you were the daughter of an unwed mother, I figured you had enough to deal with without people knowing you were only half-white. Think of all the prejudice there was against the Mexicans back then, less than the African Americans, but still a lot."

"What was the second reason?"

"You'd learned what I wanted you to learn. People are people, regardless of their color, background or abilities. Family is family regardless of bloodlines." She hugged me and pointed to the brown paper bag adoption certificate, now professionally framed and hanging on her entrance wall. "You learned very well."

I looked at her in confusion, then realization slowly set in. I *am* half Mexican, my daughter is in a serious relationship with a dark brown man whose parents were born in India, my son is a cerebral palsy quadriplegic who is gay with all sorts of friends of all colors, straight, gay, disabled, and able-bodied. Since she was young, my daughter has brought home strays and misfits looking for family. That doesn't count the dogs and cats she snuck in. Our holidays frequently look like the United Nations. And on and on. All because Hank Sawicki dared to rent a room to an unwed, pregnant nineteen-year-old in 1950.

Chapter Sixty-Eight

After the Rooming House

Okay, I'm not finished yet. In 1965, I enrolled at Josephinum Catholic High School on the Northwest side in Wicker Park. I commuted by city bus, but due to racial tensions that became too risky. Mom bought a car and she began driving and picking me up on her way to and from her shop in the gold coast area. It was a tough four years, lots of turmoil as whites tried to adjust to black kids enrolling and demanding equal rights. I tried, and for the most part succeeded, at getting along with most kids regardless of color. I think my mom's influence and underlying philosophy that people are people helped me accept and listen to the differences in cultures. It wasn't easy, but I wouldn't go back and change anything.

In 1966, we rented a lovely, large three-bedroom upper unit of a two-flat in Wicker Park. Mom's business was expanding and the commute time with taking me to school and back was proving inconvenient. There were many tears shed when we moved out of the rooming house, but it felt like it was the time to finally leave. Many of the Sawicki children already left the Back-of-the-Yards area for Roseland or even the Southwest suburbs. Now with a car, it was nothing to travel out to visit them or see Hank and Mae. Little changed in terms of family relationships. I shed more tears when, in the process of moving, I discovered I lost my dolly, Henrietta May. My bed felt empty for years and I could never figure out where I lost her.

In 1967, Mom bought a condo just off Lakeshore Drive. She also opened a small private, by appointment only, exclusive design and resale shop in the Carbon and Carbide Building on North Michigan Avenue.

I graduated high school in 1969, then attended Loyola for my Bachelor's in Accounting, got a job, passed the licensing test as a CPA, obtained my Master's in Accounting, and married a tall, handsome, red-headed Irishman, a lawyer named Tim McGuire. In addition to our careers, we purchased, rehabbed, and rented out flats and apartments. Shortly before Lacie was born in 1983, we moved to Lake Forest.

Mom became a huge hit with the ritzy women of Chicago. Designing new dresses, remaking existing ones, selling older ones on consignment, remaking and selling the consignment dresses. She kept track of all the major social events so that Mrs. A. didn't wear Mrs. B.'s former dress, or if she did, she remade it so no one could say they remembered it.

Sometime in the eighties, she figured New York City could use her services so she opened a similar business there, flying monthly to the Big Apple to consult with her assistant, another designer. Eventually, she sold that business and concentrated on designing new dresses for clients in Chicago, though some flew in from all over the country for fittings and her work.

For office space, Tim and I bought and rehabbed an old warehouse-type building on the near west side, close to where Oprah eventually bought. He runs his law practice there, he focuses on family business law (he also has an MBA, as do I) and says he sometimes feels more like a social worker than a lawyer.

I branched off from my original employer. I built a CPA firm that also focuses on family and small businesses. Our offices are in the same building where we share office services. We also lease out office space in our building.

Lacie was born in 1983. A whirlwind who has not slowed down yet. Our son Nate was born in 1988 with cerebral palsy. At that time, we sold our rental properties to free us up to spend more time at home, caring for him. On the one hand, his care seems intense, he has to be fed, toileted, dressed, bathed. However, it quickly became normal to us, even the hiring of caregivers to assist, many who became family too. He is currently studying psychology at the University of Illinois, and, when not drinking beer with friends, trying to decide what he wants to be when he grows up.

Lacie is a social worker and works with wards of the court, most who are adults and/or disabled. She is already working on her Master's degree.

As Mom says, "Who'd a thunk?"

Diary 5

Walentina Adamczyk (In Poland-Adamowicz)

Born, Warsaw, Poland, October 12, 1868
Died, Chicago, October 23, 1918
Diary discovered in 2011 under aged shelf paper in the back
apartment closet, and translated into English by first-generation Polish-
American students at the University of Illinois-Chicago.

Chapter Sixty-Nine

My Secret Life

December 12, 1895

My Darling Josef and Family,

I write this in fear of what you will think of your loving wife and mother once you know my history. Hopefully, my motherly and wifely love for you will overweigh the scales on which you judge me. I pray you will see how I overcame much to be the good wife and mother I was. I hope you will understand how I did not want this information to be told until after my death. Think of the grief it would have caused you in our neighborhood, parish and school.

The first thing to say that will shock you is that I am one hundred percent Jewish. The second is my parents were part of a white slavery and smuggling ring in the old country. The third is I both loved and hated my parents.

My mother was from a town near Krakow. She was fourteen when she married my father who was twenty-six. It was an arranged marriage between her father and my father. My father paid a good price for her so that he could place her in a brothel somewhere. Father found young, usually naïve, country girls, married them, secretly divorced them, and sold them to brothel owners, usually in the big cities of Krakow, Vilna and Warsaw.

However, for some reason, my mother's vitality and brightness intrigued him and he took her home with him to his big house in Warsaw. He never did divorce her, though I later realized he continued to illegally marry other young girls to sell. I am convinced my mother knew what her own father was doing when he sold her. She was one of five daughters and her father was also part of nefarious smuggling and white slavery operations perpetuated by a tiny group of Jews who helped give good Jews a bad name.

I am nursing Henryk as I write. He is three months old and such a beautiful baby. I am so glad he is big and looks just like Josef, his wonderful Polish father.

I was a tiny but healthy baby born October 12, 1868, twelve months after my parents' marriage. I'm not sure how I would have dealt with becoming a mother at age fifteen, but probably would have done well. I do take after my mother in spunk and energy. My father was thrilled over me and doted on me, though, thinking back, I wonder if he might have had other children elsewhere.

We lived near an exclusive area on the outskirts of Warsaw. Our home was actually two connected homes on a secluded corner. One home faced a wide, tree-lined boulevard. The other home faced a narrow, dead-end side street. There was a portico that connected the two homes whereby horses and buggies could pause to let out passengers and continue on to the stables which formed a courtyard. Our home, the front one, was three stories, though from the street it looked like a two-story with a large, windowed attic. The first story contained a small fashionable vestibule with several chairs and three doors leading into other rooms. The left door led into our large, luxurious drawing room; the middle led into a hallway that went to the dining room and kitchen and on through to the portico; the third led into my father's and his brothers' jewelry offices.

The second floor held a tub room, plus four bedrooms, including one connected to mine for my governess. The third floor was achieved by a hidden doorway with narrow stairs and included a number of small bedrooms. At the end of that hallway, another door led to a skinny, low, enclosed hall that went over the portico to the second house. I was never to go up to the third floor, but being the inquisitive child, I was, I managed to several times.

The first floor of the connected second house possessed several small sitting rooms, all opulent, one with a hand-carved wooden bar for spirits, two tub rooms for customer baths, a kitchen and dining area accessible only to the staff, and a laundry area that opened onto the outside next to the stable's courtyard. The second floor contained a number of small, but well-appointed bedrooms. The third was filled with many, small, basic bedrooms, similar to the ones on the third floor of my home.

My early years were spent in luxury. A governess, Agata, doted on me. Other women cleaned, cooked, washed our clothes and were thrilled to be around me. My young mother loved being with me, but frequently remonstrated with the staff not to spoil me. My father was gone a lot, but when he was home, he insisted on walking me around the neighborhood, or taking me to synagogue, even though I had to sit with my mother on the other side of the screen.

By the time I was six, I possessed a basic understanding of the family businesses. By the time I was eight, I understood it well. My world collapsed when we fled Warsaw.

The family business was several generations old. My grandfather increased it and set up the separate, but interrelated divisions with his three sons. I only recall meeting him a few times when I was four. One uncle, I called him Guesthouse Uncle, lived in the attached guest house. That's what we called it. It was a brothel. He was in charge of the women. He trained them in good deportment, personal cleanliness, learning to carry on good conversations, eating healthy, tracking their menses. Apparently, my Jewish family understood a woman's cycle, or tried to, in order to avoid pregnancy. He attempted to keep the women fresh, make them feel important.

There were a number of brothels in Warsaw, but ours was high class, and one of the most exclusive. Women who had bad attitudes, allowed themselves to become slovenly or dull were transferred to other brothels the extended family owned. Some were sold to the common ones. Though there were some legal regulations and inspections, Guesthouse Uncle was also in charge of bribing the local police and city officials, plus gifting the desk staff at the nice hotels to provide discreet referrals.

My other uncle, I called him Jewelry Uncle, was in charge of the jewelry business. He owned a well-respected store in downtown Warsaw and an expansive home where he lived. He reviewed the jewels coming into our home. It was he who decided which ones to sell in his store, to wholesale to other stores in other cities or to hold in one of the secret safes until such time it was felt secure to sell them.

My father was the procurer. He traveled extensively throughout Eastern Europe, sometimes Western, finding jewelry, valuables and coins. Some, he bought from thieves, some, he swapped for, some, he bought from unsuspecting folk. Some, he outright stole.

On his travels, he also procured young women, usually aged fourteen to sixteen, occasionally seventeen or eighteen. Unlike my mother, most were simple, but all were mesmerized by his charm, good looks and wealth. Some girls, he bought from their fathers, others he sweet-talked their widowed mothers into allowing them to move to the city by promising them jobs to help support their destitute families. Others, he kidnapped. He brought only the best ones to my uncle in the guest house. The rest he sold to other brothels.

One night when I was around six, I awoke to sounds of a horse neighing. I ran into my governess' room, but her bed was empty, as was my mother's. I ran downstairs to the portico to see my father handing a bag to my jeweler uncle and three young women disembarking from the carriage, their eyes wide with fear and wonderment. I watched my mother and governess run up and hug them. "You'll be fine, we'll take good care of you," my mother said. Soon other women from the third floors came down in their nightclothes and ushered the new girls inside.

"Come, let's eat and give you a bath," one said on their way inside. "You will get used to our work and we are well taken care of. Please, don't be afraid."

I will never forget how confused one of the girls looked. She couldn't have been more than thirteen.

Shortly after that experience, I realized how, on several days or evenings during most weeks, my mother would be absent from our house for two or three hours, but the governess would be with me. Other days, my mother would be with me and the governess absent. One evening, while my mother was sorting jewelry with my uncle, I snuck up to the secret door and ran down the third floor hallway toward the portico door. Just as I got there, my governess came through the door from the guest house, wearing a gorgeous robe opened to show a revealing thin negligee.

"What are you doing up here? You are never to be on the third floor." She was very upset with me. She took my hand and firmly led me to my room, but she didn't inform my mother. I remember several of the girls, who on occasion worked around the house, probably during their menses or fertile times, smiling at me and patting my head. A day or so later, when I was on my bed and supposed to be reading while the governess sat in her room, stitching, I heard Mother slip down the hall. I snuck to my door and watched her, wearing a beautiful robe, enter the secret door. She too was gone for several hours. Later, after my world totally fell apart, Father told me both women were sought after by some of the top officials and businessmen in Warsaw and commanded the highest prices. Neither wanted me left without one of them present, which was the reason they split their limited time with the select men.

Agata, my governess, was Catholic, as were many of the girls in the brothel. My father procured Jewish, Catholic, Protestant, and Eastern Orthodox girls. On Fridays, I went to Temple with my parents where I heard the prayers and learned our orthodox Jewish customs, many of which we didn't follow. On Sundays, I attended a Catholic service with Agata where I learned the prayers, holidays and all about the saints. It didn't seem confusing to me, I already spoke Polish, German, Yiddish and some Russian. Knowing two religions seemed normal. My life was contained in the home with only occasional jaunts into the city. I didn't attend school. The tutors came to me.

I just realized the tutors were the same ones who worked with the girls in the guesthouse, trying to improve their knowledge of history, languages, basic math and social abilities. The brothel girls were not to remain simple, or just cheap whores, but women who a gentleman could converse with. Single gentlemen occasionally took their choice girl to social functions. Occasionally, one asked to marry their favorite and were allowed to, after paying a steep price to my uncle who helped invent a relevant history for the girl that would be accepted by society.

It was the fall of 1876, I was almost eight, when my entitled, secretive child's world came apart, nearly twenty years ago. It hardly seems possible all of the changes I have experienced. Today, here I sit, rocking a beautiful baby, married to a wonderful man who accepted without judgement my background in the baths, who now knows I am Jewish and loves me too much to care, he even knows a bit of my scoundrel family. He will learn much more when he reads this.

Eugenia, my brilliant six-year-old daughter, just arrived home from school and is begging to hold her brother. The rooming house has such benefits. The women's matron or the men's ward take turns, in fact, they argue almost daily, over which of them will escort Eugenia across Ashland Street to and from school. Our rooming house is a fine home without all the secrets I was subjected to as a child. Well, other than my secrets I now write. I pray all will forgive me when they read this someday.

Chapter Seventy

Leaving Our Home

For several months, even as an almost eight-year-old child, I was aware of increasing tension in our home and amongst the staff. Jews were under more and more pressure to leave Prussia. Even the Poles, especially the peasants, were being treated badly. Jeweler Uncle's business was declining as fewer non-Jews shopped with him, forcing him to wholesale his merchandise further away. My father reported being challenged more frequently as he traveled, ostensibly to purchase jewelry.

One day, Mother and my two uncles received word that Father was imprisoned for bilking a widow in Krakow. Mother rushed by train to him, and, after a week, managed to negotiate his release. I'm certain jewels and coins helped in the negotiations. At the same time, my guesthouse uncle was ill with fever, chills, rashes, sores and increasing weakness of his eyes and mind. The inspectors were inspecting the girls more often and telling some to leave the city. Long-term customers were stopping by to yell at him or my mother about health matters they claimed were coming from the girls. That was the first time I heard the word syphilis.

My jeweler uncle's store was inspected by city officials more frequently. They threatened to close him down or arrest him for selling suspected stolen goods, but mostly because he was Jewish.

One night, I was awakened at midnight. My parents, Agata, Jeweler Uncle, his wife, their twenty-one-year-old son, Wiktor, and nineteen-year-old daughter, Evangeline, and two of the younger, most pretty girls from the guest house, all squeezed into the carriage. We traveled as fast as we could to a train station east of Warsaw. Jeweler Uncle was afraid we would not be allowed to board at the main Warsaw station.

The train was filled with Jews and Poles leaving the country. So full, the first-class carriages were filled and we were told to squeeze onto the peasant benches. Still, there wasn't enough room for the ten of us, so Uncle handed some coins to the porter and demanded he remove several peasants which he did, causing a huge uproar and many oaths to be hurled at us, words I never heard before.

Things quieted down and a little girl sitting in front of me turned and smiled at me. When I smiled back, she spit in my face. My mother told me to wipe my face off and not to cry and for Father to be quiet. "There will be worse things in life then getting spat upon," she said.

I did not know how correct she would be, but that was my first lesson in becoming indomitable.

Our travel to the ship and on to New York is a blur of impressions seeming to arise one after the other from being only eight at the time. I remember Jeweler Uncle buying bread for all the peasants in our train car, then making them irate again by bribing another porter to bring our family some first-class food. The first-class rooms on the ship were filled, so we booked two smaller rooms in second class. The room was too small for my parents, me, Agata and the two girls, so Father moved the two girls to steerage, where he took a family berth, calling the girls his younger sisters. Now, I think he did that to make some money off the girls on board the ship as several times Mother, Agata and myself stayed on deck for hours at a time while our room was in use.

I remember an older first-class woman screaming at my mother for wearing her jewelry which was stolen several months before from her Krakow home. My mother graciously removed it and handed it to her, saying, "Oh, my. I bought this from a reputable shop in Lodz. I had no idea it might have been stolen. Please, please take it. I can only imagine how shocking this must be to you."

The woman seemed to accept the story, but later, I heard Mother hiss at Uncle for not keeping the merchandise sorted well.

Jeweler Uncle and his family decided to remain in New York. Because his reputation as an upright businessman in Warsaw was already known in the Polish Jewish areas of the city from the many prior Warsaw immigrants, he was quickly accepted and went into business with an acquaintance. Obviously, they didn't know everything about him.

My father's mysterious life was also remembered and he and my mother found it difficult to do business, especially the kind they were used to. Soon, my jeweler uncle barely acknowledged them. He discreetly helped Agata find employment in a gentlemen's club and soon, she was out of my life. The two girls disappeared almost as soon as we disembarked from the ship, much to my father's dismay.

We moved to Chicago, the Northwest side, the heart of the Polish community. The landlord threw us out of our first apartment because Father used one of the bedrooms for several girls to service men.

Jewish people were not well liked in the neighborhood, especially pimps, so at our next apartment, Mother told me we were Catholic and enrolled me in the parochial school. I did well and it provided the only stability I would have for several years.

Father disappeared when I was ten, never to be heard from again. Mother was distraught, but as usual determined to do anything possible to support me, which I learned meant selling herself. At first, it was classy men who could pay well. After a year or so, it was nearly anyone who would pay something. Still, she tried to be upbeat and positive around me, always checking about my schoolwork, making sure I was clean and comported myself in a proper manner.

Chapter Seventy-One

The Orphanage

I came home from school one afternoon, I was twelve, to find a policeman, a fully naked man, by then male nakedness was not a surprise to me, and my mother with a robe thrown around her, arguing and yelling in the living room. The man was told to dress and leave. I think he was a minor official in the area. My mother was arrested. She tried to offer the policeman a piece of jewelry she had left, but was told she was now under arrest for prostitution and bribery.

For ten days, all by myself, scared inside, but determined no one would know my mother was jailed or the reason why, I fixed my own meals, cleaned my clothes and bought groceries to cook.

One day, a social worker met me after school. "I'm sorry, but your mother will not be coming back from jail for many years. This was not her first arrest or attempt at bribery. She has avoided prior court dates. She was sentenced this morning to at least six years in prison."

I stood strong, not crying. I was shocked. What would I do now? I knew I would run out of money soon, plus the rent was due the following week. Several men knocked on my door, asking for my mother. When told she was gone out for a while, they asked through the door if I might be available. I politely told them no, but now at age twelve, I realized it was something I could do. I remembered how worn and cold my mother had become, like hard dried leather, the oil gone from her beautiful face. I determined servicing men was the last thing I would ever do to survive.

"What should I do?" I asked the social worker. "I have no relatives nearby and the ones in New York never liked me."

"I spoke with your mother. She said she loves you and is so sorry your life has turned out this way. She said she knows you can never forgive her."

At those words, I cracked. All my fear erupted and I fell into the woman's arms, crying. She held me tight, patted my back like my mother did when I was little and upset.

"Your mother said to take you to the Catholic orphanage." She paused and cleared her throat. "Next, she said you were strong, smart and resilient. 'Do anything necessary to survive,' she said to tell you. 'Always set a goal above survival. You can and will succeed. It won't be easy, but I know you will.' Those were your mother's words as they put her in the carriage to take her to the prison."

As we packed my clothes, the social worker said, "I do hope you won't have to resort to your mother's occupation to survive. Please study hard, learn skills, stay chaste and marry an honest man."

I tried, I really did. At last I succeeded, well, not at the chaste part.

I became bored in the orphanage, and cautious. I never told anyone where my mother was because then I would have to answer why. Even the nuns seemed to respect that and, if someone else asked, only replied, "Walentina's mother is simply not capable of raising her and her father has deserted the family."

Of course, some whispered my mother was demented, but better they thought that than a prostitute in jail.

I was smart, soon at the head of my class and moved up a grade where I quickly became first there, too. I organized things well, helped the girls with their chores and to find better and more efficient ways to carry them out. I was a fireball in the kitchen, doing dishes, pots and pans, helping cook.

I had to stay busy. If I didn't, I thought about my mother, my father, my prior life, the good protected, innocent life I lived till I was eight. It was during those times my anger and frustration over the reality of living in a family that dealt in kidnapping, prostitution, theft and fraud would boil over, which wasn't good. How could my family be both loving and terrible at the same time? It was a lot for a young girl to consider. It still is.

I tried to write her once a month, at the nuns' request. After several months of no replies, I only wrote her at the holidays. Once, just once, I received a reply. It arrived nearly two years after I moved to the orphanage. None of my sent letters were ever returned by the postman. 'Stay strong and use your brains. I bear much guilt for putting you into the position you find yourself, but will always love you.' That was it, not even a signature. I never heard another word from her. At first, I carried that note with me at all times. Pulling it out to read and read and cry over. One day, on my fourteenth birthday which was barely acknowledged by the nuns, though the cook's helper did make a tiny cake for me and gave it to me after I finished washing the dishes, I pulled out the note and remember asking myself—why am I hanging on to this? It's holding me back from whatever life I may have. If I see her again, fine. I love her. If I don't, well, I can't keep reading this. I tore it up, threw it down the outhouse and peed on it. I refused to feel guilty over my actions. I still don't.

At the orphanage, many of us girls enjoyed journaling, in fact, were encouraged to. I kept one in Polish and English, the usual stuff a twelve- to fourteen-year-old girl might record. I kept a second one, well hidden, in which I wrote my true feelings of loneliness, growing frustration, and yet, still my love for my parents and how confusing both emotions were. This journal, I wrote in Yiddish. Once, I was careless hiding it and a nun discovered it. (They frequently read the girls' journals and would comment if the topics drifted to boys or any hint of sex.)

"What is this?" the nun asked, waving it in my face (I can't remember her name). "What type of scribbling is this and what does it mean?"

"It's Hebrew," I said. "I was just practicing the Hebrew alphabet and some verses from the Bible."

She looked at me suspiciously. I had to think quickly. "You know we have a copy of the Bible written in Hebrew in the library. Remember? We had to look at it to see what that language looked like and how the Old Testament was first written by Moses."

She cocked her head, still suspicious.

"I just thought the letters and printing were so beautiful, I wanted to copy it." I flashed a big innocent smile.

"What does it say? Read me what you've written," she ordered sternly, like I was some spy or something.

"I can't. It's Hebrew. Only Moses or some Jewish rabbi could read it. Not me."

She harrumphed, tossed it on my bed and stalked off. I thought I saw a smile trying to crinkle her face. After that, I hid it even better. Every so often, just for appearance's sake, I would sit in the library and copy some verses out of that old, dusty, Hebrew Bible, from right to left. I had no idea what I was copying, the letters are similar, but that was about all, the pronunciation and grammar were totally different.

I was fifteen when I married the first time. It lasted all of fifteen minutes, was never officially recorded, and definitely never consummated.

Freddy's family owned a small butcher shop and grocery store three stores down from the orphanage. The orphanage bought most of their grocery items from the store, plus the owners donated everything that was getting too old to sell. Freddy made frequent deliveries of goods and donated items and usually hung out in the kitchen to joke and chat with the nuns and girls. That's where we met. It soon became obvious he was interested in me and I received a strong admonition from the headmistress, Sister Mary Josephine, to not flirt or encourage him in any way.

"Hey, Sister Agnes," he called out one day as he entered the kitchen. "Is it ever possible to take one of these young ladies out for a walk?"

"Absolutely not."

"How about three at the same time?" He was laughing.

"Well..." Sister Agnes was one of the more fun ones and was smiling at him.

"So, if three is too many and one is not enough, how about two? We'll stay on the walk and only go one block north and two blocks south. How about it? Oh, and they must be at least fifteen."

"We'll try it and see. Only it can't be the same two every day. If I hadn't known you since you were born, this wouldn't be happening."

That's how our walks started. Only three of us working in the kitchen were fifteen or older and interested in walking with him, so every day, Freddy winked at two of us. Most days, one of those winks was for me.

Freddy said he was eighteen, which impressed me. He was funny, kind and kept his word about the distances we walked. Once we were out of sight of his parent's store and the orphanage, he would take my hand

and hold it lightly till some adult yelled at us. The second girl, so excited to be out of the orphanage, wouldn't squeal on my holding hands.

The backyard of the orphanage held several swings for the young girls, a garden, two apple trees, two commode houses, and was surrounded by an old wooden fence. Several of the vertical fence boards near the commode houses fell off and were not replaced. At night, we older girls could go to the commode without permission. So, around ten at night, I began going to the commode, then slipping through the fence where Freddy waited. We would stand there, talk, joke quietly, and hold hands. One night, he kissed me. The next night, he said, "I'm in love with you. Let's run away and get married."

I hugged him hard. It sounded so romantic and I was sick of living in the orphanage and the nagging nuns. Even so, I am practical. "What would we do then? How can you support us? Where can we live?"

He hugged me tighter and kissed me. This time, our mouths opened and our tongues found each other. It didn't scare me, I knew how desire and bodies worked. Still, I pushed him back and said, "Answer me. We have to have a plan."

"I do. My oldest brother and wife live in Gary, Indiana, just over the line from Chicago. We can live with them until we're established. He and his wife will stand up with us. He said the steel mills are hiring and pay a lot better than my folks, so I'll work there. We'll be fine." He warned me not to tell anyone, that his parents couldn't know either.

Two mornings later, early, I snuck out and met Freddy. We took a number of streetcars before walking the last mile or so to Freddy's brother's home, which turned out to be the apartment of his wife's mother.

"What are you doing here? Who's she?" his brother asked.

His wife, who didn't look much older than me, smiled at me as she nursed a baby, making no effort to cover her breast. Her mother was cooking, but looked warmly at me and waved.

"Remember? I told you I wanted to get married and you said to come by and you'd help us." Freddy looked concerned, perturbed.

"Oh, yeah. You was whispering about that to me last Sunday when we was over. Just didn't think someone your age was serious." He looked me over. "She is a cute one, she old enough? You know, old enough to mate?"

I started to bristle, but Freddy interjected. "Yes, she is, and girls only gotta be ten in Indiana to get married, you even told me that."

"I know, but the man's gotta be sixteen. What you gonna do about that, little brother?"

I stared at Freddy who ignored me.

"You're going to lie for me, just like you said you would, you big asshole."

His brother laughed and shrugged his shoulders. "Well, let's get headed to the county building. Hope you got money for street fare, I been laid off for a month and am flat out broke."

The mother walked over and shook my hand, then Freddy's. "Hi, I'm Norma. You two think you're in love and ready to tie the knot?"

I shyly nodded.

"I'm thinkin' it's just teenage juices rising, especially in Freddy. Bet he's same as his older brother." She pulled me into a hug. "You sure you want to do this, or are you just running from your parents 'cuz you think they're mean?"

"I live in an orphanage, but I love Freddy," I said, but wasn't quite sure I meant it as much as I did, lying awake all night, waiting to sneak out.

"Tell you what, dear, most marriages are still better than an orphanage, even with a randy husband like Freddy will be. You two can work it out."

She kissed my cheek. I liked being in her hug. I didn't get many from adults in the orphanage.

"Tell you what, I'll go with you. My daughter shouldn't take the baby out anyway, what with all the bad air around this town. That way, I can vouch for you. Where you going after you're hitched?"

Freddy choked and stammered and looked at his brother who said, "I didn't think you'd be doing this so fast. When I told you about staying with us, I figured I'd be back to work and have a place of our own again." His face turned red as he looked away from his mother-in-law. "Guess I shoulda stayed working for Dad, at least I'd have work, but they didn't want me marrying at seventeen."

I felt Norma suck in her breath before she told him, "You are a piece of work." She laughed, squeezed me again. "Don't worry, dear, you two can stay here several nights. I'll figure something out." She shook her head, then playfully grabbed the brother by his ear. "Let's go. Hopefully, you don't have any other brothers on the way to get married. I won't have room for them."

Freddy paid for the streetcar ride. On the way, I wondered what I was doing. Getting married to another kid not much older than me, not eighteen like he told me. The steel mills weren't hiring and we didn't have a place to live. There was always the orphanage, did I want to return there? I mulled it over and over till the car stopped and Freddy grabbed my hand and enthusiastically pulled me up the steps into the large marble-floored courthouse building.

The clerk wore thick glasses low on his nose with mutton-chop sideburns that joined his mustache. He asked me my name, date of birth and address. I paused at the address. Norma quickly rattled hers off, then said, "This is my daughter. I give my permission for her to marry and ask you to waive the waiting period so this marriage can be expedited." She gave a big sigh as if she was embarrassed and disgusted with me.

The clerk nodded, asked Freddy's information and his brother vouched for his being sixteen and needing to get married. We waited while the clerk filled out some forms. Sliding the certificate over the counter, he said, "Go over to courtroom number two. When the judge is free, he'll call you in and you two pipsqueaks will be man and wife. God help us when babies can't keep their drawers on tight."

I turned toward him, ready to yell I was still a virgin, but Norma grabbed me and pulled me away. Before we could get to a bench by the courtroom, Freddy's parents rushed in. "Have you been before the judge yet? Have you slept together?"

Norma hugged me close as Freddy's mother snatched the marriage certificate out of his hand. "So, your brother lied about your age?" She turned and slapped his brother hard. "You had no right. Freddy is only fifteen." She slapped him on the other cheek as the father stood, glaring at his two sons. I think the brother was glad it was his mother who slapped him. His father looked as if he would choke him to death.

I looked into Norma's face and smiled. Relieved I wouldn't be spending the night with her, with Freddy moaning and groaning all over me. All those tingly feelings in my body I had for him, all my desire to be a woman and to know a man, disappeared as reality invaded my fifteen-year-old emotions.

I let go of Norma and took the marriage certificate out of Freddy's mother's hand. "Thank you for coming," I said. Next, I walked it over to the clerk who was smirking. "I changed my mind. I've been lied to. This boy," I emphasized the word boy, "told me he was eighteen. I refuse to be married to someone so immature, they have to lie about their age."

The clerk started to laugh, but paused, his face grew red. "B—B—But aren't you in a family way?"

"No. I am very much still a virgin." At the skeptical look on his face, I added, "Trust me, I'd know if I wasn't."

He scowled at Norma, shook his head, took the certificate from me, pulled his copy from a shelf and tore both of them up. "Looks like nothing happened here today, folks. I'm keeping your fee. I need a drink." He slid out a sign that read, 'Next Window Please' and closed his window.

I politely glanced toward my almost in-laws and marched out. As I made my way down the stairs, Norma caught up with me. She hugged me again. "You're a live wire, ain't ya? Here, let me tell you how to get the streetcars back into Chicago, it's a little confusing." I appreciated her directions as I made my way back to the orphanage. She was correct, it was confusing.

Unfortunately, or fortunately, Freddy's parents rushed over to the nuns that morning when his younger sister informed them what Freddy's plans were. He couldn't even keep his own mouth shut. I was grilled like a criminal and told I was never to leave the grounds without an adult. The nuns refused to believe I wasn't a damaged woman and pregnant till, several weeks later, I showed one of them my monthly rags. Even then, they still acted like I was a whore.

I only caught glimpses of Freddy after that. He wasn't allowed to deliver to the orphanage. Two months after he turned sixteen, with the reluctant support of his parents, he married this girl from the neighborhood who was truly pregnant. That boy really had ants in his pants.

Chapter Seventy-Two

Back of the Yards

Each year in May, a businessman stopped by the orphanage and interviewed older girls to work in his laundry business near the stockyards. The nuns appeared ready to get rid of me. I was sixteen and tired of them, so I agreed to an interview.

The man seemed a little shifty to me. The job seemed very good, too good. He kept saying it was only for the right person, someone who was smart and hardworking and liked helping people. It seemed to me the requirements were very particular for a job cleaning people's clothes. He assured me the reason he was so specific was after learning the various laundry duties, I would sometimes be meeting the public to collect and return their laundry. He said my living quarters would be small, the food better than the orphanage and I would have one day off per week. Two dollars a week seemed fair compared to earning nothing for cooking, doing dishes and laundry for the orphanage.

A week later, I rode beside him on the streetcar down Ashland Street. We talked little on the ride. I watched the city change from poor to decent homes and back to tenements, filthy streets, dirty alleys, and on into the overwhelming smells of the stockyards and packing plants.

I'm finally out on my own, I thought. I don't remember feeling excitement or dread. Maybe numbness. I knew I would never see my mother again. A social worker visited me in the orphanage shortly after my marriage attempt to Freddy. She informed me that my mother was charged and again convicted of prostituting herself. This time inside the prison with various guards and male staff. Of course, she noted, the men weren't charged or convicted of anything. The worker told me my mother said she was trying to earn some money to send to me.

Considering my one response from her, I doubted the reason. I didn't respond. If the social worker expected me to cry, I didn't. I couldn't. I wouldn't. I wasn't sure I loved my mother anymore, I blamed her for turning back to prostitution. Even though I recognized she knew of little else. I considered how prostitution could be a decent occupation, if done in a high-class manner with the girls having a say over their choices. Still, I couldn't convince myself the girls I knew from my uncle's and parent's endeavors had a lot of say, though I knew some considered their lives as a step up from the poverty they knew as children.

I had no easy answers, thinking about my mother. Part of me was angry at her, part of me sorry for her, down deep, a part of me has always loved her. I knew she loved me, how she possessed few options after my father deserted us. Though very competent and knowledgeable about the jewelry business, as a woman she could do little. I also thought she carried a streak of rebellion, of defiance, of living life on her terms and no one else's. Like gypsies who can't settle down and conform, I think the generations of Jewish white slavers and thieves were inbred in her and she didn't want to escape from it. Maybe she couldn't see another way out.

Shortly before meeting the laundry man, I was informed my mother died of pneumonia and was buried in a pauper's field. She was thirty-one. I've looked several times, but could never find her grave.

At Forty-fifth Street, the man and I climbed down from the car, walked a block west to Marshfield and south to a narrow, wooden building with steamed-up front windows. The man led me up a skinny stairway to a dark third floor hallway with tiny bedrooms. He opened a door where a double bed stood tight against the wall. A washstand with two drawers held a pitcher and bowl, plus six hooks were screwed on the wall to hold clothes. From the clothes hanging on three of the hooks, it was evident I would be sharing the room.

"Your roommate's name is Zelda," he said. "You can unpack later, put that smock on. Breakfast is at six, dinner at twelve-thirty and supper at seven, if the work is finished. It's served on the second floor, rear of the building." He eyed my body as I slipped the smock on over my head. Patting my rump, he said, "You're very pretty and could make more money here in the future."

I stepped back from him, not sure what he meant, but realizing there may be more to the place than simply doing laundry. He took me downstairs to a room filled with large tubs, fires, irons, noise and steam, and introduced me to Velma, a heavyset woman who liked to laugh.

"So, another new recruit for the house of pleasure," she said. She hugged me and waved the man away. "She's in good hands, I'll show her the ropes."

Her words further deepened my sense that this place might be more than about clean clothes.

The first four weeks were a blur of hot, difficult work. I learned to operate all the stations and equipment used to launder bedsheets, pillowcases and other linens. Big pots over fires to wash, then rinse, using wood bats to turn and tumble the laundry. There was an ironing area where we kept irons on a large stove to heat up while we used another one over a long ironing board, constantly exchanging them while keeping the sheets from dragging on the floor. Mangle boxes were also used which were faster, but also required a lot of muscle.

Daily, horses and wagons pulled in through the alley and unloaded dirty laundry from area hotels and rooming houses and picked up the clean replacements packaged neatly in the same bags, now clean. Shortly, I realized bags of laundry were also being carried over several times a day from a building across the alley.

As I grew more acquainted with my surroundings, I noticed women running back and forth from the same building with small bundles of clothing to the other laundry room where individual clothing was cleaned.

"So, have you had the talk yet?" Zelda asked me one night as we collapsed into bed.

Zelda and I got along well. She was eighteen, tall with black hair and big brown eyes. She said her father was a ship captain from Greece whom she rarely saw and her mother Polish, but she was raised Polish Catholic, not far from the orphanage.

"What talk? Am I not doing a good job?"

"You're one of the best workers. Everyone can see that. No, it's not about your work. Velma's going to meet with you soon about other types of work. She does with many of the girls, especially the orphans or ones from destitute families like mine."

Some of my nagging thoughts started to come forward in my tired mind. "What other types of work are there?"

326

"Well, next, she'll probably switch you to the personal laundry area. After you've busted your butt there a while, you'll start picking up and delivering some of the personal laundry from the building across the alley. They're the ones who own this business."

"Then what?" I asked with a sinking feeling.

She giggled. "Then they will ask you to deliver the laundry into one of the rooms, the baths."

"So? Why is that funny?"

"Because that's where some girls give men a bath. While they're doing that, we're cleaning their clothes. Get it?" She giggled harder.

I thought I did, but wanted to hear it from her lips. "No, what's funny about that?"

"Because the men are naked, sitting in the tub and the girl is washing him all over. I mean, all of him." She waited for me to comment, but I didn't. "Between his legs. The man's thing. I watched today. It was the first time I saw a man's piece."

"You mean his penis?"

"Yes, and it was big!"

I shuddered. My suspicions were correct. "Is that all they do? Bathe them? Wash their penis?"

"Well, today, I watched the girl wash it till he started moaning like a hurt cow and then it squirted stuff."

"Anything else?"

"Yes, there are other rooms upstairs where girls take men, but we can't watch them. I've heard if you like giving baths, some men will want to take you upstairs and—and—you know, do it to you."

This girl's naïveté amazed me, but, few other girls had the background I did. "You mean they have sex."

"Yes, that's what my sister says. She liked it for a while, got some nice tips, dressed fancy, wore jewelry. Until she got pregnant. Now, she's at home and nobody speaks to her because she has a baby and isn't married." She was quiet a moment. "Walentina, don't let on that I told you this stuff. I mostly know it because my sister told me and Velma told me today, I start giving men baths next week. I'm scared."

I didn't know how to reply. I was quiet, sad. I'd ended up in a brothel. I knew the system, at last realized there was more to the information the man shared with me at the orphanage, especially his remarks about looking for bright young women who liked to help people.

I turned toward the wall and pretended to sleep. My mind raced. How did I allow myself to end up in this situation? How could I get out? What other jobs could an orphan get? I assumed my father was dead. If not, he was as good as dead to me. The bastard. Leaving us destitute, taking all the jewels of value, leaving none for us to survive on.

What happens if I can't get out of prostitution? That question bothered me greatly. Was I to continue in the way of my parents, grandparents and generations before them? Jewish white slavery and prostitution? I started to cry. Silently, I thought, but Zelda rolled over and put her long arms around me and pulled me into a hug. She held me till I realized she was crying, too.

"You're smart, you've got schooling and can read and write and figure," Zelda said. "Everyone can see that. You'll figure a way out, but I'm not. I don't want to end up with some baby whose father I can't remember." She cried harder.

Now it was my turn to hold and rock her.

I thought for some time. How could I help her when I didn't know how I could help myself? "Did your sister ever say some of the girls married a man they met?"

"She did. The owners were very unhappy about it when it did happen." She sniffled. "My sister said you got more money if the same guys asked for you and came back regularly. She fell in love with a guy who she thought was in love with her and wanted to get her out of the place. But she got pregnant and he said he couldn't marry someone whose baby might not be his. She couldn't be sure so he quit seeing her."

We both cried again, careful not to be loud. Velma slept two doors down from us. "Oh, Zelda," I said, "I think the answer might be to marry some man as soon as you can. You're smarter than you think you are. Pick some lonely guy that comes in for a bath and is too shy to ask you to have sex. Ask him to marry you, then start cooking and making babies like you want to."

She sucked in her breath. "Thank you."

We turned back over and she went to sleep. Before I did, I started to make a plan. I'd be damned if I would continue in my family's life of prostitution. I would do it on my terms and would get out at the first opportunity I could and make the best of my life, no matter what happened.

Zelda moved out the next week. Once you were a bath girl, you were housed across the alley in nicer rooms above the brothel rooms. "Velma," I said the next morning, "when do I move across the alley? I'm tired of slaving over laundry."

She looked at me in surprise.

"Look, I know that's a whorehouse. I don't want to be a whore, but I can give men baths. Great baths that they'll keep coming back for and I can send them on to the back-room girls."

Velma chuckled. "You are a bright one, aren't you?" She thought a moment. "All right. I'll make an appointment to talk with the bossman and see about you moving over. I'm not sure they'll want someone as cute as you only doing baths, though."

"Take me with you. I can negotiate for myself. If I have to eventually give up my virginity it will be on my terms, not his." I watched her gulp, her eyes got large with fear.

"I—I—don't know. We've never met face-to-face. It's almost like a confessional. Wiktor sits behind a screen and you talk. I don't know his last name. It begins with Adam something."

The name Wiktor Adam-something stuck in my mind. "I don't need to see his face, I might spit in it. Just take me with you, otherwise I'll fall into a pot and disfigure my face. What good will I be to him if that happens?" I smirked, but she looked at me as if I was serious.

Negotiations

Three days later, Velma and I climbed a maze of stairs into a dark office. A small window let in enough light to see a clothesline dividing the room with several layers of sheets hung over it. We sat down on wooden chairs. Velma was nervous, so much so, I thought she might collapse.

"Who the hell do you think you are that you can negotiate your terms with me?" His voice was relatively young, yet throaty, with a heavy East European accent and sounded familiar. Very familiar.

"Mister Wiktor Adamowicz, I am one who, though young, well understands how brothels operate," I said, hoping I sounded as haughty as I meant to. There was silence, other than him clearing his throat. "My name is Walentina. Walentina Adamczyk. In Warsaw, my last name was Adamowicz, the same as yours."

This time, there was coughing and choking and gasping, but no words. I heard a drink being sipped and could smell a cigar being lit. Velma stared at me, her eyes so big, I thought they would fall out. Her mouth was open wide enough for me to see nearly to her gullet. I put my finger to my lips to indicate for her not to talk.

"Wiktor, you need to start writing this down," I said. "One, I will remain a bath girl until I decide who to sleep with my first time." I paused until I heard the sounds of a pen and ink being readied. "Two, I will receive the full fifty percent of the money I bring in each week. You will not hold most of it back as collateral so that I will stay." I waited till I heard the pen nib scratching. "Three, I will set and receive the entire virgin surcharge fee, the brothel will not get any of it. Lastly, four, make a second copy of this, sign both, and slide them under the sheet where I'll sign both and leave one."

The only sound was the scratching of nib on paper. Finally, two sheets of paper slipped under the sheets and I compared them, then signed. "Velma will not mention this occasion to anyone."

She mumbled she wouldn't and I motioned for her to leave the room.

"Wiktor, we will speak in Yiddish, now," I said. "You are my first cousin from Warsaw, correct?"

He said yes. Told me his mother and sister died in New York shortly after our arrival. He and his father, my jeweler uncle, moved to Chicago where his father fenced jewelry downtown and underwrote the purchase of this brothel. My father wanted to help him, but was shot while procuring girls in St. Louis and died. I asked all sorts of questions, mostly about the operation. Did they force the girls to service men every day of the month or were they attempting to schedule them to avoid pregnancy? Were they monitoring the girl's menses? Were they providing sponges to absorb the men's juices and avoid pregnancy? Did they have a competent abortionist? Were customers who didn't take a bath first required to wash their privates before coupling?

"You ask too many fucking questions," he finally yelled. "You're a whore and, just like your mother, you'll always be one. This is Chicago, not Warsaw, and I will run this place the way I want to. Now get out, start bathing those men and don't wait too long to lose your precious little flower." I heard him stand and stomp away. "I've bent as far as I can for you, and only because we're cousins. If you tell anyone, this deal is off. Now go." A door slammed.

Bathing Men

I started bathing men the next day. To tell you the truth, I didn't mind it, even enjoyed it at times. I've come to realize my views regarding sex are different from much of society. Not just for men, but for women as well. We each should be able to enjoy and control our own lives, and that includes our private parts. Guess I'm not so Victorian, I think that's the word.

Anyway, if I've told you this much, I'm sure some will wonder about my first time. I was determined I would pick the person and not allow the madam to assign me some fat slob, or randy kid, or married man whose wife shut down on him, probably because he was a poor lover or for fear of pregnancy. All willing to pay a high price for a virgin.

One evening, a young man, Lawrence, about eighteen, came in, smelling of the yards, but so did everyone. He was shy, all embarrassed when I told him to strip off his drawers. Once in the water, he was nervous and skittish every time I tried to wash his neck. "Why are you so nervous?" I asked.

"I've never been naked in front of a woman or touched by one since I was a baby."

"Didn't you want to? Isn't that why you came here?"

He nodded.

331

"Why don't you tell me about yourself? Why you're in Chicago? Your family."

He did. A sweet guy, farm kid from Wisconsin, who needed work. As he chatted, he slowly relaxed. Finally, he said, "The reason I came here is so I have more experience with girls. Someday, I plan to marry and don't want to be a shy fumbling fool on my wedding night." Next, he blushed. "I don't have a girlfriend now, never have. Just guess I'm anxious to find out more."

He was very relaxed when I finished bathing him. I was quiet a moment as I considered how I just finished my monthly. To his surprise, I bent over and kissed him on the lips. Several times. His eyes bugged out as I locked the door, took off all my clothes and stood in front of him. I climbed in the tub with him and led his hands to all areas of my body, even showing him how to please a woman with just his fingers.

"Sit still," I said as I straddled him and slid myself down onto him as he gasped. I went slowly, I wanted to be in control and didn't want to hurt myself on my first time. Afterward, we cuddled till the water chilled. He returned several times, sometimes for a bath only, once for another shared one with me.

I didn't mind losing my virginity, I lost it jointly with a sweet man who I hoped would be a good lover to his wife. He better be. I introduced him to Zelda who snuck out in the middle of the night. They're married and living in East Chicago now, making babies.

Marriage—Twice More

Shortly after Lawrence, I met Drabik. He seemed charming, with some rough edges. He also had a lot of money. I knew, I checked his pockets. Rather than take him to a girl in the back rooms after his bath, I took him myself and he seemed a reasonable lover. He came back two days later and asked for me personally, Lilly, which was my bathhouse name. I treated him royally. Afterward, snuggled in his arms, I told him I wanted to get out of the brothel life and asked if he knew of any jobs where I could meet an honorable man to marry.

He cleared his throat, hugged me, and said, "I'm an honorable man. You're beautiful, why don't you marry me? I'm building a house. I have money from investments so you won't have to work."

I pretended to think about it a moment, then said, "I'd love to be your wife. Just so you know, I've only had sex with one other man, the rest of the time I only did the baths." I snuck out that night, we stayed in a downtown hotel for several days, got married and had a decent time.

He brought me to his home he was building. It turned out to be a basement and he changed from a nice man with rough edges to a tyrant with nothing good about him. He hit me the fourth day of our marriage and it never stopped. Thank God the bastard hung himself, or I might be in prison for murder.

I met Josef at the baths, just once. Didn't see him again for about a year, until he bought the lot next to ours and pulled me out of the rubble after the framing collapsed from Drabik hanging himself.

Josef saved my life. We married and built the rooming house. I hope to have more children, I certainly have lost a few. Josef is so patient and understanding.

Now, you know my entire story. I hope my being an unwilling prostitute trying to survive brings you no shame. I also hope you are not angry with me for not informing you I was Jewish. After the persecution Jews suffered in Eastern Europe and the attitudes toward them by Catholics and many others here in Chicago, I wanted my children to have the best life possible. I can't imagine Eugenia and this beautiful baby Henryk being teased or tormented for being half Jewish.

Diary 6

Manny Rodriguez

March, 17, 1940–June 8, 2009
Diary written in Ledger Four

Chapter Seventy-Three

July 2005

What the hell? I've been reading all these damn diaries and secret letters for years. Now, I might as well add my own. Just in case my hair-brained dream comes true that Andres takes this dump of a place and takes the time to read all this crazy, mushy stuff I'm planning to write. I hope Josh and he stay together, but will wait and see.

The diaries are interesting, been keeping me entertained in my old age and I'm sixty-five now. I just hope I can hang on long enough for Andres to want the place. If not, maybe I'll douse the place with gasoline, light the match and use my old twelve-gauge one last time on myself. Hell, ain't it the Indians, the ones by the Indian Ocean, that fire their bodies? I'll write the insurance policy to go to the AIDS foundation, or that Brown clinic that deals with gays and did so much good during the epidemic.

I know the secrets of this old place. Most of them. One hundred and twenty years of stories and secrets. I've read every single diary and letter. Well, maybe not. Katie mentioned she lost a diary, so that might be around. If it is, it's really hidden. That thing of Walentina's, I'm not sure it exists anymore, maybe it got thrown out with some old dresser or box of stuff. Anyway, I have looked at every photo in the place, too. Maybe if I get time, I'll organize all that stuff, but that could take more time than I've got. Something's wrong in my lungs, but I'm going to wait a while to go to the doctor. What's a doctor going to tell me? Quit smoking? Feels like it's too late for that.

My mind is still good, not like my brother Art-the-fart claims, the *pendejo*. I can figure math and dates good, write pretty decent even in English, especially in the morning after some coffee clears my head from the wine I drink at night.

Now, I cross myself, even though I know it doesn't do a damn thing, I hope to live long enough to write my own secrets about me and this old place. It's too bad I can't come back from the grave or the oven just to see the looks on some faces when, or if, they read this crap.

I've been in love—true love—two times in my life. A third time with a woman, a different kind of love. Came close with a couple of other men, in the eighties and nineties, but those conditions were unique, didn't allow time for each other to figure things out. Anyway, I must start. Just do it. Isn't that what that fancy shoe company says? Just Do It.

Chapter Seventy-Four

Young Life

Primero, I will tell about my birth family and how I came to be the dangly arm faggot I am. I will provide a little dictionary so my terms don't confuse you. Mother means my birth mother who died hours after my birth. Dad means my birth father, who I thank for the sperm which created me, but little else. *Mi abuela* is my mother's mother. I'll call her grandma. She tried hard to parent me, as well as *mi abuelo*, my mother's father whom I'll call grandpa. *Tato* is my dad's father and *Tata* his mother. Both loved me and also tried hard to parent me, a very difficult task.

Tato and Tata, my dad's parents, looked like their Spaniard ancestors and were very proud they could trace their heritage back to Spain. I refused to study history seriously, but know that somehow, they ended up on the United States side of the border and their US citizenship goes back a long way. Tato is a dentist with offices in San Diego and Tijuana.

Dad was a hotshot dental student in Mexico City, home on a summer vacation, when his sperm found my mother's egg.

My mother was fifteen and assisted her mother, my grandma, as a housekeeper and cook in Tato's big house. My mother's side stood very small, Mestizo, with lots of native Indian blood still floating through their veins. They were Mexican citizens who lived just over the border in Tijuana and walked or rode the bus to work every day. Sometimes they slept over.

Dad was home from dental school in the summer of 1939, he was twenty-one. He and my mother were friends, if the owner's son can be friends with the poor hired help's child. Ha ha. He taught her to read and write when they were younger. That summer, he must have taught her how his *pene* could perform magic tricks because when he came home from school at Christmas, both parents, strict Catholics that they were, insisted on a quiet wedding. I understand my mother was thrilled, but I never heard if my dad felt the same way. I doubt it.

On Easter Sunday, 1940, my mother was scrubbing dishes and went into labor early. I was born on a wicker divan on the covered back patio. My mother bled out shortly afterward and died. The doctor couldn't arrive in time to save her. My father was away at school. They named me Manuel Easter. No one could tell me why they chose Easter for my middle name, but maybe in the confusion, the joy and sadness of a birth and death, they thought something might resurrect, I don't know.

Both Tata and Grandma decided to raise me together. After all, they were together nearly every day and got along very well. That worked till Tata's sugar became worse and she could barely move around. So, Grandma carried me between their home in Tijuana and the big house in San Diego.

I was a handful, walking at ten months, climbing everything, breaking precious objects. Everyone said my dad was devastated at the death of his young wife. I was too young to know, but I do know I developed a *mal* attitude toward him. He would come home every few months and want to see me all cleaned up and acting like a perfect child. He would try to discipline me, spank me, tie me into a chair till I ate my entire meal, get mad at me for spilling *leche* and my *frijoles*. By the time I was two, Tata was dead and I only came to the big house when my dad was home to visit.

Grandma had three other older daughters, my aunts. They each lived close to the other in a Tijuana barrio, not far from one of the dumps, a very poor area. Grandma started leaving me with one of my aunts, who would pass me on to another. By the time I was three, I ran the streets, showing up at one of their homes to eat and sleep. No one worried about me. If they did, I yelled and swore at them till they laughed. I was not very big then either, more Mestizo than Spaniard.

Chapter Seventy-Five

My Dad and My Arm

One day in July, 1944, Grandma told me to stay in the house, take a sponge bath and put my cleanest clothes on. My dad was coming to see me. She said if I left the house, she would beat my ass. I was four years old. She left for Tato's house and Papa left to dig at the dump. I realize now they did not want to see my dad. Why else wouldn't they have waited a few extra minutes? Especially knowing what they knew.

I can remember wondering why I didn't go with Grandma to see Dad at the big house, but at four, I was too young to figure it out, though it seemed suspicious when she and Grandpa hugged me and started crying when they left.

My aunt waited with me out front of our little shack of a house. My dad showed up in a big shiny car. My aunt nodded at him, she hated him, and said she was going to her home. He picked me up and said we were going to Chicago. He was going to marry a woman there and would set up a new dental practice.

"I'm not going," I said. He tried to hug me tighter, but I slipped out of his grasp and stood in front of him. "I hate you, I'm not going."

"You are my son and you will do what I tell you. Now get your ragged ass in that car." He lunged to grab me, but I stepped back.

"No. You can't make me." This time, I remember yelling as loud as I could, shaking my fist at him.

He kept lunging for me and I kept dancing back just out of his reach. He had one leg shorter than the other and wore a one-inch lift on his left shoe, which is what probably kept him out of the war. Still, it never bothered him much from playing soccer or baseball.

I saw an opening and ran into the dirt lane. He was quite fast and followed me. I was laughing at him like it was a game and went racing around the car. He chased me several rounds, till it felt like I was chasing him. At one point, I came racing around the trunk behind him, but he stopped and yanked the back door open so fast I couldn't get out of his way. He grabbed me by my left arm as I tried to duck around him.

Shaking me and dangling me just by my arm, he swore and yelled again, "You are going with me." He tried to swing me into the open door, like you swing a heavy bag of beans onto a cart, but I jerked in midair on him and felt something pop in my shoulder. It broke his grip enough that he had to grab me with both hands. He threw me to the ground and my chest hit a rock in the road. It broke that skinny bone at the top of your chest that goes between your shoulders, my *clavicula*.

I screamed in pain, but still jumped up and took off, trying to run. He grabbed me with both hands, again by my left arm, and jerked with all his might, trying to swing me around and throw me in the car. Shrieking, I bit into his hand. I tasted blood and clenched tighter. Finally, he screamed from my sharp teeth and threw me to the ground. He slammed the back door shut and said, "Better you run the streets in Tijuana than Chicago." He climbed in and drove off.

I made it to someone's dirty yard and collapsed, throwing up, nearly passing out. One of the neighbor girls, about eleven, carried me, moaning in pain, into the shade of her shack and brought me some water. I must have slept or passed out. When I woke, it was dark, the girl brought me some beans in a taco and helped feed me. I told her not to take me home. The next day, Grandpa found me. Someone told him what happened. He carried me to their home. Some medical person, definitely not a doctor, probably some old lady in the barrio who helped deliver babies or assisted people with medical problems, put smelly leaves and mustard on me and wrapped my shoulder and upper chest with gauze and tape. She told me to lie in the most comfortable position I could, to drink water, take aspirin and it would heal back together.

Grandpa wanted to take me to a real doctor, to tell Tato to find a good doctor, but Grandma felt too frightened to tell him how his son acted toward his own child and the damage he caused. Though friendly, he was still her boss and thought the sun rose and set on his only child, a child who could never do any wrong. Even knocking up my mother was nothing more than a son spreading his oats. He was sorry my mother died, but still, she was hired help. Grandma said Tato was still upset over the death of his wife and she felt like she was walking on needles around him. At that point, no one knew it would be twelve years before I saw Tato and he wept when he saw my arm dangling. He thought I was in Chicago with my dad that entire time.

Chapter Seventy-Six

The Streets of Tijuana

Soon, I had little pain, my shoulder grew where it was, though I had little use of my arm. I adapted myself to using my good arm. It did not slow me down. I ran the streets, rarely went to school, stole food from the market stalls to eat, slept at one of my aunts or Grandma's. They each knew I would stay with one of them. Grandpa tried to rein me in occasionally, made me go with him and help him with whatever he was doing, usually yard work or basic home repairs for people with money. I liked going with him, learned a lot, but the streets kept pulling me back.

I followed older kids to the tourist area of Tijuana. One of them showed me how to pick pockets or purses. I was a fast learner. After several successful attempts, he told me I had to give him half and he would protect me. I called him a *mamon*. He laughed, said, "You can make some good money doing that, too. Some of those sailors like getting their *pene* cleaned by boys."

I was ten. It struck me that guys actually did that and it wasn't just swear words from wild-ass barrio boys.

I made good money picking pockets till Grandpa found out and shamed me about being dishonest. "Stealing is not honest. Any more money you bring home, we will throw to the pigs." I'd been telling them I got it by begging with a tin cup held in my dangle arm and limping like my legs were crippled, which I did occasionally. They didn't like that method, but I guess it was more honest than picking.

I was twelve when I realized I was truly different from most of the other guys around me. Hair was sprouting all over my small body, stuff squirted out of my *pene* when I was sleeping, and all the other boys talked about nothing but breasts and pussy.

I didn't get it till I secretly followed my two cousins to the main strip where all the tourists and sailors flowed in. Both of my cousins were just sixteen and beautiful. I watched them approach several sailors, giggle, wiggle their hips, and lead them to a cheap motel off some alley. I stayed just out of sight. Their second time, I snuck up to the building and watched them through the gaps in the curtains. Seeing the girls naked was boring. Seeing the men naked was not. I wanted to be in there with the men, minus my cousins. Those men were so beautiful, I could hardly keep myself in my pants, watching.

The fourth time my cousins picked up sailors, I again followed them, this time, to a different room. I sat outside, listening. The curtains on this room covered the entire window so I couldn't see in. All at once, one cousin screamed, "Give us back our money and don't take my purse."

I yanked out my switchblade, kicked on the door and busted in. Both girls were in their underwear, but the men were dressed and one held both their purses over his head as the girls screamed and reached for them. When the men saw me with a knife, one ran out the door, the other sneered, "Am I supposed to be afraid of a broken little shrimp with a knife?"

I rushed him, kicked him in his *cojones*, grabbed the purses from him, and backed him into the corner, his eyes wide, his hands up. "Pay them the money, for both of you," I said.

Instead, he made a dash for the door and I swung my knife, slashing him in his ass. He screamed and dropped to the floor. The girls rushed to dress as I picked his pocket, tossed the wallet to the girls and we ran like hell.

We ran till we were tired and stopped at a sidewalk cafe. Glancing in the wallet, my cousin pulled out thirty dollars, a lot of money in 1952. The girls checked their purses which still held their money. We ordered a big meal and split the money left over.

"Are you all right, little cousin?"

"*Si*, I am fine. I don't think I killed him."

"You didn't, you saved our lives, or at least our money." They both giggled, then we all laughed like crazy.

Today, I cringe when I think about it, but then, well, that was our life.

"So, little cousin, did you like what you saw through the window?"

I nodded and blushed.

"Naked girls look good to you? You're now at the age where you notice things like that."

I shook my head, not sure what to say. At that point, I realized I was a homo. I had to be if I liked seeing men naked and not women. I sipped my Coke and looked at the dirt sidewalk.

"So, Manny, when you sit in the outhouse, pumping your little stick, you're not thinking about girls?" Both smirked and giggled, but became silent as I nodded.

We stayed quiet. I wanted to melt into the dirt like spilled ice cream.

One of them patted my good arm. "It's okay. Some men are made that way. You're special."

I smiled, relieved. "Do you need me to protect you tomorrow?"

"Are you coming along to protect us, or peek at the naked sailors?" We almost choked on our *frijoles*, laughing. "Maybe you could do both. We liked having you follow us."

One of their purses spilled open as we stood to leave. Several rubbers fell out. I stared at them in surprise.

"Oh, come on. You don't know what these are?"

"Sort of, but sort of not."

"You know the white stuff you spurt out, playing with yourself?"

I nodded, embarrassed again.

"Well, that contains little sperms that swim up the woman and make her pregnant. If we can get a man to wear a rubber over his hard *pene,* it catches his stuff and we can't get pregnant."

"What happens if they won't?"

Jumping up, the other one said, trying to laugh, "That's a problem. It means we both will probably get pregnant someday. We will have to find a man desperate for a wife who will pretend not to know the first baby isn't his. Later we will make lots of babies and pray our girls don't do what we did when we got old enough to open our legs to men who whistle at us and say we're cute. Like our mothers and their mothers did."

We were quiet, walking back to the barrio.

Chapter Seventy-Seven

Selling Myself

By fourteen, I filled out, almost to my adult size, and was handsome, charming and streetwise. I'm bragging, but it's true. I also learned about advertising. I wore tight, very tight, white or light pants, sandals and a snug white t-shirt. Usually I wore a light blue hanky barely sticking out of my pants. In my right front pocket, it announced I liked to suck, in my left, it meant I wanted to be sucked.

I was blessed with a sizable package. Back then, we said hung like a horse. Anyway, I learned young that a good display is important when selling things.

Men interested in such things would look at my eyes and face, smile, see my arm, start to turn away, then drop their mouths open in amazement as their eyes took in my hanky and crotch. To enhance their view and speed up the process, I began tucking my dangle-arm into a cloth sling. If asked, I said my arm was healing after an injury. After that, no one cared.

I made good money. By fifteen, I rented a tiny room near the strip, a short walk from the bus and train stations where most of my business seemed to be. I wore a key ring poking out of my left back pocket, signifying I had a room. My room gave me privacy and safety. I could charge more. The right back pocket of my tight pants also displayed the imprint of my switch-blade. I earned a reputation amongst the hoodlums and whores as a person not to mess with.

I took lots of money home to Grandma and Grandpa. I told them I earned it honestly, selling goods and services, and not from thievery.

Chapter Seventy-Eight

Tato
Summer 1956

One day when I was sixteen, Grandma said, "Go see your tato, he is getting old, he wants to see you, he now knows what your dad did to you. Don't wait. He loves you."

I showed up at Tato's in my tightest white pants and snuggest t-shirt. On the outside, I was cocky and acted like I didn't care about anything. On the inside, I wondered why he wanted to see me. Why didn't he know his son was a jerk who injured me for life? Why did he wait twelve years to ask for me? Why did Grandma never take me back to the big house or say Tato was interested in me?

"Manuel, Manuel. So good to see you." With tears in his eyes, he wheezed and coughed and led me out back to the patio where I was born. A place I slightly recalled playing around as a four-year-old. "Turn around, let me get a good look at you. You are a handsome young man."

He motioned for me to sit down, poured me a beer and sat down next to me. We sipped our beer in silence. Finally, he patted my leg. "I just returned from Chicago. I did not know you did not live there. On my first and only trip years ago, your father told me you were away, traveling with his friends who had kids your age. Last week, your father told me the truth, that you didn't live with him. After that he said your grandma and grandpa wouldn't let you leave and were afraid to tell me because of the injuries you received living in the barrio. I learned the truth from your grandma upon my return. I am so sorry for what happened twelve years ago. My son was a bastard to treat you like that."

I just looked at him. Why did it take twelve years to find this out? Why did not Grandma tell him? She was here six days a week. Did Tato and Dad not communicate? Was I so unimportant, neither thought to mention me? Did my grandma even mention me to him—tell him how I was growing? How could they avoid talking about me for twelve fucking years? It was then that I thought, would Tato have believed her? Would he believe his pride and joy, his only son, only child, the big successful

Chicago dentist, could behave so badly? I nodded, then looked away. Afraid my face might reveal my inner frustration and pain.

"I think your grandma was afraid to tell me the truth about my son, that he was too strict and mean to you when you were little. He didn't want you for anything other than to brag and show you off as his possession. It's partly my fault, too. I wanted to believe in the good things about my only son, would never admit there might have been bad things about him. Talking with him on the phone to Chicago, he always lied, said you were fine and changed the subject or bragged of little Arturo. I will call him and yell at him. Tell him you are a handsome young man who might have lost his way selling himself on the streets. I'll also tell him it's his fault." He paused, studied the fuchsia, scarlet bugler and showy penstemon growing around the yard. "I think your grandma feared telling me about you still being in Tijuana. I was not always kind to her after your tata died. By the time I was over her death and nicer, well..." He looked again at the flowers. "Well, maybe her fear went so deep she couldn't talk about you. By then it was too late to fix your arm. When I spoke on the phone to Arturo, he always said you were fine. I would repeat that to her if she was around. She always nodded and looked away. I thought her reaction was because she missed you." He sighed. "I realize now she didn't want me to be embarrassed over the actions of my ignorant, selfish son. When I returned from Chicago last week, I asked her to tell me the whole story. She told me everything. Next, how they suspected you were selling yourself, but wouldn't say anything to you. I think partly it was because of the guilt they carried for not getting you proper medical help or informing me. I'm sorry I made her afraid of me."

I stayed quiet. Feeling confused. How could I respond?

Tato's voice cracked as he said, "Again, I am sorry. I hope you can forgive me."

His words made me wince. He did care about me. Still, I didn't know how to answer, so I reached over and patted his brown-spotted hand. I noticed the gold ring set with tiny diamonds around a black onyx stone. It was beautiful. He put his other hand over mine and clasped it. Squeezed it hard. Unconsciously, I rubbed the ring with my thumb

Looking at me, his eyes blurry, he said, "That ring is special. Your tata bought it for me when we married." He cleared his throat. "Now, what about your future? What are you going to do with your life? How long can you make a living selling yourself?"

My cheeks started burning. I coughed, pulled my hand from his, it was getting sweaty, my heart beat faster. Quickly, I sipped some beer. I didn't look at him, couldn't, didn't dare. He wasn't angry, but his question cut to my heart.

Finally, I shrugged my shoulders. When I looked at him, there were tears in my eyes, too.

"You are my grandson. You have a proud heritage. Selling your body sucking others is not a profession or an honest livelihood." He stopped talking and looked away, his face contorted in pain. "I'm not telling you to like women."

I waited. What was I supposed to do? Give up my subsistence? It wasn't painful work, I was a specialist. Most of the time, it was enjoyable, fun even. I met many cool men, most sailors, but also some businessmen from both sides of the border. I was proud to say no one touched my ass. Deep down, I was saving that for someone special. I had a deep yearning for love and would know when it was time to settle down with one man. That seemed a long time off.

"I want you to move in with me. I want you to learn, get a basic education. You are smart. I will find a school for you or hire tutors."

I nodded. Getting off the streets didn't sound too bad, but still. "Will I be locked in here?"

He chuckled. "I don't think anyone can ever lock you into anything. I know I can't take the streets out of you, but I'm hoping to supplement your learning so that you see other opportunities." He reached over and patted my good shoulder, lightly touched my cheek. "Maybe the house would seem too confining. You could also sleep on the screen porch off the garage. It's up to you."

I stood up. I needed some space to think. "Tato, I need to go for a walk. You are kind, but I have to consider this. It would be a big change. Also, I would not be making any money if I was going to school."

"Grandson, please walk. Take your time. Your grandma left food for us to enjoy when you get back. I think you can do some work for me or my friends. I understand you don't want charity."

My head almost ached as I walked. On the one hand, for twelve years, my existence was ignored or hidden by the adults who should have been communicating about me and making sure I was being raised well. Yet, I was not an easy child to corral, and more importantly, now, at last the truth was out. Was I ready to give up the only life I truly knew? What would happen if Tato, I and Grandma had a falling out? Several blocks east, I came upon new homes being built. The workmen were still at one of them. I paused to watch. I was always fascinated with construction and repairs. Occasionally, very occasionally, I still assisted Grandpa. Watching these men work impressed upon me how much I didn't know. I stepped closer to the activity.

"Hey! If you're going to stand there, watching us, at least make yourself useful. Bring me that extension cord lying by you."

I grabbed the cord, noted where the outlet was, ran it over, connected it, re-hooked it to the cord of the power hand-saw and started laying out more cord so the man could move further away. "You need more help?"

"Um, if you weren't wearing those white pants, I'd tell you to start cleaning up. We made a mess today and I don't want the trash blowing around."

"They'll wash. Where are the bags?"

He pointed to them inside the garage and I hustled around, picking up trash. As the men finished up for the day, I helped them lower their ladders, store their tools in the truck and garage and coil the cords. It felt good to do this kind of work.

"Enrique," said the boss man, sticking his hand out to mine. "Want a *Modelo Negro*?"

"I'm Manny. Thank you." I took a long sip.

He eyed me, looking me over from head to toe. "You always dress to show off your dick?" He spat in the dirt. "None of us here are interested. Except maybe Lucas, we're not too sure about him." He laughed and nodded to a curly-haired man a little older than me who blushed and looked away.

"I have clothes for other work. I like working with my hands and want to learn carpentry. I'll work cheap if you teach me."

He looked at my dangle arm, the fingers slightly curled. "Looks to me like you only got one hand, how much can you really do?"

"Enrique," one of the men yelled. "Didn't you see him? I didn't know he had a bad arm till you handed him that beer."

"You'll be surprised," I said to Enrique. "Tell you what. I work two days for free, just beer at the end. If I'm worth it, you hire me cheap and help teach me. If I'm not, well, I still won't give you the beer back, unless you want it as piss in the ground."

They all laughed and waved their beers at me.

Enrique shook my hand. "I don't need you full time. Come at six-thirty in the morning and help us set up and get started, then come back late afternoon to clean up. You do good with that for a few days, the guys and I will start showing you stuff."

The men jumped in the truck and left. As I walked across the dirt yard, I glanced back and noticed Lucas slipping into the garage. We each turned and he stepped toward me. "I stay here to guard the tools and supplies," he said softly. "Where do you live?"

I pointed down the street. "Three blocks. Guess I'm going to be staying with my grandfather. He's trying to get me away from my life in Tijuana." I looked away. There was something about this man I found attractive. Not like some guy to service for money, but as a friend. Just thinking that sounded strange.

"I have some *frijoles* and tacos. I could share some if you like."

"Thank you, but Tato has food waiting." I gave Lucas a slight wave and left.

Chapter Seventy-Nine

Learning and Working

On the walk back, I realized I wanted to work with my hands, but I needed to improve my writing and reading skills too. The idea of attending school for hours day after day did not appeal to me, sounded boring, and I knew I would not last, especially with my recent life feeling so vivid. I thought about living luxuriously in Tato's large home. It felt stifling, too much of a contrast from my tiny room hidden off an alley with a cot and several nails to hang my few clothes on. Besides, there were pictures of my father all over the house. None of my mother and only several of me at three years of age with my shoulder and arm whole.

Tato and I ate in silence on the patio. His look indicated he was waiting for an answer. I cleared my throat. "Tato, I think I want to stay here and try it, see what happens. I want to stay on the porch."

"I agree. Making you live inside the big house with me might feel like a prison and I don't want to be your warden." He lit a cigar, waved the smoke out of his eyes and smiled. "Did you see the new houses going up? Is that where you were?"

"I did, they offered me a job after I helped them clean up and put things away." I looked for a reaction from Tato, but he just looked at me to continue. "Tato, I don't think I could do school full time. Is there a way I could learn a few hours a day and work the other hours, learning carpentry skills?"

"Did you meet Enrique? Is he the man who offered a job? If so, he is a good man and will teach you much."

"Yes, he's the one. I liked him. He was impressed with how I jumped in and helped. He only wants me several hours in the morning and late afternoon, after siesta."

"Tomorrow, I will find a tutor to come two hours during the day for several days a week. Now, come inside. We will check my closets and your father's for some work clothes for you."

I grinned. "Yeah, Enrique was not impressed with my other work clothes."

Tato snorted, tapped his cigar on the tray and grabbed my good hand to pull himself up. We went upstairs where we found several pairs of pants, shirts, and a pair of old shoes suitable for construction work. I took some underwear too, but wasn't sure I was ready to start wearing those as well. Besides, they were old man boxer types.

Tato found an old alarm clock. "Here, you will need this. I doubt if you are used to getting up early to work like this. Do I need to instruct you on how to use it?" He slapped it on top of my pile of clothes and chuckled, his voice, old, deep and raspy from his Cuban cigars.

There was a comfortable daybed already made up on the porch behind the garage. I took a shower, slipped into a pair of jeans and tried to relax. By this time of evening, I was used to being out and strutting myself, sizing up potential men who looked at me, checking to see if and where they wore handkerchiefs. Now I was restless. This felt strange. I was living across the yard from the patio where I was born, my mother died, now, my grandma was cooking and cleaning for Tato and me. Her suspecting all along how I was earning my money, but not saying anything. Not that I would have listened if she had. All the secrets, the elephant in the room, between her and Tato for twelve years about me were now in the open. My own father lying, saying I was fine. How long could I try this? Should I just slip out and leave now? Disappear? I slipped my sandals on and wandered outside, along the garage to the street. In the dim light, I noticed a man walking east, about a hundred feet away. He had curly hair. I gave a low whistle. The man paused and glanced over his shoulder as if to make sure it was safe. It was Lucas. We both broke into wide smiles and walked toward each other.

"I couldn't sleep, so went for a walk, something I do most nights. It gets boring in an empty, half-built house with no TV. I listen to the radio a lot."

"Do you have a home? Where are your parents?"

He looked at the ground, kicked a stone with his boot. "I don't have a home. Not anymore."

I waited for him to say more, but he didn't. I didn't know what to say either. Finally, I pointed back to the garage. "That is my tato's place. I sleep on the porch of the garage. I haven't had much of a home either."

His eyes opened wide. "Wow! Your tato must have money. Why did you say you haven't had much of a home either? This place is beautiful."

"He is a dentist, but I have not seen him in twelve years. I just came to him today. It's a long story. I have been on my own most of my life on the Tijuana streets."

"How did you survive?"

"Sucking men."

"Wasn't that a hard life?"

I slapped his shoulder and laughed coarsely. "Only if they weren't hard."

He didn't laugh or respond.

We continued walking in the quiet of the night. I wanted to take his hand, hold it. I started to reach my right hand toward him, but stopped myself. Holding hands? Isn't that what people in love did? I never held hands with anyone. I'd never kissed any of the men. Several wanted to. They tried. I told them I didn't kiss and if they needed that, to go find a lover they could cuddle with all night. Like I said, I was a specialist. I didn't want to be in love with the person. Being in love was weak. Holding hands, kissing, hugging, making out would have confused things. Still, why was I so confused next to Lucas?

Walking around that night, like the moon filtering through the clouds, I glimpsed how the only person whose love I truly wanted as a young child tore my arm out of its socket and my loving grandparents were too afraid to tell the person who might have helped, my tato. That night, I realized love in families can be difficult. Today, I know that is still true.

Lucas sighed and looked at me. He slid closer, his fingers reached for mine. I snatched my hand away. "Please don't." I abruptly turned and walked back to my bed on the porch.

Chapter Eighty

A Job

I woke long before the alarm went off, slipped into the kitchen for some coffee and *conchas* and arrived at the work site at six. I walked through the half-finished house and noticed Lucas curled in a blanket in the corner of what would become the kitchen. An urge struck me to crawl down beside him, to snuggle, to feel his sleepy arms around me, to trace his cheeks with my fingers. I shook my head till those thoughts cleared and went to the garage where I started moving the equipment and supplies I thought we might need outside.

I worked till ten a.m., came back to Tato's place, where Grandma was busy cooking. "So, you stayed over. Does this mean you're off the streets now? Going to use your intelligence and skills in your brain rather than that little brain between your legs?"

I bristled and was going to snap at her, but instead said, "Maybe. I'm going to try. We'll see what happens."

"You know," she looked at me, her eyes moist. "The head on your shoulders is tough, like a coconut's. Inside is good stuff. You are the only one who can crack it open and let the good stuff come out." She handed me a cup of coffee and poured rich milk into it and added sugar. "I am sorry we didn't tell Tato when your shoulder happened. It was wrong, I see now. But I can't go back and change things. You are the only one who can change yourself. It's not fair, but it's life."

"Grandma, do you have a picture of my mother?"

She gasped, turned and walked outside and started to hang clothes on the lines, including my scrubbed tight white pants. They hung there, still damp, waiting for me to put them on and run, which I was tempted to do. Why didn't she respond? She didn't answer my question. Is asking about my mother some kind of secret? I didn't run. Instead, I walked out to my screen porch thinking about what Grandma just said. How do you change yourself? Especially if you have a hard head.

After siesta, I worked till dusk. Lucas and I barely spoke to each other, though I noticed him intently watching me. That evening, Tato told me he made arrangements with a tutor, a woman, who would work with me from eleven to one o'clock four days a week, then cut back to two or three days when she thought I was catching up.

After eating, on my way out of the kitchen, I noticed the stack of my clothes neatly folded, including another pair of work pants. Next to the pile was a pair of new work boots. My white skinny pants were on the bottom of the pile. On top was a snapshot of my mother, big-pregnant with me, smiling, her hands around her stomach, cradling me. I picked up the boots and stacked the clothes on top, except the white pants. I left them there. I didn't want them staring at me from the shelf next to my bed where I placed my clothes. I never saw them again. I did see my mother and me. Every day. I still do.

That Saturday afternoon, Enrique handed out pay envelopes. He gave me one. "I know you said you would work two days for free, but after seeing your hustle, I would be dishonest to take advantage of you. Monday, I will teach you to install the rafters and stringers that will hold the terra-cotta roof tiles."

I woke up at six on Sunday. What would I do all day? I wished I'd saved my white pants, I could have spent the day in Tijuana, cruising and making money. I remembered there was trash still around the work site. After some coffee and a *concha*, I put my new boots on and wandered up the street. Partway there, I met Lucas, wearing board shorts, a clean blue t-shirt, sandals, with a towel rolled under his arm and carrying a transistor radio.

"Hi. I am going to catch the bus to the beach. Why don't you join me?"

I shook my head. "I was going to the site to clean up some more."

"It's already done." His eyes looked wistful. "Please join me, the water should be warm for swimming. There are food vendors there. It's a nice way to spend a day."

"I don't have a suit. I don't have any shorts." My face flushed as I looked at the ground. "I n—n—never learned to swim."

"So? Doesn't your tato have an old suit you could borrow?" He waited, then asked, "What will you do if you don't go with me? Sit and stare at your tato all day? Listen to opera? Visit your friends across the border?"

I introduced Lucas to Tato. Blushing, I asked if he had a swimsuit I could borrow. "Grandma is off today. I'll find you something." Looking at the surprised look on Lucas's face, he explained, "Grandma is Manny's maternal grandmother who has worked for me since beach sand was invented. I am his paternal grandfather. My son married her daughter who died after giving birth. It's a complicated story, but at last, I am in his life, I hope for a long time."

Lucas still looked confused.

Riding the bus next to Lucas, my mind raced. What would happen? Why did I have ants crawling around inside my stomach? Why did I like it when our shoulders bumped when the bus lurched around a corner? "How old are you?"

He smiled at my abruptness. "I am seventeen, nearly eighteen. And you?"

"Sixteen." We were both silent again. We found a quiet section on the beach. Lucas slipped off his shirt and shorts. Thankfully, his swimsuit was a boxer kind and not a tight nylon type. I slipped off my shirt, then realized my suit was rolled in the towel. Unrolling it, I gasped. Tato's swimsuit was a tiny nylon one. I started to stuff it into my shorts pocket and heard Lucas say, "Umm, maybe we should wait another day to go swimming."

I nodded as my face caught on fire. He was right, I would have attracted attention, but somehow, I didn't want that today. I couldn't relax. I'd never been to a beach before. How could people just lie around in the sun? I tossed and turned on my towel. About twenty feet away, several Navy boys flopped out towels and peeled down to their suits. More guys joined them, some in tiny nylon suits. It was too much. "Lucas, I'm sorry, but I can't stay here. I feel very antsy." I jumped up, pulled my shirt on, rolled my towel up and took off running through the sand for the bus stop.

When Lucas caught up with me, I whirled on him, my fist up, ready to punch his nose. He backed off, confusion in his eyes.

"What's wrong? What did I do?"

"I don't know, but keep the fuck away from me. I have to go

someplace."

Squaring his shoulders, he glared at me. "Where are you going? Home? Which home? Your tato's or your streets home? You have to learn you can't taste or get sucked by every guy you see in a tight suit. Grow up." He spun around and marched back toward the beach.

I rode the busses all afternoon, getting transfers, waiting in the main station till the next bus departed, forcing myself to stay out of the bathrooms and not look for hankies. I saw much of San Diego, realized how different most of it was from my side of the border.

Tato asked how my day was. Where was Lucas? I glared at him, pulled the swimsuit out of my pocket. "I left Lucas at the beach hours ago. Here. I can't wear this. I won't wear this in public. Not anymore. I want another style."

He shook his head, his face furrowed, his eyes confused. A small smile eventually broke through. "I see. Did you learn something today? Something about yourself? Sometimes pain is good. I hope you haven't hurt Lucas in the process."

"Fuck Lucas," I said and stormed out to my porch.

Chapter Eighty-One

My Education

The next morning, I didn't look at Lucas, tried to avoid him, not sure what all my emotions were. They swarmed around like bees to nectar. I needed to carry and set a ladder up. As I grabbed it, Lucas picked up one end. I started to jerk it away. I didn't need his help. He hung on tight till I looked at him. "We still have to work together," he said. "Don't act so stubborn. You'll figure yourself out. We are still co-workers. We have to be."

I wanted to shove the ladder at him, push him over, stomp away. I did until I saw his gentle smile and warm eyes. I nodded. Together, we carried it and placed it and began lugging roof tiles up it. Working together, even smiling.

I left the site at eleven to meet my tutor, Mrs. Lopez. She was a white Spaniard, an older woman with wire-framed glasses, steel-gray hair, wearing a bright red and yellow dress and carrying a large basket with books and papers. She was brisk. "First, you will read to me. I will start out with very simple books, ask you questions for comprehension, and move up to more difficult books till I have a good idea of your ability. We will do the same with math. I will tell you a story and ask that you write it down for me with as much detail as possible."

When we finished, she said, "I am impressed with your reading, your comprehension, and you well understand the basic concepts of math, including fractions. Unfortunately, your handwriting is atrocious."

I hung my head, looked at the floor. I've always felt like I should write with my left hand, but that is impossible.

She must have read my mind. Grasping my chin, she lifted my face till I looked her in the eyes, "I will work with you until you feel comfortable writing with your right hand. Okay?"

I nodded slightly. Her hand still on my chin, she nodded my head vigorously for me. "That's the type of nod I want. Oh, one other thing. I will speak with your grandfather about locating a physical therapist for your hand and arm. Maybe with some work, we can slow down the

atrophy of your muscles and teach you ways to use it more effectively."
Patting my head like a small child, she grinned, "However, that will still
not improve your handwriting with your right hand. You must work hard
at that and I have strict standards I expect you to meet."

I wouldn't admit it to anyone, but I loved her. I also didn't tell the
guys at work why I insisted on only working till eleven four days a week.

Suddenly, I was busier than I'd ever been. Working, weekly
physical therapy, tutoring and homework gradually led me out of my
desire to return to the streets. It helped even more when, several weeks
after beginning my tutoring, Mrs. Lopez invited me to her home for a
Sunday afternoon.

She showed me her library room, shelf upon shelf filled with
books. More than I ever saw. "I was going to send you to the public
library, but most are closed on Sundays. I think I may have enough here
you will find interesting."

Now, in addition to everything else, I was reading books.
Mysteries, history—much of that was dry and I skimmed them—novels,
romance, though most were boring, it was always a man and a woman. I
read slowly in either language, which was frustrating at times. Now,
looking back, I recognize it helped me, which became important in the
eighties and nineties, of which I hope to write more about later.

One day, Mrs. Lopez handed me a brand-new book, *Giovanni's
Room*, by James Baldwin. "This may be controversial, but I think you
might enjoy it." I struggled through it and slowly realized after several
readings how all homosexuals come to a recognition of themselves and
self-acceptance. I still have the book.

On Sunday, March 24th, 1957, Tato told me to dress neatly, long
pants, dress shirt and shoes. By then, I had such items of clothing, though
not many. His friend, driving a light green, 1951 Lincoln Cosmopolitan
convertible, picked us up and drove us through the border crossing into
Tijuana and to my grandpa's and grandma's shack. They joined me in the
spacious back seat. Grandpa carried a bouquet of flowers. We drove to a
cemetery. To my mother's grave. It was a place I had never been before.
The headstone was marble and much nicer than the others around it.

"Thank you, Tato," Grandma said. "We could never have afforded such a nice grave or cemetery."

"She was my son's wife and the mother of my grandson. It was the least I could do." Turning to me, Tato said, "Grandson, today is the actual date of your birth and your mother's death. I come here every year on this date. I am so glad to have you with us." Suddenly, he pulled me into a hug. His body felt frail. I could hear his chest rasping, sense his heart beating. I knew time was catching up with him. He continued to hold me, not speaking, as if he did, he might cry or lose his grip on me.

Grandma and Grandpa sniffled, then patted my back. It was awkward, yet beautiful.

We drove back across the border to an A and W Root Beer stand and ate. "This was your mother's favorite place to eat," said Grandma. "I used to tease her that you would be born holding a handful of onion rings and burping root beer."

I broke the silence and my own sadness by burping.

Chapter Eighty-Two

Eighteenth Birthday

April 6, 1958 was Easter and Tato asked Grandma to prepare a special meal in honor of my eighteenth birthday. It seemed normal to always celebrate my birthday on Easter, even if I now knew the actual date. Two weeks before, March, 24th, we made the pilgrimage to Mother's grave and afterword, ate chili dogs, onion rings and drank root beer. That Easter, he handed me an envelope. Inside was my birth certificate which showed my actual date of birth, the record of my U.S. Citizenship, and a copy of my dual Mexican citizenship, plus a set of car keys. "You have done well, grandson, I am proud of you." He pointed to a 1946 Plymouth Deluxe Club Coupe sitting in the drive. I sat down, my mouth open. Tato blew smoke toward my mouth and laughed as I coughed.

I did work hard, both at learning and at carpentry. The past six months, Enrique sent me to his rental properties to maintain them for him, fixing plumbing, hanging doors, painting, replacing broken windows, rewiring electrical boxes, even replacing small asphalt shingle roofs which were not that common in San Diego, but I later learned, would be in Chicago.

Lucas and I maintained a cordial, but distant working relationship. I still yearned to be close to him. I wanted to kiss him, hold his hand, cuddle in a bed, make love, not just have sex, but I held back. I was afraid.

After learning to drive and getting my license, I rigged car top carriers on my coupe and began to purchase old ladders to carry and used tools. Tato yelled at me, "I buy you a classic coupe and you turn it into a goddamn truck. I should have bought you the old station wagon the guy wanted to sell me." He spat into the flower pot next to his cigar stand, then winked at me. He was getting very weak and his cough was terrible.

In Love

One evening, after the other guys left the house we were working on, Lucas asked if I wanted to go for a walk across the empty lots Enrique

361

planned to develop in the future. Somehow, our hands slipped together as we navigated across the hard dirt, filled with clumps of weeds and brush.

"You've grown up, haven't you?" He squeezed my hand.

"I think so, I'm not trying to hit you or run away from you." I squeezed him back as we both stopped walking.

"Are you ready to be kissed?"

I nodded and slipped my right arm around his neck and drew his head down to mine. We pecked at each other a few times, each time longer, until our lips met in full. We walked back to my car, stopping to hug and kiss, our kisses getting longer and deeper. I slid the front seat forward of my car and we climbed into the back seat. It was big, spacious, lots of head room, not like the narrow, cramped spaces in today's cars. I don't know how kids have sex in cars today. Oh, that's right, their parents aren't home and they have comfortable beds available.

Soon we were naked and exploring with our hands and mouths till we exploded, gasping and panting and shivering in the chilled air, the old Plymouth's windows steamy.

"That was beautiful," I finally whispered. "I never knew kissing and hugging was so wonderful."

"There's more to love than just sex." Lucas kissed my cheek and hugged me tighter.

I felt chilled. I reached around till I found a mostly clean painter's drop cloth and pulled it around us.

"I think I've been in love with you since we met, but I knew you weren't ready," Lucas said. "I knew you needed time to get away from your former life in Tijuana."

"Love? You love me?"

"Yes, I hope I didn't say that too soon. Please don't take off running naked through the fields. I'd hate to wait another two years."

I laughed as my mind twirled. Love? He loves me? What is love? Can I trust it? Risk it? "Lucas, I'm not sure about love. What it means, how it acts, how I should act. All I can say is I will try to learn about loving you. I think I do, but having so little of it in my life..."

Lucas nuzzled my cheek. Kissed tears from my face. "That's fair enough. You see, I knew about family love, acceptance, structure and consistency till I was fifteen. My father caught me and a neighbor boy kissing. He threw me out of the house, told me I deserved death, that I couldn't come home till I repented. By then, I knew who I was. What could I repent of? Being myself?"

I hugged him tight. I had no idea about his family life. I knew he didn't act like a street kid. Lucas seemed to have more security in his life that showed in his mature way of dealing with people and work. And with me.

"Enrique is my mother's cousin. He found me, said he would have empty homes he needed security for and he would train me in carpentry."

During the cooler months at Tato's, I slept inside the garage in a small bedroom Grandma helped me arrange by hanging blankets and rugs. Neither she nor Tato asked me to move inside the big house, even though everyone knew I was no longer running the streets. Somehow, living inside still seemed too confining, especially with all the pictures of Dad staring at me from nearly every room. I was never sure how Grandma dealt with it. Plus, I thought it might seem weird to have my grandma caring for me as the housekeeper. Even though she did the same things for me, living on the garage porch. I'm too old to figure that out now.

Lucas started arriving to see me late at night, varying the times so any thief surveilling the home sites wouldn't suspect a pattern. We ate and talked and slept together till early morning when he would slip out.

Several weeks later, I kissed him. "I am in love with you."

He kissed me back and pulled me closer to him.

"I want you inside me. I have waited till I knew I was in love. Now I am."

His eyes shot open in surprise. "You've waited? That's beautiful. I've only done that a time or two. I want you in me as well. We'll have to go slow and it might take several times before it's good for us."

After several tries, it became wonderful.

Chapter Eighty-Three

Tato Dies

In June, 1958, Tato was spending more time in bed. He asked me not to go to work one day and sit by him. "I'm throwing a party, a going-away party," he hacked, coughed and spat into an old mug Grandma kept close to him for such purposes. "It's this Sunday. I've invited all my friends, even some enemies, over. We're going to roast a pig in the back yard, have lots of sangria and whiskey and beer. We'll tell tall stories, bad jokes and sing."

"But, Tato, you're not well enough to go anywhere, let alone throw a big party."

"Two weeks ago, I saw my doctor, then several more. They're all quacks, but I think they are right. I have lung cancer and it's spread to most of my systems. You know, my glands, my liver, my spine. They even said my brain and I told them no one could tell the difference in the way I acted, so they must be full of shit. They said people will be able to tell soon and I have four to six weeks to live."

I put my head in my hands. It was too much. My tato dying?

"It's true, grandson. You must keep this a secret. No one else knows, not even your grandma, not even your father, the asshole in Chicago. None of my friends are to know. It's a going-away party. I plan to leave on a cruise ship for two months around the world. That's what I'm saying and that's what you will say, too."

"But why? Why not tell the truth?"

He hacked and coughed up a wad of phlegm and blood. "Because I want people to remember me as being close to normal. I don't give a damn about lots of people coming to my funeral, saying all kinds of nice crap about me after I'm gone. I want to laugh and joke with them like old times." He paused to get his breath. "After I die? Well, I think people will be glad they saw me alive and not in a casket, smelling of lilies and death."

The party went better than I imagined it would. I think most of Tato's friends knew this was his way of saying good-bye, but they appreciated the time with him. There was much singing, telling jokes, eating and laughing. Tato was thrilled. "To think I got to see all my friends and neighbors. Did you see the way they danced? I even managed to stand and shake my hips a bit. You and Lucas out danced everybody. How much tequila did we go through? Never mind, I don't want to know. Better down our guts than in flowers rotting around my casket." I couldn't help laughing with him. It was a great time, a good way to say goodbye, still I felt his sadness over leaving this world.

The day after the party, Tato asked me what I wanted him to leave me in his will. "Nothing," I said. "You have given me so much these past two years, plus the car. I personally want nothing from you." I thought a moment. "Other than to make sure Grandma is taken care of."

"Grandma will be well taken care of."

He was quiet for a long time. Finally, he hacked some more hard, long, breath-gasping sounds, before muttering, "Where will you go when I die?"

I was quiet. It was a hard question. Where would I go? What would I do? "I'm not sure, probably find a place to stay, work for Enrique full time till I can start my own business." I didn't add, stay with Lucas, get a place and start a future together.

His head sagged back onto the pillow. Weakly, he asked me to sit down on the edge of his bed. I did.

"Shortly after I die, you should get the hell away from here. Go to Chicago. Even if your father is an asshole, he is still your father and you have an eight-year-old brother who might need you someday." He dozed off for several minutes. Just as I started to stand, he muttered, "Do not stay here. Tijuana life can suck you back in. Find a new life in Chicago. Take Lucas with you."

Three days later, he went into a coma and died one week later. Per his instructions, I phoned his lawyer, told him Tato died. All the arrangements for the funeral were already made, including that the lawyer would notify my dad. Thank goodness. Tato willed Grandma and Grandpa his small dental building in Tijuana. It had an apartment attached behind it for them to live in and a long-term lease for the dental office in front. As expected, Tato did not leave anything to me in his will. However, I was shocked when his lawyer handed me a brown envelope containing his old tiny swimsuit, his black onyx and diamond ring on a gold chain, and two thousand dollars in cash with a shakily written note dated the day after his party. "Your past and your future. Keep on loving."

I placed the chain around my neck and wore it for years, till the chain wore through. It and the ring are now in the drawer with all the photos.

Chapter Eighty-Four

Lucas

Lucas and I made plans to find an apartment together. Not an easy task in a Navy town where lots of landlords didn't want to rent to two Mexicans. I was still staying nights in the garage and porch, but the realtors were already showing the place, so I kept all my tools and belongings inside my car.

One Monday, two weeks after Tato's funeral, Lucas took Enrique's truck to pick up supplies for the new house we were working on. He didn't return. At first, I didn't worry. Traffic might have been heavy, the lumber yard might not have had the items in stock and he had to look elsewhere. He didn't return by siesta time. Enrique was worried, he needed his truck to get home to his family. At seven p.m., a policeman drove up, looking for anyone who knew a Lucas Cervante. Someone ran a red light and crashed into him, he was in surgery. Enrique and I sped to the hospital.

Lucas was in critical condition, with both arms and a leg broken, plus a severe head injury. Something he would have survived today simply because he'd been wearing a seatbelt and with today's car safety features, but not in the 1950s.

He never regained consciousness and died one week later. He had no insurance and neither did Enrique. I paid his hospital bill after using all of Lucas's cash I could find on him or in his few belongings. I was shocked how little he was being paid by Enrique. I paid for a plot and the cheapest funeral possible when it became obvious family members weren't going to. His parents never visited the hospital.

Chapter Eighty-Five

The Drive

I had eight hundred dollars left to my name when I bought an atlas and headed east toward Chicago. I have no memory of driving the nearly twenty-two hundred miles, of sleeping in the car, buying food and coffee along the way, getting gas. I couldn't tell you about the mountains I must have seen, the deserts, the prairies and farmland, everything that the map said was there is a blank in my mind. Though, I can tell you I cried and cried. I do recall several horns honking at me as I crossed the middle line into the oncoming lane, my eyes blurred with moisture.

I sobbed about Lucas. About finding love, about our dreaming of a future together, two faggots who didn't care what the world thought about us. I cried about Tato and finding his love twelve years late, yet still finding it. I cried about realizing how he rescued me, turned my life around, knew enough to guide me instead of order me around, believed in me, put people like Mrs. Lopez in my life, even accepted that I was a homo.

By the time Route 66 carried me into Joliet, Illinois, I was cried out, worn out, and smelled of body odor, cigarettes, stale coffee and the banana peels tossed on the floor.

I found a motel, shaved, showered and walked across the street to a restaurant. The menu was decidedly different from any I'd seen in San Diego and Tijuana. Chicken fried steak? Mostaccoli with sausages? I had a hamburger, fries and a malt. I slept like a dead man. In the morning, over coffee, I noted my route into the city, into the neighborhood where my dad lived with his wife and my half-brother, Art.

The traffic became outrageous the further into the city I drove. My nerves were on end. The slower I drove, the angrier the other drivers became. I drove Archer Avenue and turned north on Ashland to Twenty-Second and looked around till I found the address in an area called Pilsen. It was a small two-flat. Nothing what I expected from a hot shot dentist.

Chapter Eighty-Six

Meeting my Step-mother and Dad

A tall, slender, attractive woman answered the door, a curious look on her face.

"I am Manny Rodriguez, your stepson." I waited as she gasped.

"Oh, my. Oh, my God. Please come in. I was not expecting you."

"I'm sorry, but since my grandfather died..."

"He died? When? Why did no one tell us?" She led me inside, through a richly furnished living room, to the kitchen. Sitting down, she put her head in her hands for several minutes. "Oh my, I'm sorry. Please sit down. You drove all the way to tell us this in person? I must go call my husband. He will be shocked."

I wondered if the lawyer didn't contact them, but he was one of Tato's best friends and knew my dad well.

She stood and dialed a black rotary phone on the counter. "This is Maria, please put Dr. Rodriguez on, it's an emergency." She waited, twisting a long strand of her black wavy hair around her finger, pausing occasionally to brush a stray bang away from her face. "Arturo, your son Manuel just arrived and tells me your father died. What? You knew that and didn't tell me? You son of a bitch."

She listened a few moments. Nodding at me, she asked, "He wants to know if you plan on living with us? If so, how long? He says we're moving soon, maybe to the suburbs."

I shrugged. I didn't know how to answer.

"He doesn't know. You go back to your all-important work and I'll talk with him. He's a good-looking young man. What? Husband, you are crazy, talking that way." She slammed the receiver into the cradle, sat and shook her head as tears slipped down her cheeks. "I gave up dental technician school in my last three months. I was only nineteen and married him, and helped him start his practice. Now, he never tells me anything."

It struck me how she was only ten years older than me with an eight-year-old son. Dad's a bit older than her, he must like the young ones.

She stepped to the sink and poured two glasses of water and handed me one. "He knew his father died. The lawyer contacted him about his inheritance and he's already trying to spend it on another house." She looked at me strangely. "He said to not let you be alone with Art Junior, my son, your half brother." She choked a bit. "He said you're a flaming faggot, a homo who likes little boys, and you were a child prostitute who ran the streets of Tijuana." She broke into sobs.

I waited till her crying subsided. I remembered Tato's words about yelling at Dad. He must have implied I was a homo, but I knew he never said anything about me liking little boys. What a jerk. Carefully, I replied, "It is true I am a homosexual. It is not true I like young boys, my half brother is safe around me. I did run around, I had little family supervision till Tato found out I did not move to Chicago and he gave me guidance and direction. He was a wonderful man."

We were both quiet, sipping our water. Somehow, I felt this woman was also a victim of my father. She refilled our waters and offered me a pastry. "Why did your mother's family not allow you to come with your father to Chicago? Arturo said they hid you and refused to let you go. That you were injured and they were ashamed to let him know so they hid you till after he finally left."

I stared at her. What the hell? How much should this poor woman have to learn in one day? I waited, finished the pastry, it was a gringo kind, all sugar with chocolate on top of it. "My mother's family did not hide me. They wanted me to go with him. They didn't have the time to raise me, let alone care for me the way they knew he could." I paused, considering my words. "I am the one that did not want to come with him. At four, I did not like the way he treated me on the rare occasions I saw him."

Maria's eyes raised, then squinted. She nodded for me to continue.

"I refused to get in the car. He grabbed me by my left arm and tried to throw me into the back seat. I heard my shoulder pop from the force. I managed to break his grasp, so he used both hands and threw me to the ground where I hit a rock and broke my clavicle. Still, I tried to run and he grabbed me again by my left arm, this time yanking it further out of the socket. I bit him. He let go and told me I might as well run the streets of Tijuana as in Chicago. He left me beside the road. I hid for a night before Grandpa found me. They couldn't afford proper medical help and didn't want to tell Tato how my father treated me in the past as well as this time. They didn't want to ruin his perfect image of his only child."

Maria cried, this time hard. "I loved your tato, he's a good man. When he last visited us, he became upset and left suddenly. Arturo wouldn't tell me why." I handed her the water, told her to sip, to calm down.

When she did, I said, "The truth is, I did not want to come with him. However, if I had been at Tato's home instead of in the barrio, if Tato talked to me along with Grandma and Grandpa, helped me pack, told me how much better Chicago would be with my father, it might have helped." I stood up and paced around the small kitchen. "I'm sure you would have been a good stepmother, maybe offset some of his arrogance. He treated me like I was his property and I guess I knew, even at four, I have too much Mestizo blood in me to be owned by anyone, including my father."

A smile flickered across her teary face. "Well, whether I would have been a good mother to you or not, I don't know, but I would have liked to try. I love my husband, but he is a jerk. I work hard so little Art doesn't pick up some of his habits."

Little Art came home from a friend's house. He was hard for me to read, not shy, but not open. He seemed to know of me, but had reservations about me. Shortly after, my dad raced in through the back door.

"Manuel. Thanks for telling us you were coming," he said with a sneer.

"I apologize, but things happened quickly since Tato died."

"Yes, yes, I'm sure they have. How much did he leave you in his will?"

I stared at him in shock. "N—nothing, why would he? You were his only son."

He looked at me like he didn't believe me. "Okay, here's the deal. You're welcome to live with us. I'll rent you the room in the basement for, for, let's say one hundred a month plus your share of the food Maria cooks." Glaring at me, he pointed his finger at me and yelled, "On one condition. That's none of your flaming faggot friends can ever enter this house and you are never to be alone with my son Art. Understood?"

I stared at him. I hated the bastard even more than I did at age four. Before I could say anything, Maria jumped up and stomped over to him. Looking down at him, she was about three inches taller than him, she put her finger in his face. "You are never to speak like that again about your son in front of my son. Manuel will be welcome any time in our home. He can attend any and all of our holiday and family gatherings he so chooses to." She clenched her fist. "You are disgusting. Charging your own son to live in your house. He's only eighteen. You lied to me about him. You are the one that injured him, not his family."

She turned and walked over to me. Putting her arms around me, she whispered into my ear, loud enough for Dad and little Art to hear, "I am so sorry for the way you have been treated. I do hope you will stay in touch in spite of such rudeness." Looking at her husband, she added, "Just go back to the office. At least the people there you cause pain to aren't your family."

Dad slunk out the door. Maria wrote her phone number on a slip of paper and tucked it between my shriveled left fingers. "Call me when you get settled or if I can be of help. There's a YMCA out on the South side." She pulled the paper back out of my fingers, ran to her phone book and looked it up in the yellow pages and added the address before stuffing the slip back. "I've heard they will let Mexicans live there. Do you have money?"

"I do, enough to hold me till I find work." As she hugged me, I whispered, "I will keep in touch. You're a good person. Thank you."

I stepped down the front steps and stood next to my car, the address of the YMCA clutched between my fingers. I was exhausted. My own father told me I couldn't be around my half brother, he wanted to charge me to stay with them, and he lied to Maria who was a wonderful woman. Why in hell should I stay in Chicago? Too tired to think straight, I decided to drive to the YMCA, get a couple of good night's sleep and find enough work to give me some cash to get back to San Diego. That was as far as I could think at that moment.

Chapter Eighty-Seven

111th Street YMCA

I still remember the smells and sounds of the 111th Street YMCA while waiting to get a room. Scents of potatoes, sausages, and cooked vegetables mixed with that of chlorine from the swimming pool. Several men sat in the front lobby area, listening to a baseball game on the radio. Several argued companionably about President Eisenhower. On the other side of the lobby, five or six men read quietly in a room with books and magazines and newspapers. Other men bustled in and out of a door that said locker rooms.

I stood behind a tall man with white hair. Not old-man white hair, but almost pure white. I overheard him speaking to the clerk about leaving a message for someone. Realizing someone was behind him, he turned to me. "Oh, excuse me. I don't want to hold you up, I'm just waiting to attend a meeting with Morris, he's the director here." Sticking out his hand, he said, "I'm Mike. Mike McGuire."

He wore extremely thick glasses and his bluish eyes wavered behind them as if trying to get in all the sights and light they could. I realized he was an albino, someone who is born without pigmentation in his skin and it affects their vision. I took his hand, gave him my name and stepped to the counter while Mike waited to the side.

The clerk told me if I wanted a membership, I would have to wait a few minutes till the membership clerk came back, but I could start filling out the papers. "No, I would like to rent a room for several days."

He frowned and coughed a little. Turning away, he began looking through a drawer file system. "All I got is up on da fourth floor, a small one."

"That's fine."

He hemmed and hawed and shuffled some papers around. Reluctantly, he slid a small card and pencil across. "Can you write in English? We don't read spic around here."

I noticed Mike's head snap up and he inched a step closer to me. "I write English well enough," I said, feeling a little irritated at the man's attitude. "Also, I have tools in my car, is it safe to park on the street?"

"Look, fella, we don't guarantee no guarded parking lot for what yer paying. You do got American dollars, right?"

Mike's palm slapped the counter with a crack. I jumped. His face red and his eyes wavering even more, he stuck his head in front of the clerk. "That is not the way we register guests in this YMCA. Now, why are you putting him on the fourth floor? Most of those rooms are waiting to be fixed up."

The man's face flushed almost as red as Mike's. "I—I was goin to put him next to Moses. You know, so da two of 'em could have some company."

A pudgy man entered the office from a side door. "What's goin on? Hi there, how ya doin?" He reached past the clerk to shake my hand. "My name's Clancy." Glancing down at the key and room card, he turned to the other clerk, "Why you puttin him in dere? I'm sure glad yer shift is over and I don't have to look at yer ugly mug." He yanked the key and record away and handed me another key. "Youse is in tree-fifteen. Been here before?"

I shook my head. I didn't care what floor I roomed on, but obviously, the first guy was placing me somewhere undesirable.

"Okay. See dat stairway over here? We ain't got no elevator, this ain't da Ritz. So, youse go up to da terd floor, turn right, take a left and yer room faces da east. Da sun will wake ya up. Ha."

I thanked him, picked up my small bag and turned to go.

"Oh, ya. If youse hungry, da cafateria is down dat hallway by da readin' room. Food's damn good and cheap, too." He slapped his belly as if to prove it.

As I walked away, I heard Mike say, "Thank you, Clancy. I'm waiting for Morris to drive me to our evening Lion's Club meeting. I think I'll have a conversation with him on what I just observed."

"You do dat, Mike. I been tryin' to talk sense in Jerry's head, but it's hard for him to grasp things is changin'."

I went up to my room. It was small and clean. I was glad I wouldn't need my alarm clock. The weather looked like another sunny day in the morning. I checked out the men's shower and toilet area and walked downstairs. Mike was still waiting by the front desk, looking at a small notebook, the kind that fits in your pocket. I studied him a minute. He was well-dressed, navy blue business suit, white shirt, light blue tie, wingtips shined, light blue socks. He was a good-looking man. Maybe I overlooked his handicap, if that's what being albino can be called. It sounded like he didn't drive. Maybe I overlooked it because I overlook mine, don't think much of it. I wondered why he was upset over the way I was first being treated. Did he work here? He showed no compulsion about jumping into the situation. He looked up at me and smiled. "So, how did you find your room?"

"It was fine. My next step is getting something to eat, then find a newspaper and look for a job."

A man who had been listening to the ball game stepped over, still keeping his head toward the radio. "Hi, I'm Norbert. They're hirin' over at the Ford." He nodded, still not looking squarely at me. "That's east and south of here a ways. Word's already spread you're from California." He laughed. "There ain't too many secrets around this place, so if you're runnin' from the law, you better keep going." I must have still looked confused, because he added, "Dumb Jerry, the first clerk, told someone you was a spic from California."

"Well, I'm a Mexican from San Diego. He doesn't know I also grew up in Tijuana. Now, that should add to the rumors."

Mike looked at me closer.

I kind of liked his looking at me as I asked, "So, they're hiring at Ford, what are they looking for? I'm pretty handy."

Norbert turned to face me, and I saw his expression change as he took in my arm. "Oh, shit. I'm sorry. I didn't catch that yer a cripple. Ford ain't gonna hire you. I shoulda kept my big mouth shut till I fully met'cha." He stuck out his hand and we shook. "Hope you ain't offended."

"I'm not, been used to it since I was four, but they must have some jobs a skilled one-armed guy can do."

"They do, more in the janitorial areas or office, not on the lines. Running the presses and equipment takes two good arms and hands." He looked at the floor a moment. "The thing is, guys get hurt, injured there, some bad enough they can't work on the line, so the union tries to make sure they get the less skilled positions. That's why they ain't gonna take no new people on who are crips." He shrugged and went back to his seat to listen to the game.

"Norbert's a good man," Mike said. "He knows what's going on in the area. Trust me, if he hears of something, he'll track you down." He looked at the desk again, but Clancy shook his head. "Well, Morris is on a call to our camp up in Michigan, Camp Pinewood, and they must have a lot to discuss." Turning back to face me, he asked, "What type of work you looking for?"

"I can do about anything building-related. Basic plumbing, electrical, maintenance, janitorial, repairs, new construction, roofing." I glanced at the windows in the lobby. "Washing windows, this place needs it badly."

He chuckled. "Yes, they do. Let me talk with Morris on our way to the meeting. Maybe he can work something out. Give you a couple nights free if you do some of these windows. He'll let Clancy know later this evening and he'll give you a message. I'll check around for other jobs at the meeting tonight. A bunch of local business guys will be there."

I walked down to the cafeteria. A hefty woman, sweet baby face, light-brown stringy hair falling out of the twisted bun on her head and wearing white-framed glasses with silver sparkles beamed at me. "You be the guy from California?"

I nodded. Good grief, am I the first man from California to stay here? Well, maybe the first Mexican from California, or both.

"So, whacha want? Clancy, he's my fiancé, called down and said to treat ya good for da way dumb Jerry tried to shove you up to da fourth floor." She shook her head in disgust.

"Who's Moses? Why did Jerry think I should be by him?"

Her face reddened and she lowered her eyes a moment. "Moses has lived here for twenty years, he's old and won't move down to da terd level so they can paint and fix his room up. Says it's fine the way it is." She paused, as if not sure how to go on. Taking a big breath, she said, "Well, Moses is a nigger, a real good one, I mean he's colored, and..."

"And Jerry wanted to put the Mexican and the colored guys next

376

to each other." I shook my head as I noticed moisture in her eyes. "I get it, but some people don't, do they?"

She nodded.

"So, I'd like some..." I rattled off some names of food in Spanish. "Can you fix me that, please?"

Her eyes got wide, she wasn't sure if I was kidding or serious. "We ain't got none of dat stuff. You tryin' to be funny or somepin?"

"Oh, and I'd like some sangria and cervesa to drink." I let my eyes smile at her.

She giggled. "Didn't old Clancy tell ya, we serve hote quasine here? That's spose to mean fancy stuff, but we serve mostly east European and Irish, cept the grits and greens we sometimes make up special for Moses." She started dishing up a plate. "Tells ya what. I'll give ya a sample of most things we got tonight. These thuringers are great, them's the little sassages I just put on with some kraut. Oh, and we ain't got none of that sangareea stuff or Mexican beer." Her eyes laughed at me. "Fooled ya, didn't I? I knowed what Mexican is for beer, only round here, we drink Pabst Blue Ribbon." She placed the heaping plate onto a tray and slid it to me. "A quarter, please. Hey, how do ya say please in Mexican talk?"

"Por favor."

Thank God I was hungry. Ordinarily, I could not have eaten all that heavy food and overcooked vegetables. It was tasty, but I knew I needed to find a place where I could cook some of my own food. Real food. Mexican food.

I spent the evening reading the papers in the quiet room, looking for jobs and housing. It was discouraging. As I walked across the lobby toward the stairs, Clancy motioned me over.

"Hey, Morris left ya a message." He poked around the edge of his counter and lifted a pink slip. "He said start at seven-terdy as high as youse can go wit yer ladders, den our buildin' guy kin help ya out wit da highest ones."

I nodded.

"Den he said he'll give youse two nights free, mebbe more dependin' on how long it takes ya. Got it? He also said to park yer car out back. It'll be safe."

"Thank you. Say, where are you from?"

Clancy looked confused. "Me? I stay by my folks over on Hunnert 'n Fourteenth an' Prairie, by da park. Why?"

"No, I meant what country are you from. You have an accent."

"Me? Me got an accent? I ain't got no accent. You da one talks funny. Me? Dad says we hines fifty-seven mixed wit a lot of milk man." He patted his belly. "My dad's a milk man. Get it? A milk man." He laughed harder, then slapped his hand on the counter. "We American, man. We shicaago true and true. Been here since dirt. You gotta learn to talk good English, man. I ain't got no accent." He was still laughing as I left to park my car behind the building.

Chapter Eighty-Eight

The Mexican Window Washing Circus

The next morning, I was up with the sun. I walked around the building, studying the windows, their height, locating water spigots. I pulled my car near the front and unloaded my ladders and laid them next to the building. The first-floor windows I could reach from the ground, but everything above, floors two to four, would require my official Mexican extension ladders, old wooden ladders I'd found, repaired, and cobbled together. I could work safely nearly thirty-five feet. Any higher than that and I tied myself to the building. Ha ha.

Around seven, I went to the cafeteria and chose scrambled eggs and sausage, toast, and coffee. When I went to pay, the girl waved it away. "Dey said not to charge ya today, somethin' 'bout you doin the windows."

I thanked her and ate. As I put my tray with my dirty dishes on the counter near the dishwashing area, she leaned toward me and said, "I think yer gonna be the entertainment for today." She gave me a big smirky grin.

What the hell was that all about? The entertainment?

A man with wide shoulders, a flat-top haircut and black-framed eye glasses rushed up. I could tell he was fit, but then, I guess if you worked in a YMCA with a gym, you should be. "Hi, I'm Morris. What do you need from us? Hoses, squeegees, someone to hold the ladder?"

I told him I needed a hose, maybe some rags or old towels, some white vinegar and dish detergent. Said I wasn't planning on needing much help. He didn't say much, but I could see he was thinking, wondering how a small guy with a dangly arm was going to pull this off without help.

"Okay, I'll have Rev, that's our maintenance guy, meet you out front in a few minutes. He'll get you what you need." He started to turn away, stopped and looked back at me. "Say, I'm planning a meeting with Jerry today. His last chance to start acting right about his aversion to brown skin. This is the YMCA and we're changing, too. Should have years ago." I didn't know what to say, but shook his hand when he stuck it out at me.

379

A few minutes later, out by my car, a kind-looking, gray-haired man walked up. "Hi, I'm the Rev. You look like you're going to need some help today, so I'll hang around."

I nodded at him, thanked him for the supplies. I hauled my bucket, brush, squeegee and handles out of the trunk, then started to put on my leather harness. Lucas designed and tooled it and I was still breaking it in when he died.

Putting it on that first time since his death nearly knocked me to my knees. I stumbled over to the car and sat in the passenger seat, door open, feet on the ground, my head in my hands. I thought I'd cried him out of me driving across the country. Thinking about him, I'd been able to smile a few times since, maybe along with a gulp or slight choke, but still a smile, recalling his face, his touch, his bubbly personality. It all came back to me, alive one moment, waving goodbye, knowing I'd see him in an hour or so, then him in the hospital bed, the tubes, the bent bones, his head wrapped, no response to my pleadings and prayers for one week.

The harness wasn't simply a few straps of leather designed to offset my lack of use of my left arm, it was a work of art. Hand-tooled, with flowers and mountains and trees. Across the front, Manny was inscribed, across the back, Rodriguez. Scattered throughout the artwork were the letters of Lucas' name. I knew where every letter was, no one else would notice.

The harness went around my chest, just under my armpits. A two-inch strap went over my right shoulder. Over my left shoulder was a wide padded leather strap with what looked like a shelf mounted on it. The shelf was reinforced with steel between the two layers of leather and extended an inch or so beyond my twisted shoulder. Several metal slots and pins were attached near the end of the shelf. From these, I could hook a heavy stiff wire with a crook at the end to hang a bucket at my finger level, or carry a can of paint. I could also attach a wood pole—I made several lengths—which had a sturdy fork-like handle at the end.

If you've ever moved a tall ladder upright, you understand how, with the ladder standing against the building, you squat down, put your right arm through the rungs, grasp the lower rungs, then extend your left arm high over your head and grasp the rungs as high as you can reach. Using your knees, you lift the ladder straight up, and balancing it upright, slowly walk it to where you need it, usually not a great distance. This saves time in collapsing the ladder and extending it again. Of course, this won't work for extremely long ladders, but I have carried ladders in this manner extended close to twenty feet. So, think of the wooden extension resting on my leather shelf supported by the harness as a replacement for my left arm. A wooden arm.

"Manny. Manny, are you okay?" The Rev squatted in front of me, patting my knee. "I'm also a pastor, small Bible church near here. What's wrong? Why are you sad? Do you want me to pray with you?"

I smiled, wiped my eyes and stood up. "Nah, it's just that I haven't worn this harness in a while. It's kinda special. The guy, the person who made it for me, died before I came here. Car accident."

I didn't directly look at Rev, but caught his lips moving in a silent prayer. I was waiting for him to cross himself, but he didn't. Guess some pastors do things differently. What's a Bible Church? Ain't they all?

I finished snapping on the harness, hooked on the bucket with my brushes and squeegee, grabbed the handle extensions and carried them over to where I planned to begin. There was a bunch of onlookers waiting, watching my every move. It appeared that several were old guys from the Y with nothing to do, maybe others worked the late shifts, and some seemed to be neighbors passing by with little kids. Even the office girls were peeking out the front door. Rev followed me, carrying the hose and other supplies. "Rev, why are all these people out here? Is washing windows that big a deal in Chicago?"

His face turned pink, he chuckled a bit. "Well, no. It's pretty common. It's just word spread that a one-armed, spic..."

"So, a one-armed Mexican from Tijuana is the main attraction today?"

He laughed and nodded. "That's about it. There's also been a few jokes about one-armed paper hangers." At my confused look, he added, "You know, wallpaper. It comes in rolls."

It took me a moment to realize what wallpaper was. We always plastered inside our homes, but I did recall seeing some. That was when it hit me, yeah, trying to unroll and hang wallpaper with one arm would be difficult.

I decided to put on a show and have some fun. I ran to my car and pulled my tin cup out, the one I drank coffee in when driving, the one I used to panhandle with when I was little. I held it up high and called, "Senors, Senoritas, muchachas and muchachos." I rattled on in Spanish, seeing their eyes get big. "What? You no understand me?" I watched them laugh. "Okay. My name is Manny Rodriguez, I am with the window-washing circus from Tijuana, Mexico and have come to perform for you today. You do not have to buy tickets, but if you like my performance, you may leave tips in this cup. Okay?"

As they laughed, I dramatically placed the cup in the middle of the sidewalk, bowed low, then ran to my ladders. I assembled two sections on the ground, attached my wooden arm to my shoulder plate, the hook end under the ladder and carried it horizontally to the far window. I ran back, and brought the other extension back and slipped it into the iron brackets. I motioned Rev to stay clear. Carefully, with all eyes on me, I raised the ladder. I pulled the ropes to extend it, adjusted the distance from the building, and made sure the feet were solid and wouldn't slip. I removed my wooden arm and attached the wire hook. Next, I mixed the detergent, vinegar and water, chose the handle lengths I needed for the squeegee and scampered up the ladder to the fourth floor window. I carried the sloshing bucket with my left wire arm, using my right to grasp the rungs. I flew to work, brushing, squeegeeing, slipping down to the third floor, the second, jumping the last few rungs to the ground and doing the first floor window.

Rev shook his head. "I bet you could hang wallpaper, you are amazing. You truly don't need me, do you?"

"Maybe some coffee and water."

I lowered the third, the top, extension, reattached my wood arm and carefully moved the ladder to the next stack of windows. I repeated my motions and soon moved around the corner to the east side of the building which was far wider than the front was. Around noon, Morris hollered up, asking if I wanted to stop for lunch. I said no, but it would be nice if someone could bring me a sandwich and coffee and a piece of fruit.

Ten minutes later, Morris brought a covered tray and placed it on the parking curb, along with a pitcher full of ice water and a pot of coffee. "Hey," he called up. "Don't forget your tips." He laughed as he rattled my cup with the sound of change in it. "I think you got enough to afford another meal at the best cafeteria around here."

Chapter Eighty-Nine

Getting Acquainted with Mike McGuire

I climbed down, stretched, pulled off my harness, and began eating. I noticed Mike, the albino guy, watching me. Something about the way he looked at me made me wonder if he was looking at the way I worked, or like a man who likes to look at men does. I called to him, "Wanna help?"

He walked over, that cautious, sincere smile on his face I noticed and liked the first time we met. He squatted down in his pristine suit, shirt, tie and shoes. "Umm, I'm not dressed well enough for this work, but you are amazing."

"Yes, I suppose to people who think crippled people can't do much, seeing a one-armed man work is amazing. To me, it's normal. I just do what I have to do, like everyone else." I didn't snap at him, but maybe there was a little bite in my words. Working hard is what life is all about. I watched his face change as he thought a moment before I said, "See, I'd rather you were impressed with my quality of work, maybe my speed, but impressed with my work more than the fact I can do normal things everybody does, just with a weird arm."

Almost without thinking, at least that's how it seemed to me, he blurted out, "Yes, I understand all that, but *you* are amazing." I learned right then albino people can blush. His face got real red, he stammered around, "Uh, uh, I mean. Well, I meant. See, well, you are amazing."

I figured that confirmed he hadn't been referring to my work, or my abilities with only one arm, he was referring to the real me, the homo me. I thought he was going to birth a kitten, the way his mouth was working. Looking him in the eye, I said, "I am amazing, in many more ways, too."

Why did I say that? It sounded like flirting. Why would I say that with Lucas still so fresh? My God, I was just crying over him in my car. Anyway, it seemed no more words were necessary. At least I figured we each knew what the other was.

Mike covered the pitcher of water with the cloth towel, left it with the glass, picked up the tray and said, "I'll run these in. Listen, my parents are out of town for a while, I was going to eat dinner here tonight. Care to join me?"

I thought a moment. I sensed a friendly interest in me. Did I want a friend? A homo friend? What happens if he wanted more than just a friendship? Was I ready for a relationship? What the heck, there's nothing wrong with a friend. Besides, he must be rich. "Si, Señor. Only it will have to wait until when I'm done for the day. I want to finish this east side today so I only have the west side to do tomorrow morning when it's out of the sun."

"That's fine, I usually swim laps after I'm done at the bank." He marched off, whistling a little tune.

Clancy was behind the desk when I finally finished for the day and walked in, tired, aching and smelling of sweat and vinegar. He motioned me over. "Mike just called up. Said fer youse ta go downstairs. Said ya could shower down there and take a steam."

"What's downstairs? What's a steam?" I looked at him with a quizzical look.

He slapped his belly. "I fergit youse ain't been 'round a Y, have ya? Well, downstairs is the locker rooms wit showers. The business man's club has a sauna." He looked at me. "That's Swedish, dere's lots of dem folk round here, too. It's dry heat, like sittin' in hell wit'out da flames, but feels real good when ya come out. Da steam is hot, it feels good too."

I nodded. I remembered several bathhouses in Tijuana where I snuck in and serviced some of the men in and around the nooks and crannies. They had steam baths too, but I was never in one. "I'm all sweaty. What do I wear?"

He slapped his belly again. "Nuttin. Dey's all men. Some wears a towel, some don't, dey all showers in da raw. Da towels are down dere. Okay? I'm callin' down and sayin youse on yer way." He pointed me toward the sign and stairs that said locker rooms and Men's Club.

I slowly walked to the door and down the stairs. Did I truly want to be around a bunch of naked men? What was I getting myself into? I almost turned around and headed back toward my room. What would I say to Clancy if he asked, and to Mike if I saw him again, which seemed likely.

A pimply faced teenager was behind a counter. "Mike's waitin' for ya in da club."

He slid two towels and a locker key to me and pointed across the room to a wood paneled door that said, Members Only. "Don't yank on da door till it buzzes." I waited at the door till the kid buzzed me in.

"Manny. Thanks for coming down. I just got out of the pool." Mike stood just inside the door, standing between two rows of lockers. He wore a swimsuit, boxer-style. His thick glasses with the strap across the back of his head informed me he wore them swimming. "Here, put your clothes in this guest locker. Unless you got jewels and gold, you don't need to lock it up. Undress. We'll take a shower, then hit the steam."

It dawned on me that Mike was younger than I originally pegged him for. Seeing him in just a swim suit, I figured he was closer to thirty and not his forty's like I first thought. All sizes and shapes of men were in the locker area, some dressed, some not. Other than the baths, I'd never been around bunches of naked men before. Of course, back then, I was looking for business. I slowly undressed, wrapped a towel around me and followed Mike's white ass toward the shower area. Mike introduced me as his guest to a couple of the men. Several jumped to shake my hand and welcome me, a few just nodded with a look that wondered what the hell a spic was doing in their club. Seeing all the men naked, I shook my head as if getting water out of my face, but I was trying to clear old thoughts and memories. Tato's words came to me about needing a new life. For two years, I'd been living one. I wasn't going back. I couldn't believe it was only two years. Tijuana was starting to seem like another lifetime.

Mike told me to drink some water before entering the steam room. We went in and out several times. It was damn hot, but I could feel my body relaxing. We took another shower before we dressed. I must be maturing, I thought, happy to realize I was at ease around all these naked men.

After we finished dressing, Mike got a fresh dry washcloth and cleaned his glasses. "I have to wear these whenever I'm awake, even in the pool." He chuckled. "When I was a kid on the swim team, I wanted to be cool and not wear them, but after misjudging and my head hitting the end several times, I swallowed my teenage pride and wore them."

We sat and talked over dinner till they dimmed the lights. Though on the quiet side, Mike was easy to talk with. Told me about his mom's family owning a bank, his dad going to work there when they married and her being an only child, his dad taking it over when her father died. Mike had four older brothers who hated the banking business. "I wanted to be a musician, piano and violin. I was good, still am, but Father thought it impractical. After he realized my brothers would not go into the banking business, he pushed me even harder. I took my time, but eventually, I got a college degree in banking and finance." He sipped his coffee, his wavering eyes never leaving mine. "About five years ago, I realized I was actually smart and good in this business, so I buckled down. I'm now the senior vice-president and will take over when Dad retires. I'm active in the community, on the board of directors here at the Y, just trying to pay back all they did for me while I was growing up." He nudged me with his long leg under the table. "What's your story? Why'd you come here? It couldn't be for the weather or the smells."

His question threw me. My story? I hadn't thought about telling people why I left California to come to Chicago. It should be simple. I looked away for a few minutes. What do I say? How much do I tell? That I was a willing fourteen-year-old prostitute? That my own father caused my shoulder injury? That my first lover died three weeks ago? I sighed. Looking him in the eyes again, I said, "It wasn't for the weather, but my story will take a long time and may shock you. I'm an honest person, so if I tell it, I will tell it all, whether it shocks you or not."

His face grew serious. I could tell he was thinking before he said, "Tomorrow is Wednesday. Bankers don't work on Wednesday afternoons. What time will you be finished washing windows tomorrow?"

That surprised me. "Well, I think by shortly after noon. I was hoping to get a siesta, that's something else I've learned you gringos don't do around here." We both smiled. "Hey, is there anywhere around here that serves Mexican food? Man, this food is killing me."

"Are you all right?"

His question was so sincere, I couldn't help laughing. "I'm all right, but it may take several days for this heavy food to work through my system, and eating so much will probably add ten pounds. See, I need simple food, beans and rice and lots of fruit and vegetables. Fresh ones, not stuff cooked to death."

"Well, I have heard there are Mexican places to eat further north, in Pilsen." He leaned forward, his face excited. "Tell you what, can you finish, eat a light lunch and get a siesta in by, say two-thirty tomorrow? After that, maybe we could travel to Pilsen and find some food you like. An early dinner. I will treat." He paused, his face more serious. "You will have to drive. My vision isn't good enough to be safe behind the wheel."

Before I fell asleep, I thought about this friendship that seemed to be developing. Other than Lucas, I'd never had a regular friendship with someone younger than my grandparents. Would it lead to something else? Was I ready? I didn't think so. As I drifted off, I decided just a friendship might be good. Besides, Mike had many connections that might lead to a job.

The next afternoon, Mike was waiting in the lobby when I came downstairs after my siesta and shower. In the car, he was like a kid getting his first ice cream cone. He kept opening the map, though it was obvious he didn't need it. He explained Chicago's numbering system to me, pointed out different sites of significance. I recognized Back-of-the-Yards by the smell. I'd driven through it on my way from Dad and Maria's. Almost bouncing on his seat, he batted my arm. "You know I never ate Mexican food? Never, in my whole life. I am so excited." I couldn't help but laugh. It felt good to laugh with another man, seemingly a homo man. I hoped we would stay friends after I told him my story. I still wasn't sure about anything beyond friendship, or especially if I was ready for sex. Even though my body felt the need, my emotions weren't sure. Art and Maria crossed my mind as I drove close to Twenty-Second Street.

"Why are you getting quiet? You look more sober."

"*Nada*." I stopped for an old lady crossing the street. "Well, my dad lives near here and I don't want to run into him. It's part of my story."

We drove around, looking for restaurants. Mike was amazed at the small places with their handwritten signs in bright colors and the bold paint on the buildings. He thought sections of the area looked a little dirty. I told him compared to Tijuana, he hadn't seen dirt yet. He got quiet, his eyes big.

I parked the car and we walked along the street that seemed to have the most restaurants. I stuck my head in several and asked questions about what they served, all in Spanish. Mike had no idea what I was asking or looking for, but seemed to trust me. I chose a place and we went in. Tiny, with maybe five tables, clean, and the food smelled wonderful. The young woman stared at Mike, still dressed in his suit, though he'd loosened his tie. She asked if he spoke Spanish and I shook my head. She wondered if he was with *las federals*. I laughed and shook my head. "He's a banker."

She muttered they were only a little better and why were his eyes funny and his hair white. I quickly said albino and she nodded as she understood, then motioned us toward a table.

I read the menu posted on the wall to Mike in Spanish. He laughed and tried to repeat the words after me. Almost giggling, he said, "You order. This is an adventure for me. I trust you."

I ordered *pozole* to start. It's one of my favorites and is a full meal in itself, but I was starving. We had a beer, Corona, with a lime. I told the young woman where I was from and how it had been several weeks since I ate good food and my friend the banker never ate Mexican food.

"My grandmother is the cook, just a minute." She came back several minutes later. "Tata will prepare small amounts of several things so you can remember and he can learn. Okay?"

I beamed and nodded.

"She also said she will make up some sangria special just for you. This is a slow time of the day so she has time. She also said not to hurry."

I told Mike and he laughed from his excitement.

"So, are you sure you want to hear my story? It's a long walk back for you if you won't like me."

He just smiled, his eyes got warm. I was surprised how well I could read them with their twitching and his frequent blinking.

"Take your coat and vest and tie off. I don't want to tell my story to someone looking like *la federal*."

I settled back, took a sip of my Corona and slowly began with my parents, my birth, mother's death and how I was injured by my father, as well as why my other grandmother did not want to explain to my tato.

Our first platter of food arrived, containing small servings of huarache, tacos with pastor, enchilada, chilaquiles, lots of corn tortillas, beans and rice, and things I can no longer remember due to my advanced age. Ha ha.

I explained each item to Mike and he couldn't get enough of them. Several times, I told him, "The rest of this is mine!"

Of course, he laughed, so did the lady.

I continued my story when the sangria came. I spoke of running the streets, of guarding for my cousins, of selling myself, of having my own room at fifteen, of the knife I carried, of the tight pants I advertised myself with. I didn't look at Mike most of the time. I was afraid of what I might see written across his face.

A second platter arrived. I glanced at Mike and saw a mixed expression of sadness, admiration, and shock.

I quickly explained the chicken in mole sauce, the steak asada, the stuffed poblano peppers and the moletes.

I waved my hand at the woman and her grandmother to not cook anymore and told them that if I died right then, it would be as an extremely happy Mexican. They beamed with pride.

Mike asked if he could become an honorary Mexican, if not, at least a food taster. They clapped their hands and laughed when I translated, then brought out rice pudding. I have learned after eating American versions, Mexicans make the best rice pudding.

Another pitcher of sangria was placed on our table. I told Mike of Tato involving himself in my life, of guiding me lightly, but with direction. I had to swallow more sangria before talking about Lucas, how he waited till I outgrew my background before allowing himself to love me, about our wonderful few months together, about his accident and death, about my long drive here. His shoulders tensed when I told him my father offered to rent me a room in the basement for more than a house would cost to rent. I finished with Maria mentioning the Y, telling me to keep in touch with her.

When finished, I stared at the floor, embarrassed. The young woman understood enough English to grasp my loss of a good friend.

Whether she realized we were homos or not, I don't know. She brought me a small pot with cool water and a clean washcloth and whispered I could wash my face.

I heard Mike blow his nose and looked at him. His fists clenched the table, he looked like he was fighting to stay seated. "I so want to hold you right now. I—I..."

I put my hand up to stop him from saying what I thought he was going to say next. He seemed to understand and relaxed a little. He reached over for the washcloth I just used, but the young woman shouted no and brought him his own pan and cloth which broke the sadness and we all laughed a little.

Walking back to the car, Mike asked if I was all right to drive.

"*Si, Señor*. I ate enough food to absorb the sangria. Why? Are you worried about riding with a drunken Mexican?"

"I think we'd be safer with you driving drunk than with me trying to drive."

We were quiet for a good while as I navigated the traffic. Mike said it was rush hour, something we had in San Diego, but somehow it seemed worse in Chicago.

"I have an idea," he said. "I have more of my story to tell you, not like yours, but if we are to become friends, then I would like to tell you."

I said fine. I liked the idea of becoming friends, truly liked it.

"Please do not take this wrong. I try to be a man of integrity. I am a homosexual, like you, but what I am about to say should not be taken as persuasion to have sex with me. Understood?"

I nodded, confused about a wish for friendship and my physical desire. My life was changing so quickly again.

"I live with my parents, they are out of town on vacation till a week from Sunday. Why don't we go to my house for the evening and talk some more? Later, you can return to the Y. I invite you to think about staying in the house with me while you look for work and another place to live. We have a large house with many bedrooms, you could save money, plus maybe we can drive back up to Pilsen area to a grocery and bring back some food you could cook at my house. Please, my offer is with no strings attached."

I was going through a congested traffic intersection, so couldn't look at him, let alone speak. When the cars lessened, I carefully said, "I appreciate your kind offer, I will consider it."

Chapter Ninety

Mike's Story

Mike's home was brick, large, and located on several lots, surrounded by a wrought iron fence. Inside were wood panels and floors with thick rugs, fancy lights, art and pictures. In an alcove, I noticed a big grand piano, I think you call them that, with a violin on a stand next to it. It was so different from Tato's large house.

We sat in the den in comfortable chairs that faced a TV which we left off. We drank water, still too full to drink anything else.

"How old are you?" Mike asked.

"I turned eighteen at Easter. Actually, the day of Easter in nineteen-forty, but I've always considered my birthday on whatever day Easter falls."

He chuckled. "Well, you certainly seem older and wiser than eighteen." He lit a cigarette, then passed the box over to me and waited while I lit up. "I was born in May, nineteen-thirty, so I am ten years older, though after hearing your life story, I somehow feel younger. I was sickly as a child, lots of doctors, frequently changing my eyeglasses. My father realized I would not be able to play sports like my brothers, football, American football, and baseball, basketball, volleyball, tennis. I could not follow the fast movement of the balls or players. So, at age five, he taught me to swim at the Y and pushed me into swimming and running track." He took a long draw and tapped the ashes into the stand next to his chair. "As I said, I loved music and could have contented myself to play the piano and violin all day, every day. I tell you, Mother and Father frequently argued about that until a compromise was arrived at which allowed me time each day to do sport and music. Each parent pushing me hard in their favorite area. At times, I felt like an elastic band stretched between them. I suppose, like all kids, I adjusted. Here I am today, still loving swimming, jogging and music." He looked at me in a warm tender manner. "And now, Mexican food."

We were both quiet, looking into the other's eyes. I wondered about this kind man, how different our backgrounds were. How could we possibly find love? He was educated, my God, with a college degree. And he was wealthy, a gentleman in his community. And me? A simple Mexican whose main education was from the streets and the tutoring of Mrs. Lopez, not even high school. Yet, Tato's words came to me. Something about good friends are not always alike. "That way, you learn more from each other," he said. I nodded for Mike to continue.

"My father insisted I go to public school even though my brothers went to Catholic."

"Why? That doesn't make sense."

"He thought the nuns and priests would protect me, baby me too much. Public school would toughen me, make me strong, expose me to children from other backgrounds, and the teachers wouldn't have the time or the inclination to baby me as much."

He stood, stretched and lit another smoke while I also lit one. He was tall, six-one and probably weighed a solid one hundred seventy pounds. I'd seen his body naked in the locker room and he was beautiful. I remembered being surprised, pleasantly so. I think my expectations of meeting a white-haired, flickering-eyed albino dressed in a suit and tie didn't extend below the neck.

"I guess going to public school did toughen me up. I was teased a lot, especially when I had to walk up to the blackboard to read what the teacher wrote, or when a boy would quickly lob something at me, a ball, a pencil box and say, 'Think fast, Whitey.' Of course I couldn't see fast enough to catch it. One of my teachers, a male, who I now know was a homo, pulled me aside one day. 'I know you can't see well enough to use your fists because you can't see the quickness of something coming back at you, but have you thought of wrestling?'"

"I remember shaking my head. He went on to inform me he was starting a wrestling club at a local church basement and I might want to attend. I told my father who said no way, not with that man and to never be alone with him. Father signed me up for wrestling classes at the Y. I was kind of scrawny, but learned enough to occasionally take my tormentors down at school and hold them till they cried uncle. Gradually, the teasing stopped."

He refilled my water and emptied our ashtrays into a waste basket.

Sitting back down, he laughed as he continued, "I did learn a few good holds and moves, but you know what I learned the most?"

I shook my head, starting to laugh because I had a good idea what his answer would be.

"That I liked holding boys close, and the less clothes on them, the better." He slapped his leg and broke into loud, almost painful laughter. "One day, I was twelve, and Father came to watch me. Afterward, the Y wrestling instructor spoke with him. He was probably a college kid. On the walk home, Father told me I would not be going to wrestling again. He said other boys were complaining about me rubbing myself on them too much."

This time, Mike didn't laugh, nor did I.

"'You're the banker's son,' Father said. 'My name is well known in this community. You cannot become known as a faggot. I will not allow it.' When we got home, he yelled at my mother for babying me, said I was starting to act like a faggot and she needed to stop protecting me." Mike took a drink of water, drained the glass. "My music lessons were cut back, I was given private swim lessons and enrolled on a private swim club team, in addition to the Y. In junior high, I ran track and cross country. In other words, running and swimming would keep the devil from turning me homo." He walked over and opened a large, heavy door containing a large rack of wine bottles. "White or red? I need something." Without waiting for a reply, he pulled out a dark bottle, opened it and poured two small glasses.

I took a sip and looked up at him, surprised. "It's sweet."

He chuckled. "It's port." He took a sip and sat back down. "From then on, my father nagged me about how I walked, moved my arms. I don't think I presented much different than other pubescent boys who are all arms, legs and clumsy. He was extra critical. 'You are not a fairy girl,' he'd hiss. In high school, unlike my brothers, I only needed to maintain a B average because of my eyes, which was strange because my eyes had nothing to do with my brightness. My brothers had to keep an A minus average. Plus, I had to stay ultra-busy. My brothers did too, but theirs seemed self-initiated, mine enforced, like I couldn't make up my own mind, determine my own interests. One year in high school, I signed up for glee club, logical considering my love of music. Father called the school and ordered them to remove me from the group. He told them I could take marching band if I wanted, but not orchestra or glee club. I didn't take marching band. Was he crazy? Can you see me with music in front of my face trying to march, play an instrument and see?"

I shook my head in wonderment. There are different ways besides physical in which fathers and mothers can injure their children. I also remember sitting there, both of us quiet, me thinking again about the contrast in our lives. In my early teens, I was protecting my cousins turning tricks, trying to sell rubbers to their johns, giving them a discount if they wore one. Next, I was selling myself, always hustling, hiding money in my tiny room in case I didn't score, taking anything above my savings to Grandma and Grandpa, telling them I'd had a good day reselling toys, or candy or cigarette lighters. Anything but the truth. Of course, they knew what I was doing, but wouldn't say anything.

Mike must have sensed the same thing. "Quite a contrast, isn't it? What a difference between the two of us."

I could only nod.

"You spoke of Lucas, now I have to tell you about my first lover. I was sixteen and fell running cross-country, easy to do when your vision isn't great and you're running over rough ground. That night, I went to swim practice at the Y, limping and in pain. The coach said to do easy exercises in the water and not swim laps. He helped me get out of the pool a few minutes later and told me to go through the locker room to see the masseur. "He's new with us, he studied back-cracking. He thought he might be able to twist you around and plus work on some of your strains." Coach laughed as he said, "Just don't be shocked when you meet him. He's blind."

"A blind man giving massages?" I laughed out loud, then Mike did too. "Is that like a one-armed guy washing windows?"

Mike grinned and went on, "I'm in my wet swimsuit and walk through the door to his small massage room. "Hey," he yelled, "I can smell pool water, get that damn suit off and don't drip all over the floor where I might slip." He grabbed a towel and threw it toward me, told me to dry completely, then lie face down on the table." Mike took a sip of port, looked at our glasses and poured them nearly full again. "Next, he ran his hands and fingers all over me, asked me how I fell. He twisted me some odd ways, then massaged my strained leg and hip areas. It hurt, but felt good, know what I mean?"

I didn't at first. I'd never had a massage, but I nodded anyway. I remembered the physical therapy I had on my arm in San Diego and realized what he meant.

"He was very professional, even when close to my privates, though that did feel good too. He started asking me questions about my life, what I did, what I liked, what I didn't. He was easy to talk with. Said his dad pushed him too, even though he was blind since birth. He played the trumpet and piano. Next, he said he wanted to see me every day for four days, then every other day. He didn't even laugh when he said see me. I realized he saw me through his hands."

"So, how did he become your lover? It seems like the Y is not a very private place."

"Well, I did feel better and was running well again. I also felt like we became friends. I learned about his background, how he was only twenty-one, we laughed and joked a lot. We each said we didn't date girls, but never anything more than that. At my final treatment, I told him I was going to miss him, but would occasionally stop in the locker area and say hi. He got real quiet and I could see emotion on his face. He whispered, 'I've enjoyed meeting you, I'd like to be friends. I get lonely for guys close to my age. I live alone in an efficiency three blocks away so I can walk to work or take the bus in bad weather. Would you consider visiting me at my place?'

"I said yes. As I turned for the door, he touched my arm, pulled me into an embrace and kissed me. I couldn't believe it. A kiss with a man! It was wonderful and I've never forgotten it, even after twelve years. Have you forgotten your first kiss with a man?"

I shook my head, and stood up. "No, it was only three or four months ago. I—I—I really need to leave. Don't get up. Please don't."

I rushed passed him, thankful he didn't try to stand. On my way past him, he reached his hand out and gently touched mine. That's why I didn't want him to stand up. I felt like even a handshake would have ended in an embrace. Something which I couldn't have stopped or wanted to, but wasn't ready for. At least, not yet.

Chapter Ninety-One

In Love Again

I spent most of Wednesday apartment and room shopping. Same results all over that area. When the landlord saw me, he or she would say, "We just rented the room and haven't taken our sign down yet." It was discouraging. I even contemplated moving back to California, but kept thinking of Mike. I didn't want to move away from a friendship. That's what I kept telling myself. Worst case was I was sure I could find something in the Pilsen area and see Mike occasionally. The only bad thing was I wanted to be closer.

At the Y, late that afternoon, Clancy motioned me over. "Mike asked me ta ring down and tell 'im when youse got back. Okay I do dat now?"

I nodded and waited till he stepped back from the switchboard. "'Be right here,' ats what he said to tell ya."

Mike came through the door and looked at me with a curious look, trying to size up my demeanor. "I'm hungry, want to get a hot dog? There's a great little stand a block away."

"Sure, but it's my treat," I replied. I couldn't help smiling at him. I was glad to see him.

On the walk over, I told him my frustrations in finding a place to live. We were both quiet, I could tell he wanted to ask about me staying with him, but didn't want to rush me.

"Hey, Mike? If your offer is open, I'd like to stay at your place, but starting tomorrow." Nudging his arm with my shoulder, I added, "I didn't want to give up my last free night at the Y. See, I watch my pennies, just like a banker."

He laughed and shook his head. In the morning, checking out, the clerk handed me a note to stop by the bank. Mike wanted to see me.

I walked into a small, old-looking, quiet bank and noticed several buckets sitting around. It rained overnight and evidently the roof leaked.

Mike motioned me into his office. He handed me a newspaper with red circles around ads for rooming houses and efficiency apartments.

"I had one of my staff look for you. I figure Saturday and Sunday afternoon, we could drive around and look for a place."

"Thank you, but what the hell is going on with your roof? Added to that, your front windows need washing, inside and out."

He motioned for me to sit down across from him. "That's the second reason I wanted to see you. I have some work for you around here, at least for several days and maybe part time for a long time. Our building guy is old and decrepit, he can barely empty the trash, let alone repair anything. I want to show you around and see if you want to take over some things around here. I think he'll be relieved to only empty waste cans and do some light dusting."

We went through the building. I slipped my cloth sling on to hold my arm. That way, I could hold my small notebook in my left hand and make notes with my right. We went onto the flat roof where I poked and prodded. "Mike, this is shot. It has multiple layers that need to be tore off, fresh decking is needed, then the tar and gravel." I saw the look coming on his face, and quickly added, "I can't do this type of roofing, you need to hire a good roofer."

He nodded, but smiled. He understood.

Back in his office, we went over my list and I told him what needed repairing quickly, what cleaning would be needed to get things back to an easy maintenance condition, along with some future repairs and work that would need to be done as well. I gave him estimates of how long it would take me to bring things back, and to keep things up after that, probably fifteen hours a week.

"How much would you charge per hour?" Mike seemed concerned, almost overwhelmed at how much work the building needed. It was nothing major, other than the roof, but it had obviously been neglected and little supervision provided to the existing worker who was employed there since the Indians were forced out.

I looked him in the eye. "No less than you're paying the current man."

Mike's eyes flew up in shock, telling me I'd guessed right. They were paying that old guy a lot because he'd been around so long, not because he still did a good job.

I put my hand up to stop him from commenting. "You know I can work four times faster than him and get four times more accomplished. In a short time, I will be saving you money. At that point, I will also expect a raise."

His hand zoomed to his mouth, I thought he might choke. He turned away a moment, then back, this time looking me in the eyes. He slapped his forehead. "I have a college degree from one of the best university business programs in the country and you have a better grasp of economics than I do. I apologize. I was worried about telling Father I was changing building staff and preparing to deal with his nitpicking criticisms. I wasn't looking at the big picture. I wasn't thinking like the future director who will take this flea-bitten little bank into the future." Excitedly, he grabbed my hand, knocking my pencil out, and shook it like he just signed a deal with Rockefeller himself. "Can you start Monday?"

That night, I slept in a guest room. I woke up Friday morning, thinking about Lucas and Mike. How one was gone, who I missed terribly, but the other was down the hall. I would always love Lucas, but he would never be able to give back my love. Mike was alive, kind, honest and obviously entranced with me. What were the advantages of waiting? Homos finding love twice was rare. It was worth the risk, I decided, still wondering inside.

Too excited to wait till Monday to start work, I spent Saturday morning at the bank, checking supplies, cleaning equipment, making lists. The old man was there and practically cried when he met me. "I am so glad Mike is taking hold. They should have gotten rid of me years ago. His father and I go back forever. Neither one of us could pull the plug. I'm happy dusting and emptying the waste cans and helping you any way I can."

The other staff seemed intrigued with the idea of Mike hiring me. I couldn't tell if it was because I was a dangle-armed man, a Mexican, or both. Yet, several said they were tired of the place looking like a dump. I quickly washed the front windows, inside and out, winning over those clerks who doubted having a spic around.

That afternoon, we drove around, seeking rooms and efficiencies. We expanded our area to Ashland and Forty-Seventh, the Back-of-the-

Yards area. I hated the smell, but Mike said the stockyards and plants were slowly closing and it was getting better. Late that afternoon, we drove by 4822 South Justine and I remarked that the sign said efficiencies, but I was too tired of having doors closed in my face because I was a spic to get out. Told Mike I might come back later in the week.

The other reason I didn't want to get out was that I was hungry. So was Mike, not only for food, but for each other. We both sensed it. I drove back to his home where he warmed up some soup while I made a salad. Doing dishes, I asked him, "What happened with your first lover?"

"We had a wonderful six years of me sneaking over to his place. I can't tell you how many nights I snuck down the back stairway and ran over to his place, returning about five in the morning. I never got caught." He wiped his face with a napkin. "One winter, when I was twenty-two, taking university classes, living at home, he slipped getting off the bus. The driver didn't see him and the back wheels ran over his leg, severely damaging it. He had to move back home with his aging mother. He was still in a wheelchair the last I contacted him, four years ago. He asked me to quit visiting. Said a blind man in a wheelchair had nothing to offer anyone else."

"Are you over him?"

He whispered, "As much as is possible. Are you over Lucas?"

"As much as is possible."

We embraced. We didn't stop kissing and making love till Sunday night when he remembered the housekeeper would be back at seven thirty in the morning. We ran around, naked, laughing like hell, doing dishes, washing and drying our crusty sheets and the towels scattered around their huge clawfoot tub. We were out of the house by seven Monday morning. He left a note telling the housekeeper she was only needed between nine and two that week.

Chapter Ninety-Two

4822 South Justine

We worked our asses off that week, Mike meeting with the staff about improving their services and attracting new customers and me getting the place looking good. Friday morning, I realized I hadn't secured a place to live and told Mike I was taking the afternoon off, and Saturday morning if necessary, to find a place. I was starting to panic. So was he. I think because he realized we wouldn't be living together anymore.

That Friday, I stopped at several more rooming houses and small apartments and got the same results. My last stop for the day was on South Justine, the one we drove by the week prior. If that didn't work out, I planned on going further north to Pilsen, where I was sure I could find something, even if in my dad's basement.

Thank God, little Krystina was swinging on the front porch, reading a book, and her mother Katie was around the corner, and Hank and Mae weren't home. That little girl was a blessing sent directly from heaven. I still laugh at the way she wrapped old Hank around her little finger and told him I should take the efficiency so I could fix my Mexican food, whatever it was. I didn't know there was only one efficiency, nor that it was originally planned for women.

Katie. What a woman, what a mother that young lady was! She just stared at me like she saw a ghost from the past. She sent her little girl to get us some ice tea and apologized for staring. Next, like she couldn't help herself, she said I looked just like the girl's daddy. He was Mexican, they got engaged, she got pregnant. He went off to Korea and she never heard from him again. She said I was the first person other than her big brother to know the girl's daddy was Mexican. I told her I was honored to be that person and would never tell anyone else.

I finished work early the next morning, went into Mike's office to thank him and say I'd be down Monday to keep working on the place. He pointed to the couch, looked real serious, maybe sad.

"I've been thinking," he said. "It's time I moved out from home.

Tell that man to hold a small room for me near you. I'll get the housekeeper's husband to drive me up late Sunday afternoon. At least we'll be close to each other. Closer than me staying at home, missing you."

"What about your parents? Your father?"

He closed the door before saying, "Both will be shocked. I won't tell them where I'm moving, just say an apartment north of them near a bus route so I can get to work, which is mostly true. I'm not telling them about you at this point." He sighed and stretched. "Mother will cry till I tell her I'll still have dinner with them two nights a week and sometimes on Sunday. The biggest deal will be this Monday when Father comes to work and I inform him of the steps I've taken to better manage the place." He pulled me up and into a hug. "I love you," he whispered.

I kissed my answer back, walked out and drove up to my new efficiency apartment. So new, I spent several hours cleaning it, then ended up helping Hank change the oil in his car, followed by one of his homemade beers.

Mae acted like she hated me, was mad at Hank for renting to me, but I could tell she was fascinated, well, if not fascinated, at least interested in the dangle-armed Mexican her husband just rented to. Probably she was afraid what her neighbors would think of them renting to the first Mexican in the neighborhood.

That Sunday evening, Mike moved into a small room on the third floor near mine, excited as a teenager seeing his love naked for the first time. It was wonderful. No one else lived on the third floor during that time and we would basically live together in my efficiency.

Chapter One Ninety-Three

Mike's Dad

Sunday evening, after Mike moved in to the rooming house, we were in the efficiency and I was making tacos when there was a knock at the door. "It's me, Hank. I gotta take your picture." He looked slightly surprised to see Mike and me together. "Well, that's right, you two know each other. Guess this saves me banging on your door, Mike." He snapped each of us with his old Brownie camera and turned to leave.

"Hank, could you take one of us together?" Mike asked.

He threw his arm around me, like you see good friends stand. Before I could be embarrassed, old Hank turned and snapped the picture.

"Guess so," he said. "We take a snap of each resident just to keep a record. Don't know why, but my dad started it and we just keep doing it. Out of tradition, I guess. I'll get you copies when the film is used up."

He gave us a funny look and left. Weeks later, he gave us a copy of our individual picture and of the two of us together.

Monday morning at the bank, I was in the men's room, scrubbing the ceiling and walls before I tackled the floor. The place hadn't been painted in decades, nor the floors stripped and waxed. For a bank, it was a mess with the smell partially covered by deodorant blocks in the urinal. The door flew open and a tall distinguished gray-haired man stomped in. I could see Mike's resemblance. "Who are you? Where is George? Why are you doing his work?"

I dried my hand off and stuck it out to shake his. "I'm Manny. I'm the new building supervisor. Mike hired me. George will be in this afternoon to dust and empty the waste cans."

He ignored my hand. "Mike hired you? What do you mean? George is supposed to do this work. He's the only one who know how."

I pointed to the section of wall where I scrubbed off years of dust and grime. "See the difference? George was too old to do stuff like this. Next, I'm going to paint it, then strip and wax the floors. I'll do the women's room at night." I flashed my best smile. He turned and stomped out. He didn't shake my hand.

A moment later, the door flew open again, almost knocking me off the step stool and he marched to the urinal. "I still have to take a leak the minute I get here. Damn coffee." I turned and kept scrubbing the wall. He finished and washed his hands. "You said Mike hired you?" I nodded. "His eyes must be getting bad again if he can't tell you're a lazy wetback spic."

I stepped down, blocking the door, and stuck my hand out again. "I'm a Mexican born in San Diego. I'm not a wetback nor a spic and I'm sure as hell not lazy. I think your son's eyes work pretty damn good." I glared at him till he shook my hand.

I let him pass and heard him holler in the hallway for Mike. "You told me last night it was time for a change. You moved out from home, you hired a spic, you act like I'm too damn old to run this place." I figured the two of them were standing just outside the bathroom.

"Dad, do you want to go into the office to talk? I thought we covered this last night when you and Mom got home from your vacation."

It was quiet. I heard his dad say in a subdued voice, "Yes. I guess we did discuss this last night. The truth of it hit me when I came in and realized you weren't kidding around." There was another long pause. "Well, son. Guess we have been talking about you taking over for some time, but what the heck am I going to do with my time now?"

"Dad, I still have much to learn from you. Only now, I want answers to my questions, not be told to wait. Okay? I have some projects I need help on." Mike's dad must have nodded. "Dad, one more change. Now don't have a heart attack, but I switched our offices, too."

I heard his dad mutter, "Damn, boy. You finally grew yourself some balls."

That afternoon, I returned from the paint store, carrying two gallons of paint in my right hand. Mike's dad was standing in the doorway of Mike's office, a cigar in his mouth. "Mike, I'm leaving. Your mother will be shocked I came home this early. Of course, she'll probably be moaning about you not living with us, but she'll get over it. By the way, I located three contractors to give us bids on the roof." He turned and stared at me as I approached. Pulling the cigar out of his mouth, he nodded at me. "I'm still not wild about having a spic around here, but..."

"I'm a Mexican, not a spic." I said it calmly, but enunciated each word.

"I—I—I mean a Mexican. I was going to say, you sure know what you're doing. All the tellers have remarked on the changes you've made, and several fussy old lady customers also commented." He waved his cigar at me. "And George...Well, I've never seen him so happy." A grimace crossed his face. "Change is hard sometimes. Guess I need to get used to it." He turned and walked toward the rear door as Mike shot me a thumbs up.

Chapter Ninety-Four

A Manager and A Son

That first week, besides working at the bank, I walked through both upper floors of the rooming house, making notes on the condition and cleanliness, getting to know the guys on the second floor. Almost all had been there for years. I made a list of needed repairs I showed to Hank. He was surprised I'd taken the time to do it, a little embarrassed at my findings, then excited at my ideas.

"I guess I hadn't realized how much I've let the place slip," he said as we sat in his basement still—he called it his second laundry room—and enjoyed one of his home-brews.

"Nothing is major, though I have some ideas that would make the roomers extremely happy. Things they would be willing to pay more each week for."

Hank nodded, a curious look on his face.

"They told me you haven't raised their rates in well over five years, and they're willing to pay more. They know they're getting a good deal, but would like to see some upgrades."

"Such as..." He lifted his hands in question, a worried look on his face.

"Well, they would like a shower on their floor. Sitting in an old tub with a hose to rinse off does not qualify as a good shower. The toilet room should have a sink in it and desperately needs upgrading, their rooms need painting. They would love to have a back porch to sit and smoke on. The landing only holds one or two at a time."

"What's your plan? How much is this going to cost me? I ain't made of dough, you know." His eyes twinkled at his little rhyme.

I walked him up to the second floor and showed him my ideas. First, paint the rooms, paint or refinish the old dressers, install rods to hang clothes on instead of the old hooks, some were still the originals. Refinish or paint the doors, upgrade the window screens, sand and refinish the wood floors. Next, I showed him how a urinal and small sink could fit into the toilet closet with a partial wall between it and the stool.

Plus, in the tub closet, how the tub could be replaced with two shower stalls.

"Really? These guys will get naked in front of the other?"

"For Pete's sake, Hank, they get naked in front of the men over at the park fieldhouse shower room. Where the hell you think they been taking their showers several times a week?"

"Guess I am out of touch." He shook his head and leaned against the wall. "So, how much this gonna cost?"

"I'm not done yet, here's my ideas for a back porch." I explained how we could add a covered porch across the back, even screen it in. And the roof could be a deck for the third floor. Then I gave him an estimate for materials.

He sat down heavy on an old chair and wiped his brow. "What about labor? Who could do this? I ain't got time, working full time over at the Ford dealer. More importantly, I ain't got the energy like I used to."

"I have a plan," I said.

"Somehow I knew you would, let's hear it."

By the time we were done, he'd hired me to do the work, said he would add my name to the lumberyard and hardware accounts to buy materials on credit. He headed down the stairs, I turned to go up to the third floor. "C'mon," he grumped, "we need another beer."

I followed him down, out the front door, around to the side door, and into the basement.

He pulled two more beers out, sat down heavily in his soft chair and was quiet, looking up at the rafters, scratching his crotch. "I've been thinking," he finally said, taking another sip of beer. "I'm tired of this place. Oh, I love it, don't want to move, but when you said it's been over five years since I changed the rates, and the fellas been taking most of their showers over at the field house. Well..." His voice trailed off.

I waited, taking small sips of my beer. I couldn't wait to start upgrading the second floor. Hadn't told him what I thought should be done to the third. What the hell. He could almost double his income if he filled those rooms and with little added expense.

He tapped my leg with his bottle. "Wake up, boy, you got more plans floating around that head of yours, don't cha?"

I grinned and nodded.

"I don't want to hear them. Not yet. Now, here's what I'm thinking. You seem to know the guys now, why don't I just make you the manager of this old dump? You collect the rent, take in the new ones when there's space, throw 'em out when they're drunk or sneaking hookers in. What do ya say?"

"I like it, but you don't think I'm too young?"

He honked and spat a wad into the floor drain. "Hell, no. My dad started building this place at your age and I was collecting rent at age twelve. Hell, no, you're not too young. Here's what. I'll give you that efficiency for free and twenty bucks a week to manage the place. Deal?"

"What about your wife? She be okay with this?"

He struggled out of his chair, rested his hand on my shoulder, tousled my hair and laughed, "Son, I couldn't live without Mae, I love her to death, but sometimes it just takes her longer to agree with some of the brilliant decisions I make. Don't worry."

I followed him up the basement stairs, glad he couldn't see my eyes. I took a walk around the block, watched the neighbor kids being called in by their parents, the street lights flickering on, heard the water sprinklers in the gardens. I kept wiping my eyes. Hank called me son. The first time in my life a man called me son. Son! I rolled the word around my tongue. Son. My nose dripped. Son. It was as good, maybe even better, then Tato calling me grandson. Son.

I was home. A wonderful man called me son. That meant I had a parent. Only a parent calls a child son, and pats his shoulder and messes his hair. Parents have homes. Now I had a home. That thought went down so deep, I couldn't tell if it ever came out. Still can't. I leaned against a tree, lit a cigarette and stared at the gray, weather-worn, three story house and for the first time in my life, knew I was home. I was a son. I had a home.

Chapter Ninety-Five

Mike Leaves and Marries

Mike and I had a private phone line run into the efficiency. He needed a number the bank could get hold of him if there was an emergency. I liked not having to go into Hank and Mae's to order supplies. Mike did get a call late one night. The cops found the back door unlocked and the alarm not set. I drove him down there. Apparently, the last person out simply forgot. Guess he fired her the next day.

Six months after moving in, I finished the second floor. The men were thrilled. Even more so when I told them as soon as the weather broke, I was building a covered, screened back porch for them to sit and smoke on.

"How da hell you'd get old Hank to spring loose wit da dough? We alwus figured he was half Jewish."

I laughed and told them he had some reserves saved up. I didn't tell them he had a lot of reserves saved up or how he once told me, "My mom showed me how to always set money aside each month for reserves and to borrow against it when you make repairs. She was right, I got enough to rebuild the whole place. Course I ain't gonna do that."

One evening, Mike's brother James called him, told him to get home, their father had a heart attack. I drove him down. The next day, he called me. "Father's in bad shape, in a coma. I need to stay home a while with Mother, she's taking it poorly, plus her lungs are worse."

I understood, but had this sense things weren't going to be the same again. Our six months of loving and living together was going to change. I was right. His father died ten days later and Mike never moved back to the rooming house. He moved his few possessions home, but kept paying his rent. For a while, he would spend Wednesday afternoons and nights with me and sometimes Sunday nights. That lasted until his mother got worse with her emphysema and he became much busier now that he was the bank president. Still, it was a workable relationship and we loved each other. Just not as frequently.

Nine months after that, Mike began coming less often. We still talked almost daily on the phone, but even our calls became shorter. One Wednesday night, after fixing a meal, I asked him what was going on.

His hand shook as he lit a cigarette. He wouldn't look me in the eyes. Finally, he said, "I owe you a big apology. I've been avoiding telling you this for several weeks. I met a woman, I'm getting married in a month."

My mouth dropped open. "Does that mean we'll never see each other again?"

He looked away with a pained expression. "Actually, once I'm married, I might be more regular in seeing you. Cara knows about you, about us."

"But how can you be married, sleeping with her and sleeping with me? I don't get it. Why the hell would any woman allow her husband to love a man?"

He took my hand. "I know, it sounds all crazy. Cara is from Ireland. She is twenty-two with two little adorable daughters, red-haired, just like her. She is here on a visitor's visa. She came to escape an abusive husband who beat the hell out of her and the babies when he was drunk. She got a divorce, but still had to leave because of the anger of his family."

"So, you're marrying her to keep her here? You still haven't answered the big question."

"Partly to keep her here and partly because I need a wife. As the president of a bank, I have many social functions and obligations and it's awkward being a bachelor who people suspect is a sissy." He squeezed my hand. "Because Cara was so abused, she wants no relations with a man. She shudders if a man takes her arm. See, it happened like this."

He went on to explain how Cara was his sister-in-law's cousin. Mike's brother invited him and his mother to dinner to meet her. Monday evening that week, Mike saw Cara and the little girls walking home from the park. They started talking and Mike walked them home. He asked her to coffee the next day. He thought it nice to have a female friend, he said. That Wednesday afternoon, he met them at the park. On Sunday, his mother invited Cara and the little girls for dinner. While Mike was showing Cara around the house, she saw the photos on his bedroom dresser of his family and nieces and nephews, plus the one of him and me taken by Hank. He started to describe them to her. "Who is that?" she asked, pointing at the one of him and me.

"A friend, a good friend."

"Are you in love with him?" she asked.

Mike was stunned at her question, said he blushed as he tried to shake his head.

Cara smiled at him, then shocked him with her words. "It's fine with me if you are. You see, I don't think I can ever get into bed with a man again. I was horribly treated by my husband. Look, look at my arms." She showed him the rash breaking out on them. "See, just thinking about being close to a man, even just speaking with you three steps into your bedroom, is causing me hives." Shaking her head, she looked at him. "I know you need a wife and I need a husband and a father for my girls. I do not need sex, in fact I think I can only sleep in separate beds, never the same one. I will be a good wife. I already respect you immensely, I enjoy being with you, and I can tell you adore my girls."

Mike said they went downstairs. At the end of the evening, he blurted to his mother he and Cara were marrying and for her to plan a small home wedding in six weeks. He looked at Cara, amazed at what he just said. She smiled and nodded.

He was right. After their wedding, we did see each other regularly, twice a week, but things were never the same. I could tell by the way he chatted about Cara and the little girls that their relationship was growing. There was no sex, but their sense of being married partners, their connection, was growing. They became good friends who loved the same things, music, dinner with friends, volunteering in the community, playing with and encouraging their children. He was becoming a true husband and father, they were becoming a family. When he adopted the girls, I knew our relationship could not continue. More and more, it was simply sexual, which, for me, was great physically, but not emotionally. He no longer spent the entire night, just several hours, all in my bed.

One evening, he arrived, chatting about his little girls while taking his clothes off, telling me to hurry and undress. I put my hand up and told him, "Mike, I will always love you. I doubt I will ever love anyone else like I have loved you, but I will not be a whore."

He looked shocked. Before he spoke, I went on, "Right now, you have the best of both worlds. You have wonderful sex with me, plus a loving wife and children for everything else. I can't do this anymore. Please leave. Stay in touch, but don't come back here again."

We kept in touch over the phone, at least monthly for years, then it slowed to nothing.

In August, 1997, the doorbell rang. An attractive red-haired woman, probably in her fifties, along with two beautiful adult daughters waited at the door.

"I'm Cara McGuire. Are you Manny?"

I brought them into the living room which didn't look much different from when Hank and Mae lived in it. They sat down.

"I wanted to tell you in person that Mike died last month, lung cancer. He was sixty-seven. He still loved you. When he knew he had only a little time left, he asked me to come in person to tell you. He said it's the least he owed you."

We sat in silence, all of us sniffling. "Before he went into a coma," the taller of the girls said, "Dad insisted on telling us girls all about you. I think we both learned more about love and that true love can happen between anyone. I'm so glad the gays are standing up for their rights now. Before this, I'd never thought much of gays. Now I know love is worth fighting for."

Cara stood and handed me a brown envelope and motioned for me to open it. Out slid several photos of the two of us I remembered being taken on Mike's Nikon camera. He could barely see through it, but loved taking it along with him and asking someone, anyone nearby, to snap pictures of him and his friends, usually me. There were pictures of us in a park, cooking in my efficiency, I think one of the roomers named Jerry took that one, me washing the bank windows, plus the one Hank took of us. A small, cheap, well-worn men's Timex watch also slipped out. One I'd bought at a flea market and given to him as a joke shortly before he married. He already owned several expensive watches. I told him this one was for slumming around with me.

"You know," Cara said, "Mike never took that watch off except to bathe or swim. He even wore it to dress-up functions. After all these years, it still works. Strange, isn't it?" She sighed and sat back down. "Several times over these many years, I could tell his mind was way off somewhere, thinking about you. Twice, he turned to me and said, 'I wish you could meet Manny in person, you would love him.' We both knew that was impossible, given the times and circumstances." She paused, swallowed, looked out the window. "Life is strange, isn't it?"

Each one of them hugged me tight. I invited them to stay for some pozole simmering on the stove, but they couldn't. I understood. Life is strange, yet still wonderful.

Chapter Ninety-Six

No Hippies Allowed

With Hank's blessings, I whipped the old house into great shape. Redid the third floor, filled it with guys. I didn't allow any hippies in. Tried a few times, but they ran out of money unless I collected it daily and that was too much work. Plus, I'd rent to one and next thing I knew, there'd be two more, at least one of them with a guitar, chanting some kind of songs. They drove my regulars nuts.

I did rent to a colored man. I write it as colored, right about then, I think they were beginning to be called blacks. Anyway, I knew it was a risk, but he was a Korean War vet, had a job, was quiet and said he didn't drink much. A couple of the guys bitched like mad.

"I ain't livin' near some nigger."

"Manny, you gonna wash the sink and shower and toilet after that nigger uses it each time? Don' you know them people stink?"

"Get him outta here or I'm leavin'."

I showed them my fist and told them to not let the door hit their ass on their way out. One guy left and came back two days later. "That other place took in hippies. Pot smoke so thick, I couldn't breathe. They slept all day and stayed up all night. This nigger is better. I'm back."

The problem was, the man didn't stay on his medications. He had mental problems and when he didn't stay on his pills, he got goofy. After a week or so, the guys started complaining he was talking and singing to himself. I asked them, "Well, is he talking race stuff? Saying he hates whitey like some of those blacks you see on NBC news yelling about?"

"Nah, Manny. Can't say it's race talk, he's just nuts."

One night, I could hear him rocking around in his bed, yelling about the angels and devils and Jesus coming, all sorts of *loco* stuff. I called his aunt the next morning and she apologized, said she'd be over and get him to the VA. "He's a wonderful man, but when he quits taking his pills, he goes crazy." She waited a minute. "I just hope you don't think this is because he's a Negro. He told me you stood up for him. I thank you very much."

It was a long time before I rented to any more blacks. I tell myself it was because not many wanted to live here, but part of me thinks it was because of fear. There was all kind of shit going on in the streets between blacks and whites. Looking back, some of them whites were worse than the blacks. I just hope I wasn't like them.

Chapter Ninety-Seven

Tommy

I learned Hank and Mae had ten kids and that the oldest one was killed in World War II. Over those first few years living there, I met the next eight. Their acceptance of me ranged. Patricia, now the oldest, saw me mowing the yard shortly after I'd moved in. She brought me out a glass of water. "Here, you need this."

I took a long drink and thanked her.

"So, you're the latest orphan my old man took in, huh?"

I wasn't sure how to respond, so slightly shrugged my shoulders.

"Well, at least you ain't pregnant like Katie was and we don't have to worry about buying another kid Christmas and birthday presents." She chuckled, her voice hoarse from cigarettes and, I figured, from yelling all the time. She motioned at me to finish my water. "So, how's Ma taking to ya? She all warm and cuddly yet?"

I smiled and shook my head, handed her the glass back.

"Don't worry, give her time. Her bark is worse than her bite. I predict someday, she'll wanna try some of that food you spics fix, peppers and all. When that happens, you'll know you're officially one of hers, even if she won't tell ya." She punched my shoulder and marched off, her large butt swaying in frayed blue jeans that looked like she never took them off.

About Tommy, the youngest, I think I saw him in person once or twice, always with his brother Mark, the priest. The crazy thing is nobody talked about Tommy. One day, must have been 1964 or so, Hank said he and Mae were going to Macomb, Illinois the next day. Taking the day off work. He said Macomb is where Western Illinois University is, closer to the Mississippi river. He didn't look at me, just kicked the edge of the sidewalk. Finally, he muttered, "Tommy goes there. Well, went there. He got into some woman trouble and tomorrow, the judge is gonna decide if he goes to jail or goes into the service."

Several months later, he mentioned Tommy was in the Marines. I figured that meant the kid was going to Vietnam. Later, I heard, the roomers pick up on lots of stuff that went around, that Tommy came home, all shined up in his uniform for one of their family gatherings. He got Krystina alone in their apartment and was trying to force himself on her when her mother stopped him with a butcher knife.

Hearing that, I almost threw up, what with me knowing Krystina and Katie so well. Hank never said a word. I didn't see Krystina as much as I did when she was little. She was active in high school, doing her mother's bookkeeping and always on the go. Still, some Sunday afternoons, I'd hear a knock on my door, a giggle and she'd bust in with a plate of fresh cookies. We'd sit around and chat, she'd update me on her busy life. I watched her grow from childhood into a beautiful, smart young woman. They moved out shortly after the last incident with Tommy, but the move was already planned. Still, I think she was thankful to be away from that memory of living in the apartment where she was almost raped.

That fall, late October, 1966, I went down to the basement to do my laundry and heard Hank and Mae crying in their kitchen, their door open to the stairs. Hank was holding Mae in his arms. He waved me away and moaned, "Tommy got killed yesterday in Vietnam. His body's coming back next week." He didn't wave me on because Mae didn't like me, by then we were good friends, but I think their grief was too great to share with anyone else at such a moment.

They held a graveside service for Tommy. All the kids and grandkids were there, including Katie and Krystina. It was sad as hell, mostly because no one knew what to say. I heard several people whispering. One said, "We thought the Marines would straighten him out. Then look what he tried to do to Krystina."

He did get a Purple Heart for saving another soldier's life, but there were rumors of him being disciplined in the Marines for incidents of fights, even for forcing himself on girls near the base. I never saw the flag or Purple Heart for Tommy until Mae showed me shortly before she died.

Hank aged quick after that. He was already retired, but helped me putz around the house, getting in the way more than he helped, but his companionship was nice. Since Tommy's death, he mostly sat around, getting fatter, or he drove out to Oakwood Cemetery to see his two boys buried there.

Chapter Ninety-Eight

My Mother Mae

By 1962, I was twenty-two or so, when Mae accepted me as her son. Not in words, but I knew a milestone was crossed.

By then, I ran the place. Hank added me to the business bank accounts. I paid the bills, made the deposits, did everything. I even hired an auditor to go over the books at the end of each year. Hank said it was a waste of money. I told him this way, he'd know if I was cheating him out of money. He said he trusted me and knew an honest man when he shook their hand and by God, I was as honest as they come. I said, "That's what they said about Ponzi, too."

He laughed and waved his hand, like, I don't give a damn what you do.

See, I didn't want any of their kids or grandkids or anyone to say I ever took advantage of Hank and Mae. No one ever did. In fact, when Mae died in 1980 and left the place to me, all the kids were glad. Patricia said, "Hell, Manny, you've done more keeping that old relic going than any of us ever did. It's your baby, and good luck to ya." Of course, she punched my shoulder, my bad one. She never worried about which one she hit.

Anyway, back to 1962 and Mae. I had a pot of pozole simmering on my stove with the window open and a small fan blowing the heat and steam out. I could smell it all over the yard where I was mowing. I noticed Mae kept looking at me through the side door that leads to the basement or up to their apartment and Katie's.

I made one pass and as I turned around, I saw her slip a plate with two big glasses of lemonade onto the bench next to the door. I made several more passes. I was quite sure the drink was for me, but wanted to see if she would tell me that in person. Why were there two? Hank wasn't helping me, in fact, he was reading the paper on the front porch swing.

She stepped outside, caught my attention and pointed at the lemonade. I shut the mower off and ambled over. She swayed on her feet, twisting her apron, looking at the ground. She reminded me of a young teen girl, too embarrassed to talk to a boy.

"This is for... Have a glass. Here, have a glass of lemonade," she said.

I picked one up, took a long drink and asked, "Who is the other one for? Hank's half asleep on the porch."

"I know, guess it's for me." She picked it up and drank. Sniffing, she asked, "What are you cooking? It smells good."

I remembered what Patricia told me—that when she ate my food, I'd know I was hers, too. Fighting to keep a straight face, I replied, "Pozole. Katie and Krystina are joining me, they love it."

She nodded and sniffed again. "It does smell good, what's in it?"

I told her the ingredients. "Why don't you join us? Hank, too. We can squeeze in my little place. Or..." I thought a minute, waited till she was looking at me, wondering what I would say next. "Or, I could bring the pot down and we could eat around your table. Katie and Krystina are doing the dishes, that's part of the deal when I cook for guests."

"Pshaw, go on. You think Hank will eat that stuff? You guys enjoy it, I've got work to do." She gathered up the glasses and marched back inside.

I finished mowing, showered and was adjusting the temperature on the stove when Krystina burst in. "Mae says to just bring the damn pot downstairs. Hank said he'll try a bit and Mae said she'll sniff it. If she likes the smell, she'll try a teaspoonful." She patted my arm. "Don't worry. I think they'll love it. If they don't, it's just more for you, me and Mom. Right?"

"Did I just hear you say damn? Should eleven-year-old girls be using such language?" I tried not to laugh.

"Yes, you did, Mr. Manny Rodriguez. I was quoting someone, not saying it on my own. So there."

She giggled and stuck her tongue out at me. On the way out the door, she said, just loud enough for me to hear, "Guess it's time I get the hell out of here."

Mae never said she loved the pozole. She just kept tasting teaspoon after teaspoon and adding the finely chopped jalapeño peppers, a little more with each taste, until her eyes watered. Hank said he loved it. There was none left for me to have leftovers the next day. The next week, Mae stopped me and asked what tacos tasted like. There were none of those left over either. The next week, I made enchiladas. After that, I can't remember for how long, but Wednesday nights became Mexican night for months, maybe even years.

I now had a father and a mother.

Chapter Ninety-Nine

Hank's Death and Sleeping with Mae
Winter 1967

Losing Tato was rough, but he was my grandfather I was only close to for two years. It was hard when he died, even harder to lose Lucas so soon after, but Hank's death was the closest to losing a true father. My real dad's death is barely a blip on my memory, so small I haven't written about it. Yes, he died several years ago.

Mae caught me coming in the house from the grocery store, said she was nervous over Hank being gone so long to the cemetery. Somehow, I had this hunch something was wrong with him. I figured a stroke or heart attack. Still thought that when I pulled up behind his car and saw him sitting sideways, feet on the ground, the door open, facing Tommy's grave. I was almost ready to turn around and drive back to the office and have them call for an ambulance, but instead I stepped closer, calling his name. One close look and touch and I knew he was dead. I knelt in front of him for several minutes, crying, telling him how much I loved him, how much he did for me, how I considered him my true father, how I'd watch out for Mae as much as needed. I went home and got Mae. She knew the second I walked through the door that he was gone.

For the first three weeks after Hank's death, one of the children or grandchildren spent the night with Mae. By the third week, only the grandkids were coming. I picked up a few comments that they were tiring of the disruption to their lives.

One night, one granddaughter, probably about twelve, waved bye to her mother in the car as she carried in her night bag. "Bye, Mom. See you at six thirty tomorrow morning," she called over her shoulder. I held the door open for her. "Oh, hi, Manny. I lost the coin toss to sleep with Grandma tonight."

"You sleep in bed with her, not in one of the bedrooms?"

"That's right. Grandma can't stand being in the bed alone. She wants someone snuggling next to her and sometimes she snores." She heaved a dramatic sigh. "This is getting to be such a pain. I know she misses him, but I wished she'd grow out of this grief stage." Said it like she was an expert on grief.

That Sunday night, about nine thirty, I was going over plans to paint and update a neighbor's two-flat. Word spread that I did good work at reasonable rates and I was able to keep busy with side jobs and still manage the rooming house. Some years before, about the time Mike married, I found a good replacement for me at the bank. There was a light, tentative rap on my door.

Mae stood there, a robe pulled around her. She was fidgeting, twisting the ties of her robe. "Umm, Manny. Could I stay by you? No one is coming to spend the night and I'm not ready to be alone yet."

"Sure, come on in. Can I make you some tea, chamomile?"

She nodded and hesitantly sat down on the couch. I served her the tea and told her I needed a few more minutes to go over my paperwork. She nodded again and seemed to relax on the couch.

A few minutes later, she touched my arm, "Manny, I didn't mean stay by you just for a little while. I meant the whole night."

I stared at her, my mouth open.

She lowered her eyes, looked at the floor. "I'm a strong lady, but after forty-seven years, I am not ready to sleep by myself. I panic in bed when I'm alone. I just tried. I'm sorry. Could you sleep by me?"

I finally managed to gasp, "That's a lot to ask. Did you mean in my bed?"

"I know it's a lot to ask and how crazy it sounds, but I want you to come down to my bed."

I didn't know how to respond. What the hell was this all about? What would people think? What would her kids think if they found out? Did I really want to spend a night in bed with a sixty-seven-year-old lady who snores? I looked at her. She was hurting, I could see her pain. I thought of the first weeks without Lucas. How dark, long and heartbreaking they were. I thought about not having Mike in bed with me anymore. Both of those men only spent months in my bed, what must it be like to spend forty-seven years then no one? Three weeks with her family wasn't long enough, I could see that, understand it.

Drawing myself up, I said, "Let me find something to sleep in." I wondered what I had besides my boxer undershorts. I didn't sleep in pajamas. In fact, I usually slept in nothing.

"Your undershorts are fine, that's all Hank slept in most of the time."

We went down the stairs, me carrying a clean pair of undershorts in my hand and hoping none of the men happened to see me. It was *loco*. Goddamn tequila drunk crazy. LSD crazy. A twenty-seven-year-old homo Mexican going to bed with a lonely sixty-seven-year-old new widow because she panicked sleeping alone.

Was it *loco*? This woman was human. She missed her husband next to her in bed. She wanted me, or someone, to sleep beside her. Was that truly crazy? Yes, it was, but I decided it was also human. What's the worst that could happen? I get a middle-of-the-night erection? That would be embarrassing. I sure as hell wouldn't get an erection thinking about her body. Not because she was old, but because she was a woman. A female. Didn't they have teeth between their legs? Even if she had been my age, I had no desire for a woman at all. I know some homos can work it up for a girl on some occasions, but not me.

We each went to the bathroom and brushed our teeth, Mae first. After brushing my teeth, I changed into my clean undershorts and went into the bedroom. Mae was on her side of the bed, lying on her left side, facing out. Wearing just my boxers, I slid in on my left side, facing her back.

She reached back and patted my hip. "Move closer, I won't bite."

I did. I heard her sniffle so I put my arm over her and snuggled even closer, basically spooning her.

"Thank you," she sniffled. "I like being held. Good night."

Her breathing slowed to a regular rate and she slipped into sleep. I thought I'd be awake all night, tossing and turning, trying not to disturb her, worrying about why the hell I was in bed with an old lady, but I didn't. I slept. Vaguely, I remember coming to in the middle of the night to find we'd rolled onto our right sides and her arm was across my body, now spooning me.

I woke to the sounds of a coffee grinder. Desperately needing to pee, and not thinking to grab my jeans, I trotted out of the bedroom, through the kitchen to the bathroom.

"Good morning, Manny. Coffee's almost ready. You look just like Hank did, rushing to the toilet in the morning."

I was moving too fast to decide if my face was turning red or not. Mae fixed eggs and bacon. She said she hadn't slept that well since Hank died. I told her I slept well too and was surprised that I did.

"Sometimes, I think humans just need to be close," she said.

I came down and slept with her each night till Friday when her grandkids came for the weekend. Sunday night, her grandkids went home. I was up in the air about sleeping with her again. On the one hand, I thought she should get over it and learn to sleep by herself. On the other hand, as weird as it sounds, I was beginning to enjoy it.

I knocked on her door. Tears came to her eyes when she saw me. "Oh, Manny, I was feeling so embarrassed about going up to see you. Could we try something different?"

"What are you thinking of?"

"Why don't we try you sleeping down here, but in one of the other bedrooms. Maybe just knowing someone is close will be enough. I hate to keep imposing on you, I feel so selfish." She waited for my response, then added, "Manny, did you enjoy sleeping with me? You always seemed to sleep very well."

I gulped, then said, "Mae, I have to be honest with you. I thought sleeping together was the weirdest thing I could do. I was afraid I'd toss and turn and drive you nuts. I also know how lonely sleeping by yourself can be, and the truth is, I enjoyed it. I did sleep well, almost better with you than without." I looked out the window at the snow coming down. "I can go either way, Mae. In your bed or in the next bedroom. Whichever works best for you."

"I didn't get much sleep with my grandkids, they're horrible to sleep with, as much as I love them. Let's sleep together tonight, then try separate beds tomorrow night."

"Sounds like a plan," I said, shaking my head at the weirdness of the conversation and my life.

After that night, I slept in Tommy's old room, now a guest room. The next week, I returned to my efficiency. Mae was ready to sleep by herself in their apartment. About ten years later, I returned to the guest room, this time for good. However, I did have coffee nearly every morning with Mae, almost until she died. At six thirty, I sat down in her kitchen as she poured the coffee, added the sugar and condensed milk like I liked. Sometimes, she made breakfast or had a roll for me. Eventually, she found a recipe for Mexican rolls and began making them. "Not sweet enough," she'd say and sprinkle a bit of sugar on hers.

Chapter One Hundred

Adopted

I never received a paper bag certificate of adoption into the Sawicki family as did Katie and Krystina. I think the first Easter shortly after Hank's death was the official ceremony.

Early that morning, a family I'd done work for called me. A basement drain backed up, could I come over and fix it, at least temporarily, till they could find a plumber. I routed it out, good enough till they could get someone in with a power router and not pay holiday rates.

Earlier in the week, Mae asked me to attend their Easter dinner and to be downstairs at eleven, after the family returned from Mass.

When I returned from routing out the basement drain, it was nearly eleven. I quick shaved and took a shower in the shower room I'd remodeled for the third floor. I was standing in my little apartment, stark naked, drying my hair when I heard Patricia's loud voice. "Manny, get your ass down..."

I pulled the towel from my face and quick lowered it to my waist as I saw Patricia opening the door. She laughed as my face turned red. "Hey, you're holding up the party, get downstairs, we're waiting on you." As she turned to leave, she said, "Bet you lock your door after you take a shower next time."

When I walked into the apartment, everybody started singing happy birthday to me. One of the grandkids brought a tiny Mexican flag they put on the cake. Another sewed an apron for me and hand-stitched on the words, pozole and tacos. They also gave me a carton of my favorite cigarettes, Camel, unfiltered.

I was thrilled. It struck home that I was officially family now. I knew I was Hank and Mae's son. When one of the little kids asked if I was their real uncle, Mae said I sure was and the other adults said, almost in unison, "He sure is," well, then I knew it was a family thing.

Another child, I can't remember who belonged to who any more, but this one was a little older, maybe the same girl who slept over with

Mae and told me it was time Grandma get over her grief, anyway, she said to the little one, "Manny is like Katie and Krys, he's adopted." She paused and got a big grin on her face. "Of course, that's a Polish adoption." Everyone laughed.

"Speech, speech," they started yelling at me. "In Polish," several called out.

Standing, I smiled and rattled off my thanks to them in Spanish. Several of the older high school-aged teens, laughed. One said, "Keep it clean, Manny. We're taking Spanish in school."

I lifted my glass of beer. "I said I was very blessed and thankful to have been adopted into this fine family, even if you are Polish. To Mae and Hank." I paused, my throat grew tight and I shook my head so I wouldn't tear up. "Especially Hank. He called me son shortly after I moved in. I'd never been called son before." I took a sip of beer, then lifted my glass again higher. "To Hank."

As if to break the silence and tears over Hank, Mae hugged me, then said loud enough for all to hear, "Of course, everyone knows I didn't call him son right away." We all laughed.

Patricia winked at me, "You bring down any of them hailopeena peppers? Ma says her cooking tastes better with em. Oh, and those sweet rolls she's been making ya are terrible. How the hell you gonna gain weight eating them?"

That birthday, and my eighteenth, I've never forgotten.

Chapter One Hundred One

Driving Miss Mae

The movie *Driving Miss Daisy* came out around 1997 and I bought a copy after the prices dropped. Every time I watch it, I think of Mae and me traveling around the country in Hank's 1956 Ford and sniffle a little, remembering the good times we had.

Our first trip was the summer after Hank died, 1967. "You know, Manny," she said one morning at coffee, "I can't remember being out of Chicago other than one time, we took the kids to the dunes in Indiana. That day, the wind was out of the west and blew the refinery and steel smells over us so thick, we could hardly see."

"So, you want to take a drive out of Chicago?" I was thinking of a day trip somewhere. Hell, I hadn't been outside of Chicago since I arrived. I didn't know where to go.

"No, Manny. I want to see Illinois, the Mississippi River, all over. I hear there's some beautiful spots and it's time I saw them." She called the Triple A office and they mailed some maps to her with different routes. She called them back and said she wanted Wisconsin, Iowa, Missouri, and Michigan, too.

Our first trip was supposed to be five days and turned into ten. Patricia agreed to check on the rooming house daily. We drove up the lakefront into Wisconsin, across that state through the driftless area, which was like seeing mountains to us, then down the Mississippi crossing into Iowa, back to Illinois, back to Missouri and finally to the Ohio River in southern Illinois. We saw the sights, ate food we'd never eaten before, and loved wandering along the side roads as close to the Mississippi as possible and through the state and national forests.

We stayed in small cabins or motels and always rented one room. If they had two beds, fine, if not, fine. We phoned Patricia each night who only laughed when Mae told her we were extending our time away. "Sure, Ma. What the hell, I ain't got nothin' better to do." Mae said she'd take her at her word and laughed, too.

Patricia was at the house when we finally pulled into the garage and unloaded our two small suitcases. "What the hell, you two. Ma, if I didn't know Manny was queerer than a three dollar bill, I'd say he was trying to marry you for all your money."

Mae laughed and said, "Well, we did have to sleep in the same bed several times. I sure as hell wasn't paying for two rooms."

"Jesus H. Christ, Ma. I ain't sayin a word to anyone else and you better not either. What will people say?" She shook her head, waited as laugh tears started down her cheeks. "You know, I bet Pa is up there, laughing his ass off over you two. The old widow and the young queer spic."

Mae said, "Well, he better get used to seeing us traveling, we're going around Lake Michigan this fall when the colors start turning."

Patricia threw her hands up in the air with a look that said her mother was nuts. I shrugged my shoulders and in the best Hogan's Hero's Sargent Schultz German accent I could muster as a Mexican, said, "I know nutting. Nutting."

Each summer, our trips grew longer and further. The first years were throughout the Midwest, then one summer to Washington, D.C. and Philadelphia. Another fall, we went to the northeast, all the way to Nova Scotia and came back through Canada.

Once, in 1976, I brought Mae flowers. It was Valentine's Day. She didn't bother to find a vase, but she did thank me. Next, she cried. I hugged her and slowly walked her over to the couch to sit down. Pointing her finger in the air as if I needed a lecture, she said, "This summer, we're going to Wyoming and Colorado to see Eugenia, Hank's sister. She's five years older than Hank, eighty-six now, going strong and still on the ranch." She reached up and poked my chest. "And I'm going to meet Arnaud. It's about time."

I had no idea who Arnaud was and Mae told me nothing else until on the long drive to Wyoming. I have to say I was surprised to no end. Yet, even then, her details were few. She showed me a brown packet stuffed with letters and several hand-written pages, and said, "You can read these after I die. Eugenia gave me the ones she wrote and I found Hank's downstairs in his shop area after he died, took me years to find them. They were tucked inside a fishing tackle box in the rafters and they explain why he got so withdrawn every Valentine's Day.

Mae didn't feel well the entire trip. I knew her sugar was high, as well as her blood pressure. She complained the pills made her feel worse than not taking them. The altitude out west didn't help, over five thousand feet. I enjoyed meeting Eugenia and her family still on the ranch. I even rode a horse. Eugenia's son-in-law told me I was a natural and I could come help them anytime I wanted. I loved the wide open spaces and huge sky. Eugenia and Mae seemed to have a lot to catch up on so I mostly stayed outside, hanging around the barn and corrals, finding things I could fix.

We were there four days, then drove down to Denver and met Arnaud. He was slender, but his close-set eyes reminded me of Hank's. He was a livestock broker, buying and selling mostly cattle. His favorite thing to do was to break and train horses on his small ranch just north of Denver. He and Mae seemed awkward at first, then I think they meshed. Mae was feeling worse. Arnaud and I became concerned over her health, so we left after only one day.

As Arnaud helped her into the Ford, Mae said, "This is a weight off my shoulders. I wished I'd dealt with meeting you sooner instead of worrying all these years about it. You made your father proud."

He replied, "Well, I've often wondered what my life would have been like if Father hadn't sent me on to Eugenia and I'd been raised in Chicago with you, but I realize what a wonderful life and family I've had with Eugenia. Besides, I don't think I could have become a horseman and horse trainer in Chicago. I love the West, it's where I was meant to be." He bent over and kissed her on the cheek. "Now, get home and get some medical attention. I love you and will call you every week to talk and catch up more."

I drove straight home, on the interstate, I-80. I hate driving interstates, but this time, it was necessary. Mae was feeling terrible. She tried to yell at me when I drove her straight to the hospital emergency room instead of home. She was too exhausted to do much more than whisper.

The hospital admitted her and kept her for two weeks, trying to get her sugar and blood pressure under control. The night before she was to come home, she had a stroke which affected her left side, mostly her arm and leg, plus her face a little, enough she slurred her words somewhat.

Chapter One Hundred Two

Caring for Mae

When she came home, the family gathered to decide what to do with her. By now, none of the kids lived in the city. They moved, along with many other white families, to the south and southwest suburbs.

They were sitting and standing around Mae who sat in a wheelchair in the living room. All chattered away about who best could care for her, who had the biggest home with the least stairs, who was home during the day, who could move their kids around to free up a bedroom big enough for a hospital bed, who could take her to physical therapy, and on and on. It was noisy. They weren't arguing, just talking loud like usual, trying to make plans.

Mae looked at me with this pleading look in her eyes. I knew what she wanted. I smiled and nodded back. I loved this woman. I caught Patricia's eye and motioned my head toward her mother. Patricia put her hand up and yelled above them, "Hey. Why don't we ask Ma what she wants?" Turning to Mae, she said a little softer, "Okay, Ma. It may be a long time before you can be by yourself. What do you want to do?"

Mae straightened herself up as much as possible. Her eyes flashing, she raised her right hand and slowly pointed at each person standing around her. Her words slurring, she said, "I ain't moving. I love you, but will never leave this place till I die. Manny can care for me and we'll be just fine." She swallowed and wiped a bit of spittle from her lips. "Now shut up and go back to your fancy homes and jobs."

Everyone turned to look at me. I stepped over to Mae, put my hand on her shoulder and said, "She's right. We'll be fine. She'll get better fast on my Mexican cooking."

Everyone was quiet, still looking at me. I think they were a little stunned that I would do something like this. Patricia stepped closer and yanked me into a rib-crushing hug. "Little brother, you are a wonderful man. We all trust you."

The rest nodded and crowded around me, patting my shoulder, hugging me, thanking me.

After they left, Mae asked, "Are you sure you want to take care of me? You are still young. Maybe you should find someone to live in and help me and you can live a normal life, find another man to love."

"Mae, you are the mother in my life I never had. I will stay with you as long as needed."

"Oh, Manny. I love you so much, you are so good to me. You are a wonderful son." She wiped her chin, dropped the lace hanky on the floor and moaned in frustration as she tried to bend over to reach it and couldn't. "Oh, Manny," she said as I placed the hanky in her hand. "I wasn't upset that I dropped the hanky, but I just realized I have yet to tell the kids about Arnaud. I still must do that."

We settled into our new lives. I moved down to an extra bedroom. Mae was in a hospital bed which made it easier to get her in and out. I drove her to physical therapy and followed up at home with more exercises. She became able to use a platform cane and limp around the house, but the use of her left arm and hand never came back. We joked about not having a working left arm between the two of us. Patricia or a grandchild came in every other Saturday and took her out for a hair appointment. I removed the big clawfoot tub in the bathroom and installed an oversized shower stall she could sit in to wash herself. After her first fall in the shower, I helped bathe her too. I also installed a taller toilet. During her last year, I needed to help her with those tasks too.

Chapter One Hundred Three

Grant

Mae's words about finding another man to love struck me hard. About six months after her stroke, I was on the second floor, cleaning the showers. I heard the door open and a new roomer asked if the other shower was clean and available. I turned to tell him yes, go ahead, but my mouth dropped open.

Grant stood there, his towel casually draped over his shoulder, naked as the day he was born. The men usually wrapped a towel around themselves or wore a robe between their room and the shower closet.

I knew Grant was good-looking when I registered him, wondered if he might be gay, but hadn't thought much of it, well, maybe a little. Told myself I was too busy. Grant booked a room for two weeks, said he was in between apartments and he was a chef at one of the Greek restaurants up on Halsted near the university.

Now, he stood in front of me, looking like a Greek god. He was absolutely one of the best-looking men I ever set eyes on. "Like what you see?" he said, smiling, his gorgeous blue eyes holding mine.

My throat dried up, I had to swallow several times to talk. "Yes." That's all that came out.

"I've got some time, want to go back to my room? All the other guys are off working."

I shook my head to clear my mind. "Umm, no. I never get involved with the roomers."

"That's too bad. I think you are sexy and would love to see more of you."

It was all I could do not to pull him into an embrace and kiss as I walked by him and shakily went down the stairs.

He moved out the following week, but left me his new address, which wasn't too far away, and a note reading, "I'm off Monday, I'll bet you could use some loving. Two p.m. After, I'll fix a snack."

That Monday, I took a shower and dressed in clean, almost new jeans and a colored t-shirt. I told Mae I had to check out a side job and caught a Halsted bus north to his place.

"I wasn't sure you'd show up," he said, opening the door, "but I'm glad you did."

"Why did you invite me?"

"I thought you were cute, hot even, the minute I saw you. Then, I was talking with one of the roomers, an old timer, I can't remember his name. He said you were becoming a monk, what with taking care of the roomers, plus the old lady who owns the place. Said you'd gotten kind of serious and maybe a little stressed. Said you could use a distraction."

I smiled, amused Jerry would say that about me and touched as well.

"So, I asked him what kind of distraction did he think you needed and he said, 'Someone like you.' Ha ha."

Jerry'd been around since before I came and knew about Mike and me. I nodded, a little embarrassed. Grant handed me a beer and motioned toward the couch. We sat down and he began asking questions about where I went for any action. I told him nowhere and he was shocked. He started listing gay bars, bath houses and areas of the city the gays were starting to congregate.

"Jesus, you have been a monk. This is the seventies, man. Gays are coming out, it's free love. You can get anything you're into. Anything. You're missing out. C'mon."

He led me to his bedroom where only a mattress was on the floor and slowly undressed me. The man's hands and mouth were exquisite. I reciprocated, but could tell he wanted more. Something held me back, I wasn't sure what, but decided I wasn't going any further.

I saw him the next Monday and he invited me to go out with him, visit one of the baths. I was amazed, guys having all kinds of sex everywhere, in dark rooms, hallways, the baths, the steam room. I don't know why I was so amazed, other than I didn't go out much and hadn't realized how things had changed. Actually, it scared me. So much so, I left. Grant waved bye at me, shook his head and called out, "Man, quit being scared. You gotta get with the times. I'll call you." He started kissing the nipples of some hairy bear of a guy. He never did call me, nor me him. I think he didn't have time to deal with a slow learning monk like me and I couldn't get over the new times. Years later, I would recall not seeing any condoms. At the time, though, it didn't strike me as odd or necessary.

Maybe I feared just jumping in without knowing anyone else than Grant. Still, it wasn't for me. Maybe I was getting old, but I knew from my tingling crotch that wasn't truly the reason. Maybe my years selling myself in Tijuana reminded me of where I'd come from. Maybe it was the fact that this was all free now. Not that I wanted to pay for it or get paid. Free love. The hippies started it and I realized it included the queers too. Why wouldn't it?

Whatever it was, as I walked to catch a bus, I realized it wasn't me. I wanted sex in a relationship, not just poking my *pene* in any available opening. Also, on that evening, I couldn't get my mind off Mae. Was she all right? Did she eat? Did she forget to turn a burner off? Could she get her nightgown on by herself? She always tried, but I usually needed to help her. What happened if she fell and couldn't get back up and was lying on the floor when I came home?

Jesus. I am a monk, though parts of me still didn't want to be.

Chapter One Hundred Four

April Fool's

Mae became a little better, then gradually deteriorated. Her sugar was a challenge to maintain, even with me doing all the cooking, controlling her portions, checking her blood and adjusting her insulin shots. Of course, that affected the blood pressure. On good days, I'd push her around the neighborhood for long walks, but she became discouraged as she saw how some of the old homes had been chopped into small apartments. The increasing numbers of Mexicans and blacks did not bother her, just the fact that there were few good jobs left in the neighborhood to employ them since the stockyards faded away and closed.

In December of 1979, I was feeding Mae dinner. She was weak and I knew she wouldn't live many more months. "Manny, weren't you the one that told me about your grandfather having a going-away party?"

I knew immediately what she was referring to. I nodded.

"I think I want one. Who cares what people say or look like when I'm gone? I want to see them. Soon."

I spoke with Patricia, told her of my grandfather's going-away party, how I didn't expect Mae to make it till summer. How she brought the idea up and wanted something soon.

She sighed. "Guess it's coming. She can't go on much longer like this." She loved the idea and suggested New Year's Day as the day for a big party with Mae.

The day before the party, Mae directed the teenagers in decorating the house. Told them they had to play some of her favorite music, big band swing, but could mix in some of theirs. She didn't want to be on a diet the day of the party and insisted Patricia and the kids cook real Polish food, full of grease, and by god, the mashed potatoes should look the way she used to make them, full of butter. She wanted fresh green beans cooked with bacon. The only flowers allowed were tulips. I made several wooden ones, painted them bright colors and mounted them above the cabinets alongside Hank's. She was thrilled. She didn't tell anyone of the secret she concocted with my help.

At the party, Mae sparkled. She wore a brand-new dress, her hair was done by a beautician who came to the house and she even had a granddaughter put her favorite jewelry on her. One of her daughters did her make up. She was upbeat, loved seeing everyone and having the old house so full, you could hardly move. Great-grandkids ran up and down the stairs and played in any empty rooms they could find. She didn't want any presents, so all the grandkids and greats made cards and drawings for her. She insisted each one get taped to the walls, cabinets and windows. "You won't have to paper the walls when I'm gone," she said, her eyes bright and happy.

About a half hour after everyone was present, Mae asked Pat to get everyone quiet. "I have a surprise for you," Mae slurred. She nodded at me and I opened the back kitchen door and Arnaud walked in. He'd been hiding in the basement.

"Hi, folks, I'm your half brother from the west," he announced with a big smile on his face.

Patricia, Pat, said, "Ma, who the hell did you adopt now?"

"He can tell you his story, he's not related to me but he is to each of you children," Mae replied.

There were confused looks and several murmurs of, what now? The family waited quietly for Arnaud to speak.

"As you know, our father Hank, was in World War One." He grinned as he noticed the expressions of understanding float across several faces. "He fell in love with my mother. They were madly in love, but he needed to return to care for his father. Their last night together was supposed to be a short dinner, but the train was delayed and they spent the night together with no protection. My mother never told Hank of me, wanted to wait till I was a young man. She died of cancer when I was thirteen. Her relatives were killed in the war so, before she died, she made arrangements to send me to Hank." He paused as the murmurs began, waited till they were quiet to continue. "I know, how come you never saw me? I spent one night hidden upstairs, then he put me on a train to Wyoming where Eugenia and her husband adopted me. Over the years, Hank and I communicated. He frequently referred to his guilt over never

441

telling Mae or you kids, my half siblings."

"Ma, is this true? When did you find out? Why didn't you tell us?" Joey asked.

"I found out right after Dad's death, but I spent over ten years trying to find all the letters he hid about it. I wanted to know the whole story before I told anyone. On our trip to Wyoming, Manny and I visited Arnaud, but I was too sick to stay long. As you know, that was when I got sick and almost did the same thing Hank did, didn't tell you guys. I figured at my age, I'd give you one more shock. Now get to know your brother. He's wonderful and I wish he became part of this clan much sooner."

The noise of questions, exclamations, welcomes and laughter over Hank's secret filled the room to the point Mae asked me to take her out on the front porch for several minutes. "I think they accepted him," Mae muttered, twisting her head to wink up at me. "What a life, huh? What a family!"

We returned inside to lower decibels, but still an aura of excitement. Everyone became quiet when, as tears ran down their cheeks, each of the eight remaining children of Hank and Mae stood and said something they would never forget about her. Next, Arnaud stepped forward. "You can never know how much I have wanted to know Mae, my biological siblings and their families. Yes, Eugenia's family is mine and it is wonderful, but now I feel completely whole. Thank you for accepting me. I will be in town for several days so I hope I can get to your homes, in fact, Mae told me to ask who's going to take me in tonight."

That night, after everything was cleaned up by the family, which Mae directed, she collapsed in my arms as I lifted into her bed. She was so exhausted, I could hardly change her into her nightgown. I thought she was asleep, but she moved her good hand and pointed at me. "Now that's what I call a going-away party, and a welcome party."

~ * ~

Mae died on April first, 1980. She was mentally sharp up until her last breath. The day before, she whispered in her slurry voice, her oxygen

442

pumping in the background, "You're going to love this, I'm going out tomorrow, April Fool's Day. Don't tell anyone to come over. I want to die in peace, not with a bunch of loud Polacks around me." She gasped for more air. "Afterward, tell em all to laugh like hell."

"Oh, Mae. I think you'll make it to summer, why are you talking about going out tomorrow?"

She pointed her finger at me, like a mother at a small child. "Don't ask me how I know, I just know. Besides, April Fool's Day has always been one of my favorite holidays." She managed to wink at me, then said, "Trust me. It's gonna happen. Nothing you can say will change it."

I called Patricia and told her about Mae saying she would die tomorrow, on April Fool's, and not wanting a bunch of loudmouths hanging around, waiting and carrying on.

She was quiet a long while. "Well, I'm guessing the old girl knows. I agree. I don't blame her for wanting it quiet, we've all seen her several times since January." She gave a big sigh. "I'll spread the word she may leave us tomorrow and she ordered us to laugh."

In the end, the only people with her were Katie, Krystina, and myself. Spur of the moment, they got together and drove out to see Mae, who was thrilled.

"To think," Mae rasped after they arrived. "my last day is with my adopted kids. I couldn't have planned it any better." Their eyes got big and they looked at me, surprised. I nodded as if to say, she's still in charge.

Mae continued to smile and squeeze our hands for about an hour, then slipped off to sleep. Another hour and her breathing slowed until it simply quit. Dust to dust. She was gone. Finally, with Hank, after thirteen long years apart. Both probably laughing at the April Fool's joke she pulled off.

I called Patricia and told her, once again, Mae was right. Told her who was with her at Mae's last breath. She was quiet, I could hear some sniffles. Finally, she said, "I agree with Ma, it was wonderful you guys could be there. Better than the rest of us." She cleared her throat and started laughing. Low at first, then louder, sounding more and more like her coarse belly laughs. I heard her hand slap the counter or wall. "Goddammit, that old woman was something else, wasn't she? Hanging on till April first, just so everyone could have a good laugh. Damn, we come from good stock. Don't we, Manny?"

I was crying too hard to reply, but I'm sure Patricia knew my head was nodding in agreement.

Chapter One Hundred Five

Fixing Up

After Mae died, I threw myself into getting the house back in shape and finding more side jobs. Rooming houses, especially old ones in transitioning neighborhoods, weren't as popular anymore. I figured I had an advantage as several other ones closed in the area.

Old Hank didn't have much saved for retirement, especially for Mae to last this long, plus maintain the house. Part of it was my fault. I knew the reserves were declining, but kept transferring money into Mae's personal account.

That's how we financed most of our trips. We even flew to Florida for two weeks one winter and stayed at a very nice resort. She loved flying, but hated Florida. "Who would want to live down here in all this heat and humidity? All these old people do is walk the beach and pick shells. Makes no sense to me." It was sixty-five degrees the time we were there. I loved it.

My personal finances were low too, not broke, but my bank balances were less than I liked. While the house reserves held enough to do some remodeling and pay several years property taxes, they still needed to be built up if I was to have any kind of future with the old place.

I had insulation blown into all the walls and attic, installed a new high-efficient, separate furnace for the second and third floors, repainted all the rooms and replaced the mattresses. I also installed a large exhaust fan on each floor to improve circulation in the warm months. I advertised wider and once again filled the old place with a decent bunch of men. It was a mix, mostly white, but some black and Mexicans. This time, no one complained about the mix, guess it seemed more normal. Occasionally, I'd think one of them might be gay, but all the guys seemed to move on quicker than before when a rooming house might become a longer-term home.

When out and about, working my side jobs, shopping, and so

forth, I kept my eyes open for another gay man to become friends with and maybe lovers. By the early eighties, I was scared to death of AIDS. So, I didn't look too closely. Definitely didn't hit the bars and baths. Guess keeping my eyes open was mostly wishful thinking.

Chapter One Hundred Six

Grant Returns

I think it was late fall of 1983, I had the place filled, other than the efficiency unit. I rarely put anyone in there, not sure why. Maybe too many memories with Mike. Anyway, in November, one cold evening, the doorbell rang. It was Grant. Only he didn't look like a Greek god any more. In fact, if it wasn't for his gorgeous blue eyes, now all sunk in, I wouldn't have known it was him. He'd lost weight, didn't stand straight and tall like he used to, didn't have that cocky, 'look at me, I'm beautiful' sense about him.

"I need help. Can I come in?"

I led him in to the kitchen and gave him a glass of water.

"I'm sick. I can only work part-time now. I lost my apartment and need a cheap place to stay. You're my last hope."

He's got the AIDS, I thought. What the hell can I do for him? "What about your family? Can't you go with them?"

He sighed, took a sip and teared up. "They won't have me. They never accepted I was gay, but when I told them I got AIDS, they said I deserved it. It was God's punishment and they never wanted to see me again."

"All I have is the efficiency, my old place, on the third floor. Can you climb the steps?"

"Yeah, I won't have to make more than one trip on the days I work and I can fix my own food in there. Thank you."

"Don't tell anyone what you got. Okay? Just stay to yourself, and don't screw aro..."

"Don't worry. I'm too sick for sex."

That was on a Wednesday night. On Friday, he was taking a shower during the day and didn't pull the curtain tight. One of the other guys went to take one in the stall next to him and noticed all the bumps and marks on his skin.

"You got the AIDS, doncha?" he yelled. "You fuckin faggot. I'm gettin' the hell outta here." He ran to his room, dressed, packed and beat on my door till I came. "Give me my cash back. I ain't livin' next to no faggot with the AIDS."

I told him I wasn't refunding his money and the only way he could catch AIDS was through sex or sharing needles. He wouldn't listen, said he'd fix my wagon and stomped out.

That evening, he showed back up, stood out front on the sidewalk and told each guy coming in that Grant had AIDS. He moved out and they should too. Five of them left that night. Over the next week, every one of the other roomers did as well.

Several neighbors heard. They called me, left threatening notes in my mail box or taped to my door. I took the rooming house sign down and stopped the ads in the papers.

The next week, Grant lost his job when he called in sick. He asked me to drive him up to the North side to the Brown Clinic for gay people. He was too weak to ride the busses by himself. Once there, I received an education in AIDS, including how to care for him. The doctor and nurses just assumed Grant and I were a couple and I would care for him as long as possible. I started to tell them otherwise, but caught a glimpse of Grant's face. Where the hell could he go? Who else could care for him? I just nodded and started asking as many questions as I could think of.

On our way out, the doctor pulled me aside. "What do you do?" he asked. "Do you speak Spanish?"

"I own a rooming house that is now empty except for Grant and the couple in the back apartment. Yes, I'm Mexican."

He shook his head. "Everyone move out because of Grant?"

I nodded.

"That's a tough one. Fear is such a bad thing." I thought he was going to leave, but instead, he stepped closer to me. "Listen, I need your help. We have a young Mexican woman, an illegal, doesn't speak English, her baby will probably die this week from AIDS. Her husband is dying from it, he exchanged needles, that's how he acquired it and passed it on through sex." He stared into my eyes as if determining how much to ask of me.

I nodded to go on.

"She needs a place to stay. She has no one. She's Catholic and

448

can't tell her sisters who are in Chicago and refuses to tell her parents back in Mexico or return to them. Can you take her in? Probably next week?"

I stood there, stunned. A social worker walked over and told me everything the doctor just said, only in Spanish.

"I get it. I get it." I paused, upset. What the heck should I do? "You realize Grant and I are not a couple. Six years ago, he spent two weeks in the rooming house and he showed back up on my porch last week. I'll take care of him. Now you want me to take a girl home? This is *loco*."

"We're desperate," the doctor said. "We have few options for people as it is, and for illegals, virtually none." Putting his arm around my shoulders, he said, "At the risk of seeming rude, you're not going to be renting out any rooms with an AIDS patient there anyway. You have the space and you're a good man or you wouldn't have brought Grant here. The social worker will investigate to see if there's some government funds we can give you to help a little."

I drove Grant home, didn't even try to help him to the third floor, just moved him into the side bedroom.

The couple who rented the back apartment for the past eight years moved out three days later, refusing to listen to me or read the papers I brought from the clinic.

A week later, Grant and I brought Luisa home, a seventeen-year-old girl whose baby died three days before and whose twenty-two-year-old husband would die two weeks later. I put her in Tommy's old room.

Sorting pills, cooking, bathing Grant, holding Luisa's hand as she sobbed out her grief, sometimes holding her and rocking her in Mae's old rocker and taking them to appointments at Brown became my life. Luisa was still able to do some cooking and cleaning. She became a little sister I never had.

I told none of the Sawicki kids what was going on. They long since ceased just popping in, but did make sure I was invited to all the big family gatherings usually out in Orland Park. When I managed to attend, I said nothing about my current residents. Just said business was fair and I was keeping busy. The big reunions stopped after Pat died. I didn't have time to notice.

A month after Luisa moved in, the social worker called to tell me about someone else needing housing. "He's twenty-three, illegal, can't tell his relatives because he's never told them he was gay and needs a place. Louis is still working, we're hoping some of the new drugs will help him not get worse, but there's no way he can live where he is. Can you take him?"

I was quiet, then said, "Now I have a Luisa and a Louis? Can he live on the second floor?"

She laughed. "You're wonderful. Louis will be fine upstairs. He will be driven out tomorrow by one of our volunteers. She says she knows you."

I could think of no woman I possibly knew who would be volunteering with AIDS people. Nina Sawicki was a nurse who delivered babies and went on to get college degrees and now taught nursing at some university. I was sure it wasn't her.

I watched from the living room the next day, as a small, yellow, sporty car parked in front and a young man unfolded from the passenger seat, slender, walking straight and proud, wearing tight pants and carrying a suitcase, but looking scared. I jumped when I saw the woman stretch out of the driver's seat. Mexican, tall, short dark curly hair with streaks of gray, plus a huge smile as she waved at me. It was my stepmom, Maria!

She said, as we hugged, "Oh, Manny, it has been so long, at least three years or more since we talked." Pushing me back, she asked, "Are you in health?"

I nodded, said I was fine. I told Louis where to take his case and to check out the bathroom situation upstairs and to come back down. We stood in the entryway, my living room door open, Luisa and Grant standing a few steps inside, looking at us.

Maria touched my arm. "So much has happened! When Art Junior hit high school, I went back to college and earned my degree in nursing. When he started college, I divorced you boys' father, and took the bastard to the cleaners for money. What a jerk. I have been working as a nurse supervisor at Northwestern and started volunteering at Brown Clinic two years ago." She told me more, lots more, about their life. Finally, she said, "Oh, you're an uncle. Art Junior and Bella, his wife, had a baby boy in

October, 1981. Art Junior is also a dentist and is already talking like the baby will be the third generation Rodriguez dentist. They named him Andres. He'll be the only child, because Art Junior had a vasectomy shortly after the baby was born. Said one was enough. His wife barely speaks English and seems simple, but it's because of her upbringing. She's a lot younger than him. He's become a jerk, almost as bad as your father."

I didn't know what to say, but waved her into the living room, along with Louis who was back from checking out his room. Maria checked the medications of the three kids and listened to their hearts, pulses; gave them a check over, asked all kinds of questions and made notes.

I got some coffee going and Luisa set out some rolls from the Mexican bakery, then we sat in the living room. The AIDS kids, quiet, looked from Maria to me. She and I not sure where to start. It had been a long time since we spoke, even longer since we saw each other in person.

Shy little Luisa broke the silence. In Spanish, she asked, "How do you two know each other?" I translated for Grant.

Maria smiled. "Well, I'm actually Manny's stepmother." Their eyes grew large in surprise. "I didn't raise Manny. He's ten years older than the son I had with their father. And it's been many years since we were together for a holiday meal and probably three years since we spoke on the phone. Right, Manny?"

I nodded, feeling guilty for not pushing a relationship harder with her. She is such a marvelous person. But, as she mentioned, her life had taken many changes, too.

"So, Manny. Can you tell me how or why you agreed to care for these three wonderful people? What happened to the couple who owned this place?"

Grant spoke up. "I met Manny some years back when I roomed here for a short time. I tried to entice him into the gay scene which was really hot then. He decided to stay a monk and care for the old lady who owned the place."

He waited while I translated for Luisa. Louis seemed comfortable in both languages.

"Then I got infected. I hid it for a while and was in denial, but became too sick to do much. My family wanted nothing to do with me. I lost my apartment, could only work part-time, had no place to go, so showed up here. Within a week of moving in, all the other roomers moved out and the Brown staff asked him to take in Luisa. Now Louis. Manny is a brave man."

Maria smiled at me, her eyes tender. She shook her head slightly. "My, my. Who owns this place now?"

"I do," I said. I quickly told them about the Sawickis, Hank's death, our travels, Mae's illness and her dying in 1980 and willing me the place. How I fixed it back up and had it full again and was busy taking on side jobs. I paused. I didn't want to make Grant feel guilty, so I added, "Now I have three people living here who need me. I'm not sure how good I can be for them, but I will try. You never know what life may bring."

Maria said softly, "I remember the last time we saw each other, all those years ago, how at home you felt here. You've come a long way. You've learned well."

"What do you mean, learned well?"

"You finally got to experience what a family, a true family, is. Didn't you?"

I nodded.

There were tears in her eyes as she pointed to Grant, Luisa and Louis. "I can tell. Why else would you do this?"

They looked at me with expressions that said, yeah, why did you do this?

I waited. I wasn't certain myself why I did this. I thought of Tato, how he intervened in my life, how Hank took me in and called me son, how Mae loved me. "Well, I sure as hell didn't plan this. It wasn't on my calendar or list of things I wanted to do." I smiled. So did the kids as Maria watched me intently, almost hanging on my words. I leaned forward in the old recliner, trying to think what to say next. "I guess you three were dropped in my lap, kind of like a big stork flew over and gave me fully grown triplets." Luisa giggled when Louis translated. "Now that you are here, you're here. All I can say is that I will do everything I can to care for you." I stood and blew my nose. "Sometimes I guess family is where the stork drops you, no matter what size you are. That's what happened to me before."

I turned to rush to the kitchen to get the coffee and rolls, didn't want them to see the water in my eyes, but Luisa put her hand up to stop me. "Señor Manny, you mean we can stay here till, till we...I mean, you won't get rid of us when we get sicker?" Louis translated for Grant, who smiled as if he already knew the answer.

I emphatically shook my head. Maria pulled them up and into a hug. She looked at me with tears in her eyes and opened her arm inviting me to join them. Slowly I stepped over and joined the group embrace.

"What happens," Maria whispered, looking at me, "if the stork brings more kids, Mexican ones?"

Luisa answered in Spanish, "We will help Señor Manny as much as we can. They can be family, too." Louis again translated for Grant.

Gruffly, I said, "You just can't call me Daddy, Papa, Tato, Tio or Señor. I'm Manny."

Chapter One Hundred Seven

Last Days as a Rooming House

That was the beginning of the AIDS rooming house years. Not officially, not publicly. Maybe the Underground AIDS Rooming House for Wetbacks would be a more accurate name. Those years are now one long blur. Certain memories poke through when I look at the photos of each person we took in. They're in a separate album that's bound to confuse the hell out of anyone until they read this. Can you imagine finding the other pictures of regular people, then this album of barely alive, wasted skeletons?

One of the memories that sticks out is how Maria, Andres' grandmother, quit her nurse supervising job, sold her condo, and moved into the back apartment to help with the AIDS kids that kept arriving. Other than Grant who was the first to die, they were all illegal Mexicans and isolated from their families.

Shots, pills, doctor visits, diapers, laundry, cooking, cleaning, social workers, filling out forms in English and Spanish, dealing with undertakers, and holding people in our arms, or their hands, as they died was my life from 1983 to 1995. Not all died. As the medications and cocktails improved, so did their lives. I still receive letters and occasional visits from AIDS patients who spent time with us, especially in the nineties when the medication breakthroughs started. I would have to count the names in the register to tell you how many people stayed here those years. I would need a lot more whiskey to do so. I have no desire to stir up those memories or think of what it cost me in money, lost income, and my health. Though, I'm guessing, my health problems are mostly from my Camels and hand-rolled cigarettes. I'm addicted and it's too late to quit. I ain't going to a doctor either, even if Medicare pays for it.

After the last AIDS kid left—I call them kids, they were all under thirty-five—I was too worn out to jump back into fixing the place up again. Besides, the neighborhood was changing like crazy. It wasn't because the Mexicans and blacks moved in, but the goddamn gangs started running around.

I began doing side jobs and rented out the back apartment and pretty well kept it rented until this year. At sixty-two, I took my social security, which wasn't much. When you do side jobs most of your life, you don't put much in. I've managed to hang on to the most of the reserves I built back up, bringing in enough side work to pay the taxes and insurance on this old barn. Of course, the last few years I haven't done much of anything and lived off my savings and social security. Still, there's a bit left in the bank.

The gangs and kids got so bad, I replaced the garage walls with cement block ones to barricade in the Ford. No one's getting to that baby, it still glows and I keep it that way. I installed security lights, big bright ones with motion detectors all around the house and yard. For a while, if there was too much activity in the alley or around the house, I'd shoot off my shotgun, out the side door, up in the air. Now that got people's attention fast. Especially the cops. They looked after me, more so after we got Mexican and black cops. They never asked if I owned a gun or fired one. I think they knew it was mine and didn't care. Things are a bit better.

March 12, 2009

By now, it looks like my nephew Andres, and his partner Josh, will stick with each other. Been ten years, that's pretty remarkable in this day and age. In their early years, they showed up together at Art's and Maria's separate holiday get-togethers or at Andres' parents. They didn't spend any more time there than I did. I don't think I've seen any of them, including the boys, in over five years. Now that I got lung cancer, stage four, I want them to take this place. Lord knows what they'll do with it, maybe something with Andres' art, but they're smart and young and the neighborhood is safer than a few years back. I'll ask Father An and Father Frank to start the paperwork. Father An knows all about such stuff and they have been checking in on me since we met and they discovered the homemade beer. Same recipe from Hank's dad. It's been nice having friends, especially as I got sicker. Think they want to give me last rites some time, but I'll wait on that. Won't do any good. I'll still be dead.

455

Guess this took me longer to write than I thought it would. Hell, what else have I had to do for four years? At least it's done and they will know my story and more about this place. I'm going to call my brother, Art-the-fart, and tell him to send Andres and Josh over here. For some reason, I don't have Andres' phone number or address. I hope they like the old place. I hope they keep it and turn it into something worthwhile. There's been a lot of love pass through these walls. That's what I'd like to see continue in some manner.

Manny

Epilogue

June 8, 2013

Josh and Andres sat on a decorative bench in the flower-filled yard next to the former rooming house. The house gleamed with recent paint, new windows and a three-story addition on the back. They faced a long, low sculpture, a tree slab stripped of its bark, sanded, sealed and varnished. Day lilies floated behind it. An acrylic plate attached to the wood read,

Dedicated to Manny Rodriquez, The Sawickis, and all who lived and loved here.

May the tree of life and love ever continue in the hearts and lives of this community.

The Rooming House Gallery and Community Art Center

September, 2012

"Four years ago today, Uncle Manny died, this place became ours and our lives changed forever," Andres said, slipping his arm behind Josh and giving a quick squeeze.

Josh was quiet for several minutes before replying, "One hundred twenty-six years ago my great-great-grandparents opened this place as a rooming house. Fifty-five years ago Uncle Manny moved in here. One year ago we moved across the street and opened this place as a community art center, gallery, and family history center." He paused, leaned over and ran his fingers over the tree sculpture. He slid back under Andres' arm. "In one month, we will be the legal, adoptive parents of our three foster children and sharing a home with Mrs. T., our non-DNA, black grandmother."

Both were quiet, thinking of the changes, the struggles, and the triumphs they experienced as individuals and as a couple, along with the impact upon them of the diaries, the secrets, and the love that influenced them in their decision to form another family.

Acknowledgements

Kathie Giorgio, coach, editor, chief cheerleader and dispenser of blunt, but kind advice, shepherded me through the entire project. Thank you! (https://www.allwritersworkshop.com)

Rick Dexter, my partner, who read nearly every word I wrote, and still graciously encouraged me to spend time with all my imaginary friends. Several people read, reviewed, commented on, answered questions, and gave advice. Thank you, Marci Yoseph, Carol Schmidt, the members of the Stateline Night Writers Group in Beloit, WI lead by Jerry Peterson; Karen and Dave Dexter; Rich Horbaczewski. My inspiring dad, Don Mathis, now 92, father to many, pastor to all. This book is dedicated to Betty Jo Mathis, my late, wonderful, humorous mother, pastor's wife, poet, Mom to many and lover of mankind. It is also dedicated to, Ron Schmidt, a wonderful neighbor and true Chicago Sout'west side guy. Finally, many thanks to publishers, owner and editors, Christine Young and Arlo Young, manuscript editor Sherry Derr-Wille and the staff at Rogue Phoenix Press who kindly and professionally guided me, plus Genene of Web and Graphic Designs by Ms. G for the cover art.

About the Author

    The Rooming House Diaries is Bill's second novel and was inspired from growing up in a tiny town with large families, his life of working with diverse Chicago folk, and his interest in Chicago's immigration, neighborhoods and families. Plus, he wanted to tell more of the stories he cut from his first novel, *Face Your Fears*. Bill won the 2015 Wisconsin Writer's Association Jade Ring contest for nonfiction. He is published in *Jonathon* with Sibling Rivalry Press; the Writers Write section of *The Sun*; and won awards in several local writing-group contests. He began writing after he retired from careers in YMCA camping and foster care. Bill and his partner reside in Beloit, Wisconsin.

    Bill is working on a third novel, *The Rooming House Gallery,* a touching sequel which describes what Josh and Andres did with the old rooming house and how the diaries affected their choices in building a new family. Bill enjoys connecting with his readers. Feel free to contact him: billmathiswriter@gmail.com or visit his website www.billmathiswriteretc.com which includes further information about his published books, upcoming ones, his blog, and his interesting photography.

Want to know what Josh and Andres' did with the old rooming house?
How the diaries affected their lives?
How they decided to start a family?

Get to know Josh and Andres, their backgrounds, their relationship, and what happened to them and the old house. Watch for *The Rooming House Gallery.*

And, to learn more about Katie and Krys, also available at Rogue Phoenix Press

Face Your Fears

Face Your Fears is filled with vitality as it challenges the traditional concepts of normalcy, family, disability and love. Nate is a quadriplegic with cerebral palsy raised in a family of achievers. He must be fed, dressed and toileted, yet has unique skills and abilities he gradually becomes aware of. Jude is able-bodied, one of 10 children raised on a hardscrabble Iowa farm. He can change diapers, cook, fix equipment, milk cows, and discovers his vocation as a physical therapist. Both experience tragic teenage losses, navigate family tragedies, and come to peace with who they are individually as gay men, and eventually together.

This book shows how normal comes wrapped in different packages, yet inside each package, people are the same, whether able-bodied, disabled, black, white, brown, green or LGBTQ+.

Chapter One
Nate and Jude

Friday, June 26, 2015
Chicago, Illinois

Jude

I exit the 'L' and start jogging. I get too nervous walking, so I jog across Daley Plaza, toward the Picasso, looking through the couples, the supporters, the flags and banners, the people celebrating. Looking for a man with reddish-brown hair.

Inadvertently, I slow to a walk. This is nuts. I never envisioned feeling like this. Like a thirteen-year-old with his first kiss. It's not like I don't know him, or we just met last week. We've been together three years and this isn't a last-minute decision on my part. Today's news pushed me through my hesitation, my procrastination, reminded me of Lacie's words. Words that brought us together in the first place. Still, asking someone to marry me is a big move. I haven't thought about rings. We can figure them out later, as we go along. Like we have with everything else in our life together. I bet he'll be surprised.

I realize I'm walking and start jogging again.

Nate

I start humming. I do that when I'm nervous. I'm waiting at the East end of the Picasso, with my Pride flag. Ordinarily I'd be chatting to people, making funny-eyes at the little kids staring at me, making them smile, but not today.

The rings are tight on my finger. I designed them, and my friend made them. They're ceramic. I've had them for two months, not sure why I was waiting to ask him. When I heard the news late this morning, I knew today was the day.

I hum some more. I want to break out singing. A show tune,

maybe *Some Enchanted Evening*, in honor of the first time we met as adults. Now that would be funny. Singing would relieve my stress, but would also draw attention, which I don't need, we don't need. I didn't think asking him to marry me would make me this jittery. We've been together three years. Still, it has, and I am. I wonder if he will be shocked. I've managed to keep the rings hidden, which is amazing.

I hum some more.

Chapter Two

Nate

Nate McGuire, Age 8
October, 1996 - Suburban Chicago

Me and Mikey are going to a healing service. We're singing camp songs in the back seat of my mom's Jaguar. I'm trying to sing in my quiet voice, which Mom says is my loud voice anyway.

John Jacob Jingleheimer Schmidt...the people always shout...dah.

We sing the first round. Mikey taps my shoulder so I look over at him. He winks and points his first finger up. Not his second one, he'd get in big trouble if his mom saw him doing that. Her name is Judy Howard. She's in the front seat, talking God stuff with my mom. My mom's name is Krys McGuire. I nod. I know he means we're going to sing the second round loud, lots more loud.

We holler out, my throat even starts to hurt. *John Jacob Jingleheimer Schmidt!*

"Boys. Boys. You must sing quietly or not at all," Mom yells back at us. "Nate, your voice is far too loud, now quiet down. Judy and I can't hear ourselves think."

She's smiling so I know she's not mad. She hardly ever gets mad, just nervous and concerned about me being disabled. She usually calls it handicapped. I have CP, Cerebral Palsy. When I was little and didn't talk good, I told people I had Tee Pee, tea-a-bull-pawlly.

Now, when people stare at me in my wheelchair, I say real nice,

"My name is Nate, I have Cerebral Palsy and I'm a spastic quadriplegic. Do you have any questions I can answer about my condition?" Most people don't. I think they're surprised I can talk and think. Usually they act like they want to get away from me. One time at the mall, a big kid said he wondered why my parents took me out in public. He said I looked ugly and messed up. Only he used the 'F' word. I gave him the finger with my right hand. I have pretty good control with my right hand, but not with my left hand, or my legs. My big sister, Lacie, she's thirteen, ran up to him and yelled she'd beat the crap out of him. She really said s-h-i-t. Then Dad took us home and sent us to our rooms.

Mikey looks at me funny. His eyebrows are raised up. I remember I'm supposed to give Mom an answer. "Okay, Mom. I'll try not to yell. Hey, Mikey, let's sing the *This Land* song, only I don't know all the words."

"Oh," says Mrs. Howard. "That's by Woody Guthrie. I love that song."

Mikey starts out in his inside voice. *This land is your land...*I catch up with him. *This land is my land.* Mrs. Howard starts singing with us. *From the redwood forest...*That's as far as I can remember. Mrs. Howard keeps singing. Mom joins her and they sing all the words. Mikey and I listen. I like their voices. They sing good together.

After that, it's quiet for a while. My mind starts to be a little nervous. We've never gone to a healing service before, or even talked about one. But Mom got borned again, or saved, or something like that. Now she's sure I can be healed because she believes God can do it. She's been praying over me every night since school started. Does getting healed mean I'll walk like normys—normal kids? Will my legs and body still be stiff or jerk? Will I still need surgery for my twisty feet and legs? And when I get real big, for my back? 'Cause it's slowly getting crooked. I know I don't need my head healed. I talk good, too good, and way too loud. My mom and dad and Lacie and school teachers all say that.

Mikey told me getting healed was bull-s-h-i-t. That's what his dad said. His mom got interested after listening to my mom, so that's why they're coming along with us. Mikey has MD, Muscular Dystrophy. He looks normal, other than he can't run fast like he used to. He isn't as strong, and his back sways a little. He still pushes me around in my wheelchair. People with MD die young, usually when they're young-growed-up, like twenty or thirty. Sometimes they die just when they're teens. Like the age of his big brother Jon, he's nineteen. But not Lacie's age, she's thirteen. People with CP don't die young. Maybe Mikey should get healed before me.

Mikey and me met at camp. Lakeside Camp for Crippled Children. I was still eight, he was nine, and we were in Robin, the youngest boys' room. Mom was afraid to send me to camp. She said I was too young and too handicapped and two weeks was too long and the place was too old and the staff too unprepared. Everything was *too* wrong. Dad said it would be a good experience for me. He told Mom the camp was highly recommended by my school's Special Ed director. He said she told him she didn't like the word crippled in the name, but the staff was great. So, I went.

Mikey and me slept in old metal, hand-crank beds next to each other. It was his first time away from home, too. It was so gnarly! Mikey pushed me all over, even helped feed me sometimes. We were always together. Everybody called us the 'Robin Room Twins'. We loved each other so much. On the last morning, Mikey asked Grunt, one of the counselors, how far Northbrook, that's where Mikey lives, was from Lake Forest. That's where I live. "Well, I don't think it's very close," he said.

"You mean we live a long ways from each other? When will we get to see each other again?" I was scared I wouldn't see Mikey ever again.

"Well, I bet your parents will send you both back here next summer. You'll see each other then. That's the fun of camp, seeing each other every year." Grunt moved our bags over to the pavilion where our parents would pick us up.

"Let's go out on the trail. The woods one," Mikey whispered in my ear.

I nodded. I was feeling so sad inside me. Mikey pushed me through the screen doors out onto the smooth path. No one stopped us or asked where we were going. No one said we had to wait inside till our parents came.

"Mikey, what are we going to do? We live so far away and I won't see you for a whole year." I started crying.

Mikey came around the chair. He bent over and hugged me, then kissed me on the cheek. We liked to hug, especially me. Being eight and in a wheelchair, means I don't sit on the couch and Mom doesn't hold me on her lap much anymore. I miss it.

I touched my right fingers on his hand and he hugged me again. "Mikey, you're my bestest friend in the whole wide world!"

He put his mouth next to my ear. "Nate, you're my bestest, bestest, bestest friend in the whole universe."

Just then, I saw my parents with this other couple and the camp director walking toward us. Mom hung onto Dad's arm tight, like she was nervous. The other woman was holding the man's hand and looked scared, too.

"Hey, Mom and Dad! This is Mikey. He's my bestest friend in the whole world."

Everyone was talking at once, asking us why we weren't waiting with the other kids, saying our moms thought we'd drowned or got lost. The director told them how the whole camp is fenced in and we couldn't get to the lake or the pool without keys. Our moms were hugging and kissing us like crazy.

Finally, Mom asked, "Nate, why are you crying? I thought you'd be happy to see us."

"I am, but Mikey lives far away and I may never see him till next summer at camp and I'll miss him bad."

"Where do you live?" Mikey's dad asked mine.

"Lake Forest," Dad and Mom said at the same time. "Where do you live?"

"Northbrook." Then everyone started laughing at me, like I cracked a new joke, or said something crazy like I do a lot.

"Nate, we're close, we live a half hour away," Dad said. "Who told you we lived far apart?"

"Grunt, the counselor who talks funny."

The camp director, Ronald, laughed. He told our folks Grunt's name was actually Gunther and he was from Austria and thought all of our towns in America were far apart.

So, that's how Mr. and Mrs. Howard got to be good friends with my parents and they make sure Mikey and me have sleepovers every two to three weeks.

"Mom, how much further? This is awfully long. Huh, Mom? What time does it start?"

"We're pulling in now, and it looks like we're early. I left in plenty of time, Huntley is a long way from our house."

"Living Waters Full Gospel Church." I read the sign out loud as Mom drives in. I'm a good reader.

Mikey helps his mom unload my wheelchair from the trunk. Mom undoes my safety vest and seat belt, swings my legs out, grabs me under my arms, and pulls me to a stand. Next, she turns me and sets me into my chair and buckles me in. It's easy, but still I kind of wiggle and shake when I'm being moved, sometimes when I'm not. I think that's why my CP is called spastic.

My mom is strong. She's tiny, almost five-two. She jogs outside and works out in the exercise room they built when my room was added on. She has short dark brown hair and huge brown eyes and she smiles a lot and is always busy. Dad says on a slow day she moves at the speed of light. I don't know what that means, but Lacie says it means super-fast.

The Soccer Ball

I look around. We're in a gravel parking lot. The church seems small and kind of old. It has a long wooden ramp for wheelchairs going up the front. Mikey points to a grassy ball field with old wooden posts and a rusty fence backstop. Several kids are kicking a soccer ball around.

"Go over there, maybe you can meet some new friends," Mom says.

My folks like me and Lacie making new friends. Lacie makes more than me and is always bringing them home. She usually invites me to be with them, unless I get too loud. She says I'm not cute anymore and don't need to always be the center of attention. Her friends think I'm cute. They like my freckles and red-brown hair, even my smile and buck teeth. Sometimes they don't want me around because they're talking about girl things, like clothes and bras and periods and boys. Stuff I already heard about 'cause Dad answers my questions. Besides, Lacie tells me everything first anyway. Mom don't talk about stuff like that.

Mikey pushes my chair toward the field. A loose ball rolls toward us. Mikey kicks it back toward the boy chasing it. The boy stops it. Two other boys and a girl come up and stand by him, they say their folks are the musicians, that's why they're early. All of them stare at me, then Mikey.

"Wanna play?" the tallest boy asks Mikey. He doesn't look at me.

"Nah, I can't do much running, but I'll pass it back to you."

The kid foots a pass to Mikey. He passes the ball to one of the other kids, who sends it back. Mikey picks it up with his hands.

"C'mon," one of the kids says. "C'mon out on the field and play. You won't have to run much."

"Nah, I don't want to leave Nate."

"He's just a cripple, probably retarded, and can't do anything but sit there anyway."

I don't answer him. He's the tallest, probably around twelve or thirteen. I want to give him the finger but think that may be bad. We're near a church.

Mikey winks at me. "Maybe he can do more than you think."

I know what's coming. I have good head control for a spastic and do tons of therapy to make my neck strong. Mikey puts the ball in my lap and pushes me onto the grassy field a way. He takes the ball, backs away from me. He double-winks at me, then lobs the ball easy in an arc. I don't move or speak, just let it bounce off my head. Mikey smiles. My left leg spazzes, then my right. The other kids snicker when Mikey says, "Let's try again. Now watch closely."

"Yah, right. Look at him jerk around. You gonna just keep bouncing it off his head so he thinks he's playing?"

Mikey backs up five big steps. The kids move back with him. The big kid stands next to Mikey with a dumb s-h-i-t grin. Mikey tosses the ball with the same arc. I time it perfectly and head it straight at the kid with the big mouth. It almost smacks him in the face. He ducks and the ball hits his shoulder.

"Wow! That was hit hard."

"Head it to me." the girl yells.

"No, to me," the other boy hollers.

"Can I throw it to him?" It's the big kid.

"Heck no." I yell. "You'll throw too hard. Only Mikey can."

"You mean you can talk?"

"He gets straight A's," Mikey says.

He looks like he wants to say, 'you moron', but can't. I laugh. I don't get straight A's. I probably could, but I talk and goof off too much. Dad says he thinks I'm trying to make the other kids laugh at me so they'll be my good friends.

The girl walks up to me, twisting her hands together. She puts them behind her as if she needs to keep them still. She has long brown braids, wears girly bib overalls, and has a pink flowery shirt underneath the bib and straps. She has freckles, like I do. I think she's about my age.

"I'm Eve. Are you both here to be healed?"

I nod.

"That's good, I hope you are. I think it would be terrible to sit in a wheelchair all my life."

I try to think up an answer. Most people feel sorry for me sitting in a wheelchair. Just then Mikey says, "We're fine the way we are. Well, other than Nate, he's a nut job."

He crosses his eyes at me, a little bit. He always makes me laugh.

"Still," the girl says, "it would be nice if Jesus healed you so you could kick the ball and throw one, too. Do you have faith?"

I give her a confused look. "What do you mean?" Then I remember Mom talking and praying over me about having faith. So, I add, "Ya, I got faith. My mom prays with me every night about that."

"You have to be saved, too. You have to ask Jesus into your heart to forgive your sins. It helps if you're baptized in the spirit, too. Are you?"

Mikey rolls his eyes around, like this talk is nuts. I try not to laugh. This girl seems to care about me. "Yup, I got saved three weeks ago at a different church. I repeated this prayer, and the preacher, or priest, or whatever he's called, stuck some special oil on me. He said he was baptizing me in the ghost."

The girl gives me this huge smile like she's all happy for me.

Getting Healed

Inside the church, Mom sighs when I tell her I don't want to sit out in the aisle because there are no special spaces for wheelchairs. She pulls me out and sits me on the end of the wooden pew, next to the aisle. We're near the back, the church looks pretty full to me. Mikey sits next to me, then Judy—Mrs. Howard—then Mom.

Some people go up on the stage and start playing music, soft, not loud. There's drums, two guitars, a keyboard. I watch a girl wearing a long, plain blue dress, who looks a little older then Lacie, take a microphone. She has a beautiful voice. *Father, we adore you...*Most people stand up and join in. They sing quiet, not loud like camp songs.

Eve suddenly stands next to me. She pokes me and asks if she can sit by me. Before I can answer, she starts to squeeze her butt onto the seat between me and the end of the pew. I can't sit up by myself without something to lean against. I lop over toward Mikey who sighs and gives her a dirty look. He scoots closer to his mom, pulls me over and straightens me up.

He whispers, "Watch out, he spits and bites, too."

Eve wiggles her butt back and smiles at him like she knows he's kidding. She jumps when my leg jerks but doesn't seem weirded out. Most kids do.

Mom doesn't notice. She's standing with her hands up, waving them sideways in front of her. Most of the other people are doing the same. Her eyes are closed. Her face is looking up. She looks like she might cry.

Judy stands straight and tall, like she's in the army or something, looking around. Then she sees the words to the song showing on a white wall above the music players. She starts moving her mouth, trying to sing the words. I can tell she doesn't know them. *Spir-it, I a-dore you...How we lo-ove you.*

Mikey still sits. He nudges me and tips his head toward a woman across the aisle. She has red hair down to her waist and wears a gray dress that almost touches the floor. I like red hair. My dad's is. Mine is red-brown. Her arms and face reach toward the ceiling. Tears are coming down her cheeks. She moves back and forth in time with the music. Everyone keeps singing the same song, over and over, slower and slower. More people start crying and swaying back and forth.

Judy sits down but stays stiff. She looks confused. Mikey told me they were presbatorians, or something like that. It's another kind of church. There must be lots of kinds, 'cause Mom's been taking me to a lot of them. Bible, Assemblies, Methodusts, then she heard about this one having a healing service.

Eve leans over and whispers to Mikey and me. "They're getting into the spirit so someone will get healed tonight."

Mikey tries not to giggle.

His mom pokes her elbow into his side.

I'm confused. I don't understand this getting in the spirit stuff. Why is everyone crying if someone's going to get healed? Wouldn't they be happy? How do they know who's going to be healed? Besides Mikey, am I the only disabled person here? I kind of wish I wasn't one right now. That way, I could stand up and look around to see if anyone else is. Does it hurt when you get healed? Would it be like one big spazz, then you'd be all better? What would it be like for Mikey? Would he feel his muscles get all strong again?

I wish Dad was here. He's good at explaining things. He doesn't go to church much. He says, "I'm a holiday Catholic, Easter and Christmas is enough, especially after twelve years of nuns and priests."

The other day, I heard him tell Mom she was taking this borned again stuff too seriously. This morning at breakfast, he got upset when Mom told him she and Judy were taking us to a healing service.

Dad hardly ever gets upset, but he pushed his chair back hard and almost yelled. "Krys, this is going too far. He's fine just the way he is."

I thought he was going to say more, then he looked at Mikey and marched outside to the pool and started getting it ready for winter.

I wish Mikey could get healed. He's the one who will get worser and worser, then die. I'll have some surgeries and get a little better. I'll probably live a long time in my chair.

After lots more singing, some people talk with weird words, Eve whispers they're speaking in tongues. I hear a man ask anyone who wants to be healed to come down front. My wheelchair is back by the coat rack, so even if I wanted to, how was I going to get down there?

Mom leans over Judy and Mikey. "Nate, do you want me to get you in your chair and take you down front?"

I jerk. My eyes get big. I shake my head back and forth lots. I want to say hell no, but I don't. "No," I whisper kind of loud. "I'm not going anywhere in front of all these people."

Mom sits back down. I think she looks sad. I feel bad, maybe I should have let her, that's what she brought me here for.

An old man pushes an old woman in a wheelchair by our pew. She's wrapped up in a blanket. Her head flops to one side. Her eyes are kind of funny and her lips have got spit bubbles coming out. Her feet stick out in front and she has pink fluffy slippers on. The healing man prays real loud and talks about the stripes of Jesus healing her. I hear him say he's anointing her with oil. He repeats everything all over, but louder. Next, he asks if there is anyone else who needs healing. I'm not sure the old lady got healed, 'cause she didn't come back up the aisle walking.

All at once, Eve stands up and points down at me and Mikey. Part of me wants to head butt her for pointing us out. Part of me is scared as heck.

"Pray," Eve hisses. "Close your eyes and pray hard. You too, Mikey. Pray!"

I put my head down and close my eyes. How do you pray? Does it have to be out loud? That would be crazy with other people next to me, especially Mikey. So, I think about walking and running and swimming by myself and not being in a wheelchair. I guess that would be nice. And then, no one would have to wipe my butt or feed me, that would be good for my family. But they don't seem to mind, they never complain. It all seems regular to us. Mom's the only one who wants me normal, but it's not 'cause she's tired of helping me. I think she feels sorry for me, or sometimes guilty, which I don't understand.

Someone touches me and I jerk. I open my eyes and the healing man is leaning over us. He's old and fat. His shirt button behind his tie is popped off. He's got stains on his tie and shirt and suit coat. He says all the same things over us he did for the old woman. I get tired after a while, especially the louder he yells.

I peek at Mikey. He won't look back, which is probably good. We might start laughing. He looks a little scared and worried.

His mom sits straight as a stick. She looks upset and don't even look down at us, just stares out at nothing.

I can't see my mom, but I can hear her. She's whispering and crying real quiet.

The man dabs some oil on my forehead and my arms and legs. "Everything is in God's timing, so be prepared for a miracle at home," he says.

He does the same to Mikey and goes back up front. They take an offering. At last they sing the last song, another long one.

The service is over, and my butt hurts from sitting on the hard seat. I don't think nobody got healed. No one is talking about it. I think if I was healed, or Mikey, everyone would be excited for us. He tried, the preacher healing man really did try hard.

Judy lights a cigarette as soon as we get out the door. Mikey says she only smokes outside and when she's nervous.

Mom straps me in the car and loads the chair. She kisses me, then asks in a croaky voice, "Nate, honey, do you feel any different?"

I think a minute. I know she really wants me to feel something different. I tell my brain to tell my left hand to move, but it only jerks a little, like it always does. I wiggle my toes, or try, as usual, they don't do much, instead my legs and body spazzes. I look at her and shake my head. I look away, so I don't see how she looks, but I think it's sad. I feel bad, but I can't tell her something when it ain't true, that's lying. Once she washed my mouth out with soap for lying.

Mom closes my door and goes over by Judy, who's smoking by her door. Mikey climbs in and leans over close to me, his face almost touches mine. "I think that man was crazy! I was scared you'd get healed and I wouldn't. Then you could walk and everything and make new friends, normal friends, and not have time for me. That's why I didn't look at you in church. Are you mad because I wasn't praying you'd be healed?"

I kiss his cheek. "Mikey, you're my bestest."

He joins in, "And bestest and bestest friend in the whole universe."

We giggle, he slides over and hooks his seatbelt.

Mikey's door is still open, and he can see our moms. "They're hugging. I think they're both crying a little. Your mom's saying she feels guilty 'cuz it's her fault you're handicapped."

"It is not! Some cord was wrapped around my neck when I got

borned. She didn't do it on purpose. What's your mom saying?"

"That she's scared I'm going to die young. She doesn't think church or God will heal me and it makes her mad."

He puts his finger up for me to stay quiet.

"Nate, your mom is saying she doesn't understand why God didn't heal both of us tonight, especially after all her praying. Maybe we'll get healed at home."

He waits some more, listening to our moms. "My mom said she isn't going to hold her breath and your mom shouldn't either. Now they're hugging tight."

We're quiet. "Mikey, I'm scared you will die young, too." Mikey reaches over and touches my shoulder. I think he'd like to slide over and give me a hug, but he's buckled in and getting tired out.

"I'm okay. You're okay. Dad says we have to take it one day at a time. I think that means not to worry. So, I'm not." We don't talk anymore.

Judy closes Mikey's door and climbs in the front seat. Mom gets in and starts the car. It's cool when the car starts, it's got a big engine. It's an old Jag with a stick shift, but it's in good condition. Mom's always getting it washed and waxed. Sometimes Mom jokes she should have been a race car driver instead of a CPA and owning her own accounting business. Both our moms have tears on their cheeks, but they don't seem as sad anymore.

Judy wipes her eyes, turns and looks back at us. She smiles extra big, like she's making herself happy. "How are you boys doing?"

Mikey looks over at me, shrugs his shoulders and winks. I don't know what he's going to say, but I'm ready to laugh. In a deep voice, he says like he's an announcer or something, "Well, Mrs. Howard, I found that to be an interesting way to spend a Sunday afternoon. Almost better than watching the Bears."

He and I giggle. Both our moms look like they want to laugh and cry at the same time. Judy stretches her arm between the seats and pats Mikey on the leg. "Oh, Mikey, you always see the humor in everything, don't you? I like that about you and wish I was more like you instead of worrying all the time."

Mikey pats her hand back, then looks out the window for a while.

It's quiet till Mom turns on orchestra music, real low.

After a while, Mom clears her throat. "Nate, are you feeling anything different happening? Are you all right?" Her voice sounds shaky, but not as much as before.

"Ma." I say Ma when I want to tease her or get her attention. She doesn't like me calling her that. "Ma, I'm fine, at least I'm not worse or anything."

"That's nice, honey. I'm..."

"Hey, Ma? That man's breath smelled really gross. Maybe he was constipated or needed to brush his teeth. I thought I was going to pass out before I could get healed."

Mikey looks at me like he doesn't know what to do. Judy snorts like she sucked milk up her nose. "Oh my God! Krys, you look like you're going to lose it. Pull over someplace. Quick, there's a McDonalds."

Mom whips the Jag into Mickey D's, puts the shift in neutral and yanks up the parking brake. She and Judy burst out laughing so hard tears run down their faces and they can hardly breathe.

"Oh my God, Nate. What cabbage plant did we find you under?"

I'm glad I got Mom to laugh hard. I hope she forgets about getting me healed. My bony butt still hurts.

**FOR THE FULL INVENTORY
OF QUALITY BOOKS**:
http://www.roguephoenixpress.com

Rogue Phoenix Press
Representing Excellence in Publishing

**Quality trade paperbacks and downloads
in multiple formats,
in genres ranging from historical to contemporary romance, mystery
and science fiction.
Visit the website then bookmark it.
We add new titles each month!**